SS

Making Callaloo

ALSO BY CHARLES HENRY ROWELL

Ancestral House: The Black Short Story in the Americas and Europe

Shade: An Anthology of Fiction by Gay Men of African Descent

MAKING CALLALOO
25 YEARS OF BLACK LITERATURE

EDITED BY CHARLES HENRY ROWELL

ST. MARTIN'S PRESS ❧ NEW YORK

In memory of my mother,
Jessie Heard Rowell,
who instilled in me a love of beauty

and of my father,
Hosea Rowell,
who taught me how to create it

and for
Ms. Lois D. Boyd,
my first teacher,
who taught me
how to read and to write

www.stmartins.com

Book design by Gretchen Achilles

ISBN 0-312-28898-0 (pbk)
ISBN 0-312-29021-7 (hc)

FIRST EDITION: JANUARY 2002

10 9 8 7 6 5 4 3 2 1

Copyright Acknowledgments

Contents

FICTION

POETRY

Acknowledgments

ON THE INITIAL PUBLICATION OF *CALLALOO*

To Lelia Taylor who, by chance in a telephone conversation, gave me the name of this journal. To the late Tom Dent who assisted me in selecting manuscripts for the first issue of *Callaloo* and who did not hesitate to say *yes* when I asked him to write the introduction to the first issue of the journal. To Johnnie Mae Arrington, Mercedese Broussard, Oneada Spurlock Madison, and Verda M. Talton, whose editorial support and assistance were invaluable in the initial publication of the journal. To the late Paulette Johnson, Sybil Dunbar, Lillie Burns-Brown, Darrell K. Ardison, and the other students and members of the creative-writing workshop who helped to raise funds to begin the publication of the journal. And finally to those patrons who first gave money that allowed us to produce and publish *Callaloo*: Nicholas Canady, Jr., Eulacie S. Chateman, Henry and Thelma Cobb, Rita B. Dandridge, Margaret Danner, David Graham DuBois, Nina Gillie, Frances Grimes, Lucy C. Grisby, Trudier Harris, Ida M. Hollinger, Blyden Jackson, Montgomery W. King, Pinkie Gordon Lane, Paul and San-Su C. Lin, Clyde and Ann McHenry, Adam David Miller, Cloatiel D. Mills, Esther and Robert Moran, Charles Payne, Huel D. Perkins, Jr., Danny Pogue, Robert Earl Reed, Sonia Sanchez, C. G. Taylor, Julius E. Thompson, Alice Walker, Edward Ward, Jr., Electa Wiley, and many others.

ON THE CONTINUED PUBLICATION OF *CALLALOO*

To Norman Baylor, Chester Grundy, Robert Hemenway, and Bernard Lovely who, in a variety of ways at the University of Kentucky, helped the editor keep *Callaloo* alive and develop it beyond its very first issue. To Kathleen Balutansky, Lindon Barrett, Carrol Coates, Finnie Coleman, Colette Dabney, Rita Dove, Brent Edwards, Thomas Sayers Ellis, Percival Everett, Alice Gambrell, Kendra Hamilton, Ravi Howard, Mohamed Taleb-Khyar, Helen Elaine Lee, Bruce Morrow, Carl Phillips, Terrilynn Platt, Nathan Scott, and Reetika Vazirani who, with much love and work, supported the progress and development of *Callaloo* and its various projects during its University of Virginia years. And especially to Ginger Thornton, now managing editor, who, since 1991, has not only defended the journal from its various detractors, but who has also selflessly worked in a variety of capacities to help publish, promote, and develop the entire enterprise called *Callaloo*.

To all of these individuals, and to many others not named here, the editor is very grateful; together we have literally brought *Callaloo* into being, assured its survival, and watched over its continued evolution and success.

Foreword

BY PERCIVAL EVERETT

In Ralph Ellison's *Invisible Man,* the beleaguered protagonist watches the interaction between the college's white benefactor, Norton, and the enigmatic Trueblood, an outcast from the black community for his incestuous behavior. The hero of the novel stands witness to an emotional and psychic connection between the patronizing, clueless white man and this pitiable black man, feeling embarrassment not so much for the fact that Trueblood is representative of the black race, but because he, the hero, perceives him so. This is the awkward blind from which the black artist hunts artistic expression in this culture, wondering at turns whether she or he is betraying the race by failing to be consumed by it and whether the work, when motivated by considerations of race and racial experience, really counts as art and not merely some kind of strange public service. Later in the novel, Supercargo, clearly a reference to the super ego as well as the baggage the black American is asked to carry, stands over the unconscious Norton and exclaims our most horrible fear, "He cain't die!"

I have been asked to write the foreword for this collection of the best poetry and fiction from the journal *Callaloo* on the occasion of its twenty-fifth anniversary. I am more than a little flattered and greatly bewildered by the invitation. I will start with the pedestrian truth that for any journal to survive for twenty-five years is no mean feat. But *Callaloo* has not merely survived, it has thrived, reflecting the spirit of the literature it has supported, protected, and nurtured and to which it owes its exceptional life. Typically, a foreword like this is an expected and predictable singing of praises. I am all too capable of doing that, but where is the challenge? It would be far too easy to extol the virtues of *Callaloo*'s participation in the shaping and directing of African-American letters. The tough question, and one I do not pretend to have room to fully address here, is "Where would African-American letters be without it?" Counterfactual speculation is only amusing at best, the host of variables at any given time being so numerous and the constants being so few that any definitive judgment is all but impossible. But this is, after all, my foreword, and I will do as I wish.

Standing at the mercy of the publishing industry (unapologetically and rightly a business, and one that has no moral conscience or compass of its own, or borrowed), African-American writers were, and in some ways still are, stuck trying to supply fictions that are palatable to American culture's tastes and expectations and that do not upset the way America wants to see black people and itself. The black reading public has never been a sizeable market, and no doubt it wouldn't matter if it were, African-Americans falling as much victim to the culture as anyone else, learning the same ways, reading the same, predictable ways, and wanting to read the same, predictable literature. The market for the novels of social protest, from Wright in the 1940s to John A. Williams in the 1970s, was mostly white, middle-class, and young. Black novels were, for lack of a better term, novel: a people's statement about black life, about being black in a racist, oppressive society. It all fit neatly into the rehearsed rhetoric of the 1960s and 1970s. New York publishing houses were trying to find the next, blacker work.

Then there was *Callaloo,* publishing fiction that did not demand that race be its god, allowing writers to situate narratives in places other than the rural south or the inner-city north. The magazine became known as a forum for real, artistic expression. Without *Callaloo,* black writers would still be struggling with that extra burden (in addition to the formidable task of creating art in this culture) of repeating the party-line account of the African-American experience, an experience that is as varied as any other American experience but which has been funneled into a tiny vessel of clichés and set pieces. In its quiet, majestic way, a way that reflects the character and sensibility of its founder and editor, Charles Rowell, *Callaloo* has fought the American cultural and political impulse to contain whatever threatens it. It didn't matter what the fictions of the 1960s and 1970s said, and much of it was fine art and magnificently honest, as long as it repeated itself into impotence. Building a fence around what is threatening and controlling it is a superior oppressive operating principle.

Callaloo has judged and continues to judge work on nothing but artistic merit, however subjective such evaluative judgments must be. It was and is the place where black artists have not had to fall prey to the baggage that America keeps insisting we carry. Beyond that, the journal has finally encouraged the abandonment of the recognition of color, race, and national boundaries altogether. It has done this while still admitting, discussing, and challenging the notions of race and the realities of colonization.

Callaloo exists as it does because of the remarkable vision and tenacity of an exceptional individual. Charles Rowell has given his life to the journal and, by extension, to African-American literature and, of course, the whole of literature. I am privileged to count Charles as a friend and have enjoyed for fifteen years watching his tirades and wars and campaigns for more attention and support for *Callaloo*. And every time my cellophane-wrapped *Callaloo* arrives in the mail, I am more impressed than the last time with its substance, appearance, and character. Charles Rowell's creative hand is sure and his love of his project so true that he never shades the pages with his obvious presence, but he is there. His impact on American letters is immeasurable, though he would never admit it. We writers recognize that without the journal, much good work would go unpublished. It is where young writers find support and a place to begin and where we older writers return for comfort and a serious audience. And *Callaloo* has actively sought work from the Caribbean, South America, and Africa, seeking voices that have had no place to sound, serving writers who might otherwise have been forever silenced by circumstance.

The fictions and poems that appear in this volume underscore twenty-five years of a labor of intense love and dedication. It is more than a mere collection of fine narratives and poetry or a chronicling of African-American literary change. The works present here represent a sincere, focused, and heroic effort to allow the free and uninhibited pursuit of that which does more than anything else to define us as human, the production of art.

Introduction

BY CHARLES HENRY ROWELL

Making Callaloo: 25 Years of Black Literature, a literary anthology, marks
the twenty-fifth anniversary of the publication of the African-diaspora
journal *Callaloo*. This anthology is a gathering of what I consider to be
the very best poetry and fiction published in the journal since its initial
appearance in 1976 in Baton Rouge, Louisiana. Of course, my describing
the contents of this anthology as "the best poetry and fiction" does not
mean that I, as editor, do not admire, affirm, or enjoy the other work
we have published each quarter in the journal. Rather, my description
means that the selections I have gathered for *Making Callaloo* represent
certain kinds of artistic achievements that I judge particularly extraor-
dinary. During these times when poststructuralist studies reign as the
most engaging mode for literary and cultural studies, I realize that such
a claim as "the best of" is a bold gesture that is not without its own
consequences, not a few of which might prove to be awkward or, even
worse, disturbing. And yet, in spite of those consequences, I am prepared to argue that the selection process I have deployed for this project
is simple: It is predicated on ideational and aesthetic concerns which I
always keep in mind when I select work at a given time for a particular
issue of the journal; hence the more than twenty thousand published
pages of *Callaloo* from December 1976 through December 2000.

   Making Callaloo not only represents the periodical forum it cele-
brates; this anthology also reflects the literary scenes of the communities
it serves. *Making Callaloo* reveals the location and scope of *Callaloo*—
its mission, goals, vision, and geographical and cultural concerns. While
this anthology focuses exclusively on selective poetry and fiction published in the journal, *Callaloo* mainly publishes literature and literary
and cultural studies of the African diaspora—that is, in addition to
printing pieces of visual art, interviews, and articles dealing with cultural
politics, the journal focuses mainly on creative literature and critical

texts in English and other languages from the Caribbean, South America, Europe, and North America. Nancy Morejón (Cuba), Wilson Harris (England/Guyana), Maryse Condé (Guadeloupe), Edimilson de Almeida Pereira (Brazil), and Claire Harris (Canada/Trinidad)—these are some of the creative writers of language groups outside the United States that are included in *Making Callaloo*. Their work in *Callaloo*, along with that by African-American contributors, is an index to the infinite variety of work produced by people of African descent outside the African continent.

I have been asked more than once why I publish work by and about writers outside the United States. My answer to that xenophobic question remains the same: to make *Callaloo* an African-diaspora journal is to help expand the discourses—literary and otherwise—of peoples of African descent outside Africa by engaging the writers and their critics, however indirectly, in conversation that reaches beyond the linguistic, cultural, political, and geographical boundaries from which they speak. For example, even at its most primary level, the *Callaloo* conversation I speak of allows Haitian writers to discover what African-Brazilian writers are creating as poetry. Through the pages of *Callaloo*, black writers in England may read what is being produced by writers in Martinique, Suriname, and the Dominican Republic. Writers in Jamaica, Cuba, Guadeloupe, and Curaçao reading the pages of *Callaloo* may acquaint themselves with black literary scenes in Canada, France, and the United States. And black writers and literary critics in the United States might use *Callaloo* as the forum in which to participate in conversations on literature and culture throughout the African diaspora. Part of that larger indirect conversation continues in the pages of *Making Callaloo*. One might even say that, in part, this anthology is itself a product of that larger conversation.

Although we continue to publish writers from many parts of the African diaspora, the first commitment of *Callaloo* is to black writers in the United States. It should not come as a surprise, then, that of the nineteen fiction writers in *Making Callaloo* fourteen of them are African-Americans native to the United States and that only five of the thirty-six poets represented in this anthology were born outside the United

States. Of course, demographics, shifting racial identities, and education help to account for the disparities in numbers of writers between the United States and Brazil or Cuba, for example, helping to make African-Americans the majority in this anthology. It is obvious that the main of the work published in the journal, as in *Making Callaloo*, would be by African-American writers—and, in the journal only, about the literary culture of Black America.

For the past twenty-five years, we have tried to make *Callaloo* the standard-bearer for African-American literature, especially for poetry and fiction, and it is my hope that *Making Callaloo* reflects those efforts. Even the most casual gander through this anthology will give a reader a broad view of the kind and quality of poetry and fiction African-American writers have produced over the past twenty-five years. And that literature, as published in *Callaloo*, is commensurate with the diversity of African-American writing communities. This has not developed by accident. In our efforts to locate and publish excellent writing in *Callaloo*, we have also been mindful of the new positive functions of identity politics—identity in terms of gender, sexual practices, generational shifts, regions. Southern writers—Gerald Barrax, Alice Walker, Gayl Jones, Yusef Komunyakaa and Randall Kenan, for example—have always had a home in *Callaloo*, for the origin of the journal is the Black South. From the very beginning, too, we published women writers, sometimes mounting special sections or entire issues on individual authors (e.g., Paule Marshall, Gayl Jones, Toni Morrison, Alice Walker) and other issues on subjects pertaining to women's writing in general. A special issue of *Callaloo* (Winter 2000) devoted to gay, lesbian, transgendered, and bisexual writers brought together, for the first time in the United States, black queer writers, some of whom (like Audre Lorde, Melvin Dixon, and Carl Phillips) had already been published, from time to time, in the journal. We operate from the position that Black America is no political or social monolith, that one of its most salient characteristics is variety in cultural imperatives as well as in ideologies. We have no doubt that, over the past twenty-five years, the diversity in its social and political ideologies is reflected in *Callaloo* and, in turn, echoed in *Making Callaloo*.

I am also mindful of the artistic variety we have witnessed in the poetry and fiction by African-Americans over the last twenty-five years. In fiction, for example, Percival Everett and Helen Elaine Lee focus their narratives on characters' inner lives, for these two artists—who are concerned about the art of fiction and what it can do for the artist in the act of speaking through narratives—are not concerned about external political and social struggles, such as those with which earlier black novelists ceaselessly wrestled—e.g., with the fiction of race and its accompanying politics. During the past twenty-five years, our fiction writers have given us new kinds of characters that also reflect the thematic variety in their fiction. Then, too, Nathaniel Mackey and John Edgar Wideman offer us new experiments with language, voicing, and form in fiction, thereby challenging the concept of the prose narrative as it has been passed down to us. Likewise, Ai, in poetry, continues to give new life to the dramatic monologue and, in doing so, provides herself an altered form in which to explore the lives and minds of a number of invented and real figures, some of whom are from our not so distant past. Carl Phillips's play with the limits of language, Kevin Young's experiments with voice, and Forrest Hamer's precisions in the validation of the positive power of memory—these, along with the many others we encounter in black poetry of the last two decades, are not practices in which black poets have long been allowed to engage. The poetry and fiction in *Making Callaloo* are evidence of the importance of that freedom.

Up through the Black Arts Movement of the 1960s and 1970s, white publishers and black critics frequently tried to prescribe the subjects and forms of African-American literary texts, thus limiting the art and thematics of black literary production. Perhaps novelist Percival Everett is also speaking of the writers who publish in *Callaloo* when he says that "American Culture's defense has always been to co-opt, corral, and contain what threatens it. And so," he continues,

> African-American people find themselves told at turns that works of art represent an entire, collective experience. We are left with jacket copy with claims like "captures the black life"

or "reveals the African-American experience." Writers since the Black Arts Movement have come to appreciate and reject the American effort at containment. They have freed themselves to consider their work with purely artistic concern and execution, shaking off the insidious and bogus weights of race, representation, and loyalty.

African-American writers are now enjoying a certain kind of freedom that they have never experienced before, and that freedom has allowed them the privilege to use whatever experiences they select as the material of their art. And, most important, that freedom has also afforded them the opportunity to devote themselves to their craft, to the making of the most aesthetically sound texts their subject matter dictates. If anything, the texts gathered in *Making Callaloo* tell us this: that the writers in *Callaloo* have not committed their creative work to "the struggle"; they have allowed their literary practices to commit them to the craft of the genre in which they have elected to work with elegance and eloquence.

It is my hope that *Callaloo* has been instrumental in buying freedom for black writers. As editor of the journal, I have always worked toward providing a free and open forum for excellent writing, creative and critical. *Callaloo* has always been, I hope, a publication site that is free of the narrow ideologies which only restrict artists from exploring the limitless depths of the human mind and heart, a site free of the stereotyping clichés and commercialized fantasies of white-controlled and white-dominated publishing houses.

Another feature of current writing scenes in African-American communities is generational diversity, which replicates itself in *Making Callaloo*. The poetry of the youthful Natasha Trethewey, Brent Hayes Edwards, and Terrance Hayes is published in *Callaloo* alongside that of such long-established poets as Ed Roberson, Clarence Major, Gerald Barrax, Lucille Clifton, and Michael S. Harper. What a wonderful feeling of support and promotion a new young writer must experience from being published in the same issue of a literary journal with, for example, the distinguished Jay Wright. He, along with Clifton, Harper, and Barrax, emerged as a poet during the Black Arts Movement but, like them, he was not influenced by its dicta. Their examples as poets must have also been inspirational for the next generation, which includes Rita Dove, Ai, Toi Derricotte, Yusef Komunyakaa, and Thylias Moss.

I have no doubt, however, that the examples of Dove and Komunyakaa moved African-American poetry beyond the political rhetoric, the hollow stances, and the limiting vision of the poetry of the Black Arts Movement. Theirs is a transtraditional poetry; while their poetry honors tradition, it is not bound by it. For both Dove and Komunyakaa, tradition is where poetry begins, not where it ends. Through forms of lyricism unmatched in contemporary American poetry, Dove and Komunyakaa, like other poets of their generation, continue to produce poems which inhabit private territories rendered in familiar voices so personal that we hear echoes of ourselves. Seeing this phenomenon for the first time in African-American poetry, what could the generation of Thomas Sayers Ellis, Sharan Strange, and Forrest Hamer do but take notice and learn?

It should not surprise the reader of *Making Callaloo* to discover three generations of black American writers gathered in the anthology, for one of the central purposes of *Callaloo* continues to be the identification, encouragement, and support of new and emerging writers, as well as the publication and promotion of emerging writers along with established writers. For young writers who are publishable, *Callaloo* is also their forum, and for those who only demonstrate the potential for future publication we become more than a periodical; we become their mentors. That is, in addition to encouraging and advising writers in the latter group, we also try to nurture them by providing free and open creative-writing workshops and readings which allow them to study and visit with established black writers who teach courses in major creative-writing programs. And when these writers who show potential develop and submit publishable manuscripts to *Callaloo,* we print them. Writers such as Thomas Sayers Ellis, Elizabeth Alexander, Carl Phillips, Brenda Marie Osbey, Thomas Glave, Helen Elaine Lee, Kevin Young, and many others can vouch that *Callaloo* was the first periodical—or among the first periodicals—to publish their creative work. These cross sections of generations in *Making Callaloo* are no more or less than what readers see in *Callaloo* from one general issue to the next, as we continue to publish new and emerging writers together with older and established writers.

The interest of *Callaloo* is neither the money-driven concerns of commercial publishing houses and slick magazines nor the promotion of *whiteness* and its accompanying exclusivist aesthetic. But neither is *Callaloo* interested in any form of *blackness* that essentializes, stereotypes, or constrains black people. While its primary interest is to serve black writing communities in the United States and elsewhere in the African diaspora, *Callaloo* has no vested interest in Black Nationalism, Afrocentrism, or any other *ism*, movement, or school. Rather, *Callaloo*'s interest is the identification, publication, and promotion of the best literary texts—along with the most engaging critical writing about them and the culture from which they derive—produced in the African diaspora. Ultimately, the interest of *Callaloo* is the promotion and celebration of excellence. The texts I have selected for *Making Callaloo* are a testament to those goals.

How did we get from the first issue of *Callaloo* in 1976 to 2001 with *Making Callaloo: 25 Years of Black Literature*? The narrative which accurately answers that question has never before now been fully represented in print. And as I attempt here to present an abridged version of that narrative, I must realize that I risk being self-congratulatory, sentimental, or self-aggrandizing, acts I must take care to avoid at all costs.

I founded *Callaloo* as a Black South forum and published its first issue in 1976, when I was teaching in the Department of English at Southern University in Baton Rouge, Louisiana. Actually, I conceived the idea of a Black South literary journal during the spring of 1974, when I was on academic leave from Southern and visiting at my father's farm in Auburn, Alabama. As I look back now, I recall again, as I have done so elsewhere, that it was the annoying recognition of the urgent continuing need of a publication site to accommodate and develop black literary voices in the South that motivated me to found *Callaloo*. I was fully aware that this need resulted from two separate but related realities: 1) the White South's policies of racial exclusion, one of the tenets upon which white supremacy is predicated; and 2) the Black North's will, for some nefarious reason, to superiorize itself over black people in the South. In other words, African-American writers in the South were being systematically excluded from publishing in Southern (and most frequently by white Northern) literary journals, magazines, and publishing houses; and they were only occasionally published by black periodicals in the North, even during the 1960s and early 1970s, when short-lived black literary journals seemed to "jes gro'." But it was neither of these two unfortunate circumstances that were my immediate motivation to found *Callaloo*. Rather, as I wrote in the Editor's Note in the Fall 1998 issue of *Callaloo* (Volume 21, Number 4) devoted to Sterling Brown, it was my first and only meeting with him that fed my imagination and set me in motion toward that goal of inventing the journal.

There I was alone that March morning in 1974, ruminating after breakfast at the kitchen table in my father's home. It was one of those nature-filled mornings in rural Alabama, when all the world seemed ablaze with the music of innumerable birds and the fragrances of new life. Two or three days earlier, I had returned from Washington, D.C., where I had met and taped a long interview with Sterling Brown, who was still teaching at Howard University. To the kitchen table in my father's house I had moved books, writing paper, and a portable typewriter to begin my article on Sterling Brown and his use of the Southern folk tradition in his poetry. As I thought about what I had discovered in the interview about Sterling Brown's long career as a pioneering figure in African-American literary studies, I thought that one of the cultural needs of the Black South was a publication outlet for its writers, a forum which neither subscribed to a narrow political ideology nor attempted to dictate to authors what to write. Rather, what we needed in the South, I knew back then, was a free and open periodical whose goals would take us far beyond the prescriptive aesthetic of the Northern and urban Black Arts Movement and, at the same time, would promote the common good of black writing communities in the South. The example of Sterling Brown's various efforts to interpret, preserve, and defend

African-American literature and culture through his work as poet, literary and cultural critic, literary historian, editor, and educator very much impressed me at that time—and they later came to serve (and they still do) as a directionscore for me in my efforts to serve black writing communities through *Callaloo*. Sterling Brown's work, in other words, gave me permission to conceive, found, and edit *Callaloo*. That moment at my father's kitchen table ended with my writing letters to a few of my friends, telling them about my project and inviting them to join me in ways each thought appropriate to help bring *Callaloo* into being. Because they believed in the project, some of them did so later either by offering financial support and/or submitting manuscripts for publication consideration.

But *callaloo* was not the word I knew or thought of as a name for the journal back in 1974 or 1975. That name would come later—and by accident. Why that name, a word that is not indigenous to any region of the United States or even a part of its collective imaginary? To answer the question now would move me ahead of myself.

To found *Callaloo*, and publish, distribute, and promote its very first issue were no easy feats. Neither has it been easy to develop and maintain—given human reactions to new ventures that challenge and subvert comfortable notions about people and the world in which they live and move. After I returned from my father's farm to my teaching duties at Southern University during the autumn term of 1974, I, with support and assistance from a number of my colleagues and students, set in motion a series of activities that led to the publication of *Callaloo*, the most important of which was the organization of a non-University creative-writing workshop which served a selected number of students and residents of the city of Baton Rouge. The rapid progress those workshop members made in creating fine poems and prose narratives re-awakened in me the desire to begin a literary forum for Southern black voices. Some of my colleagues and my friend, the late Tom Dent—from whom I requested an introduction to the first issue—assisted me with editorial matters. But I quickly encountered a major obstacle: the lack of funds to pay for printing and distribution. Using some of my own money, funds raised in the community by workshop members and a few of my colleagues, and the proceeds of a fundraising campaign I launched through the mails, the journal was finally born. Without the generous financial support of these friends and colleagues, both in Louisiana and around the country, there might not be a *Callaloo* today. They, too, are responsible for the beginning of *Callaloo*.

Professor Lelia Taylor's voice played a major role in the journal's naming, for it is from her that I first heard the word *callaloo*. In a telephone conversation a few months before I made a first regional call for manuscripts, she told me that what I described as my family's version of gumbo sounded like callaloo, a souplike dish she said that her Trinidadian grandfather made for his family on special occasions. When she first uttered the word *callaloo*, I was immediately attracted to its sound; and when I later came to its English spelling, I fell in love with the unique appearance it makes on a page. Without knowing all of its cultural and spiritual implications, I knew that I would make *callaloo* the name of the journal. Actually, all I knew about the word for more than ten years was just what Lelia Taylor told me.

But I was soon to discover the essential Caribbeanness of the word. During the late 1980s when I toured different countries in the Caribbean to promote *Callaloo* the journal, I first encountered a version of callaloo in Jamaica, a leafy plant which, when cooked, reminds one of turnip or collard greens. In fact, on my spring tour, I saw the plant growing in gardens at the University of the West Indies, and in the faculty dining room on the Mona campus, on more than one morning, I ate callaloo, ackee, and salt-fish as breakfast. Before I left the United States that spring, some of my Haitian friends had told me that, in their country, callaloo is the name they gave to what we refer to as okra, but years later I was surprised to discover that what black Brazilians in Salvador da Bahia call *caruru* is similar to the souplike dish referred to as callaloo in Martinique, Guadeloupe, and Trinidad. When we combine its Brazilian and Caribbean cultural implications, the words *callaloo* and *caruru* become signs for the African diaspora—its cultural mixtures, its racial mélange, its creole peoples. Of course, I knew none of this when I first named the journal; I only knew that the sound and spelling of the word would attract the attention of North American readers. I did not even think of the obvious: that, like the Trinidadian callaloo, the journal itself was a mixture of forms—and I certainly did not know that the journal would become the site where peoples from all over the African diaspora would speak. Perhaps the ancestors were speaking to me through Lelia Taylor. Through her they gave me the gift of the name of the journal, because they must have known that I would eventually have to expand the scope of *Callaloo* from the Black South to Black America to the African diaspora.

When I moved to the University of Kentucky in 1977, I published the second issue of *Callaloo* and continued to focus it on the South until 1979, when Black American literature in general became its scope. The scope of the journal would expand farther after I moved it to the University of Virginia in 1986. In fact, in 1986, the Johns Hopkins University Press became the journal's first publisher, and the scope of *Callaloo* expanded to include the whole of the African diaspora as its province. But since 1977 *Callaloo* has been more than a literary journal—it has become a journal of necessity.

As I made clear in my Editor's Note in the Fall 1999 issue of *Callaloo*, the journal has actually been a *de facto* literary and cultural center, organizing and coordinating a variety of activities which serve to exhibit, critique, and promote black literary culture in the United States and abroad. One of its most important projects was the publication of the now defunct series of creative texts in which new and established poets and fiction writers published their books. Jay Wright's *Explication/Interpretations* and *Elaine's Book,* Elizabeth Alexander's *The Venus Hottentot,* Melvin Dixon's *Change of Territory,* and Rita Dove's *Fifth Sunday* (short stories), for example, were published in the series. In addition to sponsoring creative-writing workshops at historically black colleges and universities, *Callaloo* has also sponsored reading and lecture series and literary conferences at a number of sites. There is a long distance between the Casa de las Américas in Havana, Cuba, and my father's kitchen table, and even farther from our farm in Auburn, Alabama, is the Federal University in Belo Horizonte, Brazil. One might even ask, *What has my father's kitchen table to do with Joseph Papp's Public Theater in New York or with the Library of Congress in Washington, D.C.?* The answer is "a lot," for the very forum I conceived at my father's kitchen table is the only American literary journal to organize and coordinate literary and cultural activities at these and other sites throughout the African diaspora.

As *Making Callaloo* suggests and the pages of the journal demonstrate, *Callaloo* is not merely a quarter of a century's record of literary productions in the African diaspora. The journal has been an active and decisive participant in those productions, especially in the United States. Quietly and, often, indirectly *Callaloo,* which is first and foremost a publication site, has acted as an arbiter of literary taste, while serving as a promoter and a nurturer for new and emerging writers. But *Callaloo* also serves the academic community; the journal is also equally selective in its publication of literary and cultural criticism. To celebrate a quarter century of *Callaloo* is also to chart the history of the rise of African-American literature and literary studies to the state of legitimacy within the American academy as areas of serious academic study. In short, for the past twenty-five years, *Callaloo* has not been a passive periodical. During this quarter century, we have tried to make it an active force, working in the interest of the literature, art, and culture of the African diaspora. And in our pursuit of excellence during the next quarter century, we shall strive to make *Callaloo* even more active.

FICTION

My Singular Irene

BY JOSÉ ALCÁNTARA ALMÁNZAR

Life is unjust and treacherous this way. One makes an effort to walk a clear and straight path, to work like an animal much more than eight hours—which is the usual, to study vehemently, to have a job that will permit one to live decently, to respect the law, to marry as God commands, to be, in short, an honorable citizen, and when one begins to establish himself, to progress, with a house although bought on credit and the car almost paid for, one starts wondering why things like this are not happening to others. I'm not saying it because of the manner in which Irene went away (it is still hard to believe it and I have only returned to the scene of the events because it seems a lie to me that she has left the comfort of her house without any regrets), but it is rather because of what occurs to one on the day least expected.

Irene had asked me to take her on an outing in the country. The trips along the Mirador and a few beers in the restaurant at the lake no longer satisfied her; she wanted to see the countryside in full daylight, put her bare feet in the water of a stream, climb a mountain to feel like an amateur mountain-climber, and to catch butterflies. Since women have their whims and poor Irene very seldom asked me for things and, except for when she visited her mother, she spent weeks and months tied to the house taking care that everything was in order on my return from a trip, it seemed not a bad idea to appease her. A little peaceful trip to the country was not bad for me either. The idea was for us to go to Cibao; there the vegetation is pure and one feels transplanted to a so-called "nice" place. But as I was not completely recuperated from my last attack of bronchitis and the coolness that makes one sick still is found in those hills in March, I told Irene that we would go to the south. Perhaps we would arrive in Barahona and on our return we would pass through Ocoa, where my wife's family lives. It seemed incredible to her that I myself would propose a route and carefully plan

My Singular Irene   3 the trip. It had to be that way. As a professional traveler I did not like improvisations, I take care to plan my trips, make a list of the participants, gather the backlogged invoices, and make a little map of the places where I am going to stop. If any one of those clients who talks up a storm detains me more than necessary, I have a devil of a remedy to put things back into perspective again. But to start out without a plan, never.

I began to pack the clothes and to wonder about what we would do. I saw her so full of anticipation that I began to think of my luck in having married her. When we got married I thought she was so unwilling to fulfill her duties as a wife that I would never have believed then that we would become a perfect pair. The only point on which we did not agree was the matter of being in the street, walking about, or visiting. I had to be firm and demand more attachment to the household. At first she accepted my imposition unwillingly. Then she demonstrated how much she was assimilating my way of thinking and accepted that I was right. I was not going to permit my wife to run around as if she had no one to protect her. Not that. And no visitors either. Sisters and mothers who are the only ones that I trust were allowed in my house. Friends in the street, the cafeterias, the stadium. In an instant she packed the suitcase and made the necessary arrangements for the trip while I took the car to the station to have them fill it and give it a wash, all because in the south there is such a drought and such dust at the beginning of Lent, and anyway the car was going to come back a complete wreck. Upon my arrival at the house, she was already at the door, dressed in white pants and a bluish green little blouse—as she would say—that I had brought her from abroad. She was wearing a scarf that covered her ears and made her face an adorned melon, a puppet doll. To me she seemed happy, spontaneous, prepared to go with me to the end of the world. When I saw her smiling face I thought she was a happily married woman, and I threw my arm around her shoulder. She leaned against my chest for a moment, holding me with both hands.

It was the end of March, a clear day like today, exactly the same; therefore I believe I am going to come across her at any moment, that she is going to tell me to forgive her for the foolishness she did, that we should go back to the way it was before, to our lives of mutual understanding. The first thing I did was not to leave the house immediately. We took a turn around the area and went back to the gas station to have the boys check the oil and to take a look at the water in the radiator. My car was O.K., but it is always better to be sure, when in doubt. Irene started to become impatient: she lowered the window, put the package of novels that she was carrying in her hand on the back seat, looking around everywhere. I knew that she was nervous and that she would have gladly smoked a cigarette, but I had forbidden her to do it and out of consideration she didn't dare. We went back to the house again, only to be sure that no one was lurking around it. I didn't want them to rob me of the stereo equipment I had just bought or the shotgun that my uncle had given me.

At times Irene did not comprehend my reasons and I can understand that because the poor girl never had much sense. It is regrettable to say that at this moment, but it is true. I had chosen her for that, and that is the way I want her. A woman who thinks too much can become dangerous. She will invent things, she will plot, live discontentedly; in short, she will ruin her husband's life. Irene was almost perfect; she didn't think too much, although she often showed signs of weariness, of wanting to escape. That's why I bought her the television, for her to entertain herself at home. I bought her the best brand, ceasing to bet on the horses for weeks. My trips kept me from taking her to the movies frequently. After we moved to the suburbs, downtown was too far away, I generally felt tired and fell asleep with the newspaper on my knees before nine in the evening. I didn't want her to feel restless; therefore, I bought the television and everything that she ever needed. I satisfied her whims as much as possible, as I also did during the trip. I have no regrets at all.

After we passed the distillery we headed toward the south. On that side of the city it seemed that we were going to run into Haina, with those massive construction projects. I have taken the precaution of saving, getting a plot from the State and requesting a loan from the bank to build my house with the comforts that I have always dreamed of. In my profession (I am an accountant, but I have my own business: the promotion and sales of home appliances) one cannot afford the luxury of chance. Irene observed everything with the curiosity of a lepidoptera: her big eyes, from which two large mascaraed eyelashes emerged, attentive to the changes of the highway. Her antennae stuck out of the window and were examining pieces of recently painted buildings, weeds growing in the road, naked children at the doors of the ranches. She was enjoying the outing, sucking in the hint of aridity that was now being announced on both sides of the highway. Upon passing the bridge she wanted me to let her get out to look over the river. I said no. I had seen the road, the bridge, the highway, the tollbooth so many times that her interest meant very little to me. Everything touched her, made her sit up in the seat, carelessly stick her head out the window and say goodbye to a stranger who greeted her, or burst into a flurry of innocent words of satisfaction.

Before reaching San Cristobal I knew that the outing was not going to come out all good. She insisted on getting out to see the little hill where there were wild daisies. We were enjoying ourselves, I shouldn't be so selfish; I stopped the car and waited for her to cut some daisies. In San Cristobal we stopped to have breakfast. Irene was hungry. The diner was a typical one for a village: four or five tables with checkered table cloths and a fat cook dispatching orders from behind the counter. I had planned to go to a more expensive place but in a town everything is the same and in the diners one has to wait less. Ten minutes after being in the place, the fat lady came with two steaming dishes and large cups of coffee with cream. Irene stirred the sugar slowly, smiling at me after each stir she made in her cup. Since she didn't like hot dishes I thought she was cooling the coffee. Two little "tigers" came and stopped in the entrance to the business and were taking us in with their eyes. Irene smiled at them, winked, and they covered their bashful faces. The fat lady yelled three expletives at them, frightening them away immediately. After a short while they were watching us again. I tried to finish quickly and I told Irene to hurry, but the "pushover" took the plate and the cup, got up and went to give them to the little tykes. They swallowed everything in a gulp and the fat lady took the dishes from them because she assured us that they were capable of walking away with them in the wink of an eye.

"Don't bother the young lady," the fat lady said to me in nice words. "If that pleases her, let her do it. Apparently she is even pregnant."

I thought it was not worth the trouble to tell her that it would have pleased me very much to entrust her with a girdle for her to hold in that immense stomach. Irene was content. It was a crime to spoil a moment for her. Between San Cristobal and Bani I punished her a little to make her aware of her immaturity; I kept quiet. Irene was most aloof from the hassle, playing with the daisies. The south was now being noticed in the dust on the highway, the hovels on the hills, the dry shell on the roads. Some cows crossed the road and I was obliged to put on the brakes. With that Irene got out of the car and ran toward one side of the road, in the direction of the hill. She ran, shouting and jumping. I rolled up the window, moved the car toward the emergency lane and struck out after her on foot. In view of the fact that lately I am a little stout—not a little, very stout—the race took quite a bit of my breath away and I could not catch her except upon reaching the top of the hill. The poor fool opened her arms, spinning around screaming, forgetting about the cliff.

"Irene, you must be losing your mind."

Almost without paying me any attention, lost in a different world, unknown to me, Irene came down. In the car she continued with her stupidity and opened the window. I felt like going back, to leave her at home and go out with my friends. That did not resolve the problem. On the other hand, the fact that Irene was behaving like an idiot pricked my curiosity and moreover she didn't even give an explanation. I felt hot when we reached Bani. We were no longer speaking: she being stupid, with her foolishness; I paying attention to the road. The car filled up with tension. I took off my jacket and loosened my tie. Irene smiled, took the jacket and put it without folding it on the seat. The car bounced like a frog each time it would hit a pothole in the road. No sooner than the car had come to a halt, Irene rushed to the edge of the bridge, applauding like a child for God knows what new foolish reason. She began to undress: she took off her shoes, and seated on a rock, she put her feet in the current of the river. Worst of all the water wet her pants and she seemed not to be aware of anything. She yelled for me to accompany her. It was a relief for me to discover that she was still conscious of my existence, but a moment later she seemed to lose awareness of everything around her. She took off her pants and blouse, preparing to throw herself into the water.

"IRENE!"

She didn't even look at me. Nor did I know if she still heard my shouts. With an insane happiness she splashed in the water; she was not the Irene that I had known, the one that had brought peace to my life as a bachelor. I didn't recognize her. From then on everything got worse. I feared that she would drown and went to rescue her.

"Irene, have you gone crazy?"

Between her whoops and uncontainable laughter I took her out of the water. She was almost in the raw because her underwear had stuck to her body in such a way that anyone would need no other encouragement to attack her. We ended up taking our clothes off near the car. I rubbed her with a towel and took the clothes from the suitcase. In the car, Irene made no response to my chastisements. Her naked body awakened old anxieties in me, sweet moments not experienced for many days. Her fresh skin, the cologne discreetly rubbed on alluring spots, made me forget the anger that I was feeling because of so many strange events. The road continued to be solitary, perturbed only by the chatter of water in the river and the cicadas. There was a way to calm that sudden anxiety and no man can escape it. Irene did not react; my caresses became violent without results, and she gave in disinterestedly. It was the first time that had occurred in our married life; it was a defeat on my own turf, but that was not my fault. Irene was going to form part of a different world and she was being transformed.

Unfortunately, that day the butterflies were gathering. The butterflies were the seducers that stole her from my life. Very near Bani thousands of butterflies came out of the side roads and smashed against the windshield or instinctively avoided the glass. Irene participated in the simple grace of the insects. Her eyes bugged out, she followed each precipitous flight, her hands made deceptive attempts to capture them and she gave confusing calls, invitations in code, greetings of an old friend. My patience reached its limit. That trip could not continue. Nevertheless, life has its arbitrariness and I kept my foot on the accelerator. The butterflies increased in number, the colors were multiplied; they came from the trees, they invaded the highway, they darted about crazily, wrapped in the warm breeze. Irene rolled down the window and by accident some butterflies got inside and were trapped. She knelt on the front seat and bent over to try to capture them, leaving her backside well exposed. It was useless to struggle with that little girl. I went on a short way and stopped the car next to a clearing where thousands were fluttering about. It was too late to arrive at Azua before the sun would begin to set. It was a harsh time of day, and the heat was intense. Irene had taken off her blouse and she formed a net like those used by collectors. There was something of a ritual in her actions. To see them fly produced a pleasure in her that increased with the quantity of them. Now half naked, the blouse-net was not enough and she pulled off her skirt. I told myself that it was too much, my wife had lost her senses. I ran after her: Irene was spinning with her butterflies and I, with a devil of a panting spell, was trying to grab her so that nobody would see her that way. I don't know where so much agility and quickness came from; my efforts were in vain. A foolishness was trapping me, the butterflies were multiplying, they pursued me, I wanted to free myself and it was impossible; thousands of butterflies were leaving their cocoons and coming out to join Irene, who ran about happily, completely nude. She had taken off all her clothes and ran about impatiently among the multicolored insects. She was no longer pursuing or catching them, it was enough to run about with her friends and dance to the beat of their dance. I collapsed almost in a faint. I got up to continue my race after Mary Irene; now everything was totally confused, terribly confused: I saw a woman who was divided into others, they were several Irene-butterflies who were merging and separating. I had to rest quite awhile on the grass and wait until the insanity should pass from my wife. But she started to be transformed; an arm changed into an enormous wing, yellow, with black eye-like spots, and then the other arm did the same. She made four turns and then two big antennae came out that moved to each side. The friend-butterflies were celebrating the enrollment of my wife into the butterfly order, of which she would be, undoubtedly, an important member. Her thorax changed into an ashen trunk, covered with small hairs, her legs were converted into two twisted feet. Horrifying! Irene changed into a horrendous butterfly! I stood up and fell again, powerless now. She would leave me, she would take flight and leave me. The gigantic Irene Butterfly smiled at me, diminished, and disappeared with the others.

I am at the site of the events, waiting for Irene's return. She has to return. She cannot deny me the peace that her company always offered me.

—Translated from the Spanish by Joe F. Scott

The Evening and the Morning and the Night

BY OCTAVIA E. BUTLER

When I was fifteen and trying to show my independence by getting careless with my diet, my parents took me to a Duryea-Gode disease ward. They wanted me to see, they said, where I was headed if I wasn't careful. In fact, it was where I was headed no matter what. It was only a matter of when: now or later. My parents were putting in their vote for later.

I won't describe the ward. It's enough to say that when they brought me home, I cut my wrists. I did a thorough job of it, old Roman style in a bathtub of warm water. Almost made it. My father dislocated his shoulder breaking down the bathroom door. He and I never forgave each other for that day.

The disease got him almost three years later—just before I went off to college. It was sudden. It doesn't happen that way often. Most people notice themselves beginning to drift—or their relatives notice—and they make arrangements with their chosen institution. People who are noticed and who resist going in can be locked up for a week's observation. I don't doubt that that observation period breaks up a few families. Sending someone away for what turns out to be a false alarm. . . . Well, it isn't the sort of thing the victim is likely to forgive or forget. On the other hand, not sending someone away in time—missing the signs or having a person go off suddenly without signs—is inevitably dangerous for the victim. I've never heard of it going as badly, though, as it did in my family. People normally injure only themselves when their time comes—unless someone is stupid enough to try to handle them without the necessary drugs or restraints.

My father . . . killed my mother, then killed himself. I wasn't home when it happened. I had stayed at school later than usual rehearsing graduation exercises. By the time I got home, there were cops everywhere. There was an ambulance, and two attendants were wheeling someone out on a stretcher—someone covered. More than covered. Almost . . . bagged.

The cops wouldn't let me in. I didn't find out until later exactly what had happened. I wish I'd never found out. Dad had killed Mom then skinned her completely. At least, that's how I hope it happened. I mean I hope he killed her first. He broke some of her ribs, damaged her heart. Digging.

Then he began tearing at himself, through skin and bone, digging. He had managed to reach his own heart before he died. It was an especially bad example of the kind of thing that makes people afraid of us. It gets some of us into trouble for picking at a pimple or even for daydreaming. It has inspired restrictive laws, created problems with jobs, housing, schools. The Duryea-Code Disease Foundation has spent millions telling the world that people like my father don't exist.

A long time later, when I had gotten myself together as best I could, I went to college—to the University of Southern California—on a Dilg scholarship. Dilg is the retreat you try to send your out-of-control DGD relatives to. It's run by controlled DGDs like me, like my parents while they lived. God knows how any controlled DGD stands it. Anyway, the place has a waiting list miles long. My parents put me on it after my suicide attempt, but chances were, I'd be dead by the time my name came up.

I can't say why I went to college—except that I had been going to school all my life and I didn't know what else to do. I didn't go with any particular hope. Hell, I knew what I was in for eventually. I was just marking time. Whatever I did was just marking time. If people were willing to pay me to go to school and mark time, why not do it?

The weird part was, I worked hard, got top grades. If you work hard enough at something that doesn't matter, you can forget for a while about the things that do.

Sometimes I thought about trying suicide again. How was it I'd had the courage when I was fifteen but didn't have it now? Two DGD parents—both religious, both as opposed to abortion as they were to suicide. So they had trusted God and the promises of modern medicine and had a child. But how could I look at what had happened to them and trust anything?

I majored in biology. Non-DGDs say something about our disease makes us good at the sciences—genetics, molecular biology, biochemistry. . . . That something was terror. Terror and a kind of driving hopelessness. Some of us went bad and became destructive before we had to—yes, we did produce more than our share of criminals. And some of us went good—spectacularly—and made scientific and medical history. These last kept the doors at least partly open for the rest of us. They made discoveries in genetics, found cures for a couple of rare diseases, made advances in the fight against other diseases that weren't so rare—including, ironically, some forms of cancer. But they'd found nothing to help themselves. There had been nothing since the latest improvements in the diet, and those came just before I was born. They, like the original diet, gave more DGDs the courage to have children. They were supposed to do for DGDs what insulin had done for diabetics—give us a normal or nearly normal life span. Maybe they had worked for someone somewhere. They hadn't worked for anyone I knew.

Biology School was a pain in the usual ways. I didn't eat in public anymore, didn't like the way people stared at my biscuits—cleverly dubbed "dog biscuits" in every school I'd ever attended. You'd think university students would be more creative. I didn't like the way people edged away from me when they caught sight of my emblem. I'd begun wearing it on a chain around my neck and putting it down inside my blouse, but people managed to notice it anyway. People who don't eat in public, who drink nothing more interesting than water, who smoke nothing at all—people like that are suspicious. Or rather, they make others suspicious. Sooner or later, one of those others, finding my fingers and wrists bare, would take an interest in my chain. That would be that. I couldn't hide the emblem in my purse. If anything happened to me, medical people had to see it in time to avoid giving me the medications they might use on a normal person. It isn't just ordinary food we have to avoid, but about a quarter of a *Physicians' Desk Reference* of widely used drugs. Every now and then there are news stories about people who stopped carrying their emblems—probably trying to pass as normal. Then they have an accident. By the time anyone realizes there is anything wrong, it's too late. So I wore my emblem. And one way or another, people got a look at it or got the word from someone who had. "She *is*!" Yeah.

At the beginning of my third year, four other DGDs and I decided to rent a house together. We'd all had enough of being lepers twenty-four hours a day. There was an English major. He wanted to be a writer and tell our story from the inside—which had only been done thirty or forty times before. There was a special-education major who hoped the handicapped would accept her more readily than the able-bodied, a premed who planned to go into research, and a chemistry major who didn't really know what she wanted to do.

Two men and three women. All we had in common was our disease, plus a weird combination of stubborn intensity about whatever we happened to be doing and hopeless cynicism about everything else. Healthy people say no one can concentrate like a DGD. Healthy people have all the time in the world for stupid generalizations and short attention spans.

We did our work, came up for air now and then, ate our biscuits, and attended classes. Our only problem was housecleaning. We worked out a schedule of who would clean what when, who would deal with the yard, whatever. We all agreed on it; then, except for me, everyone seemed to forget about it. I found myself going around reminding people to vacuum, clean the bathroom, mow the lawn. . . . I figured they'd all hate me in no time, but I wasn't going to be their maid, and I wasn't going to live in filth. Nobody complained. Nobody even seemed annoyed. They just came up out of their academic daze, cleaned, mopped, mowed, and went back to it. I got into the habit of running around in the evening reminding people. It didn't bother me if it didn't bother them.

"How'd you get to be housemother?" a visiting DGD asked.

I shrugged. "Who cares? The house works." It did. It worked so well that this new guy wanted to move in. He was a friend of one of the others, and another premed. Not bad looking.

"So do I get in or don't I?" he asked.

"As far as I'm concerned, you do," I said. I did what his friend should have done—introduced him around, then, after he left, talked to the others to make sure nobody had any real objections. He seemed to fit right in. He forgot to clean the toilet or mow the lawn, just like the others. His name was Alan Chi. I thought Chi was a Chinese name, and I wondered. But he told me his father was Nigerian and that in Ibo, the word meant a kind of guardian angel or personal god. He said his own personal god hadn't been looking out for him very well to let him be born to two DGD parents. Him too.

I don't think it was much more than that similarity that drew us together at first. Sure, I liked the way he looked, but I was used to liking someone's looks and having him run like hell when he found out what I was. It took me a while to get used to the fact that Alan wasn't going anywhere.

I told him about my visit to the DGD ward when I was fifteen—and my suicide attempt afterward. I had never told anyone else. I was surprised at how relieved it made me feel to tell him. And somehow his reaction didn't surprise me.

"Why didn't you try again?" he asked. We were alone in the living room.

"At first, because of my parents," I said. "My father in particular. I couldn't do that to him again."

"And after him?"

"Fear. Inertia."

He nodded. "When I do it, there'll be no half measures. No being rescued, no waking up in a hospital later."

"You mean to do it?"

"The day I realize I've started to drift. Thank God we get some warning."

"Not necessarily."

"Yes, we do. I've done a lot of reading. Even talked to a couple of doctors. Don't believe the rumors non-DGDs invent."

I looked away, stared into the scarred, empty fireplace. I told him exactly how my father had died—something else I'd never voluntarily told anyone.

He sighed. "Jesus!"

We looked at each other.

"What are you going to do?" he asked.

"I don't know."

He extended a dark, square hand, and I took it and moved closer to him. He was a dark, square man—my height, half again my weight, and none of it fat. He was so bitter sometimes, he scared me.

"My mother started to drift when I was three," he said. "My father only lasted a few months longer. I heard he died a couple of years after he went into the hospital. If the two of them had had any sense, they would have had me aborted the minute my mother realized she was pregnant. But she wanted a kid no matter what. And she was Catholic." He shook his head. "Hell, they should pass a law to sterilize the lot of us."

"They?" I said.

"No, but—"

"More like us to wind up chewing their fingers off in some DGD ward."

"I don't want kids, but I don't want someone else telling me I can't have any."

He stared at me until I began to feel stupid and defensive. I moved away from him.

"Do you want someone else telling you what to do with your body?" I asked.

"No need," he said. "I had that taken care of as soon as I was old enough."

This left me staring. I'd thought about sterilization. What DGD hasn't? But I didn't know anyone else our age who had actually gone through with it. That would be like killing part of yourself—even though it wasn't a part you intended to use. Killing part of yourself when so much of you was already dead.

"The damned disease could be wiped out in one generation," he said, "but people are still animals when it comes to breeding. Still following mindless urges, like dogs and cats."

My impulse was to get up and go away, leave him to wallow in his bitterness and depression alone. But I stayed. He seemed to want to live even less than I did. I wondered how he'd made it this far.

"Are you looking forward to doing research?" I probed. "Do you believe you'll be able to—"

"No."

I blinked. The word was as cold and dead a sound as I'd ever heard.

"I don't believe in anything," he said.

I took him to bed. He was the only other double DGD I had ever met, and if nobody did anything for him, he wouldn't last much longer. I couldn't just let him slip away. For a while, maybe we could be each other's reasons for staying alive.

He was a good student—for the same reason I was. And he seemed to shed some of his bitterness as time passed. Being around him helped me understand why, against all sanity, two DGDs would lock in on each other and start talking about marriage. Who else would have us?

We probably wouldn't last very long, anyway. These days, most DGDs make it to forty, at least. But then, most of them don't have two DGD parents. As bright as Alan was, he might not get into medical school because of his double inheritance. No one would tell him his bad genes were keeping him out, of course, but we both knew what his chances were. Better to train doctors who were likely to live long enough to put their training to use.

Alan's mother had been sent to Dilg. He hadn't seen her or been able to get any information about her from his grandparents while he was at home. By the time he left for college, he'd stopped asking questions. Maybe it was hearing about my parents that made him start again. I was with him when he called Dilg. Until that moment, he hadn't even know whether his mother was still alive. Surprisingly, she was.

"Dilg must be good," I said when he hung up. "People don't usually . . . I mean . . ."

"Yeah, I know," he said. "People don't usually live long once they're out of control. Dilg is different." We had gone to my room, where he turned a chair backward and sat down. "Dilg is what the others ought to be, if you can believe the literature."

"Dilg is a giant DGD ward," I said. "It's richer—probably better at sucking in the donations—and it's run by people who can expect to become patients eventually. Apart from that, what's different?"

"I've read about it," he said. "So should you. They've got some new treatment. They don't just shut people away to die the way the others do."

"What else is there to do with them?" *With us.*

"I don't know. It sounded like they have some kind of . . . sheltered workshop. They've got patients doing things."

"A new drug to control the self-destructiveness?"

"I don't think so. We would have heard about that."

"What else could it be?"

"I'm going up to find out. Will you come with me?"

"You're going up to see your mother."

He took a ragged breath. "Yeah. Will you come with me?"

I went to one of my windows and stared out at the weeds. We let them thrive in the backyard. In the front we mowed them, along with the few patches of grass.

"I told you my DGD-ward experience."

"You're not fifteen now. And Dilg isn't some zoo of a ward."

"It's got to be, no matter what they tell the public. And I'm not sure I can stand it."

He got up, came to stand next to me. "Will you try?"

I didn't say anything. I focused on our reflections in the window glass—the two of us together. It looked right, felt right. He put his arm around me, and I leaned back against him. Our being together had been as good for me as it seemed to have been for him. It had given me something to go on besides inertia and fear. I knew I would go with him. It felt like the right thing to do.

"I can't say how I'll act when we get there," I said.

"I can't say how I'll act, either," he admitted. "Especially . . . when I see her."

He made the appointment for the next Saturday afternoon. You make appointments to go to Dilg unless you're a government inspector of some kind. That is the custom, and Dilg gets away with it.

We left L.A. in the rain early Saturday morning. Rain followed us off and on up the coast as far as Santa Barbara. Dilg was hidden away in the hills not far from San Jose. We could have reached it faster by driving up I-5, but neither of us were in the mood for all that bleakness. As it was, we arrived at 1 P.M. to be met by two armed gate guards. One of these phoned the main building and verified our appointment. Then the other took the wheel from Alan.

"Sorry," he said. "But no one is permitted inside without an escort. We'll meet your guide at the garage."

None of this surprised me. Dilg is a place where not only the patients but much of the staff has DGD. A maximum security prison wouldn't have been as potentially dangerous. On the other hand, I'd never heard of anyone getting chewed up here. Hospitals and rest homes had accidents. Dilg didn't. It was beautiful—an old estate. One that didn't make sense in these days of high taxes. It had been owned by the Dilg family. Oil, chemicals, pharmaceuticals. Ironically, they had even owned part of the late, unlamented Hedeon Laboratories. They'd had a briefly profitable interest in Hedeonco: the magic bullet, the cure for a large percentage of the world's cancer and a number of serious viral diseases—and the cause of Duryea-Gode disease. If one of your parents was treated with Hedeonco and you were conceived after the treatments, you had DGD. If you had kids, you passed it on to them. Not everyone was equally affected. They didn't all commit suicide or murder, but they all mutilated themselves to some degree if they could. And they all drifted—went off into a world of their own and stopped responding to their surroundings.

Anyway, the only Dilg son of his generation had had his life saved by Hedeonco. Then he had watched four of his children die before Doctors Kenneth Duryea and Jan Gode came up with a decent understanding of the problem and a partial solution: the diet. They gave Richard Dilg a way of keeping his next two children alive. He gave the big, cumbersome estate over to the care of DGD patients.

So the main building was an elaborate old mansion. There were other, newer buildings, more like guesthouses than institutional buildings. And there were wooded hills all around. Nice country. Green. The ocean wasn't far away. There was an old garage and a small parking lot. Waiting in the lot was a tall old woman. Our guard pulled up near her, let us out, then parked the car in the half-empty garage.

"Hello," the woman said, extending her hand. "I'm Beatrice Alcantara." The hand was cool and dry and startlingly strong. I thought the woman was DGD, but her age threw me. She appeared to be about sixty, and I had never seen a DGD that old. I wasn't sure why I thought she was DGD. If she was, she must have been an experimental model— one of the first to survive.

"Is it Doctor or Ms.?" Alan asked.

"It's Beatrice," she said. "I am a doctor, but we don't use titles much here."

I glanced at Alan, was surprised to see him smiling at her. He tended to go a long time between smiles. I looked at Beatrice and couldn't see anything to smile about. As we introduced ourselves, I realized I didn't like her. I couldn't see any reason for that either, but my feelings were my feelings. I didn't like her.

"I assume neither of you have been here before," she said, smiling down at us. She was at least six feet tall, and straight.

We shook our heads. "Let's go in the front way, then. I want to prepare you for what we do here. I don't want you to believe you've come to a hospital."

I frowned at her, wondering what else there was to believe. Dilg was called a retreat, but what difference did names make?

The house close up looked like one of the old-style public buildings— massive, baroque front with a single, domed tower reaching three stories above the three-story house. Wings of the house stretched for some distance to the right and left of the tower, then cornered and stretched back twice as far. The front doors were huge—one set of wrought iron and one of heavy wood. Neither appeared to be locked. Beatrice pulled open the iron door, pushed the wooden one, and gestured us in.

Inside, the house was an art museum—huge, high-ceilinged, tile-floored. There were marble columns and niches in which sculpture stood or paintings hung. There was other sculpture displayed around the rooms. At one end of the rooms there was a broad staircase leading up to a gallery that went around the rooms. There more art was displayed. "All that was made here," Beatrice said. "Some of it is even sold from here. Most goes to galleries in the Bay Area or down around L.A. Our only problem is turning out too much of it."

"You mean the patients do this?" I asked.

The old woman nodded. "This and much more. Our people work instead of tearing at themselves or staring into space. One of them invented the p.v. locks that protect this place. Though I almost wish he hadn't. It's gotten us more government attention than we like."

"What kind of locks?" I asked.

"Sorry. Palmprint-voiceprint. The first and the best. We have the patent." She looked at Alan. "Would you like to see what your mother does?"

"Wait a minute," he said. "You're telling us out-of-control DGDs create art and invent things?"

"And that lock," I said. "I've never heard of anything like that. I didn't even see a lock."

"The lock is new," she said. "There have been a few news stories about it. It's not the kind of thing most people would buy for their homes. Too expensive. So it's of limited interest. People tend to look at what's doing at Dilg in the way they look at the efforts of idiots savants. Interesting, incomprehensible, but not really important. Those likely to be interested in the lock and able to afford it know about it." She took a deep breath, faced Alan again. "Oh, yes, DGDs create things. At least they do here."

"Out-of-control DGDs."

"Yes."

"I expected to find them weaving baskets or something—at best. I know what DGD wards are like."

"So do I," she said. "I know what they're like in hospitals, and I know what it's like here." She waved a hand toward an abstract painting that looked like a photo I had once seen of the Orion Nebula. Darkness broken by a great cloud of light and color. "Here we can help them channel their energies. They can create something beautiful, useful, even something worthless. But they create. They don't destroy."

"Why?" Alan demanded. "It can't be some drug. We would have heard."

"It's no drug."

"Then what is it? Why haven't other hospitals—?"

"Alan," she said. "Wait."

He stood frowning at her.

"Do you want to see your mother?

"Of course I want to see her!"

"Good. Come with me. Things will sort themselves out."

She led us to a corridor past offices where people talked to one another, waved to Beatrice, worked with computers. . . . They could have been anywhere. I wondered how many of them were controlled DGDs. I also wondered what kind of game the old woman was playing with her secrets. We passed through rooms so beautiful and perfectly kept it was obvious they were rarely used. Then at a broad, heavy door, she stopped us.

"Look at anything you like as we go on," she said. "But don't touch anything or anyone. And remember that some of the people you'll see injured themselves before they came to us. They still bear the scars of those injuries. Some of those scars may be difficult to look at, but you'll be in no danger. Keep that in mind. No one here will harm you." She pushed the door open and gestured us in.

Scars didn't bother me much. Disability didn't bother me. It was the act of self-mutilation that scared me. It was someone attacking her own arm as though it were a wild animal. It was someone who had torn at himself and been restrained or drugged off and on for so long that he barely had a recognizable human feature left, but he was still trying with what he did have to dig into his own flesh. Those are a couple of the things I saw at the DGD ward when I was fifteen. Even then I could have stood it better if I hadn't felt I was looking into a kind of temporal mirror.

I wasn't aware of walking through that doorway. I wouldn't have thought I could do it. The old woman said something, though, and I found myself on the other side of the door with the door closing behind me. I turned to stare at her.

She put her hand on my arm. "It's all right," she said quietly. "That door looks like a wall to a great many people."

I backed away from her, out of her reach, repelled by her touch. Shaking hands had been enough, for God's sake.

Something in her seemed to come to attention as she watched me. It made her even straighter. Deliberately, but for no apparent reason, she stepped toward Alan, touched him the way people do sometimes when they brush past—a kind of tactile "Excuse me." In that wide, empty corridor, it was totally unnecessary. For some reason, she wanted to touch him and wanted me to see. What did she think she was doing? Flirting at her age? I glared at her, found myself suppressing an irrational urge to shove her away from him. The violence of the urge amazed me.

Beatrice smiled and turned away. "This way," she said. Alan put his arm around me and tried to lead me after her.

"Wait a minute," I said, not moving.

Beatrice glanced around.

"What just happened?" I asked. I was ready for her to lie—to say nothing happened, pretend not to know what I was talking about.

"Are you planning to study medicine?" she asked.

"What? What does that have to do—?"

"Study medicine. You may be able to do a great deal of good." She strode away, taking long steps so that we had to hurry to keep up. She led us through a room in which some people worked at computer terminals and others with pencils and paper. It would have been an ordinary scene except that some people had half their faces ruined or had only one hand or leg or had other obvious scars. But they were all in control now. They were working. They were intent but not intent on self-destruction. Not one was digging into or tearing away flesh. When we had passed through this room and into a small, ornate sitting room, Alan grasped Beatrice's arm.

"What is it?" he demanded. "What do you do for them?"

She patted his hand, setting my teeth on edge. "I will tell you," she said. "I want you to know. But I want you to see your mother first." To my surprise, he nodded, let it go at that.

"Sit a moment," she said to us.

We sat in comfortable, matching upholstered chairs, Alan looking reasonably relaxed. What was it about the old lady that relaxed him but put me on edge? Maybe she reminded him of his grandmother or something. She didn't remind me of anyone. And what was that nonsense about studying medicine?

"I wanted you to pass through at least one workroom before we talked about your mother—and about the two of you." She turned to face me. "You've had a bad experience at a hospital or a rest home?"

I looked away from her, not wanting to think about it. Hadn't the people in that mock office been enough of a reminder? Horror film office. Nightmare office.

"It's all right," she said. "You don't have to go into detail. Just outline it for me."

I obeyed slowly, against my will, all the while wondering why I was doing it.

She nodded, unsurprised. "Harsh, loving people, your parents. Are they alive?"

"No."

"Were they both DGD?"

"Yes, but . . . yes."

"Of course. Aside from the obvious ugliness of your hospital experience and its implications for the future, what impressed you about the people in the ward?"

I didn't know what to answer. What did she want? Why did she want anything from me? She should have been concerned with Alan and his mother.

"Did you see people unrestrained?"

"Yes," I whispered. "One woman. I don't know how it happened that she was free. She ran up to us and slammed into my father without moving him. He was a big man. She bounced off, fell, and . . . began tearing at herself. She bit her own arm and . . . swallowed the flesh she'd bitten away. She tore at the wound she'd made with the nails of her other hand. She . . . I screamed at her to stop." I hugged myself, remembering the young woman, bloody, cannibalizing herself as she lay at our feet, digging into her own flesh. Digging. "They try so hard, fight so hard to get out."

"Out of what?" Alan demanded.

I looked at him, hardly seeing him.

"Lynn," he said gently. "Out of what?"

I shook my head. "Their restraints, their disease, the ward, their bodies . . ."

He glanced at Beatrice, then spoke to me again. "Did the girl talk?"

"No. She screamed."

He turned away from me uncomfortably. "Is this important?" he asked Beatrice.

"Very," she said.

"Well . . . can we talk about it after I see my mother?"

"Then and now." She spoke to me. "Did the girl stop what she was doing when you told her to?"

"The nurses had her a moment later. It didn't matter."

"It mattered. Did she stop?"

"Yes."

"According to the literature, they rarely respond to anyone," Alan said.

"True." Beatrice gave him a sad smile. "Your mother will probably respond to you, though."

"Is she? . . ." He glanced back at the nightmare office. "Is she as controlled as those people?"

"Yes, though she hasn't always been. Your mother works with clay now. She loves shapes and textures and—"

"She's blind," Alan said, voicing the suspicion as though it were fact. Beatrice's words had sent my thoughts in the same direction. Beatrice hesitated. "Yes," she said finally. "And for . . . the usual reason. I had intended to prepare you slowly."

"I've done a lot of reading."

I hadn't done much reading, but I knew what the usual reason was. The woman had gouged, ripped, or otherwise destroyed her eyes. She would be badly scarred. I got up, went over to sit on the arm of Alan's chair. I rested my hand on his shoulder, and he reached up and held it there.

"Can we see her now?" he asked.

Beatrice got up. "This way," she said.

We passed through more workrooms. People painted; assembled machinery; sculpted in wood, stone; even composed and played music. Almost no one noticed us. The patients were true to their disease in that respect. They weren't ignoring us. They clearly didn't know we existed. Only the few controlled-DGD guards gave themselves away by waving or speaking to Beatrice. I watched a woman work quickly, knowledgeably, with a power saw. She obviously understood the perimeters of her body, was not so dissociated as to perceive herself as trapped in something she needed to dig her way out of. What had Dilg done for these people that other hospitals did not do? And how could Dilg withhold its treatment from the others?

"Over there we make our own diet foods," Beatrice said, pointing through a window toward one of the guesthouses. "We permit more variety and make fewer mistakes than the commercial preparers. No ordinary person can concentrate on work the way our people can."

I turned to face her. "What are you saying? That the bigots are right? That we have some special gift?"

"Yes," she said. "It's hardly a bad characteristic, is it?"

"It's what people say whenever one of us does well at something. It's their way of denying us credit for our work."

"Yes. But people occasionally come to the right conclusions for the wrong reasons." I shrugged, not interested in arguing with her about it.

"Alan?" she said. He looked at her.

"Your mother is in the next room."

He swallowed, nodded. We both followed her into the room.

Naomi Chi was a small woman, hair still dark, fingers long and thin, graceful as they shaped the clay. Her face was a ruin. Not only her eyes but most of her nose and one ear were gone. What was left was badly scarred. "Her parents were poor," Beatrice said. "I don't know how much they told you, Alan, but they went through all the money they had, trying to keep her at a decent place. Her mother felt so guilty, you know. She was the one who had cancer and took the drug. . . . Eventually, they had to put Naomi in one of those state-approved, custodial-care places. You know the kind. For a while, it was all the government would pay for. Places like that . . . well, sometimes if patients were really troublesome—especially the ones who kept breaking free—they'd put them in a bare room and let them finish themselves. The only things those places took good care of were the maggots, the cockroaches, and the rats."

I shuddered. "I've heard there are still places like that."

"There are," Beatrice said, "kept open by greed and indifference." She looked at Alan. "Your mother survived for three months in one of those places. I took her from it myself. Later I was instrumental in having that particular place closed."

"You took her?" I asked.

"Dilg didn't exist then, but I was working with a group of controlled DGDs in L.A. Naomi's parents heard about us and asked us to take her. A lot of people didn't trust us then. Only a few of us were medically trained. All of us were young, idealistic, and ignorant. We began in an old frame house with a leaky roof. Naomi's parents were grabbing at straws. So were we. And by pure luck, we grabbed a good one. We were able to prove ourselves to the Dilg family and take over these quarters."

"Prove what?" I asked.

She turned to look at Alan and his mother. Alan was staring at Naomi's ruined face, at the ropy, discolored scar tissue. Naomi was shaping the image of an old woman and two children. The gaunt, lined face of the old woman was remarkably vivid—detailed in a way that seemed impossible for a blind sculptress.

Naomi seemed unaware of us. Her total attention remained on her work. Alan forgot about what Beatrice had told us and reached out to touch the scarred face.

Beatrice let it happen. Naomi did not seem to notice. "If I get her attention for you," Beatrice said, "we'll be breaking her routine. We'll have to stay with her until she gets back into it without hurting herself. About half an hour."

"You can get her attention?" he asked.

"Yes."

"Can she? . . ." Alan swallowed. "I've never heard of anything like this. Can she talk?"

"Yes. She may not choose to, though. And if she does, she'll do it very slowly."

"Do it. Get her attention."

"She'll want to touch you."

"That all right. Do it."

Beatrice took Naomi's hands and held them still, away from the wet clay. For several seconds Naomi tugged at her captive hands, as though unable to understand why they did not move as she wished.

Beatrice stepped closer and spoke quietly. "Stop, Naomi." And Naomi was still, blind face turned toward Beatrice in an attitude of attentive waiting. Totally focused waiting.

"Company, Naomi."

After a few seconds, Naomi made a wordless sound.

Beatrice gestured Alan to her side, gave Naomi one of his hands. It didn't bother me this time when she touched him. I was too interested in what was happening. Naomi examined Alan's hand minutely, then followed the arm up to the shoulder, the neck, the face. Holding his face between her hands, she made a sound. It may have been a word, but I couldn't understand it. All I could think of was the danger of those hands. I thought of my father's hands.

"His name is Alan Chi, Naomi. He's your son." Several seconds passed.

"Son?" she said. This time the word was quite distinct, though her lips had split in many places and had healed badly. "Son?" she repeated anxiously. "Here?"

"He's all right, Naomi. He's come to visit."

"Mother?" he said.

She reexamined his face. He had been three when she started to drift. It didn't seem possible that she could find anything in his face that she would remember. I wondered whether she remembered she had a son.

"Alan?" she said. She found his tears and paused at them. She touched her own face where there should have been an eye, then she reached back toward his eyes. An instant before I would have grabbed her hand, Beatrice did it.

"No!" Beatrice said firmly.

The hand fell limply to Naomi's side. Her face turned toward Beatrice like an antique weather vane swinging around. Beatrice stroked her hair, and Naomi said something I almost understood. Beatrice looked at Alan, who was frowning and wiping away tears.

"Hug your son," Beatrice said softly.

Naomi turned, groping, and Alan seized her in a tight, long hug. Her arms went around him slowly. She spoke words blurred by her ruined mouth but just understandable.

"Parents?" she said. "Did my parents . . . care for you?" Alan looked at her, clearly not understanding.

"She wants to know whether her parents took care of you," I said.

He glanced at me doubtfully, then looked at Beatrice.

"Yes," Beatrice said. "She just wants to know that they cared for you."

"They did," he said. "They kept their promise to you, Mother."

Several seconds passed. Naomi made sounds that even Alan took to be weeping, and he tried to comfort her.

"Who else is here?" she said finally.

This time Alan looked at me. I repeated what she had said.

"Her name is Lynn Mortimer," he said. "I'm . . ." He paused awkwardly. "She and I are going to be married."

After a time, she moved back from him and said my name. My first impulse was to go to her. I wasn't afraid or repelled by her now, but for no reason I could explain, I looked at Beatrice.

"Go," she said. "But you and I will have to talk later."

I went to Naomi, took her hand.

"Bea?" she said.

"I'm Lynn," I said softly.

She drew a quick breath. "No," she said. "No, you're . . ."

"I'm Lynn. Do you want Bea? She's here."

The Evening and the Morning and the Night

She said nothing. She put her hand to my face, explored it slowly. I let her do it, confident that I could stop her if she turned violent. But first one hand, then both, went over me very gently.

"You'll marry my son?" she said finally.

"Yes."

"Good. You'll keep him safe."

As much as possible, we'll keep each other safe. "Yes," I said.

"Good. No one will close him away from himself. No one will tie him or cage him." Her hand wandered to her own face again, nails biting in slightly.

"No," I said softly, catching her hand. "I want you to be safe, too."

The mouth moved. I think it smiled. "Son?" she said.

He understood her, took her hand.

"Clay," she said. Lynn and Alan in clay. "Bea?"

"Of course," Beatrice said. "Do you have an impression?"

"No!" It was the fastest that Naomi had answered anything. Then, almost childlike, she whispered, "Yes."

Beatrice laughed. "Touch them again if you like, Naomi. They don't mind."

We didn't. Alan closed his eyes, trusting her gentleness in a way I could not. I had no trouble accepting her touch, even so near my eyes, but I did not delude myself about her. Her gentleness could turn in an instant. Naomi's fingers twitched near Alan's eyes, and I spoke up at once, out of fear for him.

"Just touch him, Naomi. Only touch."

She froze, made an interrogative sound.

"She's all right," Alan said.

"I know," I said, not believing it. He would be all right, though, as long as someone watched her very carefully, nipped any dangerous impulses in the bud.

"Son!" she said, happily possessive. When she let him go, she demanded clay, wouldn't touch her old-woman sculpture again. Beatrice got new clay for her, leaving us to soothe her and ease her impatience. Alan began to recognize signs of impending destructive behavior. Twice he caught her hands and said no. She struggled against him until I spoke

Making Callaloo

to her. As Beatrice returned, it happened again, and Beatrice said, "No, Naomi." Obediently Naomi let her hands fall to her sides.

"What is it?" Alan demanded later when we had left Naomi safely, totally focused on her new work—clay sculptures of us. "Does she only listen to women or something?"

Beatrice took us back to the sitting room, sat us both down, but did not sit down herself. She went to a window and stared out. "Naomi only obeys certain women," she said. "And she's sometimes slow to obey. She's worse than most—probably because of the damage she managed to do to herself before I got her." Beatrice faced us, stood biting her lip and frowning. "I haven't had to give this particular speech for a while," she said. "Most DGDs have the sense not to marry each other and produce children. I hope you two aren't planning to have any—in spite of our need." She took a deep breath. "It's a pheromone. A scent. And it's sex-linked. Men who inherit the disease from their fathers have no trace of the scent. They also tend to have an easier time with the disease. But they're useless to us as staff here. Men who inherit from their mothers have as much of the scent as men get. They can be useful here because the DGDs can at least be made to notice them. The same for women who inherit from their mothers but not their fathers. It's only when two irresponsible DGDs get together and produce girl children like me or Lynn that you get someone who can really do some good in a place like this." She looked at me. "We are very rare commodities, you and I. When you finish school you'll have a very well paid job waiting for you."

"Here?" I asked.

"For training, perhaps. Beyond that, I don't know. You'll probably help start a retreat in some other part of the country. Others are badly needed." She smiled humorlessly. "People like us don't get along well together. You must realize that I don't like you any more than you like me."

I swallowed, saw her through a kind of haze for a moment. Hated her mindlessly—just for a moment.

"Sit back," she said. "Relax your body. It helps."

I obeyed, not really wanting to obey her but unable to think of anything else to do. Unable to think at all.

"We seem," she said, "to be very territorial. Dilg is a haven for me when I'm the only one of my kind here. When I'm not, it's a prison."

"All it looks like to me is an unbelievable amount of work," Alan said.

She nodded. "Almost too much." She smiled to herself. "I was one of the first double DGDs to be born. When I was old enough to understand, I thought I didn't have much time. First I tried to kill myself. Failing that, I tried to cram all the living I could into the small amount of time I assumed I had. When I got into this project, I worked as hard as I could to get it into shape before I started to drift. By now I wouldn't know what to do with myself if I weren't working."

"Why haven't you . . . drifted?" I asked.

"I don't know. There aren't enough of our kind to know what's normal for us."

"Drifting is normal for every DGD sooner or later."

"Later, then."

"Why hasn't the scent been synthesized?" Alan asked. "Why are there still concentration-camp rest homes and hospital wards?"

"There have been people trying to synthesize it since I proved what I could do with it. No one has succeeded so far. All we've been able to do is keep our eyes open for people like Lynn." She looked at me. "Dilg scholarship, right?"

"Yeah. Offered out of the blue."

"My people do a good job keeping track. You would have been contacted just before you graduated or if you dropped out."

"Is it possible," Alan said, staring at me, "that she's already doing it? Already using the scent to . . . influence people?"

"You?" Beatrice asked.

"All of us. A group of DGDs. We all live together. We're all controlled, of course, but . . ." Beatrice smiled. "It's probably the quietest house full of kids that anyone's ever seen."

I looked at Alan, and he looked away, "I'm not doing anything to them," I said. "I remind them of work they've already promised to do. That's all."

"You put them at ease," Beatrice said. "You're there. You . . . well, you leave your scent around the house. You speak to them individually. Without knowing why, they no doubt find that very comforting. Don't you, Alan?"

"I don't know," he said. "I suppose I must have. From my first visit to the house, I knew I wanted to move in. And when I first saw Lynn, I . . ." He shook his head. "Funny I thought all that was my idea."

"Will you work with us, Alan?"

"Me? You want Lynn."

"I want you both. You have no idea how many people take one look at one workroom here and turn and run. You may be the kind of young people who ought to eventually take charge of a place like Dilg."

"Whether we want it or not, eh?" he said.

Frightened, I tried to take his hand, but he moved it away. "Alan, this works," I said. "It's only a stopgap, I know. Genetic engineering will probably give us the final answers but for God's sake, this is something we can do now!"

"It's something *you* can do. Play queen bee in a retreat full of workers. I've never had any ambition to be a drone."

"A physician isn't likely to be a drone," Beatrice said.

"Would you marry one of your patients?" he demanded. "That's what Lynn would be doing if she married me—whether I become a doctor or not."

She looked away from him, stared across the room. "My husband is here," she said softly. "He's been a patient here for almost a decade. What better place for him . . . when his time came?"

"Shit!" Alan muttered. He glanced at me. "Let's get out of here!" He got up and strode across the room to the door, pulled at it, then realized it was locked. He turned to face Beatrice, his body language demanding she let him out. She went to him, took him by the shoulder, and turned him to face the door. "Try it once more," she said quietly. "You can't break it. Try."

Surprisingly, some of the hostility seemed to go out of him. "This is one of those p.v. locks?" he said.

"Yes."

I set my teeth and looked away. Let her work. She knew how to use this thing she and I both had. And for the moment, she was on my side.

I heard him make some effort with the door. The door didn't even rattle. Beatrice took his hand from it, and with her own hand flat against what appeared to be a large brass knob, she pushed the door open.

"The man who created that lock is nobody in particular," she said. "He doesn't have an unusually high I.Q., didn't even finish college. But sometime in his life he read a science-fiction story in which palmprint locks were a given. He went that story one better by creating one that responded to voice or palm. It took him years, but we were able to give him those years. The people of Dilg are problem solvers, Alan. Think of the problems you could solve!"

He looked as though he were beginning to think, beginning to understand. "I don't see how biological research can be done that way," he said. "Not with everyone acting on his own, not even aware of other researchers and their work."

"It is being done," she said, "and not in isolation. Our retreat in Colorado specializes in it and has—just barely—enough trained, controlled DGDs to see that no one really works in isolation. Our patients can still read and write—those who haven't damaged themselves too badly. They can take each other's work into account if reports are made available to them. And they can read material that comes in from the outside. They're working, Alan. The disease hasn't stopped them, won't stop them." He stared at her, seemed to be caught by her intensity—or her scent. He spoke as though his words were a strain, as though they hurt his throat. "I won't be a puppet. I won't be controlled . . . by a goddamn smell!"

"Alan—"

"I won't be what my mother is. I'd rather be dead!"

"There's no reason for you to become what your mother is."

He drew back in obvious disbelief.

"Your mother is brain damaged—thanks to the three months she spent in that custodial-care toilet. She had no speech at all when I met her. She's improved more than you can imagine. None of that has to happen to you. Work with us, and we'll see that none of it happens to you."

He hesitated, seemed less sure of himself. Even that much flexibility in him was surprising. "I'll be under your control or Lynn's," he said.

She shook her head. "Not even your mother is under my control. She's aware of me. She's able to take direction from me. She trusts me the way any blind person would trust her guide."

"There's more to it than that."

"Not here. Not any of our retreats."

"I don't believe you."

"Then you don't understand how much individuality our people retain. They know they need help, but they have minds of their own. If you want to see the abuse of power you're worried about, go to a DGD ward."

"You're better than that, I admit. Hell is probably better than that. But . . ."

"But you don't trust us."

He shrugged.

"You do, you know." She smiled. "You don't want to, but you do. That's what worries you, and it leaves you with work to do. Look into what I've said. See for yourself. We offer DGDs a chance to live and do whatever they decide is important to them. What do you have, what can you realistically hope for that's better than that?"

Silence. "I don't know what to think," he said finally.

"Go home," she said. "Decide what to think. It's the most important decision you'll ever make."

He looked at me. I went to him, not sure how he'd react, not sure he'd want me no matter what he decided.

"What are you going to do?" he asked.

The question startled me. "You have a choice," I said. "I don't. If she's right . . . how could I not wind up running a retreat?"

"Do you want to?"

I swallowed. I hadn't really faced that question yet. Did I want to spend my life in something that was basically a refined DGD ward? "No!"

"But you will."

". . . Yes." I thought for a moment, hunted for the right words. "You'd do it."

"What?"

"If the pheromone were something only men had, you would do it."

That silence again. After a time he took my hand, and we followed Beatrice out to the car. Before I could get in with him and our guard-escort, she caught my arm. I jerked away reflexively. By the time I caught myself, I had swung around as though I meant to hit her. Hell, I did mean to hit her, but I stopped myself in time. "Sorry," I said with no attempt at sincerity.

She held out a card until I took it. "My private number," she said. "Before seven or after nine, usually. You and I will communicate best by phone."

I resisted the impulse to throw the card away. God, she brought out the child in me.

Inside the car, Alan said something to the guard. I couldn't hear what it was, but the sound of his voice reminded me of him arguing with her—her logic and her scent. She had all but won him for me, and I couldn't manage even token gratitude. I spoke to her, low-voiced.

"He never really had a chance, did he?"

She looked surprised. "That's up to you. You can keep him or drive him away. I assure you, you can drive him away."

"How?"

"By imagining that he doesn't have a chance." She smiled faintly. "Phone me from your territory. We have a great deal to say to each other, and I'd rather we didn't say it as enemies."

She had lived with meeting people like me for decades. She had good control. I, on the other hand, was at the end of my control. All I could do was scramble into the car and floor my own phantom accelerator as the guard drove us to the gate. I couldn't look back at her. Until we were well away from the house, until we'd left the guard at the gate and gone off the property, I couldn't make myself look back. For long, irrational minutes, I was convinced that somehow if I turned, I would see myself standing there, gray and old, growing small in the distance, vanishing.

Making Callaloo

The Breadnut and the Breadfruit

BY MARYSE CONDÉ

I met my father when I was ten years old.

My mother had never uttered his name in my presence, and I had ended up thinking that I owed my life to her unbending will-power alone. My mother walked staunchly along life's straight and narrow path. Apparently she only strayed once to follow the unknown face of my father, who managed to seduce her before handing her back to a life of duty and religion. She was a tall woman and so severe she seemed to me to be devoid of beauty. Her forehead disappeared under a white and violet headtie. Her breasts vanished in a shapeless black dress. On her feet were a pair of plimsolls carefully whitened with blanc d'Espagne. She was laundress at the hospital in Capesterre, Marie-Galante, and every morning she used to get up at four o'clock to clean the house, cook, wash, iron and goodness knows what else. At twenty to seven she would open the heavy doors after shouting:

"Sandra! I'm off!"

Twenty minutes later, our neighbor Sandra hammered on the dividing wall and yelled: "Etiennise! Time to get up!"

Without further ado I would sit up on the mattress that I laid out each evening beside my mother's mahogany bed and reflect on the sullen day that lay ahead. Monday, Tuesday, Wednesday, Friday, and Saturday were as alike as two pins. Things were different on Thursdays and Sundays because of catechism and Sunday school.

So when I was ten my mother bent her tall figure in two and came and sat down opposite me.

"Your father's a dog who'll die like a dog in the trash heap of his life. The fact is I have to send you to the lycée in Pointe-à-Pitre. I haven't got enough money to put you in lodgings. Who would lodge you, come to that? So I shall have to ask him."

In one go I learned that I had passed my entrance exams, that I was going to leave my island backwater, and that I was going to live far from my mother. My happiness was so overwhelming that, at first, words failed me. Then I stammered out in a feigned sorrowful tone of voice: "You'll be all by yourself here."

My mother gave me a look that implied she didn't believe a word. I know now why I thought I hated my mother. Because she was alone. Never the weight of a man in her bed between the sheets drawn tight like those of a first communicant. Never the raucous laughter of a man to enlighten her evenings. Never a good fight in the early hours of the dawn! Our neighbors in tears would walk around with bruises, bumps, and split lips that spoke of pain and voluptuousness. But my mother, she modeled herself along the lines of Saint Thérèse de Lisieux and Bernadette Soubirou.

At that time—I'm talking about the end of the fifties—the town of Capesterre numbered a good many souls, how many I don't know exactly. Everything seemed drowsy. The teachers who had us recite "the River Loire has its source in the Mont Gerbier-de-Jonc," the priests who had us stumble through "One God in three distinct persons," and the town crier beating his drum "Oyez, oyez!"

Only the sea, a crazed woman with eyes of amethyst, leapt in places over the rocks and tried to take men and animals alike by the throat.

Three times a week a boat left Grand Bourg, Marie-Galante, for the actual island of Guadeloupe. It was loaded with black piglets, poultry, goats, jerricans of 55% rum, matrons with huge buttocks and children in tears. One late September morning my mother made the sign of the cross on my forehead, kissed me sparingly, and entrusted me and my few belongings to the captain. Hardly had we left the jetty on which the crowd grew smaller and smaller than my joy gave way to a feeling of panic. The sea opened up like the jaws of a monster bent on swallowing us. We were sucked into the abyss, then vomited out in disgust before being dragged back again. This merry-go-round lasted an hour and a half. Women with rosaries in hand prayed to the Virgin Mary. Finally we entered the mauve waters of the harbor with Pointe-à-Pitre shining as a backdrop.

I spent three days without seeing my father, who was away "on business" in Martinique. In his absence I got to know my stepmother, a small woman draped with jewelry and as rigid as my mother, as well as my half-sister, who was almost blonde in a pleated skirt. She ignored me disdainfully.

When he leaned against the door of the cubby hole I had been allotted in the attic, it seemed to me that the day began to dawn on my life. He was a fairly dark-skinned mulatto whose curly hair had begun to grey. A web of wrinkles surrounded his dark grey eyes. "What a damned Negress your mother is, even so!" he laughed in a sparkle of teeth. "She didn't even tell me you were born and now point blank she writes to make me 'face up to my responsibilities.' But I have to admit you're the spitting image of your father!"

I was terribly flattered I resembled such a handsome gentleman! Etienne Bellot, my father, came from an excellent family. His father had been a public notary. His elder brother had taken over his father's practice and his sister had married a magistrate. When at the age of twenty he had failed part one of the baccalauréat for the fourth time he had the brilliant idea of getting Larissa Valère, the only daughter of the big ironmonger on Market Square, with child. He was married off therefore in great pomp at the Cathedral of Saint Pierre and Saint Paul, four months before his daughter was due to be born, then appointed to replace his father-in-law who was getting on in years. Not for long! It was soon discovered that the daily takings of the ironmongery, substantial as they were, vanished into thin air among the men with whom he lost at cards in the bars of the Carenage district, the women he bedded just about everywhere and the professional cadgers. Larissa therefore took her seat at the till and stayed there from that day on.

I was not the only illegitimate child of Etienne's, even though I was the only resident one. Oh no! After Sunday school there was a stream of boys and girls of every age and every color who came to greet their begetter and receive from the hand of Larissa a brand new ten franc note that she took out of a box specially reserved for this purpose. The stream dried up for lunch and siesta only to resume in greater force from four o'clock in the afternoon until night fall. My father, who never moved from his bed on Sunday, the Lord's Day, kept his bedroom door firmly closed, never letting a smile or a caress filter through.

In fact nobody found grace in his heart except for Jessica, my almost blonde half-sister whose grey eyes, the very image of her father's, seldom looked up from her twopenny novels. I soon learned that one of Etienne's mistresses had maliciously struck Larissa down with a mysterious illness that had laid to rest two other legitimate children—both boys—and that Jessica was the couple's greatest treasure.

Larissa must have been very lovely. Now gone to seed, there remained the fern-colored eyes behind her glasses and teeth of pearl that her smile sometimes revealed. The only times she left the house were to sit straight-back at the till or to go to confession or mass. Up at four like my mother, Larissa, who had three domestics, would let no one iron her husband's drill suits, shirts, underwear, and socks. She polished his shoes herself. She prepared his coffee and served him his breakfast, the only meal he took at a fixed time. All day long he came and went, and his place remained set for hours on end while the ice turned to water in the little bucket next to his glass where the flies drowned themselves in despair. When he was at home, somebody would be waiting for him in the sitting room, on the pavement, at the wheel of a car, and he would hurry off to some mysterious rendezvous from which he returned late at night, always stumbling on the fifth stair that led to the first floor. I don't quite know how he became interested in me. For weeks he scarcely gave me a look and found it quite natural for me to be treated hardly better than a domestic, clad in Jessica's old dresses, wearing a worn-out pair of sandals and studying from her old books that were literally falling to pieces. On Sundays when Larissa was doing the distribution she used to give me two ten franc notes and I went to the "Renaissance" to watch the American films in technicolor.

One day I was sitting in the yard studying for a poetry recitation. I remember it was a poem by Emile Verhaeren:

Le bois brûlé se fendillait en braises rouges
Et deux par deux, du bout d'une planche, les gouges
Dans le ventre des fours engouffraient les pains mous.

He loomed up beside me amidst a warm smell of rum, cigarettes, and Jean-Marie Farina eau de Cologne and tore the book from my hands.

"For God's sake! The rubbish those people teach you! Do you understand anything?"

I shook my head.

"Wait there. I've got just what you need."

He plunged inside the house, stopping Larissa who was already busy laying the table: "No, honey dear, I've no time to eat." Then he came back brandishing a little thin book: "Now read that instead!" Larissa intervened and firmly took it out of his hands: "Etienne! Don't fill that child's head with rubbish!"

I never did know what book my father wanted me to read, but strangely enough, from that day on the ice was broken. He got into the habit of stopping in the dining room near the corner of the table where I did my homework and leafing through my books, commenting: "The Alps! What's got into them to teach you about the Alps? I bet you don't even know the names of the mountains in this country of ours?"

"There's the Soufrière!"

"All right, next Thursday I'll take you to the Soufrière. We'll leave as soon as it's light. I'll take Jessica along too. It will do her good to get away from the twopenny romances by Delly and Max du Veuzit! Larissa, you'll prepare a picnic hamper for us."

Larissa did not even bother to reply and went on checking the cook's accounts. "A bunch of mixed vegetables for the soup. A bunch of chives. A box of cloves."

I did not hold it against my father for not keeping his promises or for not turning up for his appointments. He was usually fast asleep when we were to leave at dawn. Or else he did not come home until midnight when we were supposed to go out in the evening. No, I did not hold it against him.

If it had not been for him I would never have dreamed, imagined, hoped, or expected anything.

If it had not been for him I would never have known that mangoes grow on mango trees, that ackees grow on ackee trees and that tamarinds grow on tamarind trees for the delight of our palates. I would never have seen that the sky is sometimes pale blue like the eyes of a baby from Europe, sometimes dark green like the back of an iguana, and sometimes black as midnight, or realized that the sea makes love to it. I would never have tasted the rose apples after a swim down by the river.

He actually only took me out once. One Saturday afternoon Larissa and Jessica had gone to pay a visit to the family and I was languishing away with one of the girl domestics who was as scared as I was in this old wooden house where the spirits were simply waiting for nightfall to haunt our sleep. My father burst in and stared at me in surprise.

"You're all alone?"

"Yes, Larissa and Jessica have gone to Saint-Claude."

"Come with me."

A woman was waiting for him on the other side of the Place de la Victoire: jet black with her lips daubed bright red and loops dancing in her ears.

"Whose child is that?" she asked in surprise.

"It's mine."

"Larissa is really going too far. It wouldn't kill her to buy two yards of cotton! Look how the child's got up!"

My father looked at me and perhaps saw me for the first time in my Cinderella rags. "You're right," he said, puzzled. "How about buying her a dress at Samyde's?"

They bought me a salmon taffeta dress trimmed with three flounces that clashed with my plimsolls which nobody thought of changing. While we walked along, the woman undid my four plaits greased with palma-christi oil that were knotted so tightly they pulled back the skin on my forehead, and rearranged them in "vanilla beans." Thus transfigured, I took my seat in the motor coach, *Mary, Mother of All the Saints,* that rumbled off to Saint Rose.

Making Callaloo

Sabrina, who was heavy with child through the doings of Dieu-donné, master sail-maker, was being married off. The priest, who was a good old devil, had closed his eyes to the bride's "hummock of truth" and agreed to give the nuptial blessing.

The wedding ceremony was being held in a spacious house circled by a veranda and built somewhat negligently amidst a tangle of bougainvillea and allamanda a few feet from the sea that gave a daily show under the sun. A table several feet long had been set up under an awning of woven coconut palms stuck here and there with little bouquets of red and yellow flowers. In each plate the women were arranging piles of black pudding, as big as two fingers, together with slices of avocado pear. A band was already playing under a tree and the flute of the hills answered the call of the *ti-bwa* and the *gwo-ka*. I did not mix with the group of children as I thought their games quite insipid. I preferred to listen in on the conversation of the grown-ups whose coarse jokes I guessed without understanding them. That's how I found myself beside my father whose tongue had been loosened by too much rum:

"We don't get two lives Etiennise. Down there under the ground there are no wooden horses and the merry-go-round has stopped turning. We're all alone, cramped in our coffins, and the worms are having a feast day. So as long as your heart keeps beating make the most of it. Don't take any notice of people who say: 'Ah, what a bitch life is! A crazed woman who knows neither rhyme nor reason. She hits outright, she hits out left, and pain is the only reality.' Let me tell you, that woman. . . ." Unfortunately somebody intervened and I never knew the end of the story. When my father returned, his mind had turned to other things.

"My parents used to tell me: 'We are mulattoes. We do not frequent niggers.' I never understood why. My best friends are niggers you know. The first woman I made love to was a negress. What a woman! Ah, what a woman! When she opened her legs, she swallowed me up! Your mother was the same. What a woman! Mme. Delpine recommended her to Larissa for the ironing as she did wonders with her instruments. And not only with them, believe me! Unfortunately, she had a serious frame of mind. Father Lebris had filled her head with all sorts of tom-foolery about Mary and virginity. She used to sleep in the attic. The afternoon I set upon her like poverty laying hands on the pauper she was reading 'The Imitation of Our Lord Jesus Christ.' You should have heard her beg me: 'Let me be, Monsieur Etienne, God will punish you. Let me be!' You bet if I let her be. . . ."

And instead of rebelling against the calvary of my poor ravished albeit raped mother, I uttered a raucous laugh. I laughed chicken-heartedly.

"Each time it was one hell of a job. I'm sure it was all pretense and she enjoyed it as much as I did. And then one morning she disappeared. Without a word of explanation. Without even asking for her wages. Larissa was furious. . . ."

Another crime to add to my list: I showed no signs of pity for my mother; neither for the terror of her discovery and her flight to her native island nor for the family lamentations, the neighbors' malicious gossip, and that pathetic gesture to cover my illegitimacy, the name of Etiennise, daughter of Etienne.

When we got home on Sunday around three o'clock in the after-noon, Larissa, who had never raised a hand against me, gave me a thorough beating, claiming that I had lost my best school dress. I know what infuriated her, it was this growing intimacy with my father.

My mother saw it immediately. Hardly had I set foot on the jetty where she was waiting than she ran her eyes over me significantly and said: "You're very much his daughter now!"

I didn't answer. I spent the Christmas holidays barricaded behind the hostile silence that I had raised between us, the unjust cruelty of which I only understood too late, much too late.

I didn't realize to what extent she was suffering. I didn't see the taut features of her face droop and slacken. The wheeze in her respi-ration, keeping back the grief, escaped my attention. Her nights were wracked with nightmares. In the mornings she would plunge into prayer.

· · ·

The intimacy with my father soon took an unexpected turn from which I obviously did not dare shy away. He entrusted me with little notes to hand to all the girls at the lycée who had caught his eye.

"Give this from me to that little yellow girl in the fourth form."

"And this one to the tall girl in the second form."

It soon became a genuine commerce of billets-doux. You would never imagine how ready they were, these young girls from a reputable family seen at church on Sundays, closely chaperoned by father, brothers, and mother and stumbling with beatitude on their return from the altar, how ready they were to listen to the improper propositions of a married man with a reputation.

I devised a daring technique. I would approach the coveted prey while she was chatting with her classmates in the school yard. I would stand squarely in front of her and hand her the note folded in four without saying a word. Somewhat surprised, but unsuspecting, she would take it from me, open it, start to read and then blush deeply as far as the color of her skin would let her. My father did not exactly treat the matter lightly:

My little darling,

Ever since I saw you on the Place de la Victoire I have been madly in love with you. If you do not want to have a death on your conscience meet me tomorrow at 5 p.m. on the second bench in the allée des Veuves. I'll be waiting for you with a red dahlia in my buttonhole. . . .

Waiting for an answer in which I hope you will accept.

The effect of such an epistle was radical. Before class was over the victim would hand me a folded sheet accepting the rendezvous. While I was in form three a new pupil arrived, Marie-Madeleine Savigny. She had just arrived from Dakar where her father had been a magistrate and her African childhood had given her an aristocratic languor. She called her sandals "samaras" and her mother's domestics "boyesses." Every able-bodied man in Pointe-à-Pitre was eaten up with desire for her, and my father more than the rest.

When I brought her the traditional billet-doux, she cast her hazel eyes over it and without a moment's hesitation tore it up, scattering the pieces of paper at the foot of a hundred-year-old sandbox tree. My father did not consider himself beaten. With me as the go-between he returned to the attack the next day and the next. By the end of the third week Marie-Madeleine had not given an inch while my father was an absolute wreck. Back home on time he would be watching for me from the balcony and then rush down the stairs as impetuous as a teenager.

"Well?"

I shook my head. "She won't even take the letter from me."

His face dropped and he became the outrageously spoiled little boy he had once been. He had been his mother's favorite, his grandmother's; his father's sisters and his mother's sisters, who showered him with kisses, turned a blind eye to his caprices and called him voluptuously "Ti-mal." In June Marie-Madeleine caused a stir by not entering for part one of the baccalauréat. A few weeks later we learned she was to marry Jean Burin des Rosiers, the fourth son of a rich white creole factory owner. Great was the stupor! What! A white creole to marry a colored girl? And not even a mulatto into the bargain! For although he was a magistrate, Mr. Savigny was but a common copper-colored nigger! As for the mother, she was half-coolie! Such an event had not occurred since 1928, the year of the terrible hurricane, when a Martin Saint Aurèle had married a Negress. But the family had turned their backs on him and the couple had lived in poverty. Whereas the Burin des Rosiers were welcoming their daughter-in-law with open arms. The world was completely upside down!

Everyone had just regained their calm when Marie-Madeleine, who no longer needed to lace herself up in corsets, exhibited at least a six-month-old belly in her flowing flowery silk dresses.

My father joined in the rush for the spoils. In the middle of a circle of lecherous listeners I heard him recount, without ever trying to deny the fact, how he had tasted Marie-Madeleine's secret delights but unlike Jean had not let himself be caught red-handed.

I spent an awful summer holiday on Marie-Galante. Since I was soon to enter the lycée in the rue Achille René-Boisneuf and take physics and chemistry with the boys, my mother got it into her head to make me a set of clothes. She went down to the Grand Bourg where she bought yards and yards of material, patterns, marking crayon, and a pair of tailor's scissors. . . . Every day when she came back from the hospital there were the unending fitting sessions. I could not bear the touch of her fidgety hands and her grumbling: "This side hangs all right. Why doesn't the other side do the same?"

On Sunday, August 15, I refused to accompany her in the flared dress she was so proud of. She looked me straight in the eyes: "If you think he worships you, why doesn't he pay for your dresses?"

It was true that for the three years or so I had been living with my father I had never seen the color of his money, except for Larissa's two little brand-new notes. I was doomed to gaze from afar at the books in the bookshops, the perfume in the perfume shops, and the ice creams at the ice-cream parlor.

Whenever she had the opportunity, my mother sent me two or three dirty banknotes with a note that always read: "I hope you are keeping well. Your affectionate maman, Nisida."

I was thus able to buy my exercise books and pens and fill my inkpot with blue ink from the seas of China.

When school started again in October my father stopped his traffic of billets-doux. I felt so frustrated, deprived as I was of my mean little mission as a go-between, that I would have gladly drawn his attention to the pretty chicks (that's how he used to call them) who scratched around untouched in the school yard. I soon discovered the key to the mystery. He had fallen head over heels in love with the very pretty wife of a Puerto-Rican tailor by the name of Artemio who had opened his small shop on the rue Frébault. Lydia was a righteous woman. Or perhaps quite simply she did not like my father. She talked freely to her husband of these constant advances that troubled her, and the husband, hotheaded as Latins are wont to be, resolved to give the brazen fellow a lesson he would not forget. He hired the services of three or four bullies, one of whom was a former boxer nicknamed "Doudou Sugar Robinson." They lay in wait one evening for my father while he was striding across the Place de la Victoire and left him lifeless at the foot of a flame tree. Around midnight Larissa was presented with an inert, bloodstained body. Transfigured, she swooped down on her husband, who was finally at her mercy. For weeks it was a constant traffic of herb teas, poultices, frictions with arnica and pond leeches destined to suck out the bad blood. Once the doctor had turned his back carrying off his sulfanilamides, in came the *obeah* man with his roots. Every Sunday after the high mass the priest popped in to describe the flames of hell to the notorious sinner.

My father never recovered from this misadventure. In his enthusiasm, Doudou Sugar Robinson had fractured his eyebrow, crushed his nasal bone and broken his jaw in three places. All this knitted together again very badly and the good souls of Pointe-à-Pitre shook their heads: "God works in mysterious ways! And he used to be such a handsome man!"

But above all, it was his pride and his morale that took a beating. My father realized he had become a laughingstock. He became easily offended and susceptible. He quarreled with his best friends. He lost that vitality that had made him so popular with the ladies. He became sad, vindictive, and whimpering.

As for me, with the typical cruelty of teenagers, I hastened to keep my distance from the hero who was no longer a hero and who shuffled around harking back to his former conquests. I began to look at him in a new light. What exactly was he worth?

I was pondering upon this when I learned that my mother had been taken to the hospital.

Less than one year later she died of cancer, having hidden the first symptoms from everyone.

—*Translated from the French by Richard Philcox*

from The Journals of Water Days 1986

BY EDWIDGE DANTICAT

We cowered beneath our beds as bullets caved in the sheets of plastic we put up as windows. My mother was choking on gun powder and tiny splinters of wood, but somehow she managed to hold in her cough. I felt her tears float across my cheeks, but I kept my eyes closed.

Outside, the military trucks roared up and down the narrow spaces between the shanties. It was different from the sound we were used to: the blare of squeaky sirens when they came on *afè ofisièl*, what they called official business.

"Jesus, Marie, Joseph. Mother Jesus, look after us."

My mother was mouthing the same prayer, her grip growing tighter on me with each refrain.

The day before, I'd seen a group of men tie a militia man to a light post, pour kerosene in his mouth, carve a hole in his chest and dive in for the heart. The heart fisherman, whose daughter had been raped and made pregnant by the militia man, he got frustrated when he couldn't find the heart and cried out that the militia man had died too soon.

The soldiers were there momentarily to revenge that death and the deaths of other militia men who had been caught by crowds and tied to poles to die. They were shooting at the seaside shanties because they weren't sure who the militia killers were, which meant they were at war with all of us.

"Jesus, Marie, Joseph. They'll drive us quickly into the ground," my mother said.

The roars of their mufflers were fading as soon as they had started. My mother grabbed my face and smacked her lips between my eyebrows.

"Jesus, Marie, Joseph. Thank you. You watched over us. But next time. Who knows next time?"

She wiped her apron across her forehead as we crawled out from the dust. A few pennies popped out of her bra and bounced on the floor. I chased the coins across the clay, slipping some in my pocket as I collected them.

"I could have gotten diarrhea from shock," she said extending her hand for the coins. "I saw you take my pennies. Don't you know how much water I need to carry on my head and sell all day long to get those pennies?"

"Can I have a cola?"

"You choose your supper. Cola or rice and beans? Rice and beans or cola?"

"Cola."

"Don't complain when you can't sleep from hunger and gas."

The neighbors were all out inspecting damage. There were large holes in most of the shanties and a dead pig squirting blood from behind a fence. We were not hit too hard, except for the blown plastic window which had come down on me like pieces of a shredded wedding veil.

Monsié Christophe's tap station had been shot through and was pumping water faster than the fat pig was pumping blood. Usually he would sell a pail of water for fifty cents to everyone except my mother who could get one out of him for forty. When breads, mangos, or straw hats didn't sell, my mother would buy a pail of water, go to the board-walk and sell it for as much as a dollar. During water rations, she could sell it for two.

Monsié Christophe's large water drums were filled with as many holes as cheap lace. He quickly warmed up some tar and tried to patch up the holes. His son Tobin was helping him, but the water flooded the dry dust, mixing with the pig's blood as the ground soaked it up.

"Ronald, come over and help me here," Monsié Christophe shouted at me. "Your time won't be wasted."

The force of the water was too much and the tar too hot and sticky to hold it in.

"Come now, all of you," cried Monsié Christophe to the neighbors who had gathered to watch expectantly. "Get all the water you could possibly want. The dead in the ground have already gotten their fill."

The neighbors ran home and came back with every jug, bucket, chamber pot, and gourd they could find. They filled everything until the water overflowed.

Some of the street children slipped under a leak and bathed for the first time in weeks. My mother and I rushed back and forth between the house and the tap, filling two empty drums we usually kept outside, to collect rain water.

"Strange how blessings come," my mother said spreading her hands towards the sky. "Jesus, Marie, Joseph. Strange the way blessings come. Go down to the beach and have a cola before the devils return again tonight. Be sure to buy it from that sweet girl Rosie. I like her very much."

I walked through the alleys between the shanties to inspect the damage. Lots of holes on walls. A fallen door here. A food stand looted there, but no loss of human life. The soldiers would probably come back later at night, on official business, to arrest at random.

My friend Jo was at the beach studying for his state-run BAC exams, which if he passed meant that he could enter the university, if there had been one there to enter.

Jo sat in a low wicker chair under an umbrella, with a notebook on his lap. Whenever he found a lost tourist wallet on the floor and could afford to pay tuition, he went to school. The rest of the time, he studied on his own.

"*C'est a ce prix qu'ils mangent du suc en Europe,*" he said, batting his eyelashes at the blue waves.

"I greet his majesty," I said.

"I quote Voltaire. I speak to you of oppression, of slavery. I tell you that in Europe they eat sugar with our blood in it and you mock me with a colonial title."

"I have some pennies that I want to contribute to his majesty's education."

He turned his face towards Rosie, the food vendor, who was fidgeting at her table on the boardwalk.

"Did those bastards kill anybody?" he asked.

"They'll kill you if you sit around here tonight, like a rat in a cemetery."

"All this violence, it's a legacy of slavery. We only know hate. It's how we survived slavery and we still do it to each other. They will never touch me. They think I'm crazy and every Haitian knows that in each mad man may live a god."

"Do you want my offering or not?" I interrupted him.

"Are you in a rush? You have better things to do?"

"I don't want to leave my mother by herself after that last hit."

"Twelve years old and still Mama's baby. It's no coincidence then that you still wear short pants. A man goes through three stages in life: short pants, humanity, and then deity. If you stay in short pants, you'll never go through your manhood fast enough and in this lifetime, you'll never become a god."

"How have you done it?" I asked. "Become a god so quickly, I mean."

"I've never been a child. I was born in long pants."

I pulled the pennies out of my pocket and threw them playfully at him.

"I'll let you buy me a piece of cassava bread and a cola," he said. "I haven't eaten all day."

We walked to Rosie's stand on the boardwalk. On the way we passed a few vendors selling old clothes, shoes, bottles, cigarettes, and a girl or two—if you asked. There was an old man painting a giant canvas with monkeys, gorillas, tigers, lions, and a mulatto woman kissing a black snake.

Jo stopped to look at the painting the man was working on.

"Is that what your mother looks like?" he asked the old man.

"Which one does his mother look like?" I chimed in. "The woman or the snake?"

Jo did not hear my joke. He was already caught up in a battle with the old man.

The old vendor fired a line of spit from a gap between his teeth.

"Your mother looks like this other one," he said to Jo while pointing to the snake. "The blackie."

"Ignorance never wants to be discovered," Jo said moving on.

"Those are not our animals. We have no such animals here. Where does he get such stupid illusions?"

"He's old enough," I said. "Maybe he remembers them from Africa. They have animals like that there."

"That man was not in Africa, anymore than I was in hell. Not yet anyway. Besides, how do you know what kind of animals folks are keeping in zoos in Africa?"

"Movies."

"Where do you see movies?"

"Sometimes I sneak into the Rex theater on Champs de Mars or I watch the public television in the shanties."

"Don't you notice they put a cage around that television in the shanties? You stand with those desolates and soak in that drug they want you to take. A new public drug called television. How do you feel when you see all those people in their nice fine clothes and beautiful houses on that television screen? How does that make you feel?"

Like I want to cry.

"Personally I feel betrayed," he said. "I know I am meant for better things."

Rosie was younger than most of the people who sold lemonade and cassava on the boardwalk between the shanties and the beach. She was plump and pretty with a big round face and fish eyes.

"Rosie the cassava sandwich of my dreams please," Jo said. "Loosen up your grip on the peanut butter and don't give me cassava that's going to box with my jaws."

"Your mouth's too much for you already." Rosie smiled while squinting in the sun to get a better look at Jo's face. I guess Jo was handsome. He had very smooth dark brown skin and a scholarly face. But only when I was around girls like Rosie did I remember about his looks.

"Glad to see you both," Rosie said. "Can you watch over my table? Hear Monsié Christophe's giving free water. I have a big old steel drum that's just empty, making eyes at the sky. I want to go and fill her up."

"Go ahead." Jo winked. "We have things under control here. I'll make myself the kind of cassava sandwich that's deserving of the money I have."

Jo watched Rosie for a long time until she blended into the shanty haze and disappeared.

"She used to be the smartest girl in all our classes." He slipped into the chair behind Rosie's table.

"What happened?"

"What do you mean what happened? She's just like you. Her mother killed all her animals and sold everything she had. The money still wasn't enough and food is more important so no more school."

We had seven pennies which would buy cassava but no drinks.

Rosie had two jugs of lemonade and a line of bottled colas. The cassava was wrapped in a piece of white cloth embroidered with her name. Joe dropped the seven pennies in her payment jar as he reached for the peanut butter.

"Usually I would not eat such indigent food out in public," Jo said, "but today I am very hungry."

He spread the peanut butter across the cassava, then leaned back to eat it dry.

"We could have a cola between the two of us," I said. "Rosie would never know. Besides, it would be our payment for sitting in the hot sun watching over her things. She's getting plenty of good water for free which will be like having wealth for a few days."

"And who pays Rosie for sitting out here in the sun all day?" Jo asked. "The poor stealing from the poor is worse than the rich stealing from the poor. Eat your cassava dry like a real man, like a god."

There was a loud squeaky siren and then a small government Peugeot screeched to a halt at the curb. It was the same car that had just sped through the shanty before I had ducked for the hit.

Two militia men walked out of the car, smiling as though they had been cruising.

One of them was Victor, a boy whose mother and sister had died of Tuberculosis the year before. After his father went to the state sanatorium for treatment, Victor joined the National Security militia, for ten dollars a month, a free indigo denim uniform, white gloves, a red scarf, whistles, dark glasses, a machine gun, and a chance to march in groups, up and down in front of the National Palace, all day long, in the hot sun, during official holidays.

Even though we all grew up playing soccer with cola cans and empty coconut shells, we now had to call Victor "Sir". He was the National Security militia's new contact in the area. He could tell them who was who.

The man with him was older and fatter. As they were marching towards us, he took off his cap and lowered his sunglasses, but Victor did not.

"What can I get for you?" Jo asked, avoiding Victor's face.

The older man grabbed a jug of lemonade and gargled down a mouthful. He passed the jug to Victor, who motioned that he didn't want it. The man drank some more as Victor reached over and grabbed a bottle of banana cola.

The other guy slammed the jug down on the table and walked back to the car. Victor followed, still drinking from the bottle.

When he got to the car, Victor held the door open as he finished the cola. Then he dropped the empty bottle on his worn out dusty shoes and kicked it up in the air, in our direction. It was a credit to his soccer skills that his bottle landed in front of my feet, unbroken. I wanted to respond with equal skill and show him that he was no better than us, even with his new job.

My feet started going for the bottle, but Jo pressed his hands down on my shoulder. The strength of his fingers kept even my toes from moving.

Victor smiled and waited, as though expecting us to kick the bottle back to him, maybe accidentally smashing it into his face. We didn't budge. Victor jumped back in the car a few seconds before it shot away from the sidewalk.

"Intelligent men fight with their minds," said Jo. He poured the leftover lemonade on the cement. "I hope Rosie comes back soon."

"Where are you going to be tonight?" I asked.

"On the beach."

"You can come to the house and stay with my mother and me, if you want."

"And intrude on the little mommy/baby love nest?"

"It isn't like that."

"People have been dying from the beginning of time," he said. "You can't spend your whole life avoiding it. There are things I want to accomplish by living on the beach."

"Like what?"

"When they pass by, I want them to see me. I don't want to be invisible. I want them to have a good look at me. I want them to know me."

"Everyone knows you, but they think you're crazy."

"They think I'm crazy. Every day they give their blood to make other people's soup thicker, to make other people's coffee sweeter, other people's lives easier. What I'm doing is using my blood for myself, until it runs out."

"Are you sure you don't want to be inside tonight?"

"I told you they won't touch me," he said. "Besides, I like to keep trying my luck."

Maybe in every mad man, there does live a god, but I never want to live long enough to find this out for myself.

from Shoat Rumblin
His Sensations and Ideas

BY SAMUEL R. DELANY

PRELUDE

No advertisements, announcements, or title cards hung beside the door. Torn off along the bottom, from brown twine a six-by-eight-inch piece of shirt cardboard dangled inside the glass. On it written in blue magic marker:

Monday—Friday
10:00 am—4:00 AM
Sat.—Sun.
10:00 am—4:00 AM
$3.50

Taped to the door's lower corner, facing out (again, inside), was a wrinkled yellow theater license—at shin level. Walking along the sidewalk's outer edge, if you glanced up, you saw a facade that made it look as if the place had once been a law firm or a medical clinic. The window covering most of the second-story frontage was painted black. Scraped-up gothic gilt arched the glass:

COLUMBIA

Smaller and off center beneath, running from the B to the A: adult entertainment—probably advertisement for the people driving on the river's edge highway. Wondering about it at all, more likely you'd think it a massage parlor than a movie. From outside, it looked like a three-story office building.

You entered by a glass door, *Columbia* across the transom in flaky gold. Between green walls a stairway led to a second-floor lobby, a hallway with a peeling rubber mat, a door to the balcony, steps down to the orchestra, a third of the seats broken or missing or just collapsed to the floor.

In the last three years, five people have tried to tell me the Columbia never existed. One claimed to have lived two blocks to the north—and swore that if there'd been a straight porn theater on 12th Avenue at 24th Street that encouraged gay activity in the audience, he would have known. Highly active through the 'eighties and 'nineties, he was a gay man who'd regularly made the rounds of New York's cruisy movies, from the Metropolitan on 14th Street and the Variety on 3rd Avenue to the Hesperus, the Grotto, the Cameo, the Adonis, and the Beverly on 8th Avenue, the King and the David and the Circus on Broadway, to the Globe up on East Treemont, and half-a-dozen others he named in Queens and Brooklyn I'd never heard of.

Well, the Columbia was there.

"Shit, you *know* it was—so do I."

The city closed it, October '96, along with the Grotto and the Hesperus.

"Now *that* was one hell of a birthday present!"

It didn't look like a porno house. It didn't look like a movie theater at all.

"I was walkin' around over there three days ago . . . The goddam *building's* been torn down!"

Technically, I suppose, it wasn't. It showed out-of-focus hardcore videos from a three-color projector fixed to a beam running across the middle of its space. When you sat in most of the shallow balcony's seats, loose on their floor bolts, the sagging two-by-four cut the screen, putting now nipples, now genitals behind a black band, as if the Great God Muddle were trying to redeem triple-X for family values.

"Me and a dozen other guys, about, used to go piss in the back corner 'cause there was a hole in the floor—went down between some walls, somewhere. But that bathroom they had downstairs was *so* scuzzy—most of the time the toilets was filled with paper and diarrhea. Even *I* didn't wanna go in there. They knew about the hole, though, 'cause at night they'd come up and put lime or bleach down it or somethin'. Next mornin' it'd be scattered around the edge of the rotten boards—before another old guy'd go wet it down. A few times they nailed a piece of plankin' over it. I was always glad they did—but whenever somebody'd kick it off, I'd be back there usin' it again with everybody else."

At any time half the audience—at least any time I ever went—was homeless. The other half? They could have been anyone. They could have come from anywhere. They could have held any job. My name is Adrian Rome. I'd just moved from Bythenia, New York, into a Greenwich Village apartment on Charles Street, near the waterfront. Back then I was a glorified data-entry clerk at a non-profit social service organization, my salary supplemented, yeah, by an allowance from Dad. In June '94 I was twenty-three when, in the back balcony of the Columbia, I met my friend and life companion of the last half-dozen years—

"Hey, there, man! Sit *down*! Yeah, up here . . . with me."

—Shoat Rumblin.

Shoat was born to a white working-class family in 1968 in a moderate-sized industrial town in Ohio, that was not Cleveland, Toledo, Cincinnati, Sandusky, or Columbus. He doesn't want me to tell you the name, since, he says, it would be too easy for someone to trace him back there, where his dad still lives in a trailer park to the southeast.

How about using a made-up name for the city—or maybe putting it in another city, more or less like it, where he didn't actually live?

"Nope. Just leave it out."

Myself, I think the possibility of its getting back to his family is minimal—given what we've done to *their* names. I'm black, by the bye. But once my mom ran off, my father up-graded to a white girlfriend with whom I do *not* get along. Anyway. Five years ago when we met, Shoat was twenty-five.

He was homeless.

He reads rarely, hesitantly, with moving lips.

In that time, I've never seen him write, not even to sign his name.

We have, incidentally, an open relationship. Shoat goes. Shoat comes. (Copiously.) But these days he sleeps with me more nights than not. Nearer thirty than twenty, the both of us—and today Shoat's on the far side of it—we seem to spend more and more time together, than less.

We've taken each other everywhere, from the Metropolitan Opera, to a jerk-off theater in Passaic he learned about (after they closed down all the ones in New York), to a charity dinner my dad got me tickets for with a lot of movie people. They all thought Shoat was an actor and asked if he was interested in doing "character" work.

"Now you can take all the pictures and Polaroids and home videos you want of me jerkin' off, pissin' on guys, shittin' in guys' faces—all that nice nasty stuff people like to do. People got pictures of me doin' stuff like that all over the goddam country. But put me in front of a real movie camera, where I got to say *words* and things? Naw, that just ain't gonna *happen* . . . ! Still, it was kind of interestin' to hear they all thought I could do it."

If we're out together and someone asks him what he does, he points a thick thumb at me and says: "I keep the little feller happy."

If he's saying it to the right person, instead of pointing, he'll nod in my direction, heft his crotch—and grin.

Shoat just makes six-four—"I was eighteen when I finally caught up to my dad. He was six-four, too. My mom was five-feet-five exact—your height. Ain't that funny? Nobody but him ever thought I was gonna make it. But I broke six feet when I was fourteen"—which is eleven inches taller than I am. He has more body fur than the next three hairiest men I've *ever* known, put together.

"In jail, everybody called me 'Rugs.' Rugs Rumblin."

That's lots of brass-colored hair, already starting to thin on top when I met him, and a curly beard. Between them a twice-broken nose splashes across his face.

"*I* look more like a nigger'n you do."

He has a wide, bear-like body. The three years between nineteen and twenty-two he spent in what he calls Ohio State: ". . . Penitentiary, that is—for not driving the getaway car in a really dumb robbery *very* skillfully at all! When they caught me, I busted a cop's jaw. And got my own nose broke while I was at it." In jail he did nothing but (in his words) "lift weights and beat off."

His forearms and the backs of his hands look as if someone has glued there the unraveled hemp of dock ropes, though only once, he says, has he ever been on a boat.

"For three days—some seventy-year-old geezer rentin' a yacht, off the Mississippi coast. I stayed drunk, caught fish, and got my dick sucked; by him and about four of his business friends. They was pretty decent cocksuckers, all of 'em—even the old guy, once he let loose and took his teeth out. Three of 'em was even nice. I had fun."

A body-builder's arms and legs lurk inside that comfortable bronze bear-rug, behind enough of a gut that no one would ever call him thin. Shoat keeps himself hard with intermittent *shape-up* jobs in a couple of Bowery labor pools. He claims that other than hanging out with "Duke and the boys" (criminals all) for a year—and occasionally giving them a hand, when asked—he never even took change out of his parents' pockets. (Even I did that.) I believe him.

Other than the skilled raconteur's tendency to exaggerate, he's meticulously honest.

It would be naive to say anything about the white American underclass vs. the black American underclass. The truth is, in terms of specific and individual differences (which include the sexual), the underprivileged of this country have never been very accurately portrayed in our time: Everyone has some notion of *the characteristic,* which, as people try to give an account of *that* (Professor Marr tells me what I'm describing is the saturation, ubiquity, and tyranny of discourse), edges out the specific and the individual, even among attempts by the best intentioned.

Shoat's upbringing was not characteristic of *anybody's.*

What's important about it, what's historical about it, what makes it worth writing about and reading about is, however, that it happened— which also means, incidentally, that it *could* have happened—which, in a country this size, means lots of things like it *are* happening. The distance, the tension, the antagonism between this and the characteristic is what's important, not its closeness to or conformity with some normalizing model. And *that* (Professor Marr tells me—what I'm trying to describe, here) is sometimes called, in philosophical jargon today, a Hasler structure. I *don't* know the details.

Nobody who can read a book in the U.S. has to be told that, for every wife who leaves a husband, twenty-five husbands up and leave their wives. But that doesn't mean (one) you won't sometimes get two guys, even three, even five, whose moms left their dads, sitting around a restaurant table who start talking about it. Or that (two) what they say may not have some relevance to, or provide some insight into, the way the world works.

Sure, lots of black men and women's stories still need to be told. The irony that I'm a middle-class black guy who's become the amanuensis to a semiliterate Midwestern redneck has *not* escaped me. Or Shoat. But (three) these happen to be the stories *I've* been rolling around in bed with every night for the past few years.

They won't hurt you.

Anyway.

Over the year-and-a-half after he got out of jail, Shoat hitched to New York (by way of Florida, Illinois, New Mexico, Mississippi, Tennessee, California, Oregon, Utah, and Montana, in that order) because another prisoner had told him, *In a real city, man, you couldn't get arrested for the kind of dipshit stuff they got you in here for.* On his third homeless week in the city, he found the Columbia, and . . . well, moved in.

"They let you bring in sandwiches, fried chicken, beer, just about anything. I'd come through the door and up the steps—my dick would be out my jeans and in my fist before I was through the lobby. The security guard—you remember, that Haitian feller?—used to call me the Midnight Flasher, 'cause he saw me come in that way six or seven times. . . . And maybe I *am* somethin' of a' exhibitionist. I *know* I got a big one. I know what to do with it, too. And I ain't never minded lettin' other people know. In school, guys used to give me money to show it to 'em—I mean the straight ones."

At the Columbia he began a shy year of what once I had the bad judgment to refer to in his presence as "lackadaisical hustling," by which

I only meant he didn't always remember to ask for money. That occasioned one of his few protesting outbursts.

"What you talkin' about, hustlin'? I was *not* no hustler, man! I was *homeless*! Yeah, that means sometimes, afterwards, I'd ask if a guy could spare a couple of bucks—"

You asked *me*, the first three times we—

"—*includin'* you. But I ain't never said no to nobody just because he didn't wanna give me no money. You don't know nothing about no hustlin'—!"

I didn't think it was a *bad* thing, Shoat. I just didn't think you were serious about—

"Hey, hustlin's not bad. I *have* hustled. I told you that. On the boat there, in Mississippi, *that* was hustlin'. I made an arrangement with the ol' guy for a hundred bucks a day. I left there with a cool thousand in my jeans—the old guy's three hundred and a hundred-dollar tip from two of his friends; the other two each gimme me two-fifty. 'Cause I decided I was gonna have me some fun while I was there. Once the two of *them*—two ugly little fellers, all skinny legs and big bellies and one of 'em was bald-headed and smoked cigars—told me it's what they wanted, I'd jump on 'em any old time, three or four times a day, bring 'em down, make 'em suck my dick, fuck 'em right there on the deck in front of everybody. I'd come into where they was sleepin', pulled their legs apart—dick whip 'em and then fuck 'em again. Piss in their faces, call 'em a scumbag, and laugh at 'em while I was doin' it; walk up to 'em while they're sitting around on the deck jawin', whip it out, pee in their drink, and walk away. Man, both of them guys wanted to *marry* me by the time we got back to shore! Now *that* was hustlin'. In fact, besides the guy cookin' and the Captain (who was another faggot but who just watched and beat off sometime—he wouldn't touch nobody) there was three of us hustlin' on that boat there. The old geezer really set him up a party. But I got the biggest tips. Even the stuck-up one, who didn't have the time of day for me unless he was suckin' me off or swabbin' out my asshole with his tongue—he gimme a hundred bucks too. But, see, I was polite to him 'cause I was hustlin'. That goes with the job. The other workin' guys said I got the biggest tips 'cause I had the biggest dick and could come the most times. But *I* think it was because I had the most fun—guys *like* that: The bald guy who really liked me give me a lift up to Knoxville, afterwards. I got a motel room and a' old car and managed to live like a civilized human being for almost three damned weeks . . . I saw him a few more times, made a few more bucks. Now *that* was hustlin'—but not in the damned movie. So you can say anything you want about me and hustlin'. You just can't say I hustled *there*. I lived in that place, man. I was homeless and that was my home. How can you hustle your own home—? Guys who come in there knew I didn't have nothin', and a whole lot of them was nice to me. Real nice. One guy used to come in with a six pack, every three or four days, and leave it with me after we was finished. Half the time there'd be a twenty in the bottom of the bag. But I never said a word to him when there wasn't. And that ain't no hustler. One time when he had to go away for two weeks on a business trip to Grand Rapids—I remember it was Grand Rapids, 'cause I hitchhiked through that place once, and we talked about it—he slipped me a hundred bucks before he left. I thought it was a couple or four fives all folded up together, till after he left and I counted it. A goddam hundred dollars! I saved fifty of it and asked him if he wanted it back, when he come to the theater again three weeks later—and *that* ain't no hustler! Another little red-headed fella liked me to piss all over the two of us. About every three or four times he'd come in there, well, he'd bring me a clean pair of size forty-two/forty jeans, which I could use since there was about half a dozen other fellers, like you know, that was kind of my specialty with. Once we'd finish, I'd get up, change into his dry ones right there, and let him take the wet ones out and throw 'em in the garbage or chew on 'em or beat 'em on a rock in the river—or whatever he liked to do with 'em. And there was three or four others what was always bringing me food and stuff. One even brought a bottle of champagne and a whole turkey dinner once, on Thanksgivin'—a big plate, wrapped up in tin foil, he'd brung down from his family. And I ate it, and we drank that champagne right there, in the back row of the movie; from champagne glasses he had with him in his shoppin' bag. That was a real nice

Thanksgivin', too. But those guys was my friends, man! They weren't no johns. I told you, I always liked older guys. I mean kissin' 'em and stickin' my tongue in their faces and swappin' spit with 'em. I still don't know what I'm doin' with *you*, 'ceptin' you like a little old man, sometimes. And you always gimme a hard on."

Why *didn't* he hustle there? I asked, of course. Wasn't a thousand dollars better than a hundred?

Answer: "Ain't ten, twenty, thirty bucks a day—with fifty, sixty, a hundred there, and few weeks later, seventy, a hundred, a hundred-fifty here—better than a thousand what you spend up three-quarters of it in three days. Then nothin' for two weeks. Then twenty. Then nothing. Then nothin'. And then another nothin's on top of that? Things like that boat party don't happen a lot. Or they don't happen to me. I ain't good lookin'. I'm special, I know that. But all hustlers do is sit around and wait—and I just ain't got the patience for it. A party like that happens to a hustler two, three times in five or six years—and some of 'em, I'll tell you, go on talkin' about it for the rest of their lives. But the fact is, most of hustlin' is standin' around in the rain and bein' wet and thinkin' about how good it used to be and how good it could be and tryin' not to think about how come it's just shit now. Besides—it's hard to hustle people what really turn you on. Which is why I don't like it. So I never did too much of it, and don't do it at all no more. I don't got to. No, see: A hustler back at the movies was a guy who, when you asked him, 'Are you workin'—or are you just here to have fun?' tells you, 'Sorry, man—yeah, I'm on payroll tonight.' A hustler's a guy who, when you say, 'Hey, let's hang out, have a beer, and shoot the shit,' tells you, 'No, man! I gotta go make me some *money!*' A hustler— and there was enough of them come in that place—is a guy who runs into the movie, scopes out where the oldest guys is sittin', throws himself down in the middle, whips it out, and starts shaking it around. Then, when one of 'em looks over or makes a move, he pulls back and rubs his thumb across his fingers in a 'moulah' sign and whispers, 'Twenty . . . ?' and waits for a nod before he lets it out his hand again. Then, the second he's finished, he's standin' up and zippin' up and *out* of there, man— to score his bottle. A hustler sets a price before you get started; he don't hit you up for no handout afterwards, when you can always grin, shrug, and say, sorry. Hustlin's about prices paid for services rendered—the Great American Way! What *I* was about—and most of the other guys there, too, exceptin' the ones who didn't wanna be bothered by *nobody*—was remindin' somebody to be nice to me when I'd been nice to them. Yeah, there were some days I made out a lot better than a damned hustler. Which is why I did it that way. But other days I didn't. Gimme a couple of those, though, and I'd be down at the Shape-Up place on Third Avenue—not hustlin'. Hustlin' ain't nothin' to be ashamed of. But it ain't nothin' to be proud of neither—unless, I guess, like anything else, you do it better than a whole lot of other people. I did it good. But I do this—takin' care of you—better. So don't put me down as no goddam hustler. At least not *there*. It's not *bad*. You just ain't *sayin'* it right!"

Was Shoat worried about AIDS, once he got to the Columbia, during which time, by his own admission, he never once used a condom?

"Nope."

Why not?

" 'Cause you can't get it just from gettin' your dick sucked, or just from some bitch-boy squattin' on it and bouncin'—"

'Bitch-boy?' Shoat, *where* did you pick up a term like that?

"From a' ol' nigger I used to fuck at Ohio State. He was about sixty-five, seventy year old. But that's what *he* said he was—bouncin' up and down on it till you shoot. I can count the times I stuck needles in myself on one hand—they was always straight out the wrapper. And once I got out the slammer, I didn't let *nothin'* up my ass no more. Even you an' me. We'd been together—what? Three years, 'fore that afternoon with all the rain I come in drunk and told you, 'Come on, Little Feller. Climb up on my ass and fuck your old man'? You was one surprised lookin' nigger—you was scared, too. We rolled around here on your rug forty minutes 'fore you got a proper hardon. But I knew you'd come through. I'll tell you though, I was about three minutes away from makin' you just get on down and suck me off like usual. Course, *now* the little nigger can't get enough of it. 'Hey, there, big guy—wanna get drunk and let your little feller fuck ya?' Then I got to

dick-whip 'im back into his place. I swear though, you tickle me sometimes. But we get into that ass fuckin' thing, what? One, two, maybe
three times a year, now? And I always make you wear a condom, when
you do it." (No, *I* make me wear a condom, Shoat.) "I wouldn't be
surprised if, in a few years, though, I wasn't need'n' it once a month
instead of once a year. It's funny how that kind of gets more important
as you get older. It was the same with Buck. Anyway, you get it from
gettin' stuck: with the wrong needle or the wrong dick. You can get the
clap or the syph that way, but you can't get no AIDS just stickin' it *into*
some feller's face."

Well, how did Shoat *know* he wouldn't get it that way?

"People told me. People what knowed, too. Besides, I don't got it."
(This last is true, as I've seen him through several routine HIV tests
since we've been together.) "If you *could* get it that way, believe me, I'd
have it. If I'm with anyone except you, now, even when I'm drunk, I'll
be snoozin' on my belly and you can climb on and rub off in my butt
hair. I *always* liked that. But that's about it. You know, mostly I'm a
face to face kind of guy—at least I wanna be able to see the top of ya'
damned head. Oh. And you can't get it *suckin'* dick, neither."

Okay, how did he know *that*?

" 'Cause *you* don't got it."

I've stopped trying to read him the articles and argue.

As you may sense, Shoat and I are about as different as two guys
can be—and we like it that way. Example: I'm a fanatic about classic
Country-and-Western. I die for George Jones, Waylon Jennings, Jimmy
Buffet, Dotty West, Reba McIntyre: and, of course, Patsy, Loretta,
Tammy, and Tanya "Texas-When-I-Die" Denise Tucker—and LeAnn
Rimes! I doubt I ever would have stood by my man without it: We *give*
'em something to talk about!

"And I hate that gut-bucket hollerin' and moanin' like a spic-on-
the-rise hates beans! One night I come back here and you was playin'
that shit . . . ? I slept down on your front stairs that night. I was not
gonna come in here, while that stuff was on the radio. It's all Buck ever
played. It was on all the goddam time. When I was a kid, I was okay
with it—back then I even thought some of it was pretty. But once I got

in jail? That's *all* they played in there—by the time I got out, I just didn't wanna hear it no more! *Ever.* You will note: There is *no* Country-and-Western even mentioned in my book. Not once. I refused to. But that's because Buck—my dad—was always playin' it. You wanna know about Country-and-Western? Well, you just lay it in under everything my dad ever did, from beatin' off out in the garage to pullin' up floor-boards in the kitchen, lookin' for a dead rat—just stick it there in the background in your mind. 'Cause it was on. But it's my book, and I'm damned if I'm gonna talk about somethin' I hate so much in a story that's got my goddam name on it. I thought when I hooked up with a nigger, I was gonna be shut of that; hear me some good soul music, jazz, rhythm an' blues. Even rap—which I don't love, but I can listen to. But Country-and-fuckin'-*Western?* Damn . . . !"

There are exceptions. (Of course.) Crystal Gale is Shoat's favorite singer.

"But she's more like jazz, ain't she?"

No, Shoat, she's not.

"And I'll admit it, Ray Stevens makes me about piss myself, laughin'."

And he likes Willie.

"But he's just a singer, ain't he? He ain't really country, 'cause he's too popular. Everybody likes *him!*"

So, Shoat, you do like *some* of—

"Don't push it, little feller."

I don't push it.

By the first time Shoat came to my apartment from the theater, I'd already made notes on my computer about some of the stuff he'd told me in the Columbia in earlier weeks. Shoat's family life was, to put it obliquely, eccentric. The idea of writing a book about it came up, how-ever, only in the second year we were together. For three months, there, he got really obsessive over it—told everybody he met we were about to start on it, that I was making notes already, that we were getting it all worked out.

Not many of Shoat's plans have come to much. After three months, when I just wasn't doing it, he dropped the whole thing, stopped bringing it up. He didn't even hold it against me. I felt bad, though, because I'd thought it would be an interesting experiment. Back at Enoch State (... University, that is!) I'd written some short stories for a writing workshop, one of which actually won second prize in a contest where I hadn't known *any* of the teachers judging.

But I just didn't have the time.

Then, one Spring night, Shoat and I were out to dinner with some friends at a down-the-steps French restaurant between Eighth and Ninth on the north side of Fifty-first. With us was another white fellow from backwoods Maryland, and his lover, a black professor. (Professor Marr had just published a book with a place called Rhino*seros*, that does some pretty risquè fare.) Shoat and the other guy started swapping stories that, soon, had the rest of us too opened-mouthed to realize how astonished we were!

The next day was Saturday.

I was up before six, and, at the blue enameled bench in front of the kitchen table, on my laptop I began jotting down as much of what Shoat had told us as I could recall from the previous night. Some of it, of course, he'd told me already—so even at that point it was a composite version. About ten, when Shoat rolled out, I heard him behind me, but I was so into what I was writing, I didn't twig to what he was doing till something hot hit the back of my neck and rolled on down my shoulder—while I got another splatter on my shoulder blade.

"What the ...?" I turned around.

He was still working on it—and giving out with a few after-grunts. "You ain't ... doin' your job, man ... I got to do it all ... by myself, now?"

So I grabbed him by his (Scouts' honor) dick, pulled him around beside me down on the bench, and told him we had started writing *his* book.

"We *have*?"

And, till sometime after nine that night, the both of us, thigh to thigh at the kitchen table, we did just that—then went out for beer and burgers, and came home for one of the hottest nights we've had together.

"You think spendin' a whole day talkin' about this shit makes you hornier?"

When you're working as hard as we were, I don't know the answer to that one for sure, any more than I do about the oral transmission of AIDS.

Shoat has asked me to write this verbatim:

"This is the story of me and my dad and, I guess, my mamma, and this other guy what I'm telling to my friend, the little feller—Adrian, yeah, that's his name—and he's putting down all the words right like I say them. My Life Story—or, like the little feller says, my ideas and sensations. (He says that comes from another book he read, but like I don't wanna put my dad's city down, he don't want to name that book neither.) Though, really, it's just about the part when I was a kid, before I come to New York. Or even got in jail, yet. Though, when you get toward the end, you'll probably see it—jail, that is—coming. I wished *I* had! The little feller says he had to put in a few words I didn't actually say to make it like a real story. Also, stuff like, when I didn't remember good or didn't know what I was talking about, and just went off on a toot, he left that shit out. But he read it all back to me and all what I said he got wrong, it wasn't like that, he changed it. And anything he put in on his own I said didn't go there, he took that out, too. Though we're putting this at the beginning, we're writing it at the end, when it's all finished—which, at the end, is where he thought it should go, but I said: No, it's my story. You put it right at the start, so people will know they can trust it."

It took Shoat and me (the little fellow, again) about eighteen months, with a week off here, a week off there. The manuscript runs six-hundred-twenty-seven pages, and sometimes Shoat got tired of telling parts of it over and over so I could write it. In school, he says, it was all he could do to get down a page: "I'd make the letters big to fill it up faster. Adrian showed me how you could do that on a word processor, too. But with this story, we didn't have to. I always wondered how you wrote a book before, and now I guess I know. 'Cause we wrote one."

I would like to put in that, as amanuensis-cum-editor, I've made no attempt to keep Shoat's dialectical idiosyncrasies consistent—because he doesn't. He's been pretty much all over the country. At this point the South and the West are as evident in his speech as any peculiarities of the Ohio working-class suburb he began in.

Oh, and Shoat has asked me to include this last, linguistic note:

"I do not ordinarily use the word 'nigger' since I been growed, except when I am around real ignorant white people of a certain class—a class whose company I do not look out for much anymore. Since I went to jail, I been a lot more with black people than with white. And that's how I prefer it. The last year I was in the pokey, that got me my nose broke for the *second* time! Yes, I am a redneck born, but I am more comfortable around black people—and no *black* guy ever busted my nose! Now it's true, niggers is always askin' me to call 'em niggers. (And we won't talk about what I like 'em to call *me*!) But I only do it with the little feller 'cause he says it gives 'im a hard-on—sometimes."

I don't know. Makes me remember my roots.

Sometimes.

Anyway.

For the rest, this is Shoat Rumblin's story.

Cadillac Flambé

BY RALPH ELLISON

It had been a fine spring day made even pleasanter by the lingering of the cherry blossoms and I had gone out before dawn with some married friends and their children on a bird-watching expedition. Afterwards we had sharpened our appetites for brunch with rounds of bloody marys and bullshots. And after the beef bouillon ran out, our host, an ingenious man, had improvised a drink from chicken broth and vodka which he proclaimed the "chicken-shot." This was all very pleasant and after a few drinks my spirits were soaring. I was pleased with my friends, the brunch was excellent and varied—chili con carne, cornbread, and oysters Rockefeller, etc.—and I was pleased with my tally of birds. I had seen a bluebird, five red-breasted grosbeaks, three painted buntings, seven goldfinches, and a rousing consort of mockingbirds. In fact, I had hated to leave.

Thus it was well into the afternoon when I found myself walking past the Senator's estate. I still had my binoculars around my neck, and my tape recorder—which I had along to record bird songs—was slung over my shoulder. As I approached, the boulevard below the Senator's estate was heavy with cars, with promenading lovers, dogs on leash, old men on canes, and laughing children, all enjoying the fine weather. I had paused to notice how the Senator's lawn rises from the street level with a gradual and imperceptible elevation that makes the mansion, set far at the top, seem to float like a dream castle: an illusion intensified by the chicken-shots but which the art editor of my paper informs me is the result of a trick copied from the landscape architects who designed the gardens of the Bellevedere Palace in Vienna. But be that as it may, I was about to pass on when a young couple blocked my path, and when I saw the young fellow point up the hill and say to his young blonde of a girl, "I bet you don't know who that is up there," I brought my binoculars into play, and there, on the right-hand terrace of the mansion, I saw the Senator.

Dressed in a chef's cap, apron, and huge asbestos gloves, he was armed with a long-tined fork which he flourished broadly as he entertained the notables for whom he was preparing a barbecue. These gentlemen and ladies were lounging in their chairs or standing about in groups sipping the tall iced drinks which two white-jacketed Filipino boys were serving. The Senator was dividing his attention between the spareribs cooking in a large chrome grill-cart and displaying his great talent for mimicking his colleagues with such huge success that no one at the party was aware of what was swiftly approaching. And, in fact, neither was I.

I was about to pass on when a gleaming white Cadillac convertible, which had been moving slowly in the heavy traffic from the east, rolled abreast of me and suddenly blocked the path by climbing the curb and then continuing across the walk and onto the Senator's lawn. The top was back and the driver, smiling as though in a parade, was a well-dressed Negro man of about thirty-five, who sported the gleaming hair affected by their jazz musicians and prize-fighters, and who sat behind the wheel with that engrossed, yet relaxed, almost ceremonial attention to form that was once to be observed only among the finest horsemen. So closely did the car brush past that I could have reached out with no effort and touched the rich ivory leather upholstery. A bull fiddle rested in the back of the car. I watched the man drive smoothly up the lawn until he was some seventy-five yards below the mansion, where he braked the machine and stepped out to stand waving toward the terrace, a gallant salutation grandly given.

At first, in my innocence, I placed the man as a musician, for there was, after all, the bull fiddle; then in swift succession I thought him a chauffeur for one of the guests, a driver for a news or fashion magazine or an advertising agency or television network. For I quickly realized that a musician wouldn't have been asked to perform at the spot where the car was stopped, and that since he was alone, it was unlikely that anyone, not even the Senator, would have hired a musician to play serenades on a bull fiddle. So next I decided that the man had either been sent with equipment to be used in covering the festivities taking place on the terrace, or that he had driven the car over to be photographed against the luxurious background. The waving I interpreted as the expression of simple-minded high spirits aroused by the driver's pleasure in piloting such a luxurious automobile, the simple exuberance of a Negro allowed a role in what he considered an important public spectacle. At any rate, by now a small crowd had gathered and had begun to watch bemusedly.

Since it was widely known that the Senator is a master of the new political technology, who ignores no medium and wastes no opportunity for keeping his image ever in the public's eye, I wasn't disturbed when I saw the driver walk to the trunk and begin to remove several red objects of a certain size and place them on the grass. I wasn't using my binoculars now and thought these were small equipment cases. Unfortunately, I was mistaken.

For now, having finished unpacking, the driver stepped back behind the wheel, and suddenly I could see the top rising from its place of concealment to soar into place like the wing of some great, slow, graceful bird. Stepping out again, he picked up one of the cases—now suddenly transformed into the type of can which during the war was sometimes used to transport high-octane gasoline in Liberty ships (a highly dangerous cargo for those round bottoms and the men who shipped in them)—and, leaning carefully forward, began emptying its contents upon the shining chariot.

And thus, I thought, is gilded an eight-valved, three-hundred-and-fifty-horsepowered air-conditioned lily!

For so accustomed have we Americans become to the tricks, the shenanigans, and frauds of advertising, so adjusted to the contrived fantasies of commerce—indeed, to pseudo-events of all kinds—that I thought that the car was being drenched with a special liquid which would make it more alluring for a series of commercial photographs.

Indeed, I looked up the crowded boulevard behind me, listening for the horn of a second car or station wagon which would bring the familiar load of pretty models, harassed editors, nervous wardrobe mistresses, and elegant fashion photographers who would convert the car, the clothes, and the Senator's elegant home, into a photographic rite of spring.

And with the driver there to remind me, I even expected a few ragged colored street urchins to be brought along to form a poignant but realistic contrast to the luxurious costumes and high-fashion surroundings: an echo of the somber iconography in which the crucified Christ is flanked by a repentant and an unrepentant thief, or that in which the three Wise Eastern Kings bear their rich gifts before the humble stable of Bethlehem.

But now reality was moving too fast for the completion of this foray into the metamorphosis of religious symbolism. Using my binoculars for a closer view, I could see the driver take a small spherical object from the trunk of the car and a fuzzy tennis ball popped into focus against the dark smoothness of his fingers. This was joined by a long wooden object which he held like a conductor's baton and began forcing against the ball until it pierced. This provided the ball with a slender handle which he tested delicately for balance, drenched with liquid, and placed carefully behind the left fin of the car.

Reaching into the back seat now, he came up with a bass fiddle bow upon which he accidentally spilled the liquid, and I could see drops of fluid roping from the horsehairs and falling with an iridescent spray into the sunlight. Facing us now, he proceeded to tighten the horsehairs, working methodically, very slowly, with his head gleaming in the sunlight and beads of sweat standing over his brow.

As I watched, I became aware of the swift gathering of a crowd around me, people asking puzzled questions, and a certain tension, as during the start of a concert, was building. And I had just thought, *And now he'll bring out the fiddle*, when he opened the door and hauled it out, carrying it, with the dripping bow swinging from his right hand, up the hill some thirty feet above the car, and placed it lovingly on the grass. A gentle wind started to blow now, and I swept my glasses past his gleaming head to the mansion, and as I screwed the focus to infinity, I could see several figures spring suddenly from the shadows on the shaded terrace of the mansion's far wing. They were looking on like the spectators of a minor disturbance at a dull baseball game. Then a large woman grasped that something was out of order and I could see her mouth come open and her eyes blaze as she called out soundlessly, "Hey, you down there!" Then the driver's head cut into my field of vision and I took down the glasses and watched him moving, broad-shouldered and jaunty, up the hill to where he'd left the fiddle. For a moment he stood with his head back, his white jacket taut across his shoulders, looking toward the terrace. He waved then, and shouted words that escaped me. Then, facing the machine, he took something from his pocket and I saw him touch the flame of a cigarette lighter to the tennis ball and begin blowing gently upon it; then, waving it about like a child twirling a Fourth of July sparkler, he watched it sputter into a small blue ball of flame.

I tried, indeed I anticipated what was coming next, but I simply could not accept it! The Negro was twirling the ball on that long, black-tipped wooden needle—the kind used for knitting heavy sweaters—holding it between his thumb and fingers in the manner of a fire-eater at a circus, and I couldn't have been more surprised if he had thrown back his head and plunged the flame down his throat than by what came next. Through the glasses now I could see sweat beading out beneath his scalp line and on the flesh above the stiff hairs of his moustache as he grinned broadly and took up the fiddle bow, and before I could move he had shot his improvised, flame-tipped arrow onto the cloth top of the convertible.

"Why that black son of the devil!" someone shouted, and I had the impression of a wall of heat springing up from the grass before me. Then the flames erupted with a stunning blue roar that sent the spectators scattering. People were shouting now, and through the blue flames before me I could see the Senator and his guests running from the terrace to halt at the top of the lawn, looking down, while behind me there were screams, the grinding of brakes, the thunder of footfalls as the promenaders broke in a great spontaneous wave up the grassy slope, then sensing the danger of exploding gasoline, receded hurriedly to a safer distance below, their screams and curses ringing above the roar of the flames.

How, oh, how, I wished for a cinema camera to synchronize with my tape recorder!—which automatically I now brought into play as heavy fumes of alcohol and gasoline, those defining spirits of our age, filled the air. There before me unfolding in *tableau vivant* was surely the most unexpected picture in the year: in the foreground at the bottom of the slope, a rough semicircle of outraged faces; in the mid-foreground, up the gentle rise of the lawn, the white convertible shooting into the springtime air a radiance of intense blue flame, a flame like that of a welder's torch or perhaps of a huge fowl being flambéed in choice cognac; then on the rise above, distorted by heat and flame, the dark-skinned, white-suited driver, standing with his gleaming face expressive of high excitement as he watched the effect of his deed. Then, rising high in the background atop the grassy hill, the white-capped Senator surrounded by his notable guests—all caught in postures eloquent of surprise, shock, or indignation.

The air was filled with an overpowering smell of wood alcohol, which, as the leaping red and blue flames took firm hold, mingled with the odor of burning paint and leather. I became aware of the fact that the screaming had suddenly faded now, and I could hear the swoosh-pop-crackle-and-hiss of the fire. And with the gaily dressed crowd become silent, it was as though I were alone, isolated, observing a conflagration produced by a stroke of lightning flashed out of a clear blue springtime sky. We watched with that sense of awe similar to that with which medieval crowds must have observed the burning of a great cathedral. We were stunned by the sacrificial act and, indeed, it was as though we had become the unwilling participants in a primitive ceremony requiring the sacrifice of a beautiful object in appeasement of some terrifying and long-dormant spirit, which the black man in the white suit was summoning from a long, black sleep. And as we watched, our faces strained as though in anticipation of the spirit's materialization from the fiery metamorphosis of the white machine, a spirit that I was afraid, whatever the form in which it appeared, would be powerfully good or powerfully evil, and absolutely out of place here and now in Washington. It was, as I say, uncanny. The whole afternoon seemed to float, and when I looked again to the top of the hill the people there appeared to move in slow motion through watery waves of heat. Then I saw the Senator, with chef cap awry, raising his asbestos gloves above his head and beginning to shout. And it was then that the driver, the firebrand, went into action.

Till now, looking like the chief celebrant of an outlandish rite, he had held firmly to his middle-ground; too dangerously near the flaming convertible for anyone not protected by asbestos suiting to risk laying hands upon him, yet far enough away to highlight his human vulnerability to fire. But now as I watched him move to the left of the flames to a point allowing him an uncluttered view of the crowd, his white suit reflecting the flames, he was briefly obscured by a sudden swirl of smoke, and it was during this brief interval that I heard the voice.

Strong and hoarse and typically Negro in quality, it seemed to issue with eerie clarity from the fire itself. Then I was struggling within myself for the reporter's dedicated objectivity and holding my microphone forward as he raised both arms above his head, his long, limber fingers wide-spread as he waved toward us.

"Ladies and gentlemen," he said, "please don't be disturbed! I don't mean you any harm, and if you'll just cool it a minute I'll tell you what this is all about . . ."

He paused and the Senator's voice could be heard angrily in the background.

"Never mind that joker up there on top of the hill," the driver said. "You can listen to him when I get through. He's had too much free speech anyway. Now it's *my* turn."

And at this a man at the other end of the crowd shouted angrily and tried to break up the hill. He was grabbed by two men and an hysterical, dark-haired woman wearing a well-filled chemise-style dress, who slipped to the ground holding a leg, shouting, "No, Fleetwood. No! That crazy nigger will kill you!"

The arsonist watched with blank-faced calm as the man was dragged protesting back into the crowd. Then a shift in the breeze whipped smoke down upon us and gave rise to a flurry of coughing.

"Now believe me," the arsonist continued, "I know that it's very,

Making Callaloo

very hard for you folks to look at what I'm doing and not be disturbed, because for you it's a crime and a sin."

He laughed, swinging his fiddle bow in a shining arc as the crowd watched him fixedly.

"That's because you know that most folks can't afford to own one of these Caddies. Not even good, hard-working folks, no matter what the pictures in the papers and magazines say. So deep down it makes you feel some larceny. You feel that it's unfair that everybody who's willing to work hard can't have one for himself. That's right! And you feel that in order to get one it's OK for a man to lie and cheat and steal—yeah, even swindle his own mother *if* she's got the cash. That's the difference between what you *say* you believe and the way you *act* if you get the chance. Oh yes, because words is words, but life is hard and earnest and these here Caddies is way, way out of this world!"

Pausing, he loosened the knot in his blue and white tie so that it hung down the front of his jacket in a large loop, then wiped his brow with a blue silk handkerchief.

"I don't mean to insult you," he said, bending toward us now, the fiddle bow resting across his knee, "I'm just reminding you of the facts. Because I can see in your eyes that it's going to cost me more to get *rid* of this Caddy the way I have to do it than it cost me to get it. I don't rightly know what the price will be, but I know that when you people get scaird and shook up, you get violent.—No, wait a minute . . ." He shook his head. "That's not how I meant to say it. I'm sorry. I apologize.

"Listen, here it is: This *morning*," he shouted now, stabbing his bow toward the mansion with angry emphasis. "This morning that fellow Senator *Sunraider* up there, *he* started it when he shot off his mouth over the *radio*. That's what this is all about! I realized that things had gotten out of *control*. I realized all of a sudden that the man was *messing* . . . with . . . my *Cadillac*, and ladies and gentlemen, that's serious as all *hell* . . .

"Listen to me, y'all: A little while ago I was romping past *Richmond*, feeling fine. I had played myself three hundred and seventy-five dollars and thirty-three cents worth of gigs down in Chattanooga, and I was headed home to *Harlem* as straight as I could go. I wasn't bothering any*body*. I didn't even mean to stop by here, because this town has a way of making a man feel like he's living in a fool's *paradise*. When I'm *here* I never stop thinking about the difference between what it is and what it's *supposed* to be. In fact, I have the feeling that somebody put the *Indian* sign on this town a long, long time ago, and I don't want to be around when it takes effect. So, like I say, I wasn't even thinking about this town. I was rolling past Richmond and those whitewalls were slapping those concrete slabs and I was rolling and the wind was feeling fine on my face—and that's when I made my sad mistake. Ladies and gentlemen, I turned on the radio. I had nothing against anybody. I was just hoping to hear some Dinah, or Duke, or Hawk so that I could study their phrasing and improve my style and enjoy myself.—But what do I get? I'll tell you what I got—"

He dropped his shoulders with a sudden violent twist as his index finger jabbed toward the terrace behind him, bellowing, "I GOT THAT NO GOOD, NOWHERE SENATOR SUNRAIDER! THAT'S WHAT I GOT! AND WHAT WAS HE DOING? HE WAS TRYING TO GET THE UNITED STATES GOVERNMENT TO MESS WITH MY CADILLAC! AND WHAT'S MORE, HE WAS CALLING MY CADDY A 'COON CAGE.'

"Ladies and gentlemen, I couldn't believe my *ears*. I don't know that Senator and I know he doesn't know me from old *Bodiddly*. But just the same, there he is, talking straight to me and there was no use of my trying to dodge. Because I do live in Harlem and I lo-mo-sho do drive a Cadillac. So I had to sit there and take it like a little man. There he was, a United States SENATOR, coming through my own radio telling me what I ought to be driving, and recommending to the United States Senate and the whole country that the name of my car be changed simply because *I*, me, LeeWillie Minifees, was driving it!

"It made me feel faint. It upset my mind like a midnight telegram!

"I said to myself, 'LeeWillie, what on earth is this man *talking* about? Here you been thinking you had it *made*. You been thinking you were as free as a bird—even though a black bird. That good-rolling Jersey Turnpike is up ahead to get you home.—And now here comes this Senator putting you in a cage! What in the world is going on?'

Making Callaloo

"I got so nervous that all at once my foot weighed ninety-nine pounds, and before I knew it I was doing *seventy-five*. I was breaking the law! I guess I was really trying to get away from that voice and what the man had said. But I was rolling and I was listening. I couldn't *help* myself. What I was hearing was going against my whole heart and soul, but I was listening *anyway*. And what I heard was beginning to make me see things in a new light. Yes, and that new light was making my eyeballs ache. And all the time Senator Sunraider up in the Senate was calling my car a 'coon cage.'

"So I looked around and I saw all that fine ivory leather there. I looked at the steel and at the chrome. I looked through the windshield and saw the road unfolding and the houses and the trees was flashing by. I looked up at the top and I touched the button and let it go back to see if that awful feeling would leave me. But it wouldn't leave. The *air* was hitting my face and the *sun* was on my head and I was feeling that good old familiar feeling of *flying*—but ladies and gentlemen, it was no longer the same! Oh, no—because I could still hear that Senator playing the *dozens* with my Cadillac!

"And just then, ladies and gentlemen, I found myself rolling toward an old man who reminded me of my granddaddy by the way he was walking beside the highway behind a plow hitched to an old, white-muzzled Missouri mule. And when that old man looked up and saw me he waved. And I looked back through the mirror as I shot past him and I could see him open his mouth and say something like, 'Go on, fool!' Then him and that mule was gone even from the mirror and I was rolling on.

"And then, ladies and gentlemen, in a twinkling of an eye it struck me. A voice said to me, 'LeeWillie, that old man is right: you are a fool. And that doggone Senator Sunraider is right, LeeWillie, you are a fool in a coon cage!'

"I tell you, ladies and gentlemen, that old man and his mule both were talking to me. I said, 'What do you mean about his being right?' And they said, 'LeeWillie, look who he *is*,' and I said, 'I *know* who he is,' and they said, 'Well, LeeWillie, if a man like that, in the position he's in, can think the way he doin, then LeeWillie, you have GOT to be wrong!'

"So I said, 'Thinking like that is why you've still got that mule in your lap, man. I worked hard to get the money to buy this Caddy,' and he said, '*Money?* LeeWillie, can't you see that it ain't no longer a matter of money? Can't you see it's done gone way past the question of money? Now it's a question of whether you can afford it in terms *other than money.*'

"And I said, 'Man, what are you talking about, "terms other than money,'" and he said, 'LeeWillie, even this damn mule knows that if a man like that feels the way he's talking and can say it right out over the radio and the T.V., and from the place where he's saying it—there's got to be something drastically wrong with you for even wanting one. Son, the man's done made it mean something different. All you wanted was to have a pretty automobile, but fool, he done changed the Rules on you!'

"So against myself, ladies and gentlemen, I was forced to *agree* with the old man and the mule. That Senator up there wasn't simply degrading my Caddy. That wasn't the *point*. It's that he would low-rate a thing so truly fine as a *Cadillac* just in order to degrade *me* and my *people*. He was accusing *me* of lowering the value of the auto, when all I ever wanted was the very best!

"Oh, it hurt me to the quick, and right then and there I had me a rolling revelation. The *scales* dropped from my eyes. I had been BLIND, but the Senator up there on that hill was making me SEE. He was making me see some things I didn't *want* to see! I'd thought I was dressed real FINE, but I was as naked as a jaybird sitting on a limb in the drifting snow. I THOUGHT I was rolling past *Richmond*, but I was really trapped in a COON CAGE, running on one of those little TREADMILLS like a SQUIRREL or a HAMSTER. So now my EYEBALLS were aching. My head was in such a whirl that I shot the car up to ninety, and all I could see up ahead was the road getting NARROW. It was getting as narrow as the eye of a NEEDLE, and that needle looked like the Washington MONUMENT lying down. Yes, and I was trying to thread that Caddy straight through that eye and I didn't care if I made it or not. But while I managed to get that Caddy through I just couldn't thread that COON CAGE because it was like a two-ton knot tied in a piece of fine silk thread. The sweat was pouring off me now, ladies and gentlemen, and my brain was on fire, so I pulled off the highway and asked myself some questions, and I got myself some answers. It went this way:

" 'LeeWillie, who put you in this cage?'

" 'You put your own self in there,' a voice inside me said.

" 'But I paid for it, it's mine. I own it . . .' I said.

" 'Oh, no, LeeWillie,' the voice said, 'what you mean is that it owns *you*, that's why you're in the cage. *Admit* it, daddy; you have been NAMED. Senator Sunraider has put the badmouth, the NASTY mouth on you and now your Cadillac ain't no Caddy anymore! Let's face it, LeeWillie, from now on everytime you sit behind this wheel you're going to feel those RINGS shooting round and round your TAIL and one of those little black COON'S masks is going to settle down over your FACE, and folks standing on the streets and hanging out the windows will sing out, "HEY! THERE GOES MISTER COON AND HIS COON CAGE!" That's right, LeeWillie! And all those little husky-voiced colored CHILDREN playing in the gutters will point at you and say, "THERE GOES MISTAH GOON AND HIS COON CAGE"—and that will be right in Harlem!'

"And that did it, ladies and gentlemen; that was the capper, and THAT'S why I'm here!

"Right then and there, beside the *highway*, I made my decision. I rolled that Caddy, I made a U-turn and I stopped only long enough to get me some of that good white wood *alcohol* and good *white* gasoline, and then I headed straight here. So while some of you are upset, you can see that you don't have to be afraid because LeeWillie means nobody any harm.

"I am here, ladies and gentlemen, to make the Senator a present. Yes, sir and yes, m'am, and it's Sunday and I'm told that *confession* is good for the *soul*.—So Mister Senator," he said, turning toward the terrace above, "this is my public testimony to my coming over to your way of thinking. This is my surrender of the Coon Cage Eight! You have unconverted me from the convertible. In fact, I'm giving it to you, Senator Sunraider, and it is truly mine to give. I hope all my people will do likewise. Because after your speech they ought to run whenever they even *look* at one of these. They ought to make for the bomb shelters whenever one comes close to the curb. So I, me, LeeWillie Minifees, am setting an example and here it is. You can HAVE it, Mister Senator. I don't WANT it. Thank you KINDLY and MUCH obliged . . ."

He paused, looking toward the terrace, and at this point I saw a great burst of flame which sent the crowd scurrying backward down the hill, and the white-suited firebrand went into an ecstatic chant, waving his violin bow, shaking his gleaming head and stamping his foot:

"Listen to me, Senator: I don't want no JET! (stamp!) But thank you kindly.

"I don't want no FORD! (stamp!)

"Neither do I want a RAMBLER! (stamp!)

"I don't want no NINETY-EIGHT! (stamp!)

"Ditto the THUNDERBIRD! (stamp-stamp!)

"Yes, and keep those CHEVYS and CHRYSLERS away from me— do you (stamp!) *hear* me, Senator?

"YOU HAVE TAKEN THE BEST," he boomed, "SO, DAMMIT, TAKE ALL THE REST! Take ALL the rest!

"In fact, now I don't want anything you think is too good for me and my people. Because, just as that old man and the mule said, if a man in your position is against our having them, then there must be something WRONG in our *wanting* them. So to keep you happy, I, me, LeeWillie Minifees, am prepared to WALK. I'm ordering me some club-footed, pigeon-toed SPACE SHOES. I'd rather crawl or FLY. I'd rather save my money and wait until the A-RABS make a car. The Zulus even. Even the ESKIMOS! Oh, I'll walk and wait. I'll grab me a GREYHOUND or a FREIGHT! So you can have my coon cage, fare thee well!

"Take the TAIL FINS and the WHITEWALLS. Help yourself to the poor raped RADIO. ENJOY the automatic dimmer and the power brakes. ROLL, Mister Senator, with that fluid DRIVE. Breathe that air-conditioned AIR. There's never been a Caddy like this one and I want you to HAVE IT. Take my scientific dreamboat and enjoy that good ole GRACIOUS LIVING! The key's in the ignition and the REGISTRATION'S in the GLOVE compartment! And thank you KINDLY for freeing me from the Coon Cage. Because before I'd be in a CAGE, I'll be buried in my GRAVE—Oh! Oh!"

He broke off, listening; and I became aware of the shrilling of approaching sirens. Then he was addressing the crowd again.

"I knew," he called down with a grin, "that THOSE would be coming soon. Because they ALWAYS come when you don't NEED them. Therefore, I only hope that the Senator will beat it on down here and accept his gift before they arrive. And in the meantime, I want ALL you ladies and gentlemen to join LeeWillie in singing 'God Bless America' so that all this won't be in vain.

"I want you to understand that that was a damned GOOD Caddy and I loved her DEARLY. That's why you don't have to worry about me. I'm doing fine. Everything is copacetic. Because, remember, nothing makes a man feel better than giving AWAY something, than SACRIFICING something, that he dearly LOVES!"

And then, most outrageous of all, he threw back his head and actually sang a few bars before the noise of the short-circuited horn set the flaming car to wailing like some great prehistoric animal heard in the throes of its dying.

Behind him now, high on the terrace, the Senator and his guests were shouting, but on the arsonist sang, and the effect on the crowd was maddening. Perhaps because from the pleasurable anticipation of watching the beginning of a clever advertising stunt, they had been thrown into a panic by the deliberate burning, the bizarre immolation of the automobile. And now with a dawning of awareness they perceived that they had been forced to witness (and who could turn away?) a crude and most portentous political gesture.

So suddenly they broke past me, dashing up the hill in moblike fury, and it was most fortunate for Minifees that his duet with the expiring Cadillac was interrupted by members of the police and fire departments, who, arriving at this moment, threw a flying wedge between the flaming machine and the mob. Through the noisy action I could see him there, looming prominently in his white suit, a mocking smile flickering on his sweaty face, as the action whirled toward where he imperturbably stood his ground, still singing against the doleful wailing of the car.

He was still singing, his wrists coolly extended now in anticipation of handcuffs—when struck by a veritable football squad of asbestos-garbed policemen and swept, tumbling, in a wild tangle of arms and legs, down the slope to where I stood. It was then I noted that he wore expensive black alligator shoes.

And now, while the crowd roared its approval, I watched as LeeWillie Minifees was pinned down, lashed into a straitjacket and led toward a police car. Up the hill two policemen were running laboredly toward where the Senator stood, silently observing. About me there was much shouting and shoving as some of the crowd attempted to follow the trussed-up and still grinning arsonist but were beaten back by the police.

It was unbelievably wild. Some continued to shout threats in their outrage and frustration, while others, both men and women, filled the air with a strangely brokenhearted and forlorn sound of weeping, and the officers found it difficult to disperse them. In fact, they continued to mill angrily about even as firemen in asbestos suits broke through, dragging hoses from a roaring pumper truck and sprayed the flaming car with a foamy chemical, which left it looking like the offspring of some strange animal brought so traumatically and precipitantly to life that it wailed and sputtered in protest, both against the circumstance of its debut into the world and the foaming presence of its still-clinging afterbirth . . .

And what had triggered it? How had the Senator sparked this weird conflagration? Why, with a joke! The day before, while demanding larger appropriations for certain scientific research projects that would be of great benefit to our electronics and communications industries, and of great importance to the nation as a whole, the Senator had aroused the opposition of a liberal Senator from New York who had complained, in passing, of what he termed the extreme vapidness of our recent automobile designs, their lack of adequate safety devices, and of the slackness of our quality control standards and procedures. Well, it was in defending the automobile industry that the Senator passed the remark that triggered LeeWillie Minifees's bizarre reply.

In his rebuttal—the committee session was televised and aired over radio network—the Senator insisted that not only were our cars the best in the world, the most beautiful and efficiently designed, but that, in fact, his opponent's remarks were a gratuitous slander. Because, he asserted, the only ground which he could see for complaint lay in the circumstance that a certain make of luxury automobile had become so outrageously popular in the nation's Harlems—the archetype of which is included in his opponent's district—that he found it embarrassing to own one. And then with a face most serious in its composure he went on to state:

"We have reached a sad state of affairs, gentlemen, wherein this fine product of American skill and initiative has become so common in Harlem that much of its initial value has been sorely compromised. Indeed, I am led to suggest, and quite seriously, that legislation be drawn up to rename it the 'Coon Cage Eight.' And not at all because of its eight, super-efficient cylinders, nor because of the lean, springing strength and beauty of its general outlines. Not at all, but because it has now become such a common sight to see eight or more of our darker brethren crowded together enjoying its power, its beauty, its neo-pagan comfort, while weaving recklessly through the streets of our great cities and along our super-highways. In fact, gentlemen, I was run off the road, forced into a ditch by such a power-drunk group just the other day. It is enough to make a citizen feel alienated from his own times, from the abiding values and recent developments within his own beloved nation.

"And yet, we continue to hear complaints to the effect that these constituents of our worthy colleague are ill-housed, ill-clothed, ill-equipped and under-*treaded*! But, gentlemen, I say to you in all sincerity: Look into the streets! Look at the statistics for automobile sales! And I don't mean the economy cars, but our most expensive luxury machines. Look and see who is purchasing them! Give your attention to who it is that is creating the scarcity and removing these superb machines from the reach of those for whom they were intended! With so many of these good things, what, pray, do those people desire—is it a jet plane on every Harlem rooftop?"

Now for Senator Sunraider this had been mild and far short of his usual maliciousness. And while it aroused some slight amusement and brought replies of false indignation from some of his opponents, it was edited out, as is frequently the case, when the speech appeared in the Congressional Record and in the press. But who could have predicted that Senator Sunraider would have brought on LeeWillie Minifees's wild gesture? Perhaps he had been putting on an act, creating a happening, as they say, though I doubted it. There was something more personal behind it. Without question, the Senator's remarks were in extremely bad taste, but to cap the joke by burning an expensive car seemed so extreme a reply as to be almost metaphysical.

And yet, I reminded myself, it might simply be a case of over-reacting expressed in true Negro abandon, an extreme gesture springing from the frustration of having no adequate means of replying, or making himself heard above the majestic roar of a Senator. There was, of course, the recent incident involving a black man suffering from an impacted wisdom tooth who had been so maddened by the blaring of a moisture-shorted automobile horn which had blasted his sleep about three o'clock of an icy morning, that he ran out into the street clothed only in an old-fashioned nightshirt and blasted the hood of the offending auto-mobile with both barrels of a twelve-gauge over-and-under shotgun.

But while toothaches often lead to such extreme acts—and once in a while to suicide—LeeWillie Minifees had apparently been in no pain—or at least not in *physical* pain. And on the surface at least his speech had been projected clearly enough (allowing for the necessity to shout) and he had been smiling when they led him away. What would be his fate? I wondered; and where had they taken him? I would have to find him and question him, for his action had begun to sound in my mind with disturbing overtones which had hardly been meaningful. Rather they had been like the brief interruption one sometimes hears while listening to an F.M. broadcast of the musical *Oklahoma!*, say, with original cast, when the signal fades and a program of quite different mood from a different wave-length breaks through. It had happened but then a blast of laughter had restored us automatically to our chosen frequency.

Meiosis

BY PERCIVAL EVERETT

"This is the last stop," the conductor said, waking Tom. Tom rubbed his eyes and looked out the window. The train took a long time to actually pull into Penn Station. Tom disembarked with the other passengers, shuffling in their steps, going where they went, finding his way into the terminal building and then feeling nervous at the sight of so many people milling about. The digital clock on the schedule board flipped over and read 1:30. Tom hadn't been standing there for fifteen seconds before a heavily-biceped cop said to him, "Keep it moving, bud, there's no loitering allowed in the station." Tom walked on, noticing that many people were standing still, waiting, reading, staring at the train board, and he wondered why it was that he must keep moving. Tom took the escalator up and outside and stood in front of Madison Square Garden. There were signs touting a boxing match to be held there that evening. The photos on the posters showed two mean looking black men staring at each other. "Fight of the century," one sign read. "No prisoners," was a quote from one of the boxers, their red-leather bound hands at the ready. Tom studied the faces of the boxers and one of them turned to him as he stood there on the sidewalk. The boxer on the poster said, "The nigger is mine." Tom was very near fainting. He turned to see if anyone else had seen or heard the same as he, but all people hurried by without noticing him. When he looked back at the poster, all was as it had been.

Tom got into a taxi and said, "Take me to NBC."

The driver looked back at him and said, "Okay, pal, but first, let me see your money."

"What?"

"I want to see your money. I ain't taking you nowhere till first I see your money."

Tom pulled some bills from his jacket pocket and showed them to the driver.

"Okay, then. NBC."

The taxi driver was still admiring his tip when Tom entered the lobby of the NBC building. He walked up to the large circular reception desk and waited for the pretty blonde woman to ask him if he needed help.

"I'd like to know where I can find someone associated with the show *Virtute et Armis*," Tom said.

The woman looked through the pages of a blue, vinyl-covered loose-leaf notebook on the desk surface in front of her. "That would be studio twelve and that would be on the fifth floor. Do you have an appointment?"

"No, I want to be a contestant," Tom said.

"Well, then you don't want the studio," the woman said. "You want Marketing and Acquisitions and that's on—" She looked through the pages again. "M and A is on the third floor. The receptionist up there will help you."

Tom thanked her and walked to the bank of elevators. Tom rode up in a car with three stiff-haired women and a short, chatty man in a badly fitted suit who was carrying several coffees and a couple of pastries on a cardboard tray. He talked and talked, told that he was currently working for Cinda Hartman up on the ninth floor, but hoped to be moving to Wallace Ackerman's office, and the women paid him no attention. Tom left them when he got out on the third floor.

"Have a nice day," the man called after Tom as the doors closed.

Tom approached the next receptionist who, except for the color of her hair, was exactly the same as the receptionist in the lobby. She smiled at him and said,

"Welcome to *Virtute et Armis*."

"I'd like to be on the show," Tom said.

"Well, of course, you would," she said. She handed a single sheet form to Tom. "Fill this in and give it back to me and we'll go from there. You may sit over there at that table." She pointed across the room to a large wooden table at which sat three other black men.

Tom took the form and went to the table. He sat and picked up a pen which was tethered to the tabletop. He tried to see the faces of the other men, but they would not look up. The first question asked for his name and already he was stumped. He wanted to laugh out loud. Under the line, in parentheses, the form asked for *last* and *first* names. He wrote Tom in the appropriate place and then tried to come up with a last name. He thought to use Himes, but he was afraid that somehow he would get into trouble, more trouble. Finally he wrote, *Wahzetepe*. He didn't know why he wrote it, but it came out easily and so he said it softly to himself, "*Wah-ze-te-pe.*" If asked, he would say it was an African name, but he knew that it was a Sioux Indian word, though he didn't know its meaning. He didn't know how he knew the word, but he was sure of it as his name. The form wanted his social security number and a number supplied itself, though he knew it was bogus. 451-69-1369. He stared at the number, wondering what it meant. He recognized the center cluster of two numbers as the zodiacal sign for Cancer. But the other two clusters, 451 and 1369, made no sense to him. He lied all the way down the page, about his address, about his place of birth, about his education, claiming that he had studied at the College of William and Mary, about his hobbies, in which he included making dulcimers and box kites out of garbage bags. He took the form back to the receptionist and she accepted it happily. She then handed him a stack of pages.

"If you would answer these questions to the best of your ability, we'll be able to make a decision about your candidacy for the show," she said. "You have fifteen minutes." She looked at her watch. "Starting now."

Tom went back to the table. The first question was: Can you describe the members of the insect family *Haliplidae*? After this Tom wrote simply *yes*. Then he thought that he was being too literal and so went ahead and also supplied a description. He wrote, "The haliplids are the crawling water beetles. They are small, oval and convex and are usually yellow or brown with dark spots. They may be discerned from other aquatic beetles by their large and plate-like hind coxae." He knew that he could go on, but he felt he had to continue to the next question.

2) *Who was Ferdinand Albert Decombe?* Tom did not hesitate, but answered: "Known simply as Albert, he was made *maître de ballet* of the Paris Opera in 1829. He produced a number of ballets, among them *Le Seducteur au Village, Cendrillon* and *La Jolie Fille de Gand*."

3) *Please state the Mean Value Theorem.* "This theorem is a gener-

alization of Rolle's Theorem. It states that if the function $y=f(x)$ is continuous for $a \leq \times \leq b$ and has a derivative at each value of x for $a < \times < b$, then there is at least one point c between a and b where the tangent to the curve will be parallel to the chord through the two points $A[a, f(a)]$ and $B[b, f(b)]$."

Tom's brain felt like it was on fire. The answers came easily, though he didn't know why. But he understood it all and his brain was burning up. He was finally asked to and he did describe the single point continuous fuel injection system that Chrysler Motor Company devised in 1977. He gave a detailed, but boring response to a request for a description of the working of the concept in the Imperial automobile. But the boringness of the answer served to quiet the fire in his brain.

"Time's up," the woman called to Tom from her desk.

Tom took the test back to her.

"That's just fine," she said. "Now, you go on home and you'll be called if you're what we need."

"I don't have a phone," Tom said.

"Oh, my," the woman said.

"I'll just wait here," Tom said and went over to a sofa and sat. The receptionist was visibly troubled by his decision to remain in the office. She took what Tom thought was his test with her into another office. He picked up a popular science magazine and read an article about the army's new tank which traveled at a rate of more than 90 mph over rough terrain.

Tom was in the NBC building, in the outer offices of *Virtute et Armis*, waiting on a sofa for the receptionist to reappear at her desk. She did reappear and with her came a man in a gray suit with gray hair and a smile slathered across his face like an infection. The receptionist pointed to Tom and the gray-haired man nodded, then walked to him. Tom watched his confident stride as he approached.

"You did very well on the exam," the man said.

Tom nodded.

"It says on your sheet that you attended William and Mary. When did you graduate?"

"Actually, that's not true. I just wanted to put down something."

"My name is Damien Blanc," the man said. "I'm the producer of *Virtute et Armis*."

"I apologize about lying on the questionnaire."

"Don't concern yourself over that. This is television. Who really gives a fuck where you studied or what you studied or if you studied?" He sat down beside Tom on the sofa. "The fact of the matter, Mr. Wahzetepe—" He stopped. "May I call you Tom?"

Tom nodded.

"The fact of the matter, Tom, is that we've got a problem. You see one of our contestants for tonight's show has taken ill. So, we need a quick replacement. And here you are."

"I'm going to be on the show?"

"That's right," Blanc said. "You're going to be live on national television. You know we're one of the few live shows left." He looked at his watch. "We go on in just a little more than six hours. So, I suggest you go get some rest, get something to eat, and take it easy. Our show can be pretty grueling."

"Yes, I know." Tom couldn't believe his quick and positive fortune. He'd just arrived in town and already he was on his way to completing the mission given to him by Homer. He was indeed going to appear on *Virtute et Armis*. But as he considered this, he also recalled the ugly ends met by his predecessors. They had been terribly bright people, but had fallen to nit-picking, trick questions. Or had they simply been careless, finally not smart enough? Tom decided he would be smart enough. He would answer each question perfectly. He would succeed where the others had failed. He would do it for Homer. As he thought of Homer, he also thought of the underwear-clad policemen in the old man's cellar and the thought made him shudder.

"Are you all right?" Blanc asked.

"Yes."

"Well, then, you report back here at seven. Meet me here and I'll take you up to the fifth floor."

"Thank you," Tom said. "Thank you so much."

"No, thank you, Tom."

Tom used what money he had to get a room in a hotel. He took a cab to the Chelsea Hotel liking the name as he saw it in the phonebook and liking the smell of it as he stood in the lobby. The man at the registration desk seemed more than a little disturbed by Tom's lack of baggage and his paying cash in advance. He asked in a rather haughty fashion if Tom might not rather put the charge on his American Express. Tom said, "No."

Tom took the key and went up to his room. He stood under the steaming spray of the shower for a long time. He wanted the water to pound out the kinks in his muscles, to wash his brain clean of worry, but all the shower did was relax him enough to realize how hungry he was. He dried and dressed in his same clothes, his only clothes a green flannel shirt and khaki trousers. He called down to room service and ordered a club sandwich. He then stretched out across the bed and fell asleep while he waited for his food.

Tom was startled awake by the knock at the door. The sharply dressed man brought in the tray with his sandwich and set it on the desk. Tom looked at the bill and gave the man some money. The man smiled and left without saying a word. Tom ate quickly and felt restored. He then went back to the bed and slept again.

Tom left the hotel with no intention of returning, but he didn't tell the front desk he was leaving. He wanted the room there for him if he needed it. He didn't know why he might need it, but the precaution comforted him. His plan, Homer's plan was for him to win the money and then come straight back to Washington. He went back to the NBC building and this time went directly to the third floor where Blanc was waiting for him.

Blanc had a large smile on his pasty face and kept running his long, bony fingers through his gray hair. "Good, you're here. If you hadn't made it, I don't know what we were going to do. Come on, I'll take you upstairs and you can get made up and we'll even give you a brand new shirt and a tie. I'll bet you didn't expect that little bonus. You know, this is television, you've got to look good. *Virtute* is no low class operation. We're the big time. I can't believe how well you did on that exam. Come on." Blanc grabbed Tom's shoulders, turned him around and got him walking toward the elevators. "Here we go. Are you excited?"

"No."

"Well, you should be. This is a golden opportunity for you. There's no telling where you'll go from here. The sky is the limit. Why you might even get a recording contract or a sit-com offer."

They took the elevator up to the fifth floor and got out. They walked down the hall toward some double doors, passing on the way a black man who was mopping the floor. As the man wrung out the mop over the bucket, Tom got a brief look at his face and thought he recognized him. As the doors closed, he recognized him as a former contestant on the show.

Now, they were standing in front of a door marked *Makeup*. "They'll get you all ready in here," Blanc said, straightening his own tie. "I've got to go check on our other contestant, but you'll be just fine. You just relax and go with the flow. Just roll with it."

Tom nodded. He looked back at the double doors, wanting to go back out into the hallway and talk to Bob Jones, but Blanc ushered him into the makeup room. Two women took him from Blanc, spun him around and sat him in a chair in front of a large mirror.

One of the women had red hair and very fat cheeks, though Tom could not see the rest of her. "Just relax, honey," she said. "We haven't lost a patient yet."

The other woman was sick-looking, she was so skinny. Her cheeks were hollowed out and looked as if they might meet inside her mouth. "What size shirt do you wear?" she asked.

"A large," Tom said.

"Do you know your collar size?"

Tom shook his head.

The skinny woman sucked her teeth and said, "You are a big boy. You look like a sixteen-and-a-half to me."

"Let me see that face," the red-haired woman said, grabbing Tom's chin and turning his head this way and that. "You ain't half-bad-looking," she said, smoothing his forehead with her thumb. She reached over to the cart which was beside the chair and came back with her fingertips coated with a brown cream.

"What's that?" Tom asked.

"You ain't quite dark enough, darlin'," she said. She began to rub the compound into the skin of Tom's face. "This is TV stuff."

He watched in the mirror as his oak brown skin became chocolate brown.

"There now," the redhead said, "that's so much better."

The skinny woman came back with a white shirt. The garment had been heavily starched, but Tom struggled into it with the woman's help. The collar turned out to be just a tad tight. Tom tried without success to button the shirt at his throat.

"Here, let me help you," the skinny woman said. Her bony knuckles pressed into his adam's apple and he could not breathe. She fought with the button for several minutes and finally got it through the stiff hole. "There." She stood away.

Tom looked at the mirror and saw someone else. The contrast of the white shirt against the altered hue of his face was unsettling and confusing. He felt like a clown. "Do I have to wear this stuff on my face?" he asked.

"I'm afraid so, doll," the red-haired woman said. "I'm afraid so. Rules are rules. You wouldn't want to confuse the folks viewing at home, now would you?"

The skinny woman knotted a tie around Tom's neck, tightening it enough to squeeze his throat with the stiff collar.

"Are you ready?" This from Blanc who leaned suddenly into the room. "Hey, you look great, absolutely terrific." He walked a circle around Tom. "Nice job, girls. Real nice. He looks just right. Tom, I almost didn't recognize you."

"Me, either."

Blanc laughed loudly. "You hear that, girls. 'Me either.' This Tom is a funny one." He stopped and put his hand on Tom's shoulder. "It's time, Tom. It's time to play *Virtute et Armis.*"

Tom stood and followed Blanc out of the room and down the inner hallway to another door. A red light was on outside the door. They entered and there before them was the set of *Virtute et Armis.* Tom's breath caught in his throat. For the first time, he was nervous. He had to win this game. But he also knew how this game worked. It wasn't up to him. He had to be careful, not slip up anywhere. He was here in the studio, standing at the threshold of his future.

The studio lights were harsh. The cameras stood like hulking gorillas

　　　　　　　　　　　　　　　　　　　　　　　Making Callaloo

in front of the set. Tom had the feeling his makeup was melting and he wondered if his face was striped. There was Jack Spades, big as life, his slicked-back hair shining like it had batteries. He was wearing a plastic bib and looking over his note cards while the skinny woman from the makeup room powdered his brow. And there was the big circular board laid out on the floor, the squares of different colors appearing to Tom as his coming obstacles. His opponent was sitting in a recliner on the other side of the studio. He was receiving a manicure from a woman with long brown hair. He was a handsome man, blond with chiseled features. Tom watched as Blanc and Spades chatted. The two men looked concerned about something, one shaking his head and then the other. At one point during their conversation, Blanc pointed over at the white contestant in his recliner. Tom felt a profound loneliness. He watched the audience file in and find seats. They were all white, all blond and all staring at Tom, an ocean of blue eyes.

Jack Spades left Blanc and walked over to Tom. "Jack Spades," he introduced himself. "Welcome to the show." His smile was somehow too bright, too clean, unreal. He shook Tom's hand. "I want to wish you luck. Just relax. I'm sure you'll do fine and be a credit to your race."

Spades walked away and was replaced by Blanc. "It's time for you to go over and take your place," Blanc said. "You're supposed to stand on the red mark. When in doubt, just look for the red mark on the floor. You've seen the show, so you'll know what to do. Just listen to Jack and watch the director. He's the one in the baseball cap. Look at the camera with the red light on when you give your answers. Now, go get 'em, Tom."

Tom walked onto the set and took his place, carefully toeing the red mark. The lights fell on him and he could no longer really see the faces in the audience, but he felt the eyes watching him, could hear their breathing. The theme music poured in and Tom's opponent was introduced. "From Elkhart, Indiana, a social worker and part-time blues musician in area nightclubs, father of two and president of the PTA and his neighborhood association, Hal Dullard." Hal Dullard waved to the television audience. "And from Mississippi, Tom Wahzetepe." The camera stared at Tom and he stared back. "And now, your favorite game-show host, the gamemaster of *Virtute et Armis*, Jack Spades."

Jack Spades came trotting out and greeted the audience. "Let's jump right into the game," he said. "Mr. Dullard, if you would, please name a primary color."

"Green," said Dullard.

The studio audience gasped collectively.

The stunned Spades cleared his throat and said, "I'm afraid that's not an acceptable answer."

"Tom," Spades said. "What is *anaphase*?"

"Anaphase is the phase of nuclear division characterized by the movement of chromosomes from the spindle equator to the spindle poles. It starts with the separation of the centromeres and ends with the termination of the poleward movement of the chromosomes."

"That's correct," Spades said. "One square forward for you."

"Mr. Dullard, in the Bible, who slew Goliath?"

"That would be Solomon."

Again the studio audience moaned. Tom looked over to see Blanc holding his face in his hands.

"Incorrect," Spades said. "The answer is David." He shuffled to the next card. "Tom, name the poem from which come the following lines, then name the poet and tell us something about him:

'Weep for the tender and delicate ones
Who barefoot now tread upon thorns,
Drawing water for barbarians,
Felling trees at their commands.' "

Tom paused for a second and saw a brief smile flash across Blanc's face, then he said, "The lines are from the poem *Lament on the Devastation of the Land of Israel*. The poet's name is Joseph Ibn Abithur. He was born in the middle of the tenth century. It is claimed that he gave an Arabic explanation of the Talmud to the Caliph al-Hakim II. He was known mainly for liturgical works, prayer books of Catalonian and North African Jews."

Blanc's face was blank.

Spades shook his head and said, "Correct. One square." He then announced a commercial break during which several makeup people ran to him and attended to his perspiring brow.

Blanc made quick, long strides over to Dullard and seemed to be yelling at him in a whisper. Though they were only two squares away, Tom could not hear what was being said. He sensed hostility in the studio audience.

The director counted backwards with his fingers from five and pointed at Jack Spades.

"Welcome back," Spades said. "Mr. Dullard, let's see if we can't get you moving here. Please name the first president of the United States of America."

"Thomas Jefferson."

"Wrong," Spades said, unable to completely hide his annoyance. "That's wrong."

"Tom, what is a serial distribution field?"

"It is a field that must be built when installing a septic system on sloping land. It possesses level trenches dug along the contours of the land, each lower than the next. Connections from trench to trench are set up to transfer the sewage to the lower trench only when the sewage in the trench above reaches the top of its gravel fill." Tom thought to stop, but added, "And so, the first trench of the system must operate to full capacity before the second trench receives any flow. Also, there is no need for a distribution box."

Blanc looked as if he might scream. He looked anxiously back at the unsettled audience.

"Correct, one square," Spades said.

Dullard did not know that a gorilla was a primate. He did not know the abbreviation for Avenue. He did not know what a male chicken was called. Soon, Tom had nearly made his way around the circle and was about to lap Mr. Dullard. The studio audience had stopped breathing. Blanc was chewing aspirin like candy. Spades was sweating so badly that no amount of attention from the puff-wielding staff could hide it.

"Tom, for the game and a purse of three-hundred thousand dollars in cash, with what lines does Ralph Waldo Emerson open his essay *Self-Reliance*?"

Tom was silent for a few seconds. The studio hushed. The red light on the camera facing him bothered his eyes. He said, "He begins with:

" *'Ne te quœsiveris extra.'*

And then lines from the Epilogue to Beaumont and Fletcher's *Honest Man's Fortune*:

'Man is his own star; and the soul that can
Render an honest and perfect man
Commands all light, all influence, all fate;
Nothing to him falls early or too late.

Our acts our angels are, or good or ill,
Our fatal shadows that walk by us still.' "

Spades took a breath and was about to speak and Tom said,

"And then four lines follow, which are:
'Cast the bantling on the rocks,
Suckle him with the she-wolf's teat;
Wintered with the hawk and fox,
Power and speed be hands and feet.' "

Spades' disappointment was obvious as he formed the word, "Correct," but hardly said it out loud. "And so you, Tom Wahzetepe from somewhere in Mississippi, are our new champion."

The audience made no sounds. They were dead.

In Blanc's office, Tom sat in a stiff-backed chair in front of the man's huge desk. Spades was sitting on the leather sofa across the room, leaning over with his face in a pillow. "How could this happen?" Blanc said. He was pacing back and forth from his desk to the window. "How could something like this happen?"

Spades looked up and said, "It's not my fault. I didn't pick that Dullard guy; you did. I can't believe he was so stupid."

"He's still that stupid," Blanc said. "He'll be that stupid tomorrow. But that's beside the point. The point is that Tom here won. Tom won the game."

Spades shook his head. "He gave me everything that was on the cards. He got it all right. What was I suppose to say? I don't know any of that shit."

Blanc picked up a briefcase from behind his desk, then walked over and dropped it on Tom's lap. "Here's the money."

"Three-hundred-thousand dollars?" Tom asked.

"Hell, no," Blanc snapped. "There's seventy-five thousand dollars in there. Take it, shut up and be happy. I don't know how you did it, but you're lucky we don't drag your ass to court for cheating. You take this dough and never show your face around here again."

"I didn't cheat."

"Yeah, right. Take the money and run, boy." Blanc's hands were shaking. "You have no idea the kind of trouble you've caused us. Take the money and don't talk to anybody about it. And I mean, anybody. I want you to disappear."

Tom stood up and looked the man in the eye. "What did you call me?"

"Don't force me to call security in here," Blanc said.

Tom took the case and walked out. He took off the necktie they had put on him and tossed it at the receptionist as he passed on his way to the elevator.

Though he was eager to get back to Washington, Tom went back to the hotel and showered again. He couldn't get the water hot enough. He stepped out and still the makeup remained. He was one color on his face and the rest of him was another. He went to the bed which had been turned down. He took the mint candy from his pillow and put it on the night table. He lay there in bed, staring out the window at nothing in particular, nothing at all.

Tom rode the elevator down to the lobby of the hotel in the morning. The car was full of chubby faced white men who stared at him. He looked at each of them in turn and they looked away. He walked through the hotel toward the exit, not bothering to check out; he had already paid his bill. He owed them nothing. The briefcase felt at once heavy and light. People in the lobby stared at him, too. Out on the street, Tom had never felt so lost. It wasn't that he was in a strange city, if indeed it was strange. It wasn't the teeming people streaming by. It wasn't the flurry of snow in the air. He was somehow lost inside himself. He took a taxi to the train station.

At Penn Station, Tom sat with the case on his lap. People studied him as they passed. He made frequent glances up at the train board, watching time turn over and over.

A tall, middle-aged, black woman stopped and stood in front of him. She looked at him from different angles and he looked back at her. "Weren't you on television last night? Yeah, you're him. You're Tom! You beat them, didn't you?" She sat down next to him. "That was the greatest moment of my life. We couldn't believe you won. Going home?"

Tom nodded.

"Imagine that," she said, shaking her head. "You won on *Virtute*. You know what we say in my neighborhood? We say 'On *Virtute*, no nigger gets the lootie." She laughed. "But we can't say that now."

Tom then noticed two gray-suited men in dark glasses watching him from across the lobby. They were standing at a Dunkin Donuts, drinking coffee. He began to feel afraid. They knew about the money, he thought. He thought they might even have been sent by Blanc and the network to get their money back.

"Where are you going?" Tom asked the woman.

"I'm going to Philadelphia to visit my daughter. She's a home nurse down there. I'm riding down with my friend Clarisa. There she is. Clarisa! Over here, honey."

Clarisa was a large woman with a pretty face. She came and sat next to the first woman.

"By the way, I'm Thelma," the first woman said. She shook Tom's hand, her grip firm, her motion vigorous.

"Tom."

"I know." Thelma turned to Clarisa. "Does my friend here look familiar to you, Clarisa?"

Clarisa leaned over and studied Tom's face. "Lord, have mercy," she said. "It's not."

"It is," Thelma said. "This is Tom. He won on *Virtute*."

"Never thought I'd see it in my lifetime," Clarisa said, sitting back and fanning herself with a magazine. "No, siree."

The men were still watching from the donut stand. Tom stood. "Would you wait here until I get back?" he asked the women.

"Sure, honey," Thelma said. "Is something wrong?"

"No, I'll be right back." Tom left the women and walked over to a cutlery shop. He asked the clerk for bags. "Big paper bags," he said and when the man complained, Tom simply gave him a hundred dollars. Tom took the stack of red bags with him into the restroom and into a stall. He transferred his money from the briefcase to a bag and then used the rest of the sacks to stuff five bags. He left the case and carried the bags, three in each hand, back to Thelma and Clarisa.

"Would you do me a favor?" Tom asked Thelma as he sat back down in the same seat. "Would you carry this bag for me? It's not heavy."

"Sure." Thelma gave Clarisa a puzzled look.

"You, too, Clarisa," Tom said. "Just carry this one for me."

"Well, okay."

The suited men talked to each other and seemed to be more animated as they observed the handing over of the bags. "Just until we get on the train. Thank you so much." Then Tom walked away from the women. His train was just minutes from boarding. He walked away and set one of the bags on a stack of baggage being pushed by a porter. He then went outside the station, walked around the block: and came in through another entrance. He didn't see the two men. He waved at Thelma and Clarisa from across the room. They whispered to each other.

The boarding of the train was announced. Tom sifted through the mob and made his way to the platform. He sat in the same car as Thelma and Clarisa, but well behind them. He watched as they put the paper sacks he had given them in the overhead storage bin. He still had three with him. He felt alive. He felt like his mind was working. He knew the suits were on the train. One of the men would have to follow the women off the train in Philadelphia. Then he would leave a bag on the train and get off in Baltimore. The remaining man would have to check it out. He would try to sneak off the train at the last second. The men came through the door at the front of the car and Tom saw them first. He waved to them, got their attention. They pretended to not be interested in him and walked past him to sit three rows farther back.

Tom's mind was twisted like a rope. He could still see the faces of Blanc and Spades, but the faces were set into heads atop toy bodies and the bodies were dancing, strings extending into space from the wooden arms and legs. Tom was blindfolded, but he could see and in his mind he could no longer control his motions. He stumbled through a crowd and found himself standing in front of a mirror and in the mirror he saw two dwarfs fighting with swords and from the blades of the weapons, he could see the whole spectrum of light refracted. He followed the colors away from the fight and then back, but he found, instead of the dueling swords, a single drop of water. He walked around the drop, wanting to reach out and touch it, knowing that it was a drop and not a bubble and then he realized that he was inside a bubble, observing the drop, the center. Then he could see himself reflected in the wall of it and he was symmetrical, like a crystal of ice. He could almost see his middle, where he came from. He could almost touch his source.

The train ride seemed much slower than before. Tom couldn't relax. One of the men got up and brought back coffee and pastries from the snack car. When they were both seated again, Tom got up, took his bags with him and walked forward to get something to eat. He bought a sandwich, ate it while he stood in the club car, and left one of the bags in the overhead of another car on his way back. He smiled at Thelma and Clarisa as he walked by, but they now seemed alarmed by his behavior and did not speak to him. He went back and knelt down next to Thelma and he could tell she was terrified. "I'm sorry, Thelma," he said. "Don't worry." He gave her a wad of bills. He didn't know how much money he had handed over. "This is for you and Clarisa. Just take the bags into the station and wait for me. Please. That's all you have to do."

Thelma nodded.

As he walked away, Tom heard Clarisa say, "Lord, have mercy."

Tom sat in his seat and looked back to see one of the men walking toward him. He looked forward and held his breath. The man knelt in the aisle beside his seat just as he had knelt beside Thelma's.

"What's the story with all of the bags?" the man asked.

Tom looked at him and said, "Do I know you?"

"Yes, you know me," the man said, and with an evil grin, he added, "you've known me all my life. You are only what you are, Tom. You can't help that. But you know that, don't you?"

Tom looked away and closed his eyes. When he looked back, the man was no longer there. He looked back and saw that the two men in suits were talking like nothing had happened. Tom squeezed the armrests of his seat and pushed his head back into the cushion.

The train stopped in Philadelphia. Thelma and Clarisa grabbed the paper sacks and looked back at Tom. Tom nodded his head. He watched as one of the suited men got up and exited the train after the women. The other suit was still in his seat, still watching Tom, still staring. Tom saw his lips move and he heard a voice all around him. It said,

"We know all about you. We know where you live. We know how you breathe. We know." And then the lips weren't moving and the man was looking out the window at the platform.

Tom hoped that the women would not wait for him in the station. He was on his way to Baltimore and he laughed at himself for not wanting to cause them any inconvenience. His life was in the balance and he was concerned about their being put out.

The train slowed and then stopped in Baltimore. Tom waited and waited and just when the train was about to leave, when the boarding passengers were getting seated and the last call was made, Tom made a quick dash for the end of the car. He glanced back to see the man in the suit start to follow him, but stop as he saw the paper sack Tom had left behind in the overhead. Tom stepped from the train as it pulled away. He left one bag on the platform, on a bench next to a sleeping man with his feet wrapped in foil. He took the one with the money out to the street where he got into a taxi and asked the driver to take him to Annapolis. He gave the cabbie two hundred dollars and told him that he'd get another two once there.

Tom was floating. He had done this correctly and it felt good. He knew what he was doing. He was good at this.

In Annapolis, Tom got out of the first taxi and made the same deal with another driver to take him to Washington. The driver balked at first, but the feel of the bills quickly convinced him. The driver took Route 50 into the city and onto New York Avenue. Tom got out downtown and then walked over to 17th and up to Dupont Circle where he sat for a long time. It was nearly dusk when he remembered himself. There was a man playing guitar and singing a stupid blues song just yards from him. Across the circle, on another bench, were two men playing congo drums. Directly in front of him stood one young man, then another came up and then an elderly woman and then a middle-aged man and then a fat man with a gray beard and they were all staring at Tom.

"You're him," the fat man said. "You're Tom Wahzetepe."

"What kind of name is Wahzetepe?" the elderly woman asked. "Is it African or some made-up shit?"

Tom was terrified.

"You're a smart motherfucker," one of the kids said and then he slapped a high five with another young man.

"Nigger don't be foolin'," the second kid said.

"Did they give you your money?" the fat man asked.

"No," Tom said. "They gave me some and then tried to take it back."

"That's bullshit," the elderly woman said.

"Won't give the man his money," one of the kids said.

"That's bullshit," another voice called out.

"What should we do?" the fat man asked Tom. "You're smart. What should we do?"

In Tom's head, nothing was making sense. Everything was slowing down. The movements of the people in front of him were slow motion. The elderly woman's swearing was deep and prolonged. "Bullllllshiiiitttt," her mouth formed the word over and over. Tom felt himself standing and saw them all take a slow motion step backward. He touched the tips of his fingers together, forming a cage and opened his mouth.

"I was, no doubt, born a slave, as were each and every one of you.

I do not know my life before this moment, or at least before these last few moments. I do, however, know some things, bits of information. That is true. And all of you look on me as if I know more than you and I don't. I know how to read and from what I can tell, I have read a lot, but I cannot remember having read anything. I am shrewd and clever, it appears, and I am yet awkward and lost. I feel out of place talking to you on the street. I can't slap you a high-five without thinking that it is a foreign motion. But in my dream, I can talk the talk and walk the walk. In my dream, I am at home and comfortable with myself. But even in my dream, my comfort is undermined. I have a dream. I have a dream and it will not leave me alone. I have a dream and it will not end. It will not die. I have a dream this very moment and there is a woman in it and she is tricking me. She is tricking me just like that man in my dream tricked me. Just like the friend in my dream tricked me. I have dreams in my dream and they are bad. And *they*—you know THEY—*they* know all about me. *They* know where I am. *They* know what I do. And you, fat man, you ask me what you should do? Don't let them fingerprint you! Don't let them take your identity!"

The crowd had grown to nearly a hundred people. Tom saw a couple of slow motion policemen approaching him from across the circle. He saw the faces of the policemen he had left in the cellar of Homer's house. He pointed to the uniformed men and shouted, "No!"

The crowd turned as one and made for the cops without hesitation. The policemen stopped cold. They did not draw their weapons. They did not call to the crowd to halt. They simply turned around and ran. The crowd was growing with each second and they were chanting now,

"No fingerprints! No fingerprints!"

Tom watched from the bench as the crowd became four-hundred strong and marched around Dupont Circle. The movement of traffic choked. Cars were overturned. A fire was set in the office of Historic Trust. A plume of smoke rose into the air over the circle.

"No fingerprints! No fingerprints!"

Tom ran away from the crowd and through the streets. He could hear the mob as if they were right behind him.

Sugar Groove

Well, I got that hair cut all right—late Saturday evening.

But when I arrived in one of Aunt Eloise's custom-made automobiles, at Anchor of Zion Missionary Baptist Church, that Sunday Morning, I was still laughing out loud at the barber Williemain's joke about the hustler who died, got to Heaven through a ruse; found himself in a strait-jacket; slipped through a loop within it, you might say; only to discover the depths of the trick bag, as he sailed to save St. Peter's out-of-breath soul. Well, I can tell you one thing, I kept worrying if Williemain would clip my ears off as he spun Sugar-Groove's saga about how he got his wings clipped—almost.

It was always extremely difficult to trace the actual genesis of a story in Williemain's Barbershop, but apparently somebody had asked the question in a most declarative manner: Whatever happened to the body of Sugar-Groove, the scavenger, *after* he vanished . . . *that last time*. And this really did it.

After he tied the collar of that red, white and blue apron about my neck, pumped the handle bar of the chair so that my head was at a workable level, Williemain declared:

". . . Well, Sugar-Groove went for a joy ride. Not the kind you fools thinking about. . . . And I sure ain't spieling on Mary Poppins; nor am I riffing on them flying nuns. There's a word for it too, but I'm not telling you dudes doodle-squat—not yet."

He was a Negro hustler, and a drifter, originally from Sugar-Ditch, Mississippi, who flew North "to escape the aggravation"; I knew for a fact that Sugar-Grove had gone to prison for check forgery, in the long ago. And that at one time he had fenced for thieves. He had lived a fast, wild life; but was "converted" on his death-bed by his grand-aunt, then he died, departed, vanished, so the mythos said. Sugar-Groove had so many non-such nicknames, but all were based on Sugar. Or, should I say, sugar-soaked. There was Sugar-Ditch, for his home town, but the only others that I was aware of (Sugar-Dripper, Sugar-Dipper, Sugar-Groove, Sugar-Grove, Sugar-Spook, Sugar-Goose, Sugar-Sack, Sugar-Shank, Sugar-Swift, Sugar-Alley, Fountain-Head Sugar, Sugar-Stoker, Sugar-Stroke, Sugar-Splib, Sugar-Stagger, Sugar-Saint, Sugar-Spine, Sugar-Dick, Sugar-Stud, Sugar-Loaf, Sugar-Smoke, Sugar-Shit; or Sugar-Eyes, and Sugar-Shark) referred to various tributes paid to his revealed sexual merriment, moxy, prowess; or his cunning at dice, cards, gambling tables, games of chance, and romantic intrigue.

Anyway, just before his body was lowered into the ground, and shortly after her husband preached the funeral, Sugar-Groove's Grand-Auntie, Gracie Mae Gates, had a vision.

Grieving before her nightstand, in her grey nightgown, at the stroke of midnight, with her husband spinning the numbers, she placed a conference call to her boss, and they got Gabriel on the line (St. Peter was away on a working vacation, checking on some bankrupt securities out West), and they struck up a peculiar deal over Sugar-Groove's body, in order for his soul to migrate Heavenly in Time, on Time. There was even a divine proclamation devised to that effect, and apparently this written contract or document over his soul greatly compounded, and confounded, Sugar-Groove's status in Paradise. The covenant was quite restrictive.

Gabriel met Sugar-Groove at the gates, with a huff and a puff. Waved a wing-wand over him. Then he needled Sugar-Groove a ray-gun shot to purge his form of all earthly delights and poisons. This serum was composed of materials purloined from the Milky Way. It made the new pilgrim drowsy for a time. After the hypodermic needle to his soul, the glazed migrant was stopped off at the WING ROOM; then Sugar-Groove went slowly winging along. But soon he discovered not only did he have reason to feel he was caught up in a strait-jacket, but that certain other traffic limitations on his highway travel were unleashed from the word of the document, to scale down the availability for him of certain zooming zones.

Sugar-Groove could be seen flying down only on the right hand side of the roadway. Exact time stipulations were to be docked to his speedometer, invested up under his left wing . . . No sky-larking, skinny-dipping, or other showboating tricks; only flights to and from the PX—Paradise Exchange—were allowed, and by the way of the rear door E-X-I-T. And Sugar-Groove was to consider, as a direct order, that for him, The Fabulous Sky-Blue Freeway was "Off Limits" in his time of day.

. . . . His first week in Paradise, low and behold if old Sugar-Groove wasn't seen jetting down the left hand side of the Kingdom; up and down the "wrong" side of the track, sailing and jetting and floating and flipping and zooming 100 miles a second, on Sunday Morning, at Sabbath tolling time . . . Why by the time the 11:00 Cathedral bells peeled from Ding to Dong, Sugar-Groove traveled the distance between Oxford, Mississippi, and Harlem, *backwards* . . . getting faster and fancier each day. And don't let there be a head-wind, Sugar-Groove turned his body into one screaming eagle, going sideways.

Finally Gabriel dispatched Sugar-Groove a note of warning by carrier-pigeon that said: "You better straighten up and fly right, Sugar-Groove."

But one Saturday night brought his downfall; Sugar-Groove was out on his regular Saturday night Sublime Sail In Space and doing one of his seven layer stellar climbs—*all night long*. Why he was last seen dead-heading for the Fabulous Sky-Blue Freeway—employing his famous *Driftwood Backstroke*.

St. Peter was back now from his working vacation; this latest outrage wrinkled too much for a fleshless temple to contemplate. So, he wrinkled Sugar-Groove into his conference room—The War Room—that Monday morning, on March 21, at High Noon.

Shortly after the cock crowed, Sugar-Groove flew in.

Casting his eyes down upon his Supersonic Over-Soul timepiece, St. Peter started off:

"Negro . . . Have you lost your cotton-picking mind . . . You just got here on a wing and a prayer as it is . . . Your grand aunt prayed you into Heaven and apparently struck some shady deal between herself, her boss man and Gabriel, behind my back. But limitations were placed upon your statute in the beginning. And your travel was curtailed. Now you are breaking every rule in the good black book. So help me God, I don't think putting you on milk and honey would be a sufficient penalty . . . I'm thinking seriously about cutting down on your spare-ribs, Sugar-Groove."

However, Sugar-Groove detected some whimsey in St. Peter's pitched and whispered baritone.

"But tell me how are *you*—doing it? Particularly the way you do that little sweep around under a cloud pocket carry up through cross-around corkscrew—outside—in a floating fashion, back hipbone motion transfer over and under super sublime sail, without shaking a tail feather, breathlessly—meantime you are actually going so fast you're threatening to break the sound barrier; meanwhile you are floating backwards and doing it all on the left hand side of the road, while you seem to be zigzagging right, to the naked eye that is . . . I can't find the proper words to express the meanings of all your carryings on, your swerving cavorting . . . your . . .

" . . . You see Sugar-Groove, I've been watching you, or trying to keep up with you, from our Watch Tower Observatory Lighthouse; a rig, called The Bird Cage, lifts me to the very zenith point, where we keep our most highly prized, high-powered radar and telescope, called 'Vigil Residual' . . . I can cite every mote of motion, as a mustard-seed, around this whole Universe with those lenses . . . But, boy, you are a new kind of wonder, a rare rooster, why even some of our most upwardly mobile charioteers, living in Celestial Gardens, just off the Dixie Turnpike, are growing jealous as hell of you. So are the lily-white colored angels.

"Sugar-Groove, between you and me (and it won't fly out of the windows of this upper room on my high Word of Honor) how in the Hell do you do it?"

" . . . Oh, I don't know, sometimes I guess I just wing it."

Wiping the cloud of irritation off of his fleshless temple, St. Peter confidentially whispered:

"You have a way of flying at heights, that gives you the best cool wind advantage from a standpoint of velocity and direction . . . That's about as far as I can scale it."

Sugar-Groove said with great detachment:

"Some of the disbelievers declare as how I creates up such a wind storm that sunlight can't get to the sugar cane, on the earth below."

"Sugar-Groove, between us, now. Don't you have a magic-musical score on rhythm tucked away in one of those wings—to pitch you in time, out of time, on time, in your own time?"

"Well, Mister Peter ... Honest and true, you struck on half of my problem up in here; *and* what was written down to get me in here. But it's also how come they call me ... renamed me ... up in here ... Amazing Grace."

But just as St. Peter was about to kick the new comer out of the War Room and down the Heavenly crystal staircase, Sugar-Groove declared:

"Now hold all twelve of your milk white horses, in harness, Mister Peter. I didn't mean to ruffle up your feathers none. But if you only knew of the particular preparation ... the eye of the storm, I flew through—in my previous condition, down in Sugar-Ditch, Mississippi— you would not be surprised if I could out fly a sparrow so fast, Himself couldn't spot me on the head of a pin, dancing, and with more power than a back-stroking Eagle, on a sunshiny day—using Vigil Residual.

"And, Sir Peter, if you knew all the restrictions I got employed on me, body and soul, all up in here; you'd know exactly how come and why—for them pure white amazed angels ain't actually calling me out of my name, either."

"... Sugar-Ditch, living the life you're living up here, you'll never win your starry crown, your golden wings, nor your eternal Harmony Halo. Sugar-Ditch, I got to cut you down ... put you in the penalty box, before it's too, too late and you melt away; because there are some up here who are angling and scheming, and skinning their eyes for your hide; they want to take you for a joy-ride, all right. But they can't settle on a way to catch you since you seem to be coming from opposite directions at the same time.

"Why you make more noise than Gabriel's hounds ... that pack of wild geese, screaming through the air, at the basin of Heaven—those souls of unbaptized children screaming to get in. And we've just got to keep them on hold.

"But Sugar-Ditch, even the dumbest Negro slaving in the cotton patch knows your life hasn't been a crystal staircase. Why try to *vagabondize* Paradise?"

". . . Yes, Mister Peter, why we had us some cock-a-roaches down there, coming and going out of a baby's crib, and into potato sacks, longer than a relief check . . . they was so big and slick we had to grease down some rat traps to try to catch 'em."

"More reason why you should appreciate living in Sublime Shake-Towers, overlooking Celestial Park, with a North-East exposure. What else do you want? You fly like a migratory maniac on a mission."

". . . But Mister Peter, how am I gonna keep on the straight and narrow, roped off as I am in a strait-jacket and ever be seen—unless I *do* go for broke? Hell, I've got to out-scream the eagle to make Paradise rock."

". . . Why you should feel repressed up here, Sugar-Ditch, while you've got us all delirious, diving and dipping in the shadow of your black magic and at the same time you are blasé about the storm you are raising. . . . It's all beyond me. . . .

"Sugar-Ditch, why don't you tell me now what you think I should do for your punishment. Maybe we can strike up a deal. Hell-fire, a covenant pitched you up here into this sphere, maybe we can take out a contract on you—so that you can fly again—but with all deliberate speed, and transform your furor into a moderate breast-stroke. But for now—your wings must be clipped."

(At this point Williemain made his golden shears make a clipping sound—just above my head.)

"*Wing*! What wings?"

"Your style crippled. Problem is, Sugar-Ditch, you got all of my legion in a pure turmoil and full of contentions. You got a league of white angels demanding your scalp, wanting to string you up, and calling for an eye for an eye, tooth for a tooth, and hand for a hand, and yes, a wing for one of your wings . . . simply because you are driving them cock-eyed with your unbelievable, faithless flying like a bat out of Hell—going cross-eyed.

"Then there's a group of Negro angels arguing up a black and blue storm over how you are to be re-located, and roped off, behind the green pastures, over there on the cinder track, where the sprinters practice, way back there and past the defunct train depot."

". . . Mister Peter, now *them* dudes probably turning gray-eyed with envy. They trying to railroad me for the duration; but to tell the truth, they done spied something about my situation, some of the rest of you early settlers done missed," he said with a wry smile.

". . . And, Sugar-Ditch, if all of this wasn't ruinous enough, you got a legion of young white angels going crazy over you; painting their faces tan, over berry black and calling themselves, The Sugar-Stomping Honkie Bears, and they are trying to imitate your every turn, twist, shake, fling, hop, bop, at break-neck speed. Some are even attaching wings to their golden sandals to elevate an élan up to you, Sugar-Ditch. Why some of the young women are so frustrated, because they can't fly next to you, that they are even painting their faces the color purple.

"Sugar-Ditch, I tell you, the Hummingborgs, the Dovetails, and the Sugar-Footed Honeys are just three of the newest fan clubs, hopping a hot foot, and shaking a tail-feather in your honor. Why some are even trying to nap fry the feathers of their blonde wings, at Talmadge's Sunnyside Salon—why just imagine, they are searching all over Paradise, at this very moment for a hot iron—to be like you, so you'll love 'em and stroke 'em . . . I'm fast on to a dispensation of wearing chastity belts, throughout the kingdom—and unleashing them at 186,000 per clip. . . . But it's plainly that free-style floating, that *Driftwood Backstroke*, that's got our right wing upset up here, Sugar-Ditch. They are mightily afraid that you have devised a plan to rename Paradise—into Sugar-Ditch. They're sailing cycles of tales of flying monkeys shouldering buzzards, as jokes about you. Others are claiming you are the Founding Father of all UFO's. Then another trio recites as how you're flying and cavorting about in your union suit. That you are actually a disembodied ghost and they feel . . . How shall I say? *Spooked*!"

And yet Sugar-Groove thought to himself, that despite this situation and even his condition of feeling roped in like a hospitalized man in a strait-jacket for the criminally insane and despite his anger with his aunt for cracking a deal, this Heaven—after all was said and done—was still one helluva a place to create a land-base, for a launching pad. Man, they sure got some fabulous pads up here in Paradise: and them highways and by-ways are natural freaked-off . . . even as they are roped off.

And all St. Peter's got to do is step out on a Rock, lower his arms, spread his wings, let his coat-tails fly, flop his hands, turn some of those kingdom-come keys in his right hand and all is revealed to him about each and every angle of every arched angel's ass . . . Talk about the roof, the steeple and the people . . . so perhaps I'd better, *hush*. Just then St. Peter was saying:

". . . And furthermore, Sugar-Ditch, you have gone against *all* Heavenly slide rules, as practiced up here in Paradise, in moderation. Why you're bending Free Will out of shape, into a t-square.

"Sugar-Ditch, some of my prized dancing angels have taken to sheep-rustling along the grazing lane, inside Divine Driveway . . . and confidentially, some are cruising off the beaten pathway, near The Fabulous Sky-Blue Freeway, just off the main drag, at Midnight—like cowboys."

". . . Supreme Court of courtly high Angels blaming that on me too, I recollects, naturally."

"Sugar-Ditch, my advice on that one was—swerve those suckers over . . . make 'em wail against the wall . . . but don't lay hands upon 'em and don't shake 'em down."

"Yeah, 'cause they might get all shook up. Mister Peter, you are a scream and you got a heart cut in stone."

"Sugar-Ditch, you are not, and cannot go blameless in any of this, because we haven't had such pandemonium up here since Lucifer lost his license, tried to upset Paradise in a power play. What is to be done, Sugar-Ditch? I'm not above reason. But I'll not commit treason. Tell me—what is to be done to you—with you, about you?"

Wherein old Sugar-Groove confided, in a confessing voice:

"Mister Peter—I'll tell you true, 'cause it's hard, but it's fair . . . Don't cut me loose. Free up my wing . . .'cause you—"

"Sugar-Ditch, are you trying to talk me out of punishing you by talking me into giving you a new set of wings . . . Say wings, Sugar-Ditch, not *wing*—you may be trying to re-write the by-laws of Paradise, but we don't speak Black English in Heaven. Anyway, you're too free, as it is . . . We've given you enough rope already . . . You free-loader."

"Naw, Mister Peter. Free up my other wing. You see when I died, and they cracked this deal to send me up in here, I was issued an old patched-up set of shattered wings thrown in the Catholic Salvage section and over in the Free Will bin where other angelic vestments were tossed away, and cast asunder—for them Mohammadems and Jews to wear, if they ever could come through the eye of a needle, in time, with their eyes closed and through the deep-freeze of dangling smoked pigs. But this here pair was the frost-bite of the lot, you might say. That's when I come upon the real meaning of the difference between dis here and dat dar' that my grand-auntie useda all the time try to unravel in her broken english down there in the old country, as she did her sewing by firelight."

Now Sugar-Groove had never observed such a hushed silence in Paradise. Yet the soul of St. Peter was commencing to tremble like a tambourine; that was the only noise. Surely this couldn't be the death rattles—no, not in Heaven, that would mean *I'm Lost in Paradise*. And that would be worse than Paradise Valley in Detroit.

". . . You see Mister Peter, Sir, they (them officials) plucked up the worst of the discarded wings for me (like they was picking the strings of a timeless harp, what's out of tune, but they didn't know, I was the boy who knew how to thump and stroke, like I was praising precious silk to turn to golden notes).

"But the covenant was read out loud and off one of them runaway scrolls, it appeared to me, from way back when. And it said this: the wing on the right, Exhibit A (just my luck, cause it was the best of the paltry pair), was to be rope tied (hog-tied I oughta say) into a sailor's triple conniving knot, behind my shoulder, wrong-side out, so that the tail of the wing was strapped down about my trunk."

The natural (previously invisible) jawbone of St. Peter returned to life, shaking, rattling, his chin starting to roll. Sugar-Groove wondered if old St. Peter had a face lift on his working vacation, now as the old flesh became visible, from his fisherman days his beak looked like Rudolph the red nose reindeer. All shook up now, he dropped his keys to the kingdom; he hadn't had anything this embarrassing occur since that time those women came upon him outside the courthouse and demanded him to own up to knowing—you know who.

"... Not to ruffle your feathers, Mister Peter, Sir—but you see part of the deal they struck to let me in ... went down between Auntie and her boss man and Gabriel was—I'd have to fly about Heaven all of my days, with one wing tied with shipyard rope behind my right shoulder, whipped about my belly ... That's how come I keep a-trying to tell you I feel like a man what's circulation's been denied him, and his trunk's tied up in a strait-jacket, yea though his pedigree feels right proper down to his bloodstream."

Then, the old fisherman St. Peter started to huffing and he started to puffing.

"... And I'm going around flying off hating Auntie Gracie Mae Gates for getting me in this here fix," Sugar-Groove was saying out loud, but as much to himself, as to St. Peter.

St. Peter's face virtually fell away to invisibility again, with the charged shock of an actor, who is pitching forth at the height of his soliloquy, when all of a sudden the curtain falls upon him—making him look like a robed monk from head to toe—in his last long suit. St. Peter started to babbling in chunks and jabbering in rushes. Or, as Williemain expressed it:

"Gentlemens, you ever seed a half drunk rooster claw his way up a chicken wire fence, nailed to a barnyard (thinking he's climbing Jacob's Ladder) and trying to catch that speck of Dawn in the gleam of his red eye, just before Daybreak cracks, and purely forgetting all about how he's suppose to crow, when all of a sudden, damn if he don't hear a thunder-clap and his face falls off like it's been hit by a streak of lightning."

Furious St. Peter was jabbering:

"... You mean to tell ... No, Behind your shoulder, strapped around your back and trunk? You wingless wonder ... Gabe dispatched *The Gazette* out to interview you and tell me how one Sugar-Ditch split the scene . . . See you've even got me talking like you, all up in here, like they try to describe your antics-in-motion . . . Gabe wanted to put ashes on the tail of your wings, while you were asleep . . . to slow you down. But the problem up here of everlasting life threw that idea out of the window. (And I haven't used salt in my meals since Galilee.)

"But Sugar-Ditch—one *wing* . . . at that furious speed—you've got to be lying!"

". . . Mister Peter, if I'm lying, I'm flying . . . So you see now, what you ain't wanted to see in the beginning . . . And you know now, what you ain't seed in the end run, long or short, cause now you know you ain't seed nothing purely yet . . . And now you do at least see *how come now*. And now how come you think them white angels done purely renamed me out of my name, into Amazing Grace."

Shuttering St. Peter was furious to a gnashing of teeth. His heart trembled like a tambourine; his rattling soul had the shakes.

But he tried to recap his cool, as he jawboned:

". . . Sugar-Ditch, I'll bet a solid gold chariot—you've never shown the good Lord proper tribute—now let us see if we can commence your penalties by witnessing how swiftly and nimbly your kneebones can bend, in the name of the Lord and how supple you can dip down, as you get low, in your quick-*silver-satin-soul—I'll amaze your grace*."

Upon these last seven words, St. Peter, himself, commenced to stagger backwards in a fainting, shortness of breath, voiceless seizure, and grabbed at the flabby meat—now quite visible—beneath his heart; fell to his knees; his left eye rolled back in his head. Or, as Williemain described it:

"I tell you gentlemens, Pete's eyeballs went rolling back in his head like Al Jolson—in black face—singing *Mammy* frozen in time and space, down on one knee; and Peter's crown rolled on out the upper window. He looked like a man withering out of this world backwards . . . like a spring chill shot through a fresh white paint job. Now don't youalls start to rolling your eyeballs at me—cause you know I ain't never lied."

Now they had to rush St. Peter to the Emergency Ward; then wheel him downstairs, via the planed smooth crystal, stepless staircase into the basement of the Intensive Care Section. They knew what they had to

　　　　　　　　　　　　　　　　　　　　　　　　　　Making Callaloo

do, but how were they going to do it in time? Well, the only way they could get there in time, with St. Peter's body and soul, pitched to the long-gone light-years of Paradise, and on to that distant solar system, was to violate all traffic laws for all souls—going East by Northwest . . .

It was a track-switching maze of arched arteries and a labyrinth of stellar chaos, Sugar-Groove coolly noted, as he dug into reading the Holy Map, called The Divine Plan. For a man knows his calling and is possessed by a sense of mission, before he's actually anointed as Auntie Gracie Mae Gates had revealed to Sugar-Groove in the long ago Old Big Foot Country, in broken English, before his body and soul was dislocated by death and relocated by Chance.

Yes and soon they had to turn to what other party? The Secretary General, MeShack, decided to free up Sugar-Groove's other wing, as patched up as it was, for every breath of a second was crucial, if not critical. But then there was some immediate quibbling and quarrelling over this—because many powerful angels wanted this selfsame wing placed in the wax museum in Preservation Hall, while Sugar-Groove was away, on his mission of mercy. They argued, breathlessly, that he be given a set of customized wings, for upper stellar celestial travel, when one is called into special conference with the Head Knock. Finally, they went along with the Secretary-General.

. . . Why it's a good thing my grand-auntie taught me to sew and don, Sugar-Groove thought, as he swiftly donned the frayed patches of the newly released wing—struck by lightning, light years ago.

But still thinking about Auntie Gracie Mae Gates, as he proudly read the many routes, short cuts of that Heavenly map to get St. Peter to Divinity Hospital in time—Gabriel placed the saint upon the back of Sugar-Groove and tied St. Peter down, using the cord unknotted from the Mississippian's shoulder and trunk.

Sugar-Groove (who never called himself any of these names, but the one given to him by his Auntie Gracie Mae Gates, "Billy") now thought of his aunt's husband, Ice, the preacher, who worked on ways of trying to preserve ice from melting so quickly by digging up circular, underground vats and pits, in nearby caves, in order to forestall the ice drifting swiftly into water.

Despite his luggage and extra baggage, Sugar-Groove "Billy" spread his wings and moved in the skies. And how could he ever forget Rev. Ice Gates who once sermonized seven straight hours on the layers of Spiritual Velocity. And the pilgrim felt like a whole man, now—new born—for the first time, without touching a tap of water—and surely as one released from a strait-jacket, using the stars to navigate by, as he remembered the map, he wondered aloud how these stars were shot through by changes, in the hypnotic beauty of the Heavens . . . And he remembered as how Rev. Ice Gates often recalled seeing Halley's Comet, as a small boy, when low and behold if he didn't hear his auntie's husband, in full preaching voice zooming upwards (as if he was about to reach onto the sweet part of his favorite sermon—"Consider the Eagle") but now exploding with:

"Sugar-Dripper, Billy-boy, has you done lost your last, lightless mind? You done let being up there turn your mind into one Fool's paradise, so bad off you can't remember nothing, in its proper form . . . You may be proud the way you can read that map—but that oughta make you, even you, recollect as how even me, I who was touched by Him—could never make that Auntie of yours learn to read nor write."

And then it all came down on Sugar-Groove, as a tumbled-down mansion of bricks. Those sonofabitches, he bleated: "Why they oughta be tarred and feathered. Why I should have fed this joker a spoon of Salt Peter." But it was too late to turn back now . . . even though he longed to do so . . . turn back to what? To what form, he cried, in his furious flight. And in what form? To a new covenant, he spat in the wind, as the burden of St. Peter's body became heavier. And what form would take over his possessed wing(s)?

Now making his golden shears imitate the motion of sailing wings in space, just above my poor fool's head, Williemain spun my chair about and I found myself wondering in my swirling about: did Sugar-Groove have a last name, or a lasting name? And where did he get it? Or from whom? What was the name of his named Sire? Suddenly, I could see Sugar-Groove sky-writing his name upon the Proscenium of Paradise. But which one of his nicknames was he deploying? I needed Vigil Residual to elevate my pilgrim's progress. Suddenly, Williemain declared:

"Gentlemens, Sugar-Groove's left eye commenced to spinning like a wheel within a wheel, over the aggravation and the condemnations, and the contentions . . . and the rupture between himself and his auntie . . ."

Picking it up, Galloway Wheeler, the barber in the second chair, who was always reading chanted:

' . . . As well as the backbone breaking work of his previous condition brought up further North, now, more than he could of ever dreamed . . . and of course now this new knowledge. For Sugar-Shark swerved over and curbed in, within the regions of his heart, but what did he in the chambers of his soul look like now?'

And so, as all of the souls of Paradise watched, breathlessly, the man from Sugar-Ditch, Mississippi, was seen flying furiously through space and time, with St. Peter strapped down upon his back, face up; and the guardian-angel's wingspread and acceleration was a thing of beholding beauty, as he winged onto the Fabulous Sky-Blue Freeway through The Tunnel of Love, crisscrossing up Eros Expressway, past the North Star affixed in the Heavens, as if by blacksmith's hammer, and a squadron of aero-angels followed in the wake of Sugar-Groove's Almighty shouldering shadow.

They got there in time and saved St. Peter from suffering an eternal case of internal combustion, as well as internal shortness of breath, for the duration of his divine days in Paradise.

'But Gentlemens,' concluded Williemain ' . . . Now, I hate to scream on Divinity, but if you want to know the whole truth, here's my hand to God, no sugar-coating, it was the first time anybody ever suffered a heart spasm in Paradise and over wing(s) to boot.'

And that's when I screamed out:

'Wasn't Sugar-Groove sky-writing a new covenant across the proscenium of Paradise—when his wingless body was last seen?'

'Hell Naw, Joubert Baby-Bear Jones, the shit remains nameless, unreported in the *Heavenly Gazette* . . .'Cause all you pilgrims know, I ain't never lied.'

Whose Song?

BY THOMAS GLAVE

Yes, now they're waiting to rape her, but how can they know? The girl with strum-vales, entire forests, behind her eyes. Who has already known the touch of moondewed kisses, nightwing sighs, on her teenage skin. Cassandra. Lightskinned, lean. Lovelier to them for the light. How can they know? The darkskinned ones aren't even hardly what they want. They have been taught, have learned well and well. Them black bitches, that's some skank shit, they sing. Give you VD on the woody, make your shit fall off. How can they know? Have been taught. Cassandra, fifteen, in the light. On her way to the forests. In the light. Hasn't known a man yet. Hasn't wanted to. How can they know? She prefers Tanya's lips, the skin-touch of silk. Tanya, girlfriend, sixteen and fine, dark glider, schoolmate-lover, large-nippled-thighed. Tanya. Who makes her come and come again when the mamas are away, when houses settle back into silent time and wrens swoopflutter their wings down into the nightbird's song. Tanya and Cassandra. Kissing. Holding. Climbing and gliding. What the grown girls do, they think, belly-kissing but shy. Holding. She makes me feel my skin, burrowing in. Which one of them thinks that? Which one flies? Who can tell? Climbing and gliding. Coming. Wet. Coming. Laughing. Smelling. Girlsex, she-love, and the nightbird's song. Thrilling and trilling. Smooth bellies, giving face, brushing on and on. Cassandra. Tanya swooping down, brown girls, dusky flesh and the nightbird's song. How can they know? The boys have been watching them, have begun to know things about them watchers know or guess. The boys, touching themselves in nightly rage, watching them. Wanting more of Cassandra because she doesn't want them. Wanting to set the forests on fire, cockbrush those glens. How can they know? They are there and they are there and they are watching. Now.

Sing this tale, then, of a Sound Hill rape. Sing it, low and mournful, soft, beneath the kneeling trees on either side of the rusty bridge out

122

Making Callaloo

by Eastchester Creek; where the sun hangs low over the Sound and water meets the sky; where the departed walk along Shore Road and the joggers run; where morning rabbits leap away from the pounding joggers' step. Sing it far and wide, this sorrow song woven into the cresting nightbird's blue. Sing it, in that far-off place, far up away from it all, where the black people live and think they've at last found peace; where there are homes, small homes and large, with modest yards, fruit hedges, taxus, juniper trees; where the silver hoses, coiled, sag and lean; where the withered arms hanging out of second-story windows are the arms of that lingering ghost or aging lonely busybody everybody knows. In that northerly corner of the city where no elevated IRT train yet comes; where the infrequent buses to Orchard Beach and Pelham Bay sigh out spent lives and empty nights when they run; where the Sound pulls watersmell through troubled dreams and midnight pains, the sleeping loneliness and silence of a distant place. Sound Hill, beneath your leaning trees and waterwash, who do you grieve for now? Sound Hill girl of the trees and the girlflesh, where are you now? Will those waters of the Sound flow beside you now? Caress you with light-kisses and bless you now? The City Island currents and the birds rush by you now? O sing it. Sing it for that yellow girl, dark girl, brown girl homely or fine, everygirl displaced, neither free nor named. Sing it for that girl swinging her axe through the relentless days, suckling a child or selling her ass in the cheap hotels down by the highway truckers' stop for chump change. Sing it for this girl, swishing her skirt and T-shirt, an almost-free thing, instinctual, throwing her head back to the breeze. Her face lifted to the sky. Now, Jesus. Walk here, Lamb. In thy presence there shall be light and light. Grace. Cadence. A witness or a cry. Come, now. All together. And.

How could we know? Three boys in a car, we heard, but couldn't be neighbors of ours. Had to be from some other part of the world, we thought; the projects or the Valley. Not from here. In this place every face knows every eye, we thought, what's up here in the heart always is clear. But they were not kind nor good, neither kin nor known. If they were anything at all besides unseen, they were maimed. Three boys, three boys. In a car. Long legs, lean hands. In a car. Bitter mouths, tight asses, and the fear of fear. Boys or men and hard. In their car. Who did not like it. Did not like the way those forest eyes gazed out at those darker desert ones, at the eyes of that other who had known what it was to be dark and loathed. Yo, darkskinned bitch. So it had been said. Yo, skillet ass. Don't be cutting your eyes at me, bitch, I'll fuck your black ass up. It had been said. Ugly black bitch. You need some dick. Them eyes gone get you killed, rolling them at me like that. It had been said. Had to be, had to be from over by Edenwald, we thought. Rowdy, raunchy, no kind of class. Nasty homies on the prowl, not from this 'hood. How could we know? Three boys, fretful, frightened, angry. In a row. The burning rope had come to them long ago in willed and willful dreams, scored mean circles and scars into their once-gorgeous throats. The eyes that had once looked up in wonder from their mother's arms had been beaten, hammered into rings, dark pain-pools that belied their depth. Deeper. Where they lived, named and unnamed. How could they know? Know that those butterflies and orchids of the other world, that ice-green velvet of the other world, the precious stones that got up and wept before the unfeeling sky and the bears that slept away entire centuries with memories of that once-warm sweet milk on their lips, were not for them? So beaten, so denied, as they were and as they believed, their own hands had grown to claws over the years; savaged their own skin. Needles? Maybe, we thought. In the reviling at large, who could tell? Pipes, bottles? Vials? So we thought. Of course. Who could know, and who who knew would tell? Who who knew would sing through the veil the words of that song, about the someone-or-thing that had torn out their insides and left them there, far from the velvet and the butterflies and the orchid-time? The knower's voice, if voice it was, only whispered down bitter rains when they howled, and left us only the curve of their skulls beneath the scarred flesh on those nights, bony white, when the moon smiled.

And she, so she: alone that day. Fresh and wet still from Tanya's arms, pajama invitations and TV nights, after-dark giggles and touches, kisses, while belowstairs the mama slept through world news, terrorist bombings, cleansings ethnic and unclean. Alone that day, the day after, yellow girl, walking out by the golden grayswishing Sound, higher up along the Shore Road way and higher, higher up where no one ever walks alone, higher still by where the dead bodies every year turn up (four Puerto Rican girls—things cut up, garbage-bagged, found there last year: bloated hands, swollen knees, and the broken parts); O higher still, Cassandra, where the fat joggers run, higher still past the horse stables and the smell of hay, higher yet getting on to where the white-folks live and the sundowns die. Higher. Seeking watersmell and sheen for those forests in her eyes; seeking that summer sundown heat on her skin; seeking something away from 'hood catcalls and yo, bitch, let me in. Would you think she doesn't already know what peacefulness means, contains? She's already learned of the dangers of the too-high skirt, the things some of them say they'd like to put between her knees. The blouse that reveals, the pants that show too much hip. Ropes hers and theirs. Now seeking only a place where she can walk away, across the water if need be, away from the beer cans hurled from cars, the What's up, bitch yells and the burning circle-scars. Cassandra, Cassandra. Are you a bitch out here? The sun wexing goldsplash across her now says no. The water stretching out to Long Island summerheat on the other side says no, and the birds wheeling overhead, *okay, okay*, they cry, call down the skytone, concurring: the word is no. Peace and freedom, sea-smell and free. A dark girl's scent riding on her thighs. Cassandra. Tanya. Sing it.

But they watching. The three. Singing. Listen: a bitch ain't nothing but a ho, sing those three. Have been taught. (But by whom?) Taught and taut. Taught low and harsh, that rhythm. Fierce melody. Melody-lessness in mixture, lovelessness in joy. Drunk on flame, and who the fuck that bitch think she is anyway? they say—for they had seen her before, spoken to her and her kind; courted her favor, her attentions, in that car. Can't talk to nobody, bitch, you think you all a that? Can't speak to nobody, bitch, you think your pussy talks and shit? How could they know then?—of her forests, smoldering? Know and feel?—how in that growing silent heat those inner trees had uprooted, hurled stark branches at the outer sky? The firestorm and after-rain remained unseen. Only the lashes fluttered, and the inner earth grew hard. With those ropes choking so many of them in dreams, aware of the circles burnt into their skins, how could they know? How could they not know?

Robbie. Dee. Bernard. Three and three. Young and old. Too old for those jeans sliding down their asses. Too young for the rope and the circle's clutch. Too old to love so much their own wet dreams splashed out onto she they summoned out of that uncentered roiling world. She, summoned, to walk forth before their fire as the bitch or cunt. So they thought, would think and sing: still too young for the nursing of that keening need, the unconscious conscious wish to obliterate through vicious dreams who they were and are, have been, and are not. Blackmenbrothers, lovers, sons of strugglers. Sharecroppers, cocksuckers, black bucks and whores. Have been and are, might still be, and are not. A song. To do away with what they have and have not; what they can be, they think, are told by that outer chorus they can be—black boys, pretty boys, big dicks, tight asses, pretty boys, black scum or funky homie trash—and cannot. Their hearts replaced by gnashing teeth, dirt; the underscraping grinch, an always-howl. Robbie Dee Bernard. Who have names and eyelids, fears, homie-homes. Watching now. Looking out for a replacement for those shredded skins. Cause that bitch think she all a that, they sing. Word, got that lightskin, good hair, think she fly. Got them titties that need some dick up in between. The flavor. Not like them darkskinned bitches, they sing. (But do the words have joy?) Got to cut this bitch down to size, the chorus goes. A tune. Phat pussy. Word, G! Said hey-ho! Said a-hey-ho! Word, my brother. My nigger. Sing it.

So driving. Looking. Watching. Seeing. Their words a blue song, the undercolor of the nightbird's wing. Is it a song you have heard before? Heard it sung sweet and clear to someone you hate before? Listen:— Oh shit, yo, there she go. Right up there. Straight on. Swinging her ass like a high-yellow ho. Said hey-ho! Turn up the volume on my man J Live J. Drive up, yo. Spook the bitch. Gonna get some serious pussy outa this shit.—Driving, slowing, slowing down. Feeling the circles, feeling their own necks. Burning skins, cockheads fullstretched and hard.

Will she have a chance, dreaming of girlkisses, against that hard? In the sun. Here. And.

Pulling up.—So, Miss Lightskin, they sing, what you doing out here? Walking by yourself, you ain't scared? Ain't scared somebody gonna try to get some of your skin? Them titties looking kinda fly, girl. Come on, now. Get in.

Was it then that she felt the smoldering in those glens about to break? The sun gleaming down silver whiteheat on her back? *And O how she had only longed to walk the walk.* To continue on and on and on and through to those copses where, at the feet of that very old and most wise woman-tree of all, she might gaze into those stiller waters of minnow-fishes, minnow-girls, and there yes! quell quell quell quell quell the flames. As one of them then broke through her glens, to shout that she wasn't nothing anyway but a yellow bitch with a whole lotta attitude and a skanky cunt. As (oh yes, it was true, rivers and fire, snake daggers and black bitches, she had had enough) she flung back words on what exactly he should do with his mother's cunt, cause your mother, nigger, is the only motherfucking bitch out here. And then? Who could say or know? The 5-0 were nowhere in sight; all passing cars had passed; only the wheeling birds and that drifting sun above were witnesses to what they could not prevent. Cassandra, Cassandra.—Get in the car, bitch.——Fuck no, I won't. Leave me alone. Leave me——trying to say Fuck off, y'all leave me the fuck alone, but whose hand was that, then, grabbing for her breast? Whose hand *is* that, on her ass, pressing now, right now, up into her flesh?—Stop it, y'all. Get the fuck off before——screaming and crying. Cursing, running. Sneakered feet on asphalt, pursuit, and the laughing loud. An easy catch.—We got you now, bitch.—Who can hear? The sun can only stare, and the sky is gone.

Driving, driving, driving on. Where can they take her? Where will they? They all want some, want to be fair. Fair is fair: three dicks, one cunt. That is their song. Driving on. Pelham Bay Park?, they think. But naw, too many people, niggers and Ricans with a whole buncha kids and shit. (The sun going down. Driving on). How about under the bridge, by Eastchester Creek? That's it, G! Holding her, holding, but can't somebody slap the bitch to make her shut up? Quit crying, bitch. Goddamn. A crying-ass bitch in a little funky-ass car. Now weeping more. Driving on.—Gonna call the police, she says, crying more; choking in that way they like, for then (oh, yes, they know) in that way from smooth head to hairy base will she choke on them. They laugh.—What fucking 5-0 you gonna call, bitch? You lucky we ain't take your yellow ass over to the projects. Fuck your shit in the elevator, throw your ass off the roof. These bitches, they laugh. Just shut up and sit back. Sit back, sit back. Driving on.

Now the one they call Robbie is talking to her.—Open it, he says. Robbie, O Robbie. Eager and edgy, large-eyed and fine. Robbie, who has a name, unspoken hopes; private dreams. How can they know? Will he be dead within a year like so many others? A mirrored image in a mirror that shows them nothing? A wicked knife's slide from a brother's hand to his hidden chewed-up heart? Shattered glass, regret. Feeling now only the circle around his neck that keeps all in thrall. For now he must be a man for them. Must show the steel. Robbie don't be fronting, he prays they think, Robbie be hard. Will they like you better, Robbie, then, if you be hard? Will the big boys finally love you, take you in, Robbie, if you be hard? But it's deep sometimes, isn't it, Robbie, with all that hard? Deep and low. . . . —He knows. Knows the clear tint of that pain. Alone and lonely . . . unknown, trying to be hard. Not like it was back then *when then when he said you was pretty*. Remember? All up in his arms . . . one of your boys, Darrell J. In his arms. Where nobody couldn't see. Didn't have to be hard. Rubbing up, rubbing. Kissing up on you. Licking. Talking shit about lovelove and all a that But *naw man* he said the first time (Darrell J., summertime, 10 P.M., off the court, hotwet, crew gone home, had an extra 40, sweaty chest neck face, big hands, shoulders, smile, was fine), *just chilling whyn't you come on hang out?*—so said Darrell J. with the hands and the yo yo yo yo going on and on with them eyes and *mouth tongue up in his skin* my man—: kissing up on Robbie the second time, pretty Robbie, the third time and the fourth and the *we did and he* kissing licking holding y'all two and O Robbie Robbie Robbie. A homie's song. Feeling then. Underneath him, pretty. In his arms. *Where nobody couldn't see didn't have to be hard kissing up on him shy shy and* himinyou youinhim Robbie, Robbie. Where has the memory gone? Back then, straddling hips, homiekisses and the nightbird's song. But can't go back there, can you? To feel and feel. Gots to be hard. Can't ever touch him again, undress him, kiss his thing . . . feel it pressing against the teeth and the slow-hipped song. Black skin on skin and

—but he was holding onto me and sliding, sliding way up inside sucking coming inside me in me in hot naw didn't need no jimmy aw shit now hold on holding him and I was I was Robbie Robbie Robbie Darrell J. together we was and I we I we came we hotwet on his belly my side sliding over him under him holding and we came we but naw, man, can't even be doing that motherfucking punk shit out here. You crazy? You bugging? Niggers be getting smoked dusty for that shit. Y'all ain't never seen *me* do that. Gots to be hard.—So open it, bitch, he says. Lemme get my fingers on up in there. Awright, awright. Damn, man, he says, nobody don't got a jimmy? This bitch stinks, man, he says, know I'ma probably get some VD shit on my hands and shit. They laugh.—He a man, all right. Robbie! Ain't no faggot, yo. Not like we heard. They laugh.—Just put a sock on it, the one they call Dee says. Chillchill, yo. Everybody gonna get their chance.

And the sun. Going down, going down. Light ending now, fire and ice, blue time watersheen and the darkened plunge. Sink, golden sun. Rest your bronze head in the Sound and the sea beyond. The birds, going down, going down. Movement of trees, light swathed in leaves. Going down, going down. And.

Hard to see now, but that's OK, they say. This bitch got enough for everybody here under the bridge. No one's around now, only rusty cars and rats. Who cares if they shove that filthy rag into her mouth and tie it there? It's full of turpentine and shit, but the night doesn't care. The same night that once covered them in swamps from fiery light. Will someone come in white robes to save a lightskinned bitch this time?

Hot. Dark. On the backseat. Burning bright. Burning. On the backseat. Fire and rage.—Naw, man, Robbie, not so hard, man. You gone wear the shit out fore I get my chance. Who said that? Which one in the dark? O but can't tell, for all are hidden now, and all are hard. The motherfucking *rigorous* shit, one of them says. Shut up, bitch. Was that you, Bernard? Did you miss your daddy when he went off with the one your mama called a dirty nigger whore, Bernard? Was that where you first learned everything there was to learn, and nothing?—there, Bernard? When he punched you in the face and left you behind, little boy Bernard? You cried. Without. A song unheard. A song like the shadow-rain—wasn't it? The shadowrain that's always there so deep, deep down inside your eyes, Bernard. Cold rain inside. Tears and tears. Then fists and kicks on a black shitboy's head. Little punk-looking nigger dumped in a foster home, age ten, named Bernard. Fuckhead faggot ass, the boys there said. The ones who stuck it up in you. Again and again. The second and the third . . . —don't hurt me, don't!—screamed that one they called the faggot ass pussy bitch. You, Bernard. How could they know? Know that the little bitch punk scrunched up under the bed had seen the whole night and afterward and after alone? Bernard? *Hurts, mama. Daddy*—. Rain. Little faggot ass punk. Break his fucking face, yo. Kick his faggot ass down the stairs. Then he gone suck my dick. Suck it, bitch, fore we put this motherfucking hammer up your ass. The one you trusted most of all in that place, in all those places . . . everywhere? Bernard? The one who said he'd have your back no matter what. Little man, my man, he said. Smiling down. His teeth so white and wide. Smiling down. Smiling when he got you by the throat, sat on your chest and made you swallow it. Swallow it, bitch, he sang. Smiling down. Choking, choked. Deep inside the throat. Where has the memory gone? Something broken, then a hand. A reaching-out howl within the rain. A nightbird's rage. A punk, used up. Leave the nigger there, yo, they said. Til the next time. And the next. On the floor. Under the bed. Under. Bleeding under. You, Bernard.

The words to every song on earth are buried deep somewhere. Songs that must be sung, that must never be sung. That must be released from deep within the chest yet pulled back and held. Plaintive and low, they rail; buried forever beneath the passing flesh, alone and cold, they scream. The singer must clutch them to the heart, where they are sanctified, nurtured, healed. Songs which finally must be released yet recalled, in that place where no one except the singer ever comes, in one

Making Callaloo

hand caressing the keys of life wounded, ravaged, in the other those of the precious skin and life revealed. The three of them and Cassandra know the words. Lying beneath them now and blind, she knows the words. Tasting turpentine and fire, she knows the words.—Hell no, yo, that bitch ain't dead.—A voice.—Fucked up, yo. The rag's in her mouth, how we gone get some mouth action now?——Aw, man, fuck that shit.—Who says that?—My turn. My turn.—They know the words.

Now comes Dee. Can't even really see her, has to navigate. Wiggles his ass a little, farts softly to let off stress.—Damn, Dee, nasty motherfucker! they laugh. But he is busy, on to something. Sniffs and sniffs. At the bitch's asshole. At her cunt.—Cause yeah, yo, he says, y'all know what's up with this shit. They be saying this bitch done got into some bulldagger shit. Likes to suck pussy, bulldagger shit.—Word?—The phattest bitch around, yo, he says. Bulldagger shit.

Dee. DeeDee. Someone's boy. Has a place that's home. Eastchester, or Mount V. Has a heart that hates his skin and a mind half gone. Is ugly now, got cut up, but smoked the nigger who did it. Can't sleep at night, wanders seas; really wants to die. The lonely bottle might do it if the whiffs up don't. The empty hand might do it if the desire can't. What has been loved and not loved, what seeks still a place. The same hand, pushed by the once-winsome heart, that before painted angels, animals, miraculous creatures. Blank walls leaped into life, lightspeed and light. When (so it seemed) the whole world was light. But was discouraged, led into tunnels, and then of course was cut. The eyes went dim. Miraculous creatures. Where have the visions gone? Look, now, at that circle around his neck. Will he live? Two young ones and a dark girl waiting back there for him, frightened—will he live? Crushed angels drowned in St. Ides—will he live? When he sells the (yes, that) next week to the undercover 5-0 and is set up, will he live? When they shoot him in the back and laugh at the stain that comforts them, will he live?

But now he's happy, has found it!—the hole. The soft little hole, so tight, down there, as he reaches up to squeeze her breasts. Her eyes are closed but she knows the words. *That bitch ain't dead.* How can they know? When there is time there's time, and the time is now. Time to bang the bulldagger out of her, he sings. Listen to his song:—I'ma give you a baby, bitch. (She knows the words). Got that lightskin, think you all that, right, bitch? Word, I want me some lightskin on my dick, yo. When I get done this heifer ain't gone be *half* a ho. You know know? Gonna get mines, til you know who you dis and who you don't. Til you know we the ones in *con-trol*, sing it! Got the flavor.—Dim-eyed, banging out his rage. Now, a man. Banging out his fear like the others, ain't even hardly no faggot ass. Def jam and slam, bang bang shebam. On and on as he shoots high, shoots far . . . laughter, but then a sense of falling, careening . . . sudden fear. It doesn't matter. The song goes on.

Night. Hell, no, broods the dim, that bitch ain't dead. Hasn't uttered half a sound since they began; hasn't opened her eyes to let the night look in again; hasn't breathed to the soft beating of the nightbird's wing. The turpentine rag in place. Cassandra, Cassandra. The rag, in place. Cassandra. Is she feeling something now? Cassandra. Will they do anything more to her now? Cassandra, will they leave you there? Focusing on flies, not meeting each other's eyes, will they leave you there? Running back from the burning forests behind their own eyes, the crackling and the shame? Will they leave you there?—Push that bitch out on the ground, the one they call Dee says.—Over there, by them cars and shit.—Rusty cars, a dumping ground. So, Cassandra. Yes. They'll leave you there.

Were they afraid? Happy? Who can tell? Three dark boys, three men, driving away in a battered car. Three boy-men, unseen, flesh, minds, heart. Flame. In their car. O my God, three rapists, the pretty lady in her Volvo thinks, locking her doors at the traffic light. In their car. Blood on the backseat, cum stains, even hair. Who can tell? It's time to get open now. Time to numb the fear.—Get out the whiff, yo.—40s and a blunt.—That bitch got what she deserved.—Those words, whiffs up, retreat, *she deserved it, deserved it*—and they are gone. Mirrored images in shattered glass, desire and longing, chill throbbing, and they are gone. The circles cleaving their necks. Flesh, blood and flame. A whiff and a 40.—We fucked that bitch good, G.—Night. Nightnight. Hush dark silence. Fade. They are gone.

Cassandra. What nightbirds are searching and diving for you now? What plundered forests are waiting for you now? The girl-trees are waiting for you, and so is she. Tanya. The girl-trees. Mama. How can they know? Their eyes are waiting, searching, and will soon be gray. The rats are waiting. They are gray. Cassandra, Cassandra. When the red lights come flashing on you, will they know? Fifteen, ripped open. Will they know? Lightskinned bitch nigger ho, went that song. Will they know? Girl-trees in a burning forest . . . they will know. And the night. . . .

Where is she, they're wondering, why hasn't she come home?

They can't know what the rats and the car-carcasses know.

Cassandra? they are calling. Why don't you answer when night-voices call you home?

Night. . . .

Listen now to the many night voices calling, calling soft, *Cassandra. Come. Carrying. Up. Cassandra. Come. Out and up.* What remains is what remains. Out and up. They will carry her. A feeling of hands and light. Then the red lights will come. *Up* and *up.* But will she see? Will she hear? Will she know?

The girl-trees are screaming. That is their song.

It will not appear on tomorrow's morning news.

But then—come now, ask yourself—whose song, finally, shall this be? Of four dark girls, or four hundred, on their way to lasting fire in Sunday school? Of a broken-backed woman, legs bent? Her tune? Of a pair of hands, stitching for—(but they'll never grow). Of four brothers rapping, chugging?—a slapbeat in the chorus? Doing time? Something they should know?

A song of grieving ships, bodies, torch-lit roads?

(—*But then now O yes remember, remember well that time, face, place or thing: how those ten thousand million billion other ashes eyelids arms uncountable dark ceaseless burnt and even faces once fluttered, fluttered forever, in someone's dream unending, dream of no escape, beneath a blackblueblack sea: fluttered, flutter still and descend, now faces ashes eyelids dark reflection and skin forever flame: descend, descend over laughing crowds.*)

A song of red earth roads. Women crying and men. Red hands, gray mouths, and the circle's clutch. A song, a song. Of sorrowing suns. Of destruction, self-destruction, when eyes lay low. A song—

But whose song is it? Is it yours? Or mine?

Hers?

Or theirs . . . —?

—But a song. A heedless, feckless tune. Here, where the nighttime knows. And, well—

Yes, well—

—So, Cassandra. Now, Cassandra.

Sing it.

from Jonestown (Imagination Dead Imagine)

BY WILSON HARRIS

NOTE

The Longman Chronicle of America *tells of the "tragedy of Jonestown" and of the scene of "indescribable horror" that greeted the eyes of reporters when they arrived in Jonestown in a remote forest in Guyana in late November 1978.*

Questions are raised about the charismatic power of a cult leader to induce such self-inflicted holocaust.

My fiction possesses its trigger in such events but it is, in no respect, a historical portrait. Jonah Jones, Deacon, Francisco Bone—who appear in this excerpt—are archetypal and fictional characters. They bear no resemblance whatever to living or dead persons.

Francisco created a book of dreams in order to break the trauma he suffered in surviving the holocaust. He sees Jonestown as a recent manifestation of the enigma of vanished populations, abandoned cities, lost cultures in the Central and South Americas.

Bone is affected by a strand in the ancient Maya civilization in which the linearity of time is breached in favor of a twinning of pasts and futures. The archetypes of the past become unfathomable and are woven into "unknowns" arriving from the future. Such compressions in and of time would imply, I feel, gestating resources within the womb of tradition. Tradition, then, cannot be taken for granted. Our tendency to do so reinforces fixtures of bias that we erect into absolutes and closures that threaten the life of the Imagination.

I have adopted the phrase Imagination Dead Imagine from one of Samuel Beckett's short novels.

—Wilson Harris
July 1994

I lay in a clump of bushes like a dead man. Scarcely breathing. My head rested on a cushion of stone. I dreamt of angels ascending and descending into Jonestown. Jonestown was above me in the skeletons of the stars. No stars now at midday. Only the sunlit dead on the ground. How incredibly soft is stone when one fears flesh-and-blood!

Jonah Jones was still alive with a gun. He would appear, I knew, at any moment in the Clearing.

There was a split leaf close to my nose through which—with slightly lowered head away from my pillow—I began to count the dead bodies on the ground. They lay not far from the rude church in which they had worshipped an hour or two ago. One swore one could hear their voices still rising into the heart of the South American Forest that seemed now in me yet as remote from me as the Milky Way blotted out by sunlight . . .

I felt a mental splinter sharp as the nib of bone; and voiced my own lament in tune with their vanished voices. The voice of bone was the art of the Word, of sculpture, of painting within the holocaust.

"Good God!" the bone sang.

The bone ceased for a while its tremulous, echoing tracery of scriptures of sorrow. It ceased yet never ceased for it continued to make silent pictures until the wordlessness of the sleeping choir of the dead in the Clearing welled up around me.

A woman whose name was Marie Antoinette was clutching a mystical cup or grail of music from which she had drunk milk and sugar and deadly cyanide. Her head lolled on the ground. Her torso wore the blind sunlight of Carnival. It was the sheer ordinariness of the cup against the lips in the head that struck me to the heart, the lips' communion with Silence.

All at once the Reverend Jonah Jones, tall, commanding, came out of the rude Church of Eternity into the Clearing. His face wore an air of triumph like a general's on the field of battle. He stopped above the eloquent lips and head and the communion cup. There was a child beside her I had not seen before. A child I knew all at once. me! *Me* in another universe, a parallel universe to this. *I* was in that parallel child. Quantum hallucination. Quantum transference of psyche.

Jonah stood in the whale of the sun, he knelt, he placed a gun to

Marie Antoinette's temple that seemed in a state of divorce from the trunk of her body.

What curious memorials a bone inscribes, draws, paints, builds, sings in the mind, the exiled mind, the solitary mind and soul on the margins of doomed civilizations.

One is exiled when one refuses to obey the commandments of Conquest Mission, to think, or write in a certain way, in conformity with the realism of Death. I was a sculptor of the bone in exile now, a writer of the bone in exile now, a painter, an architect, a poet of the bone in exile now upon the margins of the Conquest Mission established by the cult Master of Ritual the Reverend Jonah Jones.

Jonah and Jones are common-or-garden names which have gained ascendancy in the Forest of my age.

I sensed the great danger I was in. I had deceived Jonah. I knew there was no persuasion or plea or dialogue on my part that could have led him back and out of the great white whale of the sun into which he was determined to go, that he wished to inhabit as the throne of conquest, and in which he sought to secrete his followers. Could one begin to explain to him that such secretion was a manifestation or a prelude to the extinction of species?

I had deceived him. I had been his comrade. I had been a close associate. But—at the last moment—I had broken the pact. I had not drunk from the cup. He was sure I was lying there amongst the dead. I had been disobedient. Would I pay dear for such treason? Had I saddled myself with the traumas of an age, the traumas of disadvantaged peoples around the globe?

At last the Reverend Jonah Jones was satisfied that the woman had been loyal. The subject of a revolution that he wished to engineer, she had surrendered to his will, she had drunk her drink to the last drop . . . No need to pull the trigger . . . He withdrew the gun from her broken body . . . Was it broken? Was it miraculously whole?

He raised the cold steel, the icy metal—cold as my pillow—to his eyes. I dreamt I was in his blindness. We were already dead. We had already pulled the trigger! But he was alive. *I was alive.* Technologies and functions of life and death seemed the most ordinary things, banal commodities of conquest. And yet my fear was such I could have vomited. Vomited the stars! The moment had arrived—Jones knew—for him to join his flock. I could not help it. My limbs began to shake. Jonah and I had been close friends within veil upon veil of sun that hid us from each other even as we thought we knew one another. We had debated points in the world's holy books, books of Rwanda, books of Bosnia, books of Palestine, books on the fall of Jerusalem, that bore on the end of Time. We had chosen South America, we had chosen Guyana, for our Conquest Mission. We had chosen—as the ancient Maya once did—the very heart of the jungle, in which to re-interpret the death of the arts, pyramidal epitaphs, painting-epitaphs, poetry-epitaphs. IMAGINATION DEAD IMAGINE.

We had chosen the ancient rainforest hinterland for our Conquest Mission because the Central and South Americas were a theatre of enigma. No place around the globe had so mirrored the paradox of vanished cultures, vanished settlements, from ancient Maya cities and causeways—long abandoned, drowned, wreathed in jungles—to invisible Atlantean arches and bridges upon which migrating peoples had moved from the North to the South, the East to the West, and left behind but the morsel of a flute (as though music possessed the secret architecture of ages after the collapse of frames in which conquistadorial priests of old sought to conscript the Imagination)—a morsel, a flute, a fury akin to the bone or splinter in my mind.

Wherein lies the mystery of music in the densities of space, the live fossil solidity of music in the song of a blackbird or reflected rhythms and compositions in the mirrored throat of a South American apparitional mocking-bird? Did the bone in a wing of the mind, a wing of the brain, inhabit a treasonable space beyond fixtures that sanction extinguished species, poisoned landscapes?

Jones did not approve of such questions but he humored me, he tolerated me. He occasionally elected me to serve on panels in the church. He was convinced of my loyalty to the Conquest Mission whatever my unrest of conscience. We dined together, Deacon, Jones, and I on the eve of the holocaust.

I was his left-hand man. Deacon was his right-hand angel. I could not deny it. We were friends. I was a traitor. I began to scorn the treasures of eternity in order to salvage a morsel of Time.

News had reached us that the Police were on Jonah's trail. They claimed he had defrauded the Bank of America.

"The Caribs ate a ritual morsel," I said, "on the eve of battle. And now that we're on the eve of the holocaust, the Jonestown holocaust, time has become invaluable."

"We shall all die rather than surrender to the corruptions and lies of the Police," said Jones.

"Die?" I said.

"Yes die," he cried.

"It's astonishing to have such a conversation."

The Carib ritual morsel melted in my mouth as if I were consuming the flesh of a high priest to unravel the secrets in Jonah's constitution. Food on such a day, such a time, imbued me with terror.

It was impossible to dismiss him as a fanatic. He was too solid, too bloody-minded. He was as sane as a Napoleon of finance. DEFRAUD BANKS? I did not believe it. Pocket millions, yes, in a crusade against violence that recruited the self-same violence in pursuit of its ends. In the light of such symmetry, violence cemented into violence, the morsel I ate burned into my tongue. Was it poison, had I already consumed poison in the name of the people? No! It was the fracture of loyalty, the disruption of loyalty, it was treason.

I was joined to Jonah Jones in the paradox of a bone, a bone-flute, a bone-morsel that I tasted in the anatomy of my mind.

I was joined to him in the splintered disruption of a pact with eternity that I had sworn to honor at his command. I was joined to him now in the fear that I sensed on the eve of disaster. I knew more searchingly and agonizingly than I had ever known before—with the morsel on my tongue—the perversity of the harmony that he inspired in his people, the perversity of symmetry and dread closure underlying the death of the arts. Perhaps I had known it all along, perhaps I *knew* my age was dying. Perhaps that was why I joined the Jonestown Church. What I had not perceived was the curious salvage of a Primitive morsel of time sprung from another kind of variable pact rooted in counter-pointed layers of a-symmetrical longing to consume the fortresses of hate within my age, cemented bias, cemented violence.

"I thought they were bloody cannibals," said Jones. "These Caribs of which you speak."

I had forgotten I had spoken of them. But he remembered. He would become, if not the Bank of America, a significant agent in the Bank of Memory when I began to shoulder the trauma I would experience the following day as I lay on my pillow of stone. His face was curiously livid, curiously bland, deceptively bland, as he projected his rage upon the vanished Caribs in thinking of the Police. So easy to orchestrate the law into scapegoats one would murder at the drop of a hat.

I turned to Jones with tears in my eyes but he did not see them.

"Are we not subject to the vocabulary of death-dealing regimes? Think of the battle cries, the marching songs, drums that counsel assault. Death coins every phrase that spells conquest . . ."

"*In counterpoint with the mystery of the victim soul, the mystery of music,*" said Deacon. "Is it not time—when time seems to be ending—to unravel the counterpoint, varieties of counterpoint, between priest and sacrificial victim, between huntsman and hunted species, between lovers and virgins of the wild . . . ?" He stopped. Was he laughing at me? Was he mocking me? Was Marie of Jonestown (with her dead child) whom I was to number amongst the dead, in the Clearing on the morrow, a despoiled Virgin?

I was startled. The truth was I disliked Jonah's right-hand angel. Disliked him intensely on the eve of the holocaust. He was, I dimly felt, at this stage, a signal for me—in the book I was to write when I survived Jonestown (a book entitled *IMAGINATION DEAD IMAGINE*)—of the riddle of the huntsman, the riddle of the hunted creature, the enigma or counterpoint of shared Passion between spoilers and despoiled.

After the holocaust his self-mockery gave way to truths one wrestles with on every ladder between heaven and earth, the truths of fictionality in birth and death, virgin space and animal bridegroom, animal masks worn by the gods when civilization is in crisis. He was to don the mask of the Scavenger or Vulture or Eagle. Jonah, at the point of death, *when Deacon shot him*, was to achieve guilt and remorse in the metamorphosis of the whale into a sun-striped tiger swimming in space. But all that lay in rehearsals and stages in my book in the future . . .

Let me however—in this opening chapter—give a trace or a clue to the burden of inconsolable grief in Beauty that tore his Voice to shreds, sliced his tongue (as mine was pierced by the Carib, cannibal morsel on the eve of the South American holocaust). *I survived to write about him in archetypal detail when he saved my life by shooting Jones in the nick of time.*

Deacon had been abandoned as an infant child in the coastland savannahs of Guyana. A rice farmer and his wife took him in. An infant fallen from the stars! Later he was inoculated by a Medicine Man of Mount Roraima with the venom of the Scorpion constellation. He gained, or appeared to gain, immunity to pain! But this was to prove the unmasking of the huntsman into the inner burden of unspoken grief suffered by victim-cultures. The price of relief from pain was to uncover all the more terrifyingly the helplessness of animals of fate destined to impart the rage of stone, or the venom of marble, into civilization for therapeutic, aesthetic purposes, it was alleged, to labor in the promotion of privileges, but never to be accepted as equal participants in sorrow or joy or ecstasy of flesh-and-blood.

Did he (the infant angel fallen from the stars, the infant angel of the precipice in civilization) bring the venom when he fell, does the venom lie in him or in despised creaturely souls that map the earth and the heavens in the intricacy of laddered feet, antennae, the intricacy of wing or feather or scale, the miraculous grotesqueries in masks of God, the terror of God, the instinctualities-in-spiritualities in the mind of God?

Grief lies in Beauty when creaturely, apparently dissonant beauty— in its infinite particularities and infinite voyaging ramifications—is so despised, so outcast into spare-part methodologies, that it offers little or no solace, and the therapies it provides become functional callouses or tools. Immunity to pain, within privileged orders, comes to mirror functional callouses or tools.

from Jonestown (Imagination Dead Imagine)   141

Grief lies in Beauty when the unmasked priest Jonah Jones, the unmasked right-hand angel Deacon, the unmasked left-hand man (myself, Francisco Bone) discover their animal, archetypal masks within the hunted creatures each pursues in himself. We are hunted, we are pursued, by repetitive catastrophe, repetitive Nemesis, and our insight into Beauty—that we may gain at the heart of terror—deepens the trial of creation to bridge a chasm in itself.

Or else we will continue to perpetuate hierarchies of brutality sponsored unwittingly perhaps by Privilege, hierarchies in which each theatre of inhumanity is placed on a scale to measure which is less horrendous or more hard-hearted than the last, the symmetry of hell . . .

The angels in my Dream-book—bringing messages I needed to interpret and re-interpret—ascended and descended as I lay on my pillow of stone on the day of the holocaust.

[The following section comes later in the fiction. Francisco Bone voyages back in his dream book on a virgin ship from the future (from Jonestown) into the past (his childhood days in Albuoystown).

The past and the future are interwoven. Francisco is nine years old in 1939 when he returns to Albuoystown burdened with the knowledge of the coming death of his mother on the day he arrives and of the ghosts of the dead he brings with him from the year 1978 (Jonestown).

I left school when the afternoon sun was still high in the western sky. I left with the heavy knowledge—knowledge I brought back into my Albuoystown childhood from Jonestown and post-Jonestown futures—of the death of my mother at the hand of a mugger that coming night. Mugger. Evangelist. Crusader. Carnival masks!

She had asked me to go straight from school to the leather shop where she worked. There was to be a Carnival procession that night in Albuoystown.

Marie felt—my mother's name was also Marie—that she could lean on my child's tall Lazarus arm as she made her way through the crowds after work. My Lazarus arm I had brought from the future and tacked on to my present/past body. I too was a creature of Carnival's reconnaissance of the past from a wave of the future . . .

I knew of quiet alleyways we could take to avoid the pressure of the processions.

It was Friday and when the shop closed at night she would draw her weekly wage. When I arrived there was a queue of shoe-makers purchasing choice leather. Each would take a sheet of leather, bend it, study its texture, pass his hand along the rough edges of the sheet, taste it with the tip of his tongue, bring it to his nostrils and inhale the bouquet of the tanned skin.

It was a studied ritual. Leather was a Carnival ritual, a sacramental alliance with the dead, dead cattle transported from interior savannahs. In due course the leather was fashioned into shoes in which the living danced with the ghosts of cattle or rode on their backs.

With my eyes that had returned in a Nemesis Bag from the future I saw the ghosts of Jonestown purchasing shoes in Albuoystown. My sacramental treaty or alliance lay with them. As Jones's left-hand man had I not ridden them in my Sleep, in my unconscious? I had wanted to save them on holocaust eve (when flocks of sheep and horses and cattle were groomed to be burnt as a sacrifice to the gods in ancient Greece) but had succeeded in saving only my own skin with the intervention of the Virgin.

The cattle lay in the Jonestown Clearing on the Day of the Dead. Cattle have human faces, tigers that burn in the sun have the faces of gods, horses weep. I could not help noticing the leather on their feet, the boot with which Deacon had kicked Jones onto his side. They reminded me of the leather in Marie's shop.

The shoe-makers bought the leather in the shop, took it away, made shoes which they brought back to the very shop to be exhibited for sale by my mother. It was a transaction that Marie understood and which she exercised with compassion for I had seen her purchase shoes out of her meagre wages and give them to barefoot beggars.

I now realized that there were two intermingling queues in the shop, one purchasing leather, the other buying shoes. Imprinted on the sole of each boot or shoe was a miniature ship of the heartland within a bubble or a fluid shop, my mother's shop.

I had seen the imprint of trade unmistakably there, trade in bodies and souls across generations and centuries, in which my mother intervened when she fell in the street with a blow to her heart and was lifted shoulder high by beggars. Such is the trade between life and death in which mothers of poverty intervene.

I had seen the imprint of trade unmistakably there on horses and cows that Jones had stabled along with the membership of the Mission whom he had provided with bunks and stalls.

Jones kept many horses which I had christened the horses of the Moon because of their flowing mane that encircled my brow and my head at times when I mingled with them.

And now as I recovered myself in the shop to which I had returned in 1939—heavy-hearted at the prospect of my mother's coming death— I inspected the crew of leather-purchasers and shoe-purchasers. If only I could seize the pendulum of the Clock ticking away remorselessly, as if it were a horse's cosmic phallus, phallic twisted ladder pointing to the Moon, or Venus, or Aphrodite, I might startle my mother's sobriety with the temperament of pagan goddesses. "Don't leave the shop tonight mother. Stay here until the full Moon drowns in the sky of dawn. I shall stay here with you until tomorrow. We shall voyage to the Moon at the bottom of the sky." I spoke through lips shaped in a child's head upon a child's body that had nevertheless returned from the age of the future.

As darkness began to fall Marie began to close the windows and doors of the shop. It was a meticulous business. There were bars to be placed on the windows. Padlocks on the doors. "I shall break through these one day," my mother said with a laugh. "How could we spend the night here Francisco? It would be jail."

"Break through and go where?" I said.

Marie looked at me sharply. She seemed to know I was testing her when I asked the question. I was seeking to confirm . . . What was I seeking to confirm? Was I seeking to confirm that the invisible Bag over my head was real? I had *seen* her coming death within the hour. But now I was unsure. Why should I not be able to stop her from leaving the shop? How did one convert the jail of fate into freedom? I wanted to say, "If you stay here you will live." But I was confused. Does the jail of fate mean life or the postponement of death, freedom death or the beginning of unimaginable life?

There was a backdoor to the shop that seemed to fall into a pit. An odd kind of sensation when one re-visits the past! The door of space itself seems on the edge of falling out of its hinges. It is the knowledge one possesses—or dreams one possesses—that provides an inkling of a chasm in creation across which one voyages.

When one stood at the backdoor the shop was tilted upwards, as on a wave, or upon a higher plane to the street below in which faces glimmered like spray in a deceptive sea of moonlight. Faces glimmered up out of the pit. Black faces seemed white. They had acquired the prize of whiteness. They were white. A desperate whiteness. A desperate illusion of immortality or eternity. White faces glimmered black, a desperate illusion that they were being swamped by immigrants. Brown faces were stained with the salt of blood, neither black nor white. How red is blood, how pale or dark is salt beneath the Ship of the Virgin?

We left the shop through the front door that led straight into the silver blood of the Moon. I saw it all through the invisible Bag of Nemesis over my head. I saw my mother's coming death written into the sacred nerves and the fibre of her body, written into the shoes she wore that the dead woman, with her child beside her in the Jonestown Clearing, had worn. It was as if I saw her walking above me on a wave as before I had seen black and white and brown faces walking below me in a pit. I saw the soles of her feet dance above me like bone in the mind clad in brown leather, white leather, black leather. Then in a flash she was beside me again and we were walking in the street that led from the front door into throngs of passersby.

Funny the things one remembers! She had bolted the door securely behind her with a green, spongy-looking padlock and deposited the key in the purse with her weekly wage. The sound of a drum reached our ear with a curious ecstatic sigh and yet a funeral note. It was so muffled, so deep, so disturbing in low range yet ferocity of pitch I tried to seal my ears against it . . .

Was this the sound that Jonah Jones had sealed his ears against in order to prosecute the pact forged with the members of the Conquest Mission, the Church of Eternity?

Had he sealed his ears against the Virgin Sirens, Virgin *regenerative* Sirens, Virgin regenerative furies? Had he listened would he have named death in himself, would he have sought to cancel an equation between eternity and the conquest of all species that he harbored in himself in the name of death? Does the regeneration of oneself and one's civilization lie through new translated rhythms of well-nigh unbearable song secreted in the furies of space?

"Death's essentialist vocabulary is conquest," I thought I heard my mother say but I was unsure of everything. "One needs to break the charisma of conquest in oneself if one is to build a new Virgin ship. The Virgin is a Blessed Fury when she secretes her involuntary pagan Shadow (and gives re-birth to our uncertain age of Shadow) in the torso and the scattered limbs of mothers of humanity upon every battle-field. . . ."

from Rutherford's Travels

BY CHARLES JOHNSON

ENTRY THE FIRST

Of all the things that drive men to sea the most common disaster, I've come to learn, is women. In my case, it was a spirited Boston schoolteacher named Isadora Bailey, who led me to become a cook aboard the *Republic*, both Isadora and my creditors, I should add, who entered into a conspiracy, a trap, a scheme so cunning that my only choices were prison, a brief stay in the stony oubliette of the Spanish Calabozo (or a long time at the bottom of the Mississippi), or marriage, which was, for a man of my temperament, worse than imprisonment—especially if you knew Isadora—so I went to sea, sailing from Louisiana on 14 April 1840, hoping a quarter year aboard a slave clipper would give this relentless woman time to reconsider, and my bill-collectors time to forget they'd ever heard the name Rutherford Calhoun. But what lay ahead in Africa, then later on the open, endless sea, was, as I shall tell you, far worse than the fortune I'd fled in New Orleans.

New Orleans, you should know, was a city tailored to my taste for the excessive, exotic fringes of life, a world-port of such extravagance in 1839 when I arrived from southern Illinois—a newly-freed bondsman, my papers in an old portmanteau, a gift from my master in Makanda—that I dropped my bags and a shock of recognition shot up my spine to my throat, rolling off my tongue in a whispered, *Here, Rutherford is home.* So it seems, those first few months to the countryboy with cotton in his hair, a great whore of a city in her glory, a kind of glandular Golden Age. She was, if not a town devoted to an almost religious pursuit of Sin, then at least to a steamy sexuality. To the newcomer she was an assault of smells: molasses commingled with mangoes in the sensually damp air, the stench of slop in muddy streets and, from the labyrinthal warehouses on the docks, the odor of Brazilian coffee and Mexican oils. And also this: the most exquisitely beautiful women in the world, thoroughbreds of pleasure created two centuries before by the French for their enjoyment. Mulattos colored like magnolia petals, griffs with breasts big as melons—women who smelled like roses all year round. Home? Brother, for a randy, Illinois Boy of three and twenty accustomed to cornfields, cow plops, and handjobs in his Master's hayloft, New Orleans wasn't home. It was Heaven. But even paradise must have its backside, too, and it is here (alas) that the newcomer comes to rest. Upstream, there were waterfront saloons and dives, a black underworld of thieves, gamblers, and ne'er-do-wells who, unlike the Creoles downstream (they sniffed down their long, Continental noses at poor, purebred Negroes like myself), didn't give a thinker's damn about my family tree and welcomed me as the world upstream would not.

In plain English, I was a petty thief.

How I fell into this life of living off others, of being a social parasite, is a long sordid story best shortened for those who, like the Greeks, prefer to keep their violence off-stage. Naturally, I looked for honest work. But arriving in the city, checking saloons and Negro bars, I found nothing. So I stole—it came as second nature to me. My Master, Reverend Peleg Chandler, had noticed this stickiness of my fingers when I was a child, and a tendency I had to tell preposterous lies for the hell of it; he was convinced I was born to be hanged and did his damnedest to reeducate said fingers in finer pursuits such as good penmanship and playing the grand piano in his parlor. A biblical scholar, he endlessly preached Old Testament virtues to me, and to this day I remember his tedious disquisitions on Neoplatonism, the evils of nominalism, genius of Aquinas, and the work of such seers as Jacob Boehme. He'd wanted me to become a Negro preacher, perhaps even a black saint like the South American priest Martin DePorres—or, for that matter, my brother Jackson. Yet, for all that theological background, I have always been drawn by nature to extremes. Since the hour of my manumission, a day of such gloom and depression that I must put off its telling for awhile, if you'll be patient with me—since that day, and what I can only call my older brother Jackson's spineless behavior in the face of freedom, I have never been able to do things halfway, and I hungered—literally *hungered*—for life in all its shades and hues: I was hooked on sensation, you might say, a lecher for perception and the nerve-knocking thrill, like a shot of opium, of new "experiences." And so, with the hateful, dull Illinois farm behind me, I drifted about New Orleans those first few months, pilfering food and picking moneybelts off tourists, but don't be too quick to pass judgment. I may be from southern Illinois, but I'm not stupid. Cityfolks lived by cheating and crime. Everyone knew this, everyone saw it, everyone talked ethics piously, then took payoffs under the table, tampered with the till, or fattened their purses by duping the poor. Shameless, you say? Perhaps so. But had I not been a thief, I would not have met Isadora and shortly thereafter found myself literally at sea.

Sometimes after working the hotels for visitors, or when I was drying out from whiskey or a piece of two-dollar tail, I would sneak off to the waterfront, and there, sitting on the rainleached pier in heavy, liquescent air, in shimmering light so soft and opalescent that sunlight could not fully pierce the fine erotic mist, limpid and luminous at dusk, I would stare out to sea, envying the sailors riding out on merchantmen on the gift of good weather, wondering if there was some far-flung port, a foreign country or island faraway at the earth's rim where a freeman could escape the vanities cityfolk called self-interest, the mediocrity they called achievement, the blatant selfishness they called individual freedom—all the bilge that made each day landside a kind of living death. I don't know if you've ever farmed in the Midwest, but if you have, you'll know that southern Illinois has scale, fields like sea swell, soil so good if you plant a stick, a year later a carriage will spring up in its place, forests and woods as wild as they were before people lost their pioneer spirit and a healthy sense of awe. Only here, on the waterfront, could I recapture that feeling. Wind off the water was like a fist of fresh air, a cleansing blow that made me feel momentarily clean. In the spill of yellow moonlight, I'd shuck off my boots and sink both feet into the water, but the pier was most beautiful, I think, in early morning when sunlight struck the wood and made it steam as moisture and mist from the night before evaporated. Then you could believe, like the ancient philosopher Thales, that the analogue for life was water, the formless, omnifix sea. Businessmen with half a hundred duties barnacled to their lives came to stare, longingly, at boats trolling up to dock. Black men, free and slave, sat quietly on rocks coated with crustacea, in the odors of oil and fish, studying an evening sky as blue as the skin of heathen Lord Krishna. And Isadora Bailey came, too, though for what reason I cannot say—her expression on the pier was unreadable—since she was, as I soon learned, a woman grounded, physically and metaphysically, in the land. I'd tipped closer to her, eyeing the beadpurse on her lap, then thought better of boosting it when I was ambushed by the innocence—the alarming trust—in her eyes when she looked up at me. I wondered, and wonder still: What's a nice girl like her doing in a city like this?

She was, in fact, as out of place in New Orleans as St. Teresa would be at an orgy with De Sade: a frugal, quiet, devoutly Christian girl, I learned, the fourth daughter of a large Boston family free since the Revolutionary War, and positively ill with eastern culture. An educated girl of twenty, she thought it best to leave home to lighten her family's burden, but found no prospects for a Negro teacher, and a female at that, in the Northeast. She came south by coach, avoiding the newfangled trains after reading an expert say that traveling at over twenty miles per hour would suffocate all aboard when the speed sucked all the air from the cars. Once in New Orleans, she took a job as a nursery governess for the children of Madame Marie Toulouse, a Creole who'd spent her young womanhood as the mistress of first a banker, then a famous actor, a minister, and finally a mortician. Why these four? As Madame Toulouse told Isadora, she'd used the principle of, "One for the money, two for the show, three to get ready, and four to go," and they'd left her generous endowments that she invested in a hotel at Royal and Saint Peters Streets. But Isadora was not, I'm afraid, any happier living in a Creole household than I would have been. They were beautiful; she was bookish. They were society here; she was, as an Easterner, the object of polite condescension—the Toulouses, in short, could afford the luxury of stupidity, the blind, cowlike, chinlifted hauteur of Beautiful People. And such luxury Isadora had never known. You had the feeling, once you knew her, that she'd gambled on knowledge as others gambled on power, believing—wrongly, I think—that she had little else to offer. She let herself get fat, for example, to end the pressure women felt from being endlessly ogled and propositioned. Men hardly noticed her, pudgy as she was, and this suited Isadora just fine. She had a religious respect for Work. She was a nervous eater, too, I guess, the sort of lonely, intelligent woman who found comfort in food, or went to restaurants simply to be treated kindly by waiters, to be fussed over and served, to be asked, "Is everything alright here?"

Yet, she *was* pretty in a prim, dry, flatbreasted way. Isadora never used make-up. At age five she had been sentenced to the straightening-comb, and since then kept her hair pinned back so tightly each glossy strand stood out like wire, which also pulled back the skin at her temples, pushing forward a nose that looked startlingly like a doorknob, and enlarging two watery, moonlike eyes that seemed ever on the verge of tears. No, she wasn't much to look at, nor was the hotel room where she lived with eight one-eyed cats, two three-legged dogs, and birds with broken wings. Her place had a sweet, attic-like odor, but looked like a petshop, and smelled like a zoo. Isadora took in these handicapped strays, unable to see then left unattended, and each time I dropped by she had something new. No, not a girl to tell the guys about, but one reassuring to be with because she had an inner brilliance, an intelligence and clarity of spirit that overwhelmed me. Generally she spoke in choriambs and iambs when she was relaxed, which created a kind of diametrical music to her speech. Did I love Isadora? Really, I couldn't say. I'd always felt people fell in love as you might fall into a hole; it was something I thought a smart man avoided.

But somedays, after weeks of whoring, and card games that lasted three days and nights, I found myself at her hotel room, drunk as Noah, broke and bottomed out, holding a bouquet of stolen flowers outside her door, eager to hear her voice, which was velvety and light like water gently rushing nearby—we'd sit and talk (she didn't like Nature walks, claiming that the only thing she knew about Nature was that it itched), her menagerie of crippled beasts crawling over her lap and mine. Those afternoons of genteel conversation (Isadora wouldn't let me do anything else) we talked of how we were both newcomers to New Orleans, or we took short walks together, we'd dine in sidewalk cafes, where we watched the Creoles. My earliest impressions of the Cabildo, the fancy-dress quadroon balls and slave auctions arranged by the firm of Hewlett & Bright each Saturday at the New Exchange Market (ghastly affairs, I must add, which made poor Isadora a bit ill), were intertwined with her voice, her reassuring, Protestant, soap-and-water smell. Aye, she was good and honest and forthright, was Isadora. Nevertheless, at other times she was intolerable. She was, after all, a *teacher*, and couldn't turn it off sometimes, that tendency to talk in propositions, or declarative sentences, to correct my southern Illinois accent, with its squashed vowels and missing consonants, and challenge everything I said on, I thought, General Principle.

"Rea-a-aly, Rutherford," she said one afternoon in her sitting room, her back to a deep-silled window where outside a pear tree was in full bloom, its fruit like a hundred green bells draped upon the branches. "You don't think you can keep this up forever, do you? The gambling and girl-chasing?" She gave her gentle, spinster's smile and, as always, looked at me with a steadier gaze than I could look at her. "You have a *mind*. And, if what you tell me is true, you've lacked for nothing in this life. Am I right in saying this? Neither in childhood education or the nourishment of a sound body and Christian character?"

I gave her a nod, for this was so. Though a slave-holder, Reverend Chandler hated slavery. He'd inherited my brother and me from his father and, out of Christian guilt, taught us more than some white men in Madanka knew, then finally released us one by one, except that Jackson stayed, more deeply bound to our Master than any of us dreamed. But I am not ready just yet to talk of Jackson Calhoun.

"So you were," Isadora asked, toying with her teacup, "blessed with reasonably pleasant surroundings and pious council?"

I nodded again, squirming a little. Always, and eerily, I had the feeling that Isadora knew more about me than I did.

"Then aren't you obliged, given these gifts, to settle down, and start a family so you can give to others in even greater measure?" Her eyes went quiet, closing as if on a vision of she and I at the altar. "My father, you know, was a little like you, Rutherford, or at least my aunties say he was. He stayed in Scolley Square, or in the pubs, looking for himself in rum and loose women until he met a woman of character—I mean my mother—who brought out his better instincts."

"What's he doing now?" I rested my teacup on my knee. "Your father."

"Well . . ." She pulled back, pausing to word this right. "Not much just now. He died last winter, you know, from heart failure."

Wonderful, I thought: the wage of the family man was coronary thrombosis. "And," I said, "he was how old?"

"Forty-nine," then Isadora hurried to add, "but he had people who *cared* for him, daughters and sons, and a wife who brought him down to earth . . ."

"Indeed," I said. "Quite far down, I'd say."

"Rutherford!" she yipped, her voice sliding up a scale. "It *hurts* me to see you in such ruin! Really, it does! Half the time I see you, you haven't eaten in two days. Or you're hung over. Or someone is chasing you for money. Or you've been in a fight! You need a family. You're not—not *common*!"

Ah, there it was, revealed at last, the one thing inside Isadora that made me shudder. It was what you heard all your blessed life from black elders and church women in flowered gowns: Don't be common. Comb your hair. Be a credit to the Race. Strive, like the Creoles, for respectability. Class. It made my insides clench. Oh yes, it mattered to me that Isadora cared, but she saw me as clay. Something she could knead beneath her tiny brown fingers into precisely the sort of creature I—after seeing my brother shackled to subservience—was determined not to become: "a gentleman of color." The phrase made me hawk, then spit in a corner of my mind. It conjured (for me) the image of an Englishman, round of belly, balding, who'd been lightly brushed with brown watercolor or cinnamon.

"No, Isadora," I shook my head. "I don't believe I'll ever get married. There's too much to do. And see. Life is too short for me to shackle myself to a mortgage and marriage." I was a breath away from adding, "And a houseful of gimped cats," but thought it best to bite my tongue.

Her eyes took on a woebegone, persecuted look, a kind of dying-duck expression she had now and then. She stared at me for the longest, then flashed, "You just won't act *right*, will you?" Touching her handkerchief to the doorknob nose, she stood suddenly, her cat leaping from her enskirted knees and bumping blindly into a candlestand. Isadora took three paces toward the door—I thought she was about to throw me out—then turned to pitch her voice back into the room. "Suppose you *have* to get married, Rutherford Calhoun!" Now her eyes burned. "What about that?"

What Isadora meant by this was a mystery to me. She couldn't be pregnant. Not her. At least not by me—she twisted my fingers whenever I reached for her knee. *Have* to marry her? It made no sense that afternoon, but not a fortnight later her meaning became horribly clear.

Near the waterfront, after a day of dodging my creditors and shooting craps, I turned a corner and found myself facing a Negro named Santos, a kind of walking wrecking-crew who pretty much ran things down on the docks for a Creole gangster known by the name of Phillipe "Papa" Zeringue. Some masters, as you know, groomed their slaves to be gladiators: the Africans with a reach, or thickness of skull, or smouldering anger that, if not checked, would result in slave rebellion. So it was with Santos. He'd been a dirt-pit wrestler on a Baton Rouge plantation, and made his master, John Ruffner, a fortune in bare-knuckle fights he arranged for him with blacks on other farms. Freed by Ruffner, undefeated, and itching for trouble, he'd come to New Orleans, and fell, as many did, into the orbit of life upstream. You have seen, perhaps, sketches of Piltdown Man? Cover him with coal dust, add deer-skin leggings and a cutaway coat tight as wet leather, and you shall have Santos's younger, undernourished *sister*.

This upright disaster was in the oval light of a lamppost on Royal Street as I passed. He was gnawing a stolen ham. Behind him, two policemen stood, tapping their nightsticks on their palms. "Come along now, Santos," said one. "Don't make trouble. That ham'll cost you a month in the Calabozo." Santos went right on chewing, his small, quick eyes half-seeled in gastronomic bliss. And then, without warning, both policemen smashed him full on both sides of his temples with their nightsticks. They'd taken halfsteps back, too, putting their waists and full weight into the swing. One nightstick broke with a sickening crack, the other vibrated in the officer's hand as if wood had struck wood. As for Santos, he only looked up sleepily. Said, "Now, what'd you do that fo'?"

No fools, the policemen flew past me, Santos's eyes on their flapping waistcoats until his gaze lighted upon me. "Illinois!" he said—or, rather his sweaty voice rumbled and rattled windows along the street. "Ain't you Rutherford Calhoun from Illinois?"

I shook my head and took a step backwards.

"Dammit, you *are* Calhoun! Don't lie! Papa been lookin' fo' you, boy!"

I touched my chest, "Me?"

"Yes, *you*, nigguh." He came forward, seizing my arm. "He wants to *talk* to you 'bout somethin' you owe him." I told him that surely he was mistaken, that indeed I owed people within a mile circumference of the city—my landlady Mrs. Dupree, Mr. Fenton, the money-lender, and the vendors, too—but I'd never *met* Papa. How could I owe him? None of this washed with Santos, a man with whom you didn't argue because he looked exactly like what he was: a weightlifter gone slightly to seed, with maybe thirty pounds of muscle alchemizing to fat on his upper body. He'd be dead by forty from the strain on his heart—the extra bulk had scrunched down his spine, I heard, shortening him by two inches, but no matter. He was bigger than me. Silently, he steered me, his right hand on the back of my collar, to a tavern owned by Papa on Chartres Street, a one-story building of English-brown brick-work, with sunken, uneven floors and windows with old, diamond-paned lattices, pushing me through the door to a table at the rear of the room where Papa sat eating a meal of drop-biscuits and blueberries with— my heart jumped!—Isadora! Of a sudden, I had that special feeling of paranoia that comes when you enter a cafe and stumble upon two women you used to sleep with—who you'd have sworn were strangers, but were now whispering together. About you, by God! She looked up as I scuffed jelly-legged to the table, and her eyes, I tell you, were indecipherable.

"Isadora," I gulped, "you *know* these people?"

She gave Papa, in fact, a very knowing smile.

"We've just met to discuss a business arrangement that affects you, Rutherford. I'm sure you'll be interested to hear what Mr. Zeringue and I have decided." Isadora touched a napkin to her lips, then stood up. "I'll wait for you outside."

She seemed to take all the available air in the room with her as she sashayed outside, mysteriously happier than I'd seen her in months. For an instant I could not catch my breath. Papa sat with a napkin tucked into his collar. He was holding a soup-spoon dripping with blueberry jelly in his right hand when I extended my hand and introduced myself; this spoon he slapped against my palm and, having nothing else to shake, I shook that. Santos roared.

"Sir, you wanted to see me abo . . ."

"Don't say nothin', Calhoun."

If there were musical instruments that fit this man's voice, that would ring from the orchestra, say, if he appeared on stage, they would be the bull-fiddle, tuba, and slide-trombone (Isadora was all strings, a soft flick of the lyre), a combination so gutteral and brutish, full of grunts and deep-throated notes, that I cannot say his voice put me at ease. Nor this room. It had the atmosphere you feel in places where some great "Murder of the Age" has taken place. My worst fears about him were confirmed. He was, in every sense of the word, the very Ur-type of Gangster. Fiftyish, a brownskinned black man with graywebbed hair, he dressed in rich burgundy waistcoats and had a princely, feudal air about him, the smell of a man who loved Gothic subterfuges and schemes, deceits and Satanic games of power. Yet, despite his wealth, and despite the extravagant riverboat parties I heard he threw—bashes that made Roman bacchanals look like a backwoods—he was a black lord in ruins, a fallen angel who, like Lucifer, controlled the lower depths of the city—the cathouses, the Negro press, the gambling dens—but held his dark kingdom, and all within it, in the greatest contempt. He was wicked. Wicked and self-serving, I thought, but why did he want to see me?

"I suppose," said Papa, as if he'd read my mind, "you wanna know why I had Santos bring you here."

Indeed, I did.

"It's simple—you owe me, Illinois." I started to protest, but his left hand flew up, and he said, "First thing you gotta learn, I reckon, is that it's *rude* to talk when I'm talkin', and that I don't mind gettin' rid of people who have the bad manners to cut me off in mid-sentence. Most people are so confused, you know, 'bout life and what's right that it ain't completely wrong to take it from 'em." He paused as a waiter came to the table, topping off his coffee, then drilled his gaze at me. "Now, you ain't one of them people, I kin tell."

"Nossir," I said.

Papa's brow went dark. "You just did it again, Calhoun."

Quietly, biting my lips, I thought, *sorry*!

"Bout this debt now," he began working a grain of food from his front teeth with his fingernail. "You know that li'l boarding-house for cullud folks run by Mrs. Dupree?"

I didn't like where this was leading, and found myself disliking him, too, but gave him a nod.

"I own it." His eyes narrowed. "Fact is, I own *her,* and she tells me you're three months behind in yo rent. And that li'l money-lender Fenton—you know him?"

I bobbed my head.

"I own him, too, so you might as well say I'm the one holdin' the bad paper, promises, and I.O.U.s that you been handin' out like flyers. It comes to mebbe fifty thousand francs, I figure, and we all know a farthing-and-sixpence hoodlum like you can't even afford the down-payment on a glass of lemonade." Looking square at me, he shook his head. "If all cullud men was like you, Calhoun, I 'spect the Race would be extinct by now."

Papa offered me a cigarette, but my hands trembled so violently that I used four friction-matches before the flame took to the end. "Now, a man *should* pay his debts, it seems to me." He placed a finger thoughtfully on one side of his nose. "That's how worldly things work, Calhoun. The Social Wheel, as I unnerstand it after forty years in business for myself, is oiled by debts, each man owing the other somethin' in a kinda web of endless obligations. Normally," he added, "if a man welched on me like you done, he'd find hisself on the riverbottom. But you are truly blessed, Calhoun. I daresay you have divine protection. You are indeed watched over and loved by one of God's very own angels."

This was all news to me. "I am?"

"Uh huh, that schoolteacher Miss Bailey has saved yo behind from Davy Jones's locker. Out of the goodness of her heart, she has come forward and offered to liquidate yo debts with her meager savings, provided you agree—as I know you will—to the simple condition of holy matrimony."

"But that's *blackmail*!"

"Yes," said Papa, nodding. "Yes, it is. I'm acquainted with the technique, son."

"She can't do this!" I sat biting my fingers in rage. "It's . . . it's criminal!"

Santos raised his eyebrows. "Look who's talkin'."

"And it's done," said Papa. "Tomorrow you and Miss Bailey will be wed. I *wouldn't* miss that ceremony, if I was you. It would cancel our arrangement, and I'd have to return Miss Bailey's money, and you'd be in debt again." His eyes bent slowly up to me. "You *do* wanna erase yo debts, don't you?"

"Nossir . . . I mean, yessir!" I eased back off my chair. "But you say the wedding is *tomorrow*?"

"At noon. And I'll be givin' Miss Bailey away. Santos heah will be yo best man." His factotum grinned. Papa reached his ringed fingers toward my hand and pumped it. "Congratulations, Calhoun. I know you two are gonna be happy together."

For the rest of that day, and most of the night, I had cold shakes and fits of fear-induced hiccoughing. Stumbling from the tavern, I felt lightheaded, ready to fall, and slapped one hand on the wall outside to steady myself. Isadora came up behind me. She threaded her arm through mine, supporting me as I walked, dazed, toward the waterfront. Yes, I'd underestimated her. She'd wiped my nose with my own handkerchief; with my own bread she'd baked me a tart. "Tell me," she squeezed my arm, "what you're thinking."

"You are not . . . hic . . . to be *believed,* Isadora!"

"Thank you." She hugged my arm tighter and rested her head on my shoulder. "I'm doing this for your own good, Rutherford."

"The hell you are! I'm *not* getting married! Never!"

"Yes, you are." Her voice was full of finality. "And someday when we are very old, have grandchildren, and you look back upon this rack-etty, freelance life you've led from the advantage of the comfortable home and family we've built together, you will thank me."

"I will . . . hic . . . *despise* you! Is that what you want? You're twisting my cullions, but you haven't won my consent!" I grabbed her arms and shook her hard enough to dislodge her hat and send her hair flying loose from its pins. "Why are you *doing* this?"

Bareheaded like that, with hair swinging in her eyes, the change came over Isadora, a collapsing of her lips inward against her teeth, the blood rising to her cheeks as if I'd suddenly struck her. One by one, she peeled my fingers off her arms, then stepped away from me, drawing up her shoulders, her hair wilder now than that of a witch.

"Because I love you . . . you fool! . . . and I don't know what to do about it because you don't love *me!* I know that! I'm not blind, Ruth-erford." She began gathering hairpins off the boardwalk, sticking them any whichaway back into her head. "It's because I'm not . . . not pretty. No, don't say it! That *is* why. Because I'm *dark.* You'd rather have a beautiful, glamorous, lightskinned wife like the women in the theatres and magazines. It's what all men want, someone they can show off and say to the world, "See, look what *I'm* humping!" But she'd worry you sorely, Rutherford—I know that—you'd be suspicious of every man who came to the house, and your friends, too, and she'd be vain and lazy and squander your money on all sorts of foolish things, and she'd hate having children, or doing housework, or being at your side when you're sick, but *I* can make you happy!" We were drawing a crowd, she noticed, and lowered her voice, sniffling a little as she tried to push her hat back into shape. "I'd hoped that you'd *learn* to love me the way I love you . . ."

"Isadora," I struggled. "It's not like that. I *do* love you. It's just that I don't want to marry *any*one . . ."

"Well, you're getting married tomorrow, or I'm taking back my money." Isadora rammed her hat—hopelessly ruined—down over her ears, her eyes still blazing. "You choose, Rutherford Calhoun, whichever way you like."

And there she left me, standing by the docks in a lather of confusion. Never in my life had anyone loved me so selflessly, as the hag in the Wife of Bath's Tale had loved her fickle knight, but despite this remarkable love, I was not, as I say, ready for marriage. I didn't feel *worthy* of her, if you must know. Fact is, her goodness shamed me. I turned into the first pub I found, one frequented by sailors, a darkly lit, rum-smelling room about fourteen feet square, with a well-sanded floor, and a lamp that hung within two feet of the tables, stinking of whale oil. The place was packed with seamen. All armed to the eyeballs with pistols and cutlasses, scowling and jabbering like pirates, squirting jets of brown tobacco-juice everywhere except in the spitoons—a den of Chinese assassins, scowling Moors, English scoundrels, Yankee adventurers, and evil-looking Arabs. In short, I felt pretty much right at home. Seated near the window beside an old mariner in a pair of shag trousers and red flannel shirt who was playing with his parrot and drinking hot brandy grog, I ordered a gin twist, then tried to untangle this knot Isadora had tightened around me.

She was as cunning as a Byzantine merchant—that was clear—but I couldn't rightly fault her. She'd known her share of grief, had Isadora. Her mother Viola, she'd told me, died when she was three, which meant that she and her sisters had no one to teach them to think like independent, menless Modern Women—it was something you *learned*, she implied, like learning how to ride a bicycle, or do the backstroke. Certainly her father couldn't help. Isaiah Bailey was a wifebeater, that's how Viola died, and, once she was buried, he started punching Isadora and her sisters around on Saturday nights after visiting his still. Yet, miraculously, Isadora had remained innocent. There was no hatred in her. Or selfishness. No vanity, or negativism. Some part of her, perhaps the part she withdrew when Isaiah started whaling on her, remained untouched, a part she fed in the local African Methodist Episcopal Church, and shored up with Scripture: a still, uncorrupted center like the Chinese lotus which, though grown in muck and mud, remained beautifully poised and pure. But shy, too. Seeing horses defecate on the street made Isadora blench. She was constitutionally unable to swear. When she was angry, her lips would form a four-letter word, then freeze, as if she'd been chewing alum. A part of me ached to be with her always, to see that only things of beauty and light came before her. Would marrying her be so bad? That night, a little before dawn, I had a vision of how that union would be in decades to come—eighteen thousand, six hundred and ninety-three cups of watery sassafras tea for breakfast, and in each of these I would find cat fur or pigeon feathers. No, it was not a vision to stir the soul that longed for high adventure.

Eight bottles of beer emptied before me; the sailors thinned out, but still I sat, knowing that each hour brought me closer to the bondage of wedlock. Behind me, I heard first a burp, then the gravelly voice of the now drunken sailor in shag trousers. "Yo ho, there, young un!" He held up a flagon of wine, his fifth, which he'd only half finished. "Ye can take this, my dear, if yuh've a mind to. Josiah Squibb's had enough for one night."

"Much obliged . . . Squibb, is it?" I took his bottle in my left hand and his thick, rough hand in my right. "You've put away quite a lot. A man would think you're going to a hanging, friend."

"Worse," said Squibb. "I'm shipping out tomorrow with Captain Ebenezer Falcon. Good as a hangin', that, to hear some men tell it. He's a descendent of Colonel Blood who stole the Crown Jewels, some say, a buccaneer at heart, and proud of it." Blearily, he lit a long-shanked pipe and studied me through eyes too bloodshot, really, to see. "Ye drink a lot y'self, boy. Got problems, have ye?"

"Marriage" I told him. "Tomorrow at noon."

"Blimey!" Squibb sat back, stunned, his chair creaking. "Ye *have* got a problem. Oh, I know about wives alright. Got a couple myself—one in Connecticut, and one in Vermont. That's *why* I ship out. What say I buy you a round?"

Josiah Squibb, I learned, had signed on as a Midshipman aboard the *Republic*, a ninety-ton square-rigger that would up-anchor and sail eastward against the prevailing winds to the barracoon or slave factory at Bangalang on the Guinea Coast, take on a cargo of Africans, and then, God willing, return in four months. "There she be," Squibb stabbed his pipestem toward the window, and the ship he showed me from this distance was strikingly beautiful, a great three-masted, full-rigged bark with a roundtuck hull, grated hatches and bulkheads cut round the deck for circulation. As it turned out, these were the last words from Squibb. Halfway through our third hooker of gin, his forehead crashed down upon the table. And his papers . . . ah, these were rolled cylindrically inside his right boot. I thought, *Naw, Calhoun, you can't do that;* but at that selfsame instant I remembered what awaited me at the altar, and I decided most definitely, *Yes, I can.*

"Bad move," said the parrot. "Very bad move."

I said, "Shut up."

Transferring Squibb's papers to my coat, I eased away from the table whilst he snored. "Thief! Thief!" shouted the parrot, but fortunately he could not shatter the cook's heavy-headed sleep. I slipped outside into a shock of cool air, and ran down the pier to a cluster of small boats— sailors called them wherries—rocking lazily to and fro on the water. I unfastened the rope to one, paddled out toward the *Republic,* then hauled myself hand-over-hand up a rope-ladder to the topgallant bulwark, and over onto a broad empty deck. The crew had not come aboard yet. Standing aft, looking back at the glittering lights ashore, I had an odd sensation, difficult to explain, that I'd boarded not a ship but a kind of fantastic, floating black Mariah, a wooden sepulchre whose timbers moaned with the memory of too many runs of black gold between the New World and the Old—moaned, I say again, because the ship, with its tiered compartments and galleys, like a crazyquilt house built by a hundred carpenters, each with a different plan, felt conscious and disapprovingly aware of my presence when I pulled back the canvass on a flatbottomed launch and lay myself down in its hull, which was long and narrow, both hands crossed on my chest. And then, waves lapping below the ship gently swung me left, then right as in a hammock, sinking me like a fish, or a stone, farther down through leagues of darkness, and mercifully to sleep.

Making Callaloo

from The Machete Woman

A Novel

BY GAYL JONES

CHAPTER ONE

It is 1637 and I'm an African born in the New World. I was once a
slave, but now they've begun to call me the Machete Woman, because
I dared to free myself. How? Everything blends into the details of one's
days. I don't want to write my story, but I must. And the sisters in this
convent have enough writing paper that they make themselves from ixtle
fiber and old pieces of cloth. They've even got palimpsests, new manuscripts written over old ones. Sometimes the old ones show through,
though. And there's one the nuns say shows a text written in the 6th
century—probably a nun's diary or a monk's journal.

And they themselves are always keeping journals, notebooks, diaries,
and the like, the ones from Spain and the ones from here in the New
World. New Spain they call it, though the Indians have got another
name for it, and it's as old a world as any other. Tlatelolco, the Indians
call it. Tlatelolco. Tlatelolco, I've heard them say, clicking the roofs of
their mouths, just like I've heard Africans do.

I suppose if it was a woman's world, they'd write other sorts of
books than journals, notebooks, and diaries. Giant tomes on philosophy,
moral and natural, like I've seen in the nun's library, but always with a
man's name attached to them. Mathematics, astronomy, alchemy, and
logic. Or maybe the diary and the notebook would be accorded greater
value, and not just thought a mere woman's book in woman's language.

But there's enough writing paper, like I said, and one of the sisters
even calls herself writing a man's book, a history of the conquest of
Mexico, a history of Hernan Cortez, the great conqueror himself, that
old devil, whom the blancos say discovered it. When I ask her if she's
heard of Tlatelolco, she says it must be some imaginary place.

"Say it again," she says.

I say the name again, clicking the roof of my mouth.

"You Africans have a wondrous way of talking," she says. "All your clicks and clacks."

But one thing that you can say that makes the sisters different from most of the señoras, the planters' wives, is that they do know how to read and write. Sometimes a planter's wife might hire a schoolboy or scholar-vagabond, a licenciado, to read to her—as long as she's chaperoned, that is—but most know as much about reading as a botfly. But the planters, they like it that way. Learned women, I've heard them say, don't make true wives or true wifehood or even true womanhood. Learned women, some would even say that that's a contradiction, to be both learned and a woman. True womanhood and learning they say that's incompatible. Same thing they say about us slaves. Learned woman, eh? The same as saying learned slave, eh? Best to keep slaves ignorant, they say, if you want a true slave. True slavehood and learning, eh? True slave or true wife, keep them both ignorant, eh? And of myself, you could say I've been both a true slave and a slave's slave.

Slavehood and learning? As for reading and writing, I've learned to read and write. And how to read and write, you may ask, in a New World such as this one where teaching a slave to read and write is a true crime, eh? Well, it was part of an experiment, the master called it, when I was a slave—a slave's slave I should say, because I not only did chores for the master but for a woman who was herself a slave. In Uruguay, a slave's slave, before I was sold to the Mexican.

Before I came here to the convent, when I was in the household of my first Mexican owner, a señora, I had to pretend I knew as much about reading and writing as a carob tree or a sand fly or most señoras.

The Uruguay owner, though, was an eccentric and a drunkard. Tall, wiry, blond, tan from the hot sun. When he got drunk, he'd call the slave children into his study and teach us our alphabets and numbers. He was often drunk and so we often learned our alphabets and numbers.

And it was funny, he didn't slur them like those poor devils who line up in front of the pulquerias. But don't think he taught us to read out of goodness or virtue, either; or villainy, if you think such teachings are crimes; it was pure curiosity. Pure inquisitiveness. He'd heard and read of other learning experiments in other parts of the New World and in the Old World too among other members of the heathen and backward races, he said, and so he wanted to have a learning experiment himself, for it was among the elite and cultured classes and intellectuals, he said, that such experiments had meaning. Though it was only when he was drunk that he was inquisitive enough to experiment on us.

When he was sober, it was enough a learning experiment just to teach his house slaves how to properly steam his salted codfish or teach his stableboys how to currycomb his horses or teach his field hands how to grow cubeb, how to dry the spicy fruit, so that he could smoke that in his pipe instead of tobacco. He imported it from Asia to the New World. A better stimulant than tobacco, he said.

The alphabets and numbers, he didn't slur any of them. It was strange. He'd talk more clearly drunk than sober. When he was sober, he acted just like any hacendado, any other plantation owner. Pious or dissolute, you never know what temper they're in, or whether they're ready for a handshake or the branding irons.

But drunk, that one's at his best as far as a slave's concerned, and even a slave's slave. That's probably why his housekeeper Zutana always made sure to keep the liquor cabinet full of everything, from homemade beer to the finest port and brandy imported from Madrid. Zutana he called her, but her real name's Fulana.

"Zutana," he'd say.

I used to think she'd correct him, but she didn't. "Fulana's my name," I kept thinking she'd say. But Fulana just let him call her Zutana.

"Zutana, bring me my pipe," he'd say.

And she'd bring it to him. He'd stuff it with cubeb, like I said, instead of tobacco. Or rather she'd stuff it with cubeb for him, light it and hand it to him.

"Señor," she'd call him, but I never heard her say his Christian name.

Being a slave's slave, it was me who'd sometimes stuff the cubeb in, then hand the pipe to her, and she'd light it, then give it to the señor.

When he was drunk, he'd say gracias. When he was sober, he'd just take the pipe and start puffing.

"Gracias."

"De nada."

Or he'd just take the pipe and start puffing. Though once I heard him say, "You're as spicy as cubeb, eh? Do you think you're the better stimulant?" But mostly he'd just take the pipe and start puffing.

I was just twelve, then, like I said, and a slave's slave, and when the eccentric wasn't drunk—his name, by the way, is Señor Pedro Herramiento, not that names matter with masters, they're all the same pedro, like iron is iron—I worked in the fields with all the other heathens— not that names matter with slaves, say the masters, we're all the same heathen, eh? Like iron is iron.

Cubeb was the Señor's personal obsession, but his chief plant was maize, which you might say's manna to the New World. I've heard that on slave ships it's called guinea corn, and in that way I guess it links the new world to the old one. Those who don't call us negroes call us guineas. Anyhow, and he had orchards. Apples, peaches, oranges, and plums. But no slave was allowed near them or near the pruning knives, which he kept locked up in a shed between the big house and the senzala, the slave's quarters.

Usually he'd hire some poor gullible fellow newly arrived from old castilla or some criollo peasant. Even with them he'd have his overseer keep an eagle's eye on them while they used the pruning knives. Then when they finished pruning, they'd return the knives to the shed, and the knives were locked up again.

Only the overseer, a rugged mulatto, and Don Pedro himself had the key to the shed. I wondered how Don Pedro could trust even a mulatto with such a key, but it was rumored that the mulatto's Don Pedro's own.

"Don Pedro's own?" I asked Zutana Fulana once when we were in the kitchen making tortillas.

"What?"

"I heard someone say that Jorge, the overseer, is Don Pedro's own."

"Hijo," she said.

She shaped a tortilla and dropped it into the frying pan.

"His own son," she explained. "When he's drunk, he swears he's his, anyhow. But when he's sober it's another story."

"So that's why he trusts him, eh?" I said.

"You'd better say that's why the boy trusts *him*. But me I don't trust him drunk or sober, for I don't know what's his true nature."

"Me, I like him when he's drunk," I said.

"Because he teaches you your alphabets and numbers, yes?"

"Yes."

I stood at the table beside her mixing water and cornmeal.

"He's more a libertine when drunk," she said.

"Libertine? what's that?"

"It's enough for you to know what liberty means, eh. Anyway, there's good comes from his drunkenness and evil too."

"What evil?"

She got a handful of lentils and dropped them in the mutton stew. The stew was bubbling. I shaped a tortilla and licked my fingers. My fingers tasted like cubeb.

"Can you tell one lentil from the other?" she asked.

"No. A lentil's a lentil."

I waited for her to explain, but she didn't.

"Liberty," she mumbled. "He knows how to treat his slaves to liberty. But it's good he teaches you your alphabets and numbers, girl. That's enough liberty for you, eh?"

"I heard him say you're as spicy as cubeb."

"Spicy? Who talks of spiciness? Why, liberty's enough for you to know, gal."

CHAPTER TWO

"Es una mujer muy simple," the nuns say of me. "She's a very simple woman," and it's the first time anyone's called me woman without the slave attached. "A simple vista es una mujer simple," says one of them. "At first sight she seems like a simple woman."

At first sight I seem simple, eh? But all of the sisters want me to say that I did what I didn't without thinking. From the time I arrived at the convent. "Lo hice sin pensar," they want me to say.

The truth is there're a million reasons and one why we do anything. Do you think Señor Pedro taught us our alphabets and numbers because he was drunk? And did he teach us without thinking? Do you think that Zutana Fulana only kept the liquor cabinet full to get him drunk? One only tries to think of all the reasons, to let them blend into the details. Like lentils in mutton stew.

Or perhaps a better metaphor's those palimpsests I told you about. New reasons written over old ones, and sometimes the old ones showing through the new. And you don't know how many layers of reasons there are.

"Lo hice sin pensar," they want me to say.

The nun who says, a simple vista, at first sight, the nun named Isabel, refuses to call me by my name. As for her, her real name's Panal, but on becoming a nun she took the name Isabel.

That's the first thing I liked about the nuns—taking new names for themselves.

"And can you take any name?" I asked.

"A saint's name. We take the names of saints."

"Like Juan?" I asked.

She smiled.

"Female saints, I mean to say. Juanita, yes, if that's a saint. It's male saints who take the names of male saints. Male saints, did I say? It's monks who take the names of male saints."

Instead, this Panal, this Isabel, she calls me by the names of volcanoes. Sometimes she calls me Sangagueja, other times it's Colima, sometimes Ceborua. Yet again I'm Popocatepetl, Ixtaccihatt, Malinche, Ajusca, 'Toluca, Orizaba, Citlaltepetl. They say that Citlaltepetl means Star Mountain or the Mountain of the Star. Surely if she knew what it meant she wouldn't call *me* that.

Star Mountain.

It's an Aztec name, though, for I've seen it on a map. And there are many volcanoes here in Mexico. You can find almost as many volcanoes on a map as cities or rivers. There are so many volcanoes, she could call me names forever.

Is it possible to insult a volcano?

And what if one dared?

Having moved from slave's slave to slave to freewoman of sorts perhaps I should take on the name of a volcano.

But I keep my old name. It's Zutana Fulana who named me, so I might as well have named myself.

"Destinaria," she said when she first saw me. And Señor Pedro, who wasn't a stickler for names anyhow, said it was as good a name as any. One Pedro's as good as another, eh. And he preferred her to name the slaves, anyhow, rather than the Señora, who had a fondness for Greek names.

"We've enough Jupiters and Minervas," I heard him say.

CHAPTER THREE

I should tell you right now, right in the beginning, right here, what I did. I should tell you right from the beginning. I shouldn't play any games with you like they do in stories that aren't true. And this story is the truest of the true. Zutana Fulana would say at least in its bare facts it's true, for every tale is as much wish and dream as reality, even the true ones.

But this is my tale: I took my machete to my mistress, my machete for cutting cane. One might say I made cane of her. She insulted me. Perhaps she thought it was as impossible to insult a slave as to insult a rock or the moon or guinea corn or even a volcano. Who knows what her thoughts were? What slave knows the thoughts of a Señora?

Once, when the Uruguay master was drunk, he put on his university cap with its borla or tassel and lectured us on how it was impossible to tell the thoughts of a slave. But it is the thoughts of the masters that I can't decipher and am always wary of, whether they wear a university cap or a barber's.

To be a slave, I suppose, means one has no sense of honor. Yet I've heard the mistress say on occasion, even to a slave, "Do you give me your word of honor?" How can one give one's word of honor who has no honor? It is illogical. But the logic of the master—or the mistress, as the case may be—always turns topsy turvy when applied to the slave. One cannot say that Mexico, that New Spain, is a land without logic. Maybe all New Worlds, as new old words, turn logic topsy turvy or inside out.

That so many volcanoes chose to inhabit here. . . . Choose, you say? Yes, I'm sure of it. Isn't that one of the choices a mountain has—to become a volcano? But I'm not a volcano, I'm human. A human woman, though I've heard my masters try to juggle that in their topsy turvy logic. Since they're human, what's alien to them must not be.

Nor am I a mountain of a woman. I'm average-sized, no larger really than my mistress. In fact, she herself envied my tiny waistline.

"How'd you get a waistline so tiny?" she once asked. She'd just stepped down from a horse she'd been riding. The groom took it, and she stood with one hand on her hip while holding her riding whip in the other. I didn't flinch, though plenty of slaves flinch as soon as they see that riding whip.

"How'd you get a waistline so tiny?" she repeated.

And you could tell she wasn't used to asking an esclavo a question more than once.

I shrugged because one doesn't know the answer to such a question. A tiny waist I was born with, I could answer. But sometimes one wonders how such a trivial question can be asked in the midst of deeper questions.

"Tonta," she declared, shaking her riding whip in the air. I felt the air sting, though I still didn't flinch. "Fool. Most women have to torture themselves for a waistline such as that. Garcia's wife has a waistline three miles round. Tres millas a la redonda."

Most women have to torture themselves for a waistline such as my own? And I knew it. She imported her corsets from Rome and it took longer to pull at the strings in them to scrinch in her waist than it did to comb out the strings of her hair.

"Tres millas a la redonda," she repeated, and I thought she'd try to encircle my waist with that whip.

She liked there to be distinctions between a mistress and her serving girl, but only when it showed off the mistress's best features. For example, she liked my African nose, for it made hers appear the greater jewel—at least according to the standards of her race. But I shouldn't paint her all one color, all bad, for when I saw her in the company of people of her own race whom she considered her equals or her betters, I caught glimpses of her better nature—it stood shoulder to shoulder with her equals, but neither stood on tiptoe nor knelt before her betters. It was only those that she considered below her who brought out her lowest nature, but should I call that the real Señora, the truer one?

Now Why Come That Is?

BY RANDALL KENAN

That squall. That squall: metallic and beastly, squalling, coming from the bottom of hell itself, a squall full of suffering and pleas for mercy, a squall so familiar since Percy's earliest days, from when he was a little boy feeding his daddy Malcolm's Poland China brood sows . . .

But he didn't want to hear it now, damn it, not now, no, for now Percy Terrell was deep inside a dream. He and Elvis were on the town—was it Memphis? New Orleans? Nashville?—he didn't really know, and it didn't really matter. Cause he was in this diner with the King after a wild night of drinking and pool—the velvet night as tangible as the sheets in which he entangled himself at this moment of the dream—at this moment when he and Elvis sat in the diner with the checkered red and white tablecloth with two blondes, one each, one for him, and one for the King; and Percy had his hand on the milky-red thigh of that big-legged gal who smiled through her smacking gum and that leg was so soft and so inviting and she smiled even bigger as Percy moved his hands up that thigh toward—

But that squalling got louder as if someone were murdering that damn hog over and over, calling Percy back to wakefulness, and Percy didn't want to wake up, not with this fine big-legged thing sitting next to him, practically begging for it, and Elvis looking on across the table through his sunglasses, his arm around his sweetie for the night.

What's your name again, hon?

Evangeline, she said.

Evangeline. What a pretty name. Yeah. Percy slid his hand a little higher. Yeah. What's that smell?

At that moment, the moment when the dreamer begins to lose the threads and fabric of his dream, Percy began to dwell more and more on that vile, that powerful and obnoxious odor. Was it the woman? No, hadn't smelled her before. She looked clean enough. And the squalling kept on and on and the smell of hog. Hog. *Hog.*

Percy sat up in the bed, wide awake. As he blinked and focused, the squalling continued, but not in the bedroom now, and presently stopped altogether. Percy swung his feet over the side of the bed, and one foot landed in something warm and slick, the sensation at once comforting and sickening, ooey and gooey and warm. His bare foot slid on the Carolina blue carpet.

"Shit."

Shit. There it was, and Percy's heart almost leapt for joy. Almost. For his foot was in a turd. But he had proof. At long last the evidence he needed.

"Rose," he called to his snoring wife, turning on the bedside lamp. "Rose," he began to shake her. "Rose, wake up. Look, Honey, look. That damn bastard has been here and he's left his calling card. *Wake up!*"

Rose Terrell smacked her mouth absently, and frowned, the sleep so deep around her eyes. "Hmmm?"

"Look, Honey, look." Percy held his soiled foot perilously close to his wife's face. "See, Rose, see it there! I wont lying. He was here. That bastard was here."

Rose opened one eye, moved it from her husband's brown-stained foot, to his gleeful face, she closed it and turned over. "Percy? Take a bath. You stink." Rose brought the sheet over her head, and almost as quickly began to snore.

Percy, a little dejected, removed his foot, and with a little hesitation began to wipe it clean with a tissue. Yet he was not completely deflated, no. He was not crazy, as his be-soiled foot and annoyed nostrils bore witness. This proof was what he had needed; he had finally gotten a physical sign, a residue; and with all the stubbornness his Scotch-Irish blood could muster, he was going to prove, at least to himself, that he was not mad: he was indeed being visited by a hog.

A reddish-brown rusty razorback, to be exact, an old boar hog with unpulled incisors long enough to be called tusks, kite-big, floppy ears, and massive testicles the size of a catcher's mitt. For now on six weeks this hog would appear out of nowhere, without warning or preamble, anywhere—in the living room, in the cab of his pick-up, at the store, entreating Percy, staring at Percy, following Percy, and the damned fool thing of it was that nobody, but Percy had—could—see it; and Percy had no idea how it came and went.

Rose Terrell had listened to Percy—who for not one minute believed the hog to be a figment of his imagination—and was absolutely unconvinced. In fact, seeing that Percy otherwise had all his faculties, she clearly just assumed Percy was fooling again—like the time he swore up and down that there was a snake in the plumbing (a very bad joke), and just ignored him. Percy could tell that was what she had figured, and had given up on her, had simply stopped commenting on the hog, even when it showed up and sat at his side all through breakfast. And now he was assured the whole thing might be a practical joke being played on him. But by who? He wasn't certain. But he'd find out in time. Got your hog right here, Mr. So Percy would play along, cause there was no way in hell she and everybody else didn't see that damned hog.

But now, now he had evidence and substance. Now he knew the whole damn thing could be explained away. Something someone else could see, smell, hell, even taste. And though, upon reflection, he had no idea what to do next, other than clean up the mess, sitting there on the side of the bed, his foot encrusted with drying excrescence, Percy Terrell felt a glimmer of something like hope, a sense that perhaps he were not going mad.

That first night he had seen it madness was far from his mind; the whole occurrence had simply been a matter of negligence, of chance, of curious curiosity. He had been at his desk around eight o'clock in his office at the back of the general store, deep in thought, pouring over tax document after tax document, trying desperately to find a mistake his fool accountant had made, cussing at this damn new machine that Rose bought him, damn thing was supposed to be fast, digital and all, but it kept losing the figures, coming up with zero or e, and . . .

Percy had heard something outside his office, in the belly of the store, something clicking on the old hardwood floor. He stopped, tilted his head to give a listen. A few more clicks. "Rose? That you?" He didn't hear the clicks. "Malcolm? Percival? Philip?" Nothing, just the refrigerator going off, a car passing by outside, the buzz of the overhead light. Percy went back to work. Presently he heard it again, but closer, decidedly a "click" or a "clock" or a "cluck" sound, of something hard, yet a bit muffled against the wood. Something walking. Percy got up to inspect. Everything looked shadow-drenched and shadow-full, the ghostly beams of the emergency lights enhancing the shadowscape, making the rows of fishing rods and gun racks and boxes of mufflers and barrels of three-penny nails and the yarn section, the bubblegum machine, the pipes and monkey wrenches and shovels and babydolls, seem about to move. Yet all was bathed in after-closing quiet, and still. Percy saw this dim world every night and he had never given it a second thought: same as it was during the day. But for some reason, this night, at this moment, he felt a little spooky.

"Who that out there?" Nothing. "Store's closed, now." By and by, Percy began to feel silly, just a tree branch knocking against the roof, and turned around and set his mind to line 27e on page 12 of whatever the hell that form was. After a bit his mind was once again stinging with the unshakeable accuracy of what his accountant had cyphered true, and how much he would not be putting in t-bills this year, when he felt a presence. Someone was standing at the door. He didn't want to give in to the surprise, and his mind instantly went to the three rifles on the wall behind him, just below the flattened rattlesnake skin he had tanned himself. If they had a gun trained on him, he wouldn't be able to reach it in time. Reluctantly he looked up.

Percy actually hollered. And flung his chair back so hard that the wall shook and the bronze gubernatorial citation he had received in 1975 fell to the ground with a clank. Had it been a human being person, Percy would have been ready, but before him stood this great big ole hog, its head jerking here and there, inspecting the place, coming back every now and again to Percy, its eyes piercing and unhumanly human.

"Git!" Percy said from the chair, collecting himself, wondering how the hell a hog got in his store. "Git on, now, git." Percy sprang to his feet, now simply annoyed, annoyed that someone had obviously left the door open or came open and this hog got in. He grabbed a broom from behind the door and waved it at the hog, no stranger to the dumb, docile nature of the creatures. "Git on, now. Git on." Wondering who it could belong to, hoping it hadn't shit in the store. Damn. Damn. Damn. The hog grunted and began to back up. In his frustration Percy hit the creature on the nose with the broom. "Git on out of here and back to where you belong!"

With that crack of the broom the hog backed up two steps and raised its head, opening its swine mouth wide and let out a piercing, brassy bellow, a bellow of outrage and anger, loud enough to make Percy step back and almost drop the broom. And with a quickness that belied its enormous size, the hog leapt and ran, the clackety-clackety of its hoofy gallop reporting against the store's walls. Percy chased after it, but soon realized he didn't hear the hog anymore. He switched on the store lights, which momentarily rendered him blind with their glare. He didn't see the hog. He searched up and down each aisle, calling it, stopping to listen, but heard nothing. After about twenty minutes, his frustration at the boil, he got on the horn and called his sons and wife and the two men who worked in the store. "No, dad. I don't know nothing about no hog." "Percy, I locked and checked all the doors fore I left. How could a hog get in there?" "Swhat I want to know, Ed!" When his youngest and dimmest son, Philip Malcolm, suggested, "Well, maybe he climbed in through the window," Percy just slammed the phone down, annoyed, angered, pissed-off beyond anything he could remember in recent memory. He sat at his desk, stomped his foot once, sighed, crammed all the tax forms and files into his satchel, turned out the lights and left.

Days passed and the memory of the mystery hog began to bore Percy with the equality of its nagging and its curiosity. He went about his days with the grim, quotidian joylessness and banal glory with which he filled each day. Rising at five to feed the dogs, watching the farm reports from Greenville, eating breakfast that Rose prepared herself since Agnes didn't arrive until eight; going to open the store, checking everything; driving around the farm, checking this, checking maybe having a meeting in Crosstown with his lawyer or his banker or the manager of the mill, lunch most days at Nellie's Cafe, a plate of barbecue that his doctor said he should at least cut back on, with a glass of ice tea—these were his days, as empty as they were full. And even Percy, Lord of York County, had dreams of going off away somewhere, maybe to go on safari, hunting big game. He had done that once, back in '52, and had a fairly good time in Kenya, got a good shot off at an antelope, but didn't bag a thing. These days it was too much trouble, especially since those uppity coloreds made it illegal. He'd met a man a few years back who said that they'd guarantee a big kill in one of those African countries, Percy forgot which one, but it would cost him somewhere in the neighborhood of fifty thousand American dollars, the man had said, and Percy had said, Thank you kindly, and goodbye, cause Malcolm Terrell didn't raise no fool. No sir. Thank you sir. So he figured he'd content himself with deer and coon and ducks and the occasional big fish, though, truth to tell, at 58, Percy Terrell was losing his taste for killing things, something he'd never admit to another soul. Some days just being in the woods of an autumn or in a boat under the big sky was reward in and of itself. Perhaps Percy was at a point that he could even admit it to himself.

A week and six days passed, and Percy had damn near forgotten about the hog—he remembered really, mostly, that feeling of horror that had involuntarily gripped him upon the sight of the thing. That afternoon he stopped by one of the twenty-three turkey houses he owned, a set of five over in Mill Swamp, where Ab Batts was fixing the feeding system that had been breaking with annoying frequency. This turkey house was about thirty yards long and Percy could see Ab bent over at work at the far end. Percy despised these dumb creatures, gobbling and gibbering about his feet and ankles, their heads just above knee level, the sight of their red and gelatinous waffles making him sometimes shiver with disgust. Turkeys were too dumb to walk out of the rain, but sometimes one would get its feathers riled and would peck at you. One tom turkey made him so mad once that he stomped it to death before Percy realized what he was doing, and which he later regretted cause the price went up that very day.

As Percy waded through the dirty white mess of jabbering poultry, kicking and shooing, he called out to Ab and Ab waved at him and went on working. As Percy got about half-way into the house, the turkeys started making more and more of a commotion, and started parting even before Percy got in their midst, bunching along the wire-mesh walls, hollering, crying even, it seemed to Percy's ears. Percy looked about, baffled and even Ab Batts jerked up, amazed at the unruly fuss. Then Ab's eyes fixed on Percy with a mild degree of consternation and puzzlement, but Percy came to see it was not he Ab had transfixed in his glare.

"Boss," yelled Ab, "What you bring a hog in here for?"

Astonished and confounded, Percy stared at Ab trying to make sure he understood what he was saying, and, as he said, "Wha . . . ," trying to understand, he looked round about him, and directly behind him stood that same damned hog, sniffing at the turkeys, whose racket was at this point of an ear-splitting quality. And ever so briefly, in the middle of this feather frenzy, this poultry pandemonium, ever so momentarily, eye to eye with this porcine beast, this stalking ham, Percy felt that he were not in Tim's Creek, North Carolina; that he was not Percival Malcolm Terrell, first and only son of Malcolm Terrell; not chairman and chief executive officer of Terrellco, Inc., county commissioner and deacon—he was a mere blip on some otherness, some twisted reality. He didn't know where he was.

Ab rushed after the hog and, after some effort, chased it from the turkey house. "Tweren't your hog, I reckon," Ab laughed off the situation, walking up to Percy who had not really moved.

"Ah . . . no." Percy rubbed his eyes, not wanting to betray himself to Ab. "No, don't know where it came from. Must a just followed me in here. Didn't even see it. Ain't that something?"

"Must a been one of Joe Richards's. He been catching the devil with his hogs. Got one of them new-fanged, fancy-dancy hog operations, over there he has, and can't keep 'em from getting out." A predicament that Ab clearly found amusing as he laughed some more.

Somehow, hearing Ab speak of the hog as a piece of a machine, a cog, an it, something that belonged to someone, and eventually on a plate, reassured Percy and filled in that momentary sense of a void; made him, oddly enough, whole again in his mind.

But that would be the last time he would feel that way for many a day, for, two days later, the hog again appeared in the back of his pick-up truck while he was driving back to Tims Creek from Crosstown. He stopped the truck and got out, worrying that the hog might vanish and convince him that he was more than a little touched. But the hog remained standing there in the bed of the truck, and Percy touched it, patted it, saying, "Whose hog are you, fella?" Feeling its warm, rough, hairy flanks flinch beneath his hand, the coarseness and the solid meat, Percy laughed outloud and shook his head and drove on to Tims Creek. He stopped at McTarr's Convenience Store in the middle of town and got out, seeing within the store Joe Batts and Tom McShane and Teddy Miller and Woodrow Johnson, standing around the microwave counter.

"Hey, ya'll," Percy said upon entering. "Anybody lost a hog?"

The men looked one to another, and all around out the window, searching with their eyes.

Woodrow took a swig of his Pepsi. "Where you see a hog, captain?"

"Out in my truck is where. Anybody heard anything about somebody losing one?"

Everyone went out to inspect the now empty truck.

"All right, now. Who took the hog out that truck?"

The men, smiling, a bit confused, watched one another, a little uneasy now.

Percy looked to see if anyone else were about. He noted a young woman filling up her compact Japanese-made piece a mess. "Hey, there. You seen anybody take a hog out this here flat bed?"

The teenager shrugged and said, "I ain't seen nothing and nobody. There wont nothing in that truck to begin with."

"There was!" Percy turned to the men, who were no longer looking him in the eye. He walked to the side of the store. Nothing. Just a lone tractor.

"All right, now." He came back before the men, who dared not look him in the face. "Where is it? There was a goddamned boar hog in this goddamned truck and I want to know which sonofabitch put it—took it—"

"Percy? You all . . ."

"Yes, I'm all right, god damn it, and when I find out who—" Percy heard himself, heard himself yelling, heard how ridiculous he was sounding, him, Percy Terrell, before these men who respected and admired him, men who he knew secretly all hated and dreaded him as well. And he caught himself, the way a snake handler catches the head of an angry snake; caught himself mid-roar, and started laughing, just like that, laughing, started exerting control of the situation and of himself. He winked, "Had you going, didn't I?" and he strolled past the men who were not laughing, yet, who followed him into the store where Percy went over to the drink cooler and hauled out a Pepsi and drank deeply, saying, "So, Tom, did you ever find that foaling mare the other night?"

Still a bit uneasy, Tom McShane sat down, clearly a mite rattled and said: "Ah, yeah, Percy, yeah I did, but it was too late, they both died. Hated to lose that mare and that colt. 'Twas a colt, you know."

The men fell into commiserating and talking about this and that, and the queer spell Percy had cast over the meeting diminished by and by, though the specter of his curious behavior clung to the air like a visible question mark. And Percy, who was Oh so loathe to admit it to himself, knew that he had no idea what the hell was going on; knew that in some inescapable way he was, at bottom, more than a little afraid.

The visitations stepped up after that in frequency and in their curious and unexpected nature. The hog would appear of its own accord now in the house—once, when he was shaving, he saw it in the mirror; once, when he and Rose were in the living room watching a World War II documentary on cable ("Rose?" "Yes, Percy," she said, not looking up from her needlepoint. "Nothing." And the hog got up, during a commercial, walked out of the room and didn't return that night.)—now in town—once in a meeting at the mill with John Buzkoswski, the general manager, the hog walked from behind the manager's desk, with him sitting at it, and the manager saw nothing, and Percy had to pretend he saw nothing; and once while attending a court proceeding over a bankrupt furniture store he owned a percentage in, Percy swore he saw the hog walk across the front of the room and expected someone to say something, anything, to acknowledge the animal. But no one said a word, not even Percy.

Every day now, the hog was sure to show, and everywhere that Percy went the hog was sure to go. He had given up asking if anyone else had seen it. He was even no longer certain that it was an elaborate practical joke that everyone was playing on him, a joke that would suddenly come to a crescendo, a punch line, and that everyone in the whole blessed county would have an enormous, gut-wrenching, wont-that-funny-as-hell laugh over and then Percy would come out looking the good sport and the business would be finished. But nothing of the sort occurred. So Percy waited, for days and days, and he became a little resigned to his swinish companion, and had even commenced to talking to it on occasion, when they were alone, sometimes in the cab of his truck, where it would sit, as tame as any dog. And, on these queer occasions, Percy would think how sanely insane it all was, and that he himself might be, without a doubt, crazy. But one stubborn and nagging fact remained: Ab had seen it. And as long as he didn't remark upon the creature, Percy's life was going along swimmingly.

However, one day his bafflement reached a new level of strangeness. He had gone over to his son Malcolm's house, where his daughter-in-law was bad-off with the flu. Rose, who was frantic with preparing and planning for a church trip to the Holy Land next month, asked Percy to take some food Agnes had prepared over to poor ailing Maria. Malcolm and Maria Terrell had five children, three boys, Percival, Malcolm III, and Richard (after Maria's father), and two girls Rose and Electra, and Percy felt awful proud of his progeny, especially the second boy who not only bore his father's name but his father's likeness, but with a sweetness the old man had never possessed. That day, as he blew the truck horn, the children all ran out the front door to greet Granddaddy Percy, and he got out of the truck and reached into his coat pockets for the treats he never forgot to bring for them—much to their mother's disquiet, who had the unfortunate lapse of good judgment to tell him to his face that she disapproved of giving candy to her children, whereupon her husband Malcolm himself made it clear that you don't object to Percy Terrell's largess, and besides a little candy won't hurt em none, and so she now just grinned and bore it, the way Percy felt she should have from the beginning—but this day the children inexplicably ran to the other side of the truck. Percy walked around to discover them cooing and cuddling with the hog; little Malcolm had clambered onto its broad back, and, to Percy's amazement, rode the hog like a miniature pachyderm.

Percy stood there with a feeling like bliss and quiet resolve. "Ya'll see that ole hog, do you?"

Rose, age 8, looked up as if to say, What kind of question is that? "Where'd you get him, Granddaddy? He's BIG!"

Percy lit a cigarette and watched the innocent gallivanting for the duration of his smoke, a guilty pleasure he had promised the doctor he'd quit, while promising himself he'd just cut back; he watched with a feeling of warmth at the sight of his issue's issue having fun, a feeling that he rarely felt, a feeling that he actually felt uncomfortable feeling, yet felt good feeling when they were around. Over it all, in the middle of it all, under it all, was the strange stalking porker, whose presence, for a few moments, he actually accepted, accepted as a queer reality, and at the moment, even enjoyed.

Presently, Percy took the food in to Maria, who, from her bed, asked what the children were doing out there, and Percy almost said, "Oh, they're just playing with my hog," the reality behind the word "my" pricking his brain as he thought it, suddenly aware of the connotations, the meaning of the word "my." My hog. "They're just playing."

After sitting for a few minutes with the mother of the children who would carry on his family name, his name, Percy kissed her upon the brow and ordered her to get better—she was a good-looking woman, even when she was under the weather—and returned to the playing children, now three of whom were perched on the back of the patient, ever-suffering, ever-enormous hog. Percy gently lifted his grandchildren off its back, one by one, and slapped its rump, "Go on, now. Git on." The hog didn't move. "Go on now, go on back to where you belong." Percy kicked it.

"Granddaddy! Don't!"

"Quiet now, honey. This ain't my hog. 'Sgot to go on back to where it came from."

"But Granddaddy . . ."

The hog turned around and looked at Percy with something that Percy felt to be an accusation. Without further adieu or prodding the hog trotted off in the direction of the house. Richard started to run after it, but Percy made him come back. "Leave him go, boy. Leave him go."

That very night the hog left his aromatic calling card.

But, as fate would have it, that next morning, Rose rose before Percy did, and she cleaned up the offending mound, leaving Percy with ring ears over letting those dogs come in the house, haven't I told you enough about that Percy, Land to Goshen! I'd swear you were brought up in a barn—Hog, hog, hog—just stop it Percy, and also leaving him right back where he started from.

Having exhausted every avenue he could consciously consider short of going to a doctor—or a vet—Percy took what, for him, was a bold and unexpected step: He went to visit Tabitha McElwaine.

All the colored folks who worked for him swore up and down about Miss Tabitha, who was known throughout five counties as the best midwife and rootworker around. They mentioned her name with reverence and a touch of awe: "Went to see Miss Tabitha bout it." As if, Percy contemplated with scorn, she was the Lord Jesus Christ Him Damn Self. When they spoke to him of her, he called them damn fools to their faces, saying they'd be better off just burning their money. "But Mr. Percy, you just don't know." "I know damn well enough that that old fool can't do nothing but make piss and deliver babies, and God can take care of that without her around!" But the colored swore by her and gave her money left and right to cure ailments and make somebody fall in love with them; to make them prosperous and to take out revenge, happily handing over hard-earned currency to that lying heifer. And if he discovered a white person doing such a thing, Percy would refuse to speak to them for years on end.

The old witch, who was about Malcolm's age, lived alone in the old McElwaine mansion that proudly stood in what was left of her granddaddy's two hundred and eight acre spread, purchased after the civil war. Now only five acres remained, the balance now belonging to the Terrell family, as his own father had seen to. Legend had it that his daddy had killed her daddy over it, and they had in turn killed Malcolm. But nobody could prove anything, and Percy kept the land, and they kept their hatred.

Percy stood there now, at the front door of the old Federal style house, improbable in its competence and simple grandeur, well kept up, recently painted, red brick and white trim, fearfully large crepe myrtle bushes ringing the yard, and Percy wondered how an ex-slave could have possibly built it alone, thinking the story to be a lie in the first place. As he stood there Percy dared not admit to himself how desperate he had to be to come to this lowliness, how perplexed and damned, and, at base, simply bored with this intrusion, this haunting; how his otherwise simple and orderly life had been thrown into chaos, and how he, Percy Terrell, was at his wit's end. How he wanted an old black woman to tell him, an old white man, what he must do to release himself. But at that time, though he knew this all to be true, he would not allow the thoughts to form in his noggin; he just moved forward with an inexorable logic and a bitter will for exorcism. So he told himself nothing, as he stood there knocking, knocking, repeatedly, annoyed and calling out, finding the door to be open and just inviting himself on in.

Grudgingly impressed again, he marveled at how finely-wrought and finely attended the house's interior had been, how cavernous its halls and rooms seemed—larger than the ones at his house—fixed up like a New Orleans cathouse with lace and doilies over the velvet up-holstered chairs and with ferns and potted plants aplenty, gossamer curtains, daguerreotypes of some solemn-looking Negroes staring down at him from the walls.

Without prologue he saw her straightway, on the other side of a big room, through yet another between them, standing by a big and dark stone fireplace. She stood there, still a tall and slim woman, her head now white with gray, a red shawl over her shoulders, wearing a long blue dress that looked modern and fine, as if she'd just ordered it out of a Speigel catalogue. Percy walked down the carpet toward her.

"Nice hog," she said, not cracking a smile or moving a muscle.

"Um," Percy grunted, not wanting to acknowledge his co-visitor, walking by his side, his head febrile with the fact of his being there, in her damn house, fighting with the inevitable fact of humility, of asking, of a need he for once could not solve with a credit card or the writing of a check.

He came within a yard of her and stopped, seemed his legs refused to take him any closer. The room sparkled with light from the windows, nothing hanty or frightening about it, as he had imagined it. He could have been standing in some resort hotel, somewhere far and away. "Look, Weird Sister, I got this little problem and I was wondering—"

"Well, Percy Terrell," she said, taking a pipe out of her pocket. "I ain't heard you call me that since 1952." She scooped and worked the pipe in a leather pouch full of tobacco.

Dismayed, Percy's eyes grew wide and even amused, "What?" he even grinned, involuntarily, so taken aback was he. " 'Weird Sister?' You remember the last time I called you that? Hell, I ain't talked to you in over thirty years."

Tabitha drew on the pipe, squinting in the cloud of sweet fog, and, blowing out the match, giving him a look as if to say, Boy you don't know your asshole from your mouth, do you? said, "I made up the year."

"Look," Percy said, after clearing his throat, feeling more than a little betrayed, more than a little stupid, more than a little. . . . "Look, I ain't got time for this. I need—"

"Know what you need. Why you came here. Answer's no."

"Huh?"

"Can't do nothing for you."

"Wait a minute. What you mean, you 'know'?"

"Want to get rid of that damn hog a yourn, don't you?"

"Can you?"

"Oh, I can," Tabitha stopped and blew out a long stream of smoke, like a ghost's train, and looked upon him vaguely with a look of pity that quickly transformed into scorn. "But you ain't gone be willing to do what you got to do to get rid of him. So why waste my time? Can't help you." She turned to the window, clearly having said all she would say.

Percy felt his face go red. When had someone last told him flat out no? No song, no dance? Refused him anything? After he had done such a thing as to actually come to this freakish old colored bitch for help, after . . . He stood there staring at this woman who had dismissed him so rudely, and it never once occurred to him that he might plead, beg, pour out his heart, that he might say *please*. He just got angrier, hotter, redder. Finding his voice he finally said, shaking, "Well, why don't you just go right on to hell then, you crazy witch. You just crazy. Ain't a bit a nothing to that old foolishness you preach. Just a old charlatan. You just go right on to hell."

He watched himself storm out of the old house, wanting to break something, wanting to burn the entire abomination to the ground, vowing to himself that he'd break that old witch one day. So twisted with hate and malice and anger was he that he couldn't even frame his own thoughts, at that moment, so inarticulate with rage, such a rejected little boy that he almost came to tears. And, indeed, at the wheel of his truck, with the hog sitting quietly, peacefully beside him, driving down and away from the old house, the unfamiliar sting and pain and torment began moistening his cheek, and he did.

By the time he reached home, twilight had darkened past dusk, and, it being a Saturday night, Rose had already left for bridge and wouldn't be back until after eleven, and he simply wanted to forget this whole business, to forget the hog, forget, indeed, the feeling the mystery of the hog precipitated within him, to forget how helpless and hopeless he was feeling. He locked himself in his study and snapped on the TV and popped "The Outlaw Josey Wales" into the VCR and opened a fresh bottle of his old friend, Jack Daniels, and took two enormous swigs before pouring four fingers neatly into a tumbler. He kicked off his shoes and loosened his belt and flopped back on the couch, before the flickering images of a West that never existed, concentrating intensely on the testosterone-deluded fantasy, and drank and drank. He had stopped drinking so much—well, during the week, now only on Fridays and Saturdays . . . except on special occasions; and he had stopped getting truly drunk . . . except on special occasions—but tonight that was exactly what he wanted, craved; he needed to erase, expunge; he lusted after what the bottle never failed to supply: power and ease and good feelings; he wanted to revisit the sweet veil of haze and be-bothered nothingness and the viscous warmth and head-fuzziness; he wanted to be released from tax codes and stupid children and orders and poultry and stocks and marriage, from maleness and the tug of gravity on his growing belly, to be released from the grey hair that he refused to dye out of a vanity stronger than fear and the red splotches and burst veins that would never vanish from his face and that signaled the end, years ago, of his virility and machismo energy; to be released from the memories of that once-youth, of his escapades and all the trouble his penis had seen and caused; away from memories of hunting and dancing and tomfoolery: released, yes, from the hog and all it seemed to signify. Percy drank. And drank. He swilled and slurped, he guzzled and gobbled, with a ferocious abandon, and with the swallowing, at his lips, and the fuzzy now-hum of his brain, somewhere in the amber liquid of the bottle, somewhere behind the black label, enlivened by the light of the TV screen, he saw his father, that old demon, with his big black hat with the huge brim, looking down upon his son with contempt. And Percy didn't want to see his father, never ever again, knew he was better than his father, could never be like his father, was a human being person unlike his father, an evil, freak of nature, yes, he built it all up from nothing, yes, he started it, murdered for it, stole and beat for it, that sonofabitch, and left Percy with the blood, but Percy had, had—no, he didn't want to think of Malcolm, so he drank, and drank some more, the fire in his belly now out-stepped by the fire in his brain, he willed himself to stop seeing Malcolm, and, stumbling up and over, switched off the VCR and turned on the CD player and fell back on the sofa to the measured twangs and lonesome cords of Hank Williams, "Goodbye Joe, me gotta go . . ." and sang with Hank (Hell, Malcolm never could sing, never sang, never would sing) laughing and goofy in the clouds and fumes of mash and Benedict, Benedictine, and the deluged fretted in Antioch, O' Antioch, where the gladrags had orgies of ragout in Shiloh, O, by the door of Doomsday, yes, in Berlin where superior werewolves were sailors with head colds who lost the compasses in that distance, that joint—what was its name?—of pus-filled pushovers who submit, submit, wogs and Zeus, yes, zilch, in shampoo, Zimbabwe! Gomorrah! Dye. Die.

And somewhere, somehere, somethere, in the misfiring synapses and purple blaze of effluvium that had seized his brain and body, somewhere just before passing out, Percy saw his hog sitting there by him, by the couch, and felt a little love in his heart for this friend of his, and reached out to pet him, and, forgetting he held a glass, dropped it, and his mind went to black.

The next morning found the Head Deacon and Chairman of the Board of Trustees of St. Thomas Aquinas Presbyterian Church of Tims Creek, Percival Malcolm Terrell, sitting on the second pew along with the rest of the congregation, with a hangover that rivaled the worse hangovers of his youth—though knowing from half a century of heavy drinking that a bad hangover makes its own history. Percy felt he was indeed still drunk, for as he rose at seven after Rose banged and banged on the door to his sanctum sanctorum for him to get up and get ready for church, and as he washed and shaved and squirted drops of Visine into his eyes, and picked at his breakfast and drank four cups of coffee, the world was still tinged with a colorless aura, things were enveloped yet within a nimbus of gauze and otherness, and though he felt sick to his stomach, the alcohol had provided, at least for a spell and at a cost, a distraction from his mental confusion, had given his mind a respite from the hog which was nowhere to be seen.

Now he sat before Pastor Bergen, who could not preach to save his life, droning on and on about the faith of Zacheus up a tree, now he was playing the role he had part-inherited and part-worked for, a role so old it was capacious and well-worn and comfortable, and took so little effort he had barely to think upon it to be it: he was it: He was King of his little fiefdom of mills and poultry plants and fields and social rungs, richer than most men dared hope to be, and feared, respected, paid homage unto. Why on earth should he worry about anything other than cancer and taxes? And as Bergen drew thankfully near the end of his overlong sermon, Percy felt more than a little better and the nausea seem to abate and his mind to clear a bit and he thought of the football game he would cheer on after dinner with the kids and he realized he had not even thought of the hog all morning. As the colored light from the stained-glass windows played against the pristine whiteness of the church walls, Percy smiled to himself.

The commotion started as a low level rumble. Whispering turned to loud talk, and somebody said, "Git it, Frank!" By the time the minister stopped in mid sentence and stared, Percy could hear people standing, some laughing, some angry, "How'd it get in here?" and before Percy could turn all the way around, he heard a grunt at his side: There was his old friend, his familiar, his companion and seeming advocate, his own and only hog. But the thing that Percy's mind latched onto was the fact that everyone saw the hog! Percy felt released. Yet, oddly enough, the hog had stopped by his side, as if to point a finger, or a snout, at him.

"What?" Percy hollered at the hog. "*What do you want from me?*"

With that the hog gave out his signature bellow and rushed toward the pulpit, around to the side and up toward the Reverend Paul Bergen. The men in the front pews, unwieldy in their Sunday-Go-to-Meeting best, all jumped to their feet, and the pastor let out a girlish yelp, gathered up his robe like a woman's frock and ran, being chased by this boar hog, its oversized genitalia jangling betwixt its legs, its big ears flapping like the wings of a bat, its mouth wide and frothing. As the men of the church chased after the hog, and the women screamed, and the children laughed with unbridled wildness, Percy was just thankful and amazed that everyone, everyone, could see the hog, at last, at long last, and he felt that the whole six week ordeal was coming to some end, was about to affix itself to a clear and final meaning.

The men tried in utter vain to grab the hog, but it proved too ornery, too sly, and kept slipping between their legs, knocking them over and down, for it was indeed, a very large hog. At one point it actually bit Pernell Roberts on the hand, which made Pernell cuss ("Goddamnit!") in church, though no one bothered to scold him, for at that instant the renegade swine chomped down on the edge of the communion tablecloth and backed up, pulling the Eucharist, the silver pitchers full of grape juice, the little glasses, the silver platters containing wafers, all crashing, clattering, tumbling down with a metal thunk and splatter. Momentarily everyone stopped, the men, the pastor, the women, the children, Percy, the hog, stopped, witnessing the spectacle as if, in that brief wrinkle in time, some clarity, some hidden codeology in this bedlam. But the hog brought an end to that sober oasis of reflection when it moved first its head, with its bedazzling speed, toward Percy and grunted derisively, giving otherworldly language to its own unquestionably blasphemous actions, and with equal speed dashed down the aisle toward the door.

Without thinking, Percy moved in front of the great mass of pork, to stop it, calling out, "Whoa!" as one would to an intelligent, malevolent, comprehending entity, "Stop," he cried. But the hog didn't stop, poking its behemoth head between Percy's spread thighs and lifting him astride its wide neck, and continuing down the way, Percy being carted along and atop, backwards, yelling, through the throng of the agitated congregation. At the threshold of the church Percy fell off, unceremoniously and hurtfully, and the hog galloped away.

Percy scrambled to his feet, and, feeling somehow personally responsible, and even possessive, he gave chase, running down the side of North Carolina Highway #50, after that great boar hog, who had just disrupted the services of St. Thomas Aquinas Presbyterian Church beyond conceivable imagination. Running, Percy didn't even give a second thought to the fact that they were running, unmistakably, inevitably, to his own home.

Though Percy's house was less than a mile from the church, he stood in the doorway breathless, his heart pounding dangerously, sweat pouring copiously down his face, for he had not run this far, or this fast, in years, not to mention the nausea he had been battling all morning. He tugged off his tie and doffed his coat to the floor, and stalked to his study. His mind was a red place, a hot place, a place of brimstone and vengeance; he was not simply angry with a thing, but with an intangible yet tangible circumstance, a situation, a tangle of happenstance and botheration. He knew there was one way to get rid of it all, a way that had never clearly presented itself before, since the creature had never acted so hatefully.

Percy marched into his study, and, perhaps due to the anger and the urgent need to strike out at something, broke the glass of his gun rack with his elbow and a rebel yell, rather than waste time looking for the key which was in his pocket. He reached for the old elephant gun he had used once in Africa in 1952, and not since, though he had kept it clean religiously. He loaded the shells, feeling the ungodly size of them in his hands, himself feeling suddenly potent with each insertion, wondering to himself why he had not done this most obvious of things long before.

Percy raised his head to the door, and, as he knew he would be, there stood his hog, his hog, insolent, inquisitive, mocking. Percy sneered at the beast, thinking and then saying out loud, for none would appreciate this outsized drama more than he, like some celluloid cowboy show in his brain: "End of the line, fella."

Percy had the hog in his sights, right between the eyes. They both stood there, stock-still for a period of time Percy could not easily name. Percy and the hog. The hog and Percy. The hog did not move, and by and by, Percy thought: What a magnificent creature. Unaccountably he began to tremble, and inadvertently he peered into the hog's eyes, into the depth of them, perhaps toward the soul of it; and to Percy it seemed the hog did the same to him. Percy's trembling increased and a feeling began to wash over him and into him, and Percy began to feel puny. Naked. Ashamed. Just as he had at that moment when he discovered that his penis was not the largest in creation and that the juice of his testicles would neither save nor solve humanity; neither save nor solve himself; that all he had he and his father had stolen and robbed for, and that he had no right to any of it; that he was next to nothing, and that the mask of his flesh, once glorious, now wrinkling and withering, would in time be dust and ash, and that he was really not very, very much at all, not even as valuable as a hog.

Percy began to cry. He could not shoot. He would not shoot. He should not shoot. He understood in this moment of pregnant possibility, this showdown, this climax of it all, what the hog was. And in a moment of quiescence and acquiescence, Percival Malcolm Terrell let it all go, let the gun slip from his hands, and slumped to the floor of his study, a feeling like exhaustion settling into his bones. The great boar hog, on scuffling hooves, came rushing, and leapt, springing impossibly, up, into the air, and Percy, in chilled fright, watched as the mammoth creature sailed, like a gargantuan football, toward him; and he could only shield his face with his hands, and quake.

A few instants later he heard Rose run into the house, calling, "Percy, are you all right? My God, Percy!" He slowly uncovered his face to see only the open window, a breeze gently troubling the sheer curtains inward, barely a billow. Percy continued to sob, though the sob had altered in its tenor and meaning: now the sob was a sweet, deep wonderful and profound sob, his body shaking, snot running down his nose. Rose walked into the room, but Percy did not really see her or hear her, so intent was he upon this newfound and peaceful feeling. He felt just like that bird in the old Hank Williams song, the one too blue to fly, and tried to mouth: "Hear that lonesome whippoorwill": but only the mumblings of a child emerged. Lonesome, O so Lonesome.

Silences

BY HELEN ELAINE LEE

From the beginning, they were consigned to narrowed space. To cubicles with proportions that seemed just right to those safely distanced by the refuge of their personal judgments. For others, these were the spaces where she and Zella had lived, squeezed and folded in by the theories that explained her fall.

Some said curiosity was her undoing. Others said the hunter had found its prey. Some said she had met with shrunken choice. And just about everyone said it was a terrible shame.

She stood at the casket, slightly bent, leaning on solid arms. Her ceremonial wig hugged her forehead where the elastic gripped too tight, and the toe of one foot rested, poised to pivot, on the polished floor. She stared, struggling with an impulse to peel back the expression of arranged peace, searching for the woman she had known. She looked for the dark eyes that could flash caustic or tender. For the warm flush of vibrant copper skin. She looked for Zella in the face before her.

The mouth once carved and full was pinched shut. Hair that was worn loose had been set into waves and dips of unsettling symmetry. All of her features looked insistent, exaggerated by the funereal makeup that, seeking desperately to recapture life, only makes more real the passing on. As she stood staring, groping for the past, she opened and closed her hands over the worn rungs of her crutches, gathering close the fragments of their forty-seven years.

The summer of 1924, the summer they had met, she had always privately called her "swan song." She had swung her corset-cinched body along the streets of St. Louis with long steady strides, smiling but never meeting the eyes of those who paused from whatever they were doing to partake of her radiance. The world would come to prefer the starved look, and her grand niece would exclaim in horror at the rounded bodies in the crumbling snapshots taken in long thigh-length bathing bloomers. But in those days, she had the ideal form, "ample and for-giving," in Zella's words. She carried herself with a sense that something wonderful might happen to her. And just freed from the weakness incarnate she had married out of carnal guilt, her step was invigorated by a newfound liberation. The final act of extrication had been to tell her father, who was puzzled by the union from the first, that she was coming home.

Since her mother's death when she was barely twelve, her father had been confused to find himself alone and raising girls. They focused on the practical demands of each day, never speaking of the void her death had left, never remembering her out loud. Her father had offered a titular guidance, had offered what he knew, from the Pullman cars that were his mobile home. She could still see him standing on the platform, his brow a map of furrowed ground. He had fumbled, with the help of his dead wife's sister, Rose, to raise them right. And when she announced her intention to return home, he stood there mutely, nodding and frowning, sticking to his policy of never asking those questions whose answers he might not want to hear.

That summer had been hers, and in her memory it inhabited a soft violet space. As with all treasured time, the lens had gradually softened, rendering indistinct the sharp edges of growth, polishing smooth the glory of her freed beauty. From the vantage point of her manicurist's table at the Marquis Barber Shop, she had surveyed the range of the possible, and for the first time in her life, she felt she owned the choice. From the spin of options, she made assessments. And she did some choosing.

She chose the dark barber who, passing by throughout the day, tormented and drew her with the economy of his attention. She chose the white patron who brought fine linens and embossed leather as barter for the pulse of life she gave. For the exotic spark that he might capture, like a firefly, within his palm. And then, to everyone's astonishment, she chose Zella, in whom she had sensed something unplaceable from the first.

Maybe it was the disregard in the set of her jaw. Or the untamed richness of her laugh. She remembered sharing the knowledge that she had thought secret with her sister, Mattie. The late-night revelation that she had met a girl who was "different."

It wasn't long before she heard Zella spoken of in curtained words, in phrases of whispered violence. BulldaggerBulldaggerBulldagger. Sealed by a switchblade fold of hands and an abruptly turned back. But her fear was heightened only for an instant, and the warnings washed right over her. She had reached through the ugly words, past the fear in other eyes, scattering an arc of their beaded unshed tears. Reaching anyway. Reaching because of. Reaching for the knowing.

There was polite speculation at first about the nature of the friendship, but others found solace in her enjoyment of the company of men. As she and Zella grew closer, some distanced themselves from the taint of the "unnatural," and, more and more, she and Zella found themselves speaking in conspiratorial tones. Heads shook slowly in condemnation, and leaned closer for details. Couldsheisshedoesshe? Photos of stilted poses that would yellow over the years in dusty attic boxes betrayed a subtle intimacy that would have rendered inquiry unnecessary.

How many distant arcs had spiraled off that early meeting, fused from passion and nearly disarming understanding? Arcs like arms that would flail and smooth and push, and draw them in again and again across the years.

It was Zella who had helped her stem the fevered blood of that stagnant day, that night of rent flesh. Zella had pleaded hopelessly against the clumsy unclean slashing out of unwanted life, begging it for her own, and had stopped in alarm, midway through the barren landscape of dry ragged brush and fallen leaves, to arrange the discarded towels and newspapers. Zella had gone for help. And that was only the beginning. Over time, she had cradled her in those places that they inhabited alone.

It was Zella whose legs had been there when her own stiffened from the infection that sped through her body when help came, but didn't matter. She had spent months suspended in traction. And more months standing in naked humiliation before rooms of white doctors who shook their heads at such ravaged beauty, while "studying" the workings of her steel pinned joints.

About her illness no one spoke. What could be said of such a thing, the causes of which were guarded and tinged with shame? Because it was easier to skirt the discomfort of tragedy and send a card, visits were infrequent and shortlived. During her one-year stay at a Boston hospital, Zella moved there in order to be near. She had helped her through that time, coming daily with flowers, pears and chocolates . . . the little things with which the confined order time.

It was Zella who had built her a house without stairs. She remembered approaching it for the first time, after leaving another hospital where she had spent two years. She had seen it from a block away, from a little circle rubbed from the frosted car window. They had been the first colored on the block, and she would never forget the look of choked rage on her neighbor's flaming face as she opened her door and stood watching them struggle to move in. The hostile stares persisted until the area began to change, and they could finally release the breaths they had held for decades. One more reason to keep to themselves. One more silent space.

They would spend forty-two years together in that house, washed in the prism of afternoon light that spilled in from the window of tiny stained glass panes. They had watched so many things pass from their living room chairs. Joe Louis and "Amos 'n Andy" in the magic word-picture times before T.V. Assassinations that had left them speechless. Stonewall and the slow gains of Sixties marches. And Bob Gibson's Cardinals. And "Porgy and Bess" on the hi-fi relegated later to the basement. And all the little changes wrought by mornings and ducks. There had been many an outburst in that room, where discussions were never tame. She would hold forth, gesticulating with impassioned hand-phrases, while Zella waited quietly for the chance to slice in with sharp concise rebuttals. How many times had she hoisted herself up, snatched her crutches, and disappeared before Zella could come up with a response?

She thought, too, of the kitchen sink, where she had stood so often, continuing with the daily tasks that move life forward. She was sure that if she added up the time she had spent there it would amount to years, passed in that familiar pose. Crutches abandoned, she stood with arms firmly placed. As she washed and chopped, she looked out through her collection of African Violets, sifting time. Assessing and reassessing the past. Imagining things to come. Zella would enter and stop short, struck by the strength of her pose, mumbling, "I don't know who's disabled and who's not."

They had taken cooking seriously, and unlike the women of today, she had never really worried about getting fat. "You can't get too much of a good thing," Zella used to say. Both had their specialties, and they were always feeling some craving coming on. Zella made homemade soup with everything leftover thrown in, and seafood was an undying passion. But no matter what season or hour, it was always time for barbecue. They had sat devouring a slab one evening thirty years ago and pledged, hands raised to the heavens, that they would never stop eating ribs. Zella used to get a notion to barbecue in the middle of January sometimes, and she would find her out there in her beaver coat and boots.

They had always believed in eating and drinking, and had hosted slews of parties in the early years. Zella mixing and passing round the designated cocktail. They had spent three weeks on Margaritas once, stuck on a double-edged Tequila rush. There had been chitterling parties on the back porch. And bridge games that extended into night, stretched by the requisite bout for biggest talker of shit. Twin titles, "Bridge" and "Shit," that Zella often won.

Gathering regularly with other sharers of clandestine love, they had celebrated the move from muted tones to full voice. Waves of unencumbered expression swept a house filled with their expanding numbers. There had been such carrying on. She would never forget the time Calvin Styles had joined into the discussion of the Kinsey Report to say that such theories were originated by the great Roman philosopher, Julius Octavius Flavius. He had everyone going, taken in by the casual nature of the lie, until Zella went for the encyclopedia. The stories that man told, you never knew what was fiction and what was fact. He wove them together deftly, scorning the effort at distinction.

There were poetry readings and charades. The contest for "Homecoming Queen" that the girls judged. And that unforgettable Sunday morning after a party that had left the floor littered with sleeping bodies, when Lanie Johnson had awakened them with a lampshade on her head to serve bacon and eggs.

Zella had been comfortable in putting aside the styles prescribed for women. Designated handsome, even as a girl, she had always featured tailored clothes. Back in the Forties, she wore pleated trousers and button-down shirts when not at work. She remembered the first pair of trousers they had bought. Marching into the Men's Department at Famous, she had scandalized the place. And then, moving directly into Lingerie, she had satisfied her passion for lace and silk. Zella had been thought so daring. So bold. And so many other things with which she didn't concern herself.

Zella had considered herself so tough. She walked alone at night, convinced that attitude was a foolproof repellant. And to her colleagues, she was a teacher, nothing more. No one would ever ask about the missing pictures of husband and kids. No one would visit her at home. She had mastered the protective device of distance early on, so that it was clear that things private were forever closed topics.

None of them knew how gentle she really was. But for her and their animals, who loved without judgment or condition, she would rearrange the stars. She had treated their cats like her own babies, feeding them only fresh liver from the deli down the street. "They live better than we do," she used to say, feigning outrage at their indolence, scolding them for not getting jobs.

What a legend Zella had been at Central High. Thousands of students had come through her classroom in forty years of teaching. She had touched so many lives. In the later years they had assigned her the "problem" students, knowing she could whip them into shape. For it was common knowledge that Ms. Bridgeforth took no shit. Soon thereafter, she tired of her role as enforcer, and figured forty years was long enough to spend at most things.

Former students of all ages stopped her on the street and called. One had phoned last month, an outstanding student who had become a teacher herself. The brilliant ones flourished under her tutelage . . . and none forgot her. People were still telling the story of the sleeping student who awoke to find a sign reading "Rest in Peace" hanging from her neck.

While Zella was at school, she turned to profit her gift for shaping fabric into clothes, tucking and pleating silks for white ladies who could afford such customized things. She felt at peace only when creating, and was mostly glad to have the time to herself. But sometimes her loneliness was something tangible, her companion. The quiet quiet time was punctuated only by the humming of the machine and her outbursts at mistakes. She was swept up with profanity for a time, calling out curses with increasing fervor. She had been surprised at the particular pleasure she had found in the word "shit."

Seeking always, always, to quiet restless hands, she had mastered the entire array of needlecrafts. Her fingers took off like hummingbirds, as if to make up for what her legs could not do. She had quilted, clothed, sweatered, and afghaned her entire family, so that Mattie's child had never known a store-bought dress until the age of 21. Sewing was something her mother had given her, and she could still see her quilting in dim evening light. She had meant to pull her weight with Zella, honing her one marketable skill, the joining of needle and thread. As soon as she moved in, she ordered a brand new Singer and set in to making slipcovers. She never wanted Zella to look back and wonder if she had been saddled with an invalid.

She had forfeited her chance to go to college by marrying right out of high school and beginning a quick slide into financial ruin. Although there had never been a lot of extra money around when she was growing up, her father and Aunt Rose had been smart with what they had. Suddenly, there wasn't enough money for rent and Billy had come home with a silver flask or a new pair of snakeskin shoes. She had known that, although his family owned the first colored drug store in St. Louis, he was spoiled and weak.

But she had had to turn his fumbling and persistent conquest into something. And besides, everyone thought that marriage might grow him up. She had tried to will their union into rightness for three years, but he moved from job to job by day, and prowled at night, propelled only by the drive to enjoy life and look good in the process. It seemed like money slipped through his fingers. Suddenly it was gone, and he had nothing to show for it. Until the day he died, people would say of Billy Sampson that he could "fuck some money up."

Despite the world of her aborted plans, she had set out to expand herself through books. Her mother had read to them ritually, and had told them stories as she finished the sewing that she took in. She remembered jumping on her bed as a little girl to recite her favorite poem with great drama, "to strive to seek to find and not to yield!" Her mother was so surprised that she forgot to scold. The books that Zella couldn't manage to bring arrived by the bookmobile that visited "shut-ins" once a week. She liked to mix up the classics and the latest offerings, and kept a record of what she read, charting her journeys into other worlds. Many a time she and Zella sat up far into the night discussing their favorites. Sharing stanzas from Robert Hayden and Keats. Arguing whether *Finnegan's Wake* was worth the try.

They had fought, venting anger in curses uttered with sweeping arms. Wounding with immediate regret. But then, they were devout about everything they did. Her jealous passion had erupted more than once at intruders, real or imagined. There was a dent in the dining room wall to memorialize one explosion. The cut glass pitcher had sailed through the air in slow motion, of its own volition, it seemed, just missing Zella's head. She had reached out to snatch it back, and then stared, shocked at what her hands had done.

Afterwards, there was only silence as they turned aside from the brush with loss. After walking around it for an entire day, she had quietly gone for the broom and dust pan and had swept the broken glass. They had been speechless for days, and then one afternoon Zella had returned from school with a bouquet of soaring birds of paradise . . . there must have been two dozen . . . and left it on the bed.

They had moved past the pain, but she had tucked it away with the other disillusionments, cordoned off with her indignation. She kept it in a place not too far back. Accessible. Where she could reach it to probe the soreness, or pull it out for view. She knew, now, how little it had mattered, and regretted that she had nurtured it so long.

Some of the best times she could remember were the scrabble bouts at the folding card table they kept in the vestibule. Both determined and fiercely competitive. Both holding out for the seven-letter word. They had had to institute a timer to keep decisions from stretching into night. In summer they had taken the board to the shaded porch with cool drinks to ease the suffocating heat. To watch for the landing of wings and the drifting down of forsythia clouds.

And there were the summer visits to see Mattie's family in Detroit. They set off at dawn with waxed-paper-lined tins of fried chicken and devilled eggs that were gone by the time they hit Louisville, entertaining themselves with word games and twenty questions as they drove. They came, like the seasons, for long spells at a time. One day in early June they would pull up to Mattie's two-family to find someone on the stoop relaying cries of "They're here" to those out back. Bedrooms were switched, furniture rearranged and projects begun. Summer curtains took shape in the dining room workshop where she sequestered herself on cooler days. Pound cakes, preserves, and watermelon pickles appeared, as she swung around the kitchen with the deftness of impassioned determination.

Since Mattie had sat hugging her knees and wide-eyed at the news of Zella's otherness, she had asked no questions. She had listened silently over the years to the things carefully selected for sharing. She figured that what her "sisser" chose must be okay, and when she heard the word "lesbian," she never thought of her. In decades of long-distance holiday calls and letters, Mattie had never failed to include Zella. She had loved her, like a sister, but had kept her distance from the hazy spaces where strange love lived.

She and Zella guarded Mattie's ignorance carefully, displaying just enough affection. Stilling touch. She had wondered often if sudden rage lurked below the surface calm. But in the rare moment when intimacy bled through, when their fingers brushed or she caught something in their eyes for which she had no comfortable name, Mattie turned and busied herself with straightening up.

With Mattie's child, the nature of her love for Zella was never broached. In their zealous protection of her niece's innocence, in their attempt to keep this child from the dangers of things sexual, they had sealed her off from understanding. The not telling grew, until it was larger than the reason why. And soon it was herself, and not her niece, that she protected. She didn't know what the exposure would mean for their love. Would it keep? Would it keep? Would she hesitate before she hugged? Would she pull away behind her eyes in confusion? In anger at her prolonged ignorance? In horror at the shame that implicitly accompanies such silence? Because she could not risk this magic, she was an accomplice in the hiding. Here she had chosen not to speak. She had chosen not to be known.

Disapprovals were never voiced at family reunions on the Cape Cod shore. No openly expressed disdain, even from those with connections more tenuous than blood. Just a veering from all dangerous ground, and the cool whispers that faded on their approach. That one unbelievable time, at the Wilson cottage, when Mattie had burst into a discussion on sleeping arrangements with, "You all need a room away from everyone else, the way you carry on," those nearby had turned away politely with raised eyebrows to gossip behind closed doors.

At times she had longed for open scorn. For the honesty of direct confrontation. And she had tried to use her mechanism for physical suffering on the psychic pain. To apply the coping game that she was already playing now with death. In an hour it will still throb. In a day it will wane. In a month it will scar. In a year it will fade. But she found that unarticulated condemnation made wounds that burned freezer sharp. Wounds that would never make scars. Wounds that would never heal.

She and Zella had grown old together. She remembered when they had first found grey pubic hair. They had laughed, saying it was time to get rid of those tired old things. And she had been shy about her scars at first, covering her nakedness even when alone. But Zella had embraced it all, seeing beauty even in her mangled joints. There had been wrinkles, sagging breasts, and sometimes a passing glance in the mirror that made you stop and look for the girl you had been. In forty years of Sunday afternoons massaging and lathering Zella's hair, she had watched it move through shades of grey into solid white.

And then the stroke came, suddenly, after all the years of encroaching decay, with so little concern for easing them into death. It had raged violently, knocking her from her chair, so that before she realized what was happening, Zella was lying at her side. Zella had lingered a few weeks, recognizing no one, in a place where antiseptic dispositions and artificial cheer were the only weapons against certain death. She had managed to struggle there to see her only once. With all of her illnesses, she had outlived Zella. They had never imagined it like this.

She stood there at the casket, back suddenly in the present. Although only a few moments had elapsed, their years together had passed before her in their richness. She glanced across the room of heavy drapery and slim armless chairs, completing her formal goodbye. And then she moved on, past the section where Zella's family sat, to stand with the close friends.

The parlor filled with eyes that evaded hers, unsure of the response to match the occasion. As she looked around and arranged her crutches to leave, she felt trapped within the walls erected by their fears. She realized that none of them would rock her from grief into acceptance. None of them knew the shape of her love. For forty-seven years, she had lived in a world of reduced proportions, exiled by their theories to untraveled silent space.

Atet A.D.*

An Excerpt

BY NATHANIEL MACKEY

———————————— 21.II.82

Dear Angel of Dust,

No doubt by now you've heard the news of Monk's death. What can one say? No doubt there'll now be outpourings of appreciation, much of it from hitherto silent sources, long overdue. It can never amount to more than too little too late. I'm reminded of how I learned of Duke's death in 1974. I was living up north at the time, in Oakland, and was in the habit of listening to the Berkeley Pacifica station, KPFA. Every weekday morning they had a program called "The Morning Concert," two hours of what's commonly called classical. So exclusively was European and Europe-derived "art music" its regimen that when I turned on the program one morning late in May and heard "Black and Tan Fantasy" I knew it could only mean one thing. Well before the announcer came on and said so I knew Duke was dead.

In any event, the way we heard that Monk had died is that Onaje called Lambert the day the news broke to ask if we'd play in a memorial gig at his club that night. It came as no surprise, Monk having been in a coma for more than a week, though that's not to say it had no impact. Still, as I've already said, what can one say? We agreed with no hesitation to take part in the gig, even though Penguin hadn't yet come out of hiding and even though we didn't know when he would. If playing the gig turned out to mean playing without him we were ready to do so.

Atet A. D. is volume three of *From A Broken Bottle Traces of Perfume Still Emanate*, a series of letters written by composer/multi-instrumentalist N., founding member of a band formerly known as the Mystic Horn Society.

Penguin's retreat, of course, had given rise to a good deal of comment, concern and speculation among us. Drennette even ventured to wonder out loud one day what kind of trip it was he was on, did he go off that way often and, if so, why do we put up with it. This struck us as a little harsh and to me at least it suggested she had a deeper emotional investment in Penguin's doings than she let on. Aunt Nancy wasted no time speaking up. She called Penguin's "trip" an "occupational hazard," repeating Baraka's line that music makes you think of a lot of weird things and that it can even make you become one of them. Clearly, she suggested, Penguin had.

I spoke up as well. Penguin's retreat, I said, struck me as related to something he once told me about Monk. I recounted his telling me of Monk getting into moods in which he'd answer the phone by grumbling, "Monk's not here," then hang up. Penguin's own telephonically announced retreat, I suggested, amounted to a kind of couvade. It was a case of sympathetic ordeal, him turning away from the world in solidarity with Monk. How it came to me to say this I can't entirely say. It simply popped into my head as I spoke. I can, however, say that I deliberately downplayed Penguin's attraction to Drennette, thinking it might be the source of her annoyance. I steered clear of his would-be rap, the aborted recitation I knew was at the root of his retreat. This doesn't, however, explain the particulars which popped into my head to take its place. Nor does it explain why I persisted along these lines even after I saw that my not mentioning his attraction to her seemed to increase instead of lessen Drennette's annoyance. I'm tempted to say that I could feel Penguin feeding me my lines, just as with "E Po Pen," but it wouldn't be true. All I felt was the pull and the appeal of the Monk angle, the fact that it so perfectly fit. (Indeed, so much so that I wondered, even as I spoke, had I gotten things wrong in "E Po Pen," thought Mingus when I should've thought Monk.)

The impromptu connection I drew between Penguin's retreat and Monk's coma seemed to be borne out by what subsequently occurred, the fact that Penguin chose to make his return at the memorial gig. We had no way, as I've already said, of knowing whether he would emerge in time for the gig. Lambert called and left a message on his machine, giving him the details, but by that night, not having heard from him, we accepted having to play without him.

A good-sized crowd showed up at Onaje's. A small place, it was pretty much packed. Considering the short notice, word had gotten around pretty well. Besides us, a number of other bands from around town took part. We each played what was supposed to be a thirty-minute set, though in most cases it turned out more like forty-five. Our set came fairly late, as we were the fifth group to play. We followed a trio led by Badi Taqsim, a pianist who's been turning a lot of heads lately. He mainly plays other people's compositions, among them a good number of standards, but the touch he puts on them is all his own. They finished up their set with a couple of pieces which really tore the place up—Monk's "Pannonica," followed by a John Lewis piece hardly anyone ever does, "Natural Affection." A wistful strain had run thru the set, held in check or bitten back, however, by Monk's ironic pluck and puckish good humor (all the pieces they played, save the last one, were Monk pieces). "Pannonica" took the standoff between wistful plaint and ironic pluck to an almost unbearable pitch before the Lewis piece exacted a surprising denouement. How piano, bass and drums could effect a breathy timbral suspension worthy of Charlie Rouse himself I'll never know, but they somehow did on the former. All the built-up tension, the austere articulacy and the sense of incomplete release, "Natural Affection" then took into another domain. The bossa nova beat, coming after the solemnity of the piece's opening chords, took most of the audience by surprise, introducing an abrupt, dilated liquidity, an agile dilation finessed on several fronts at once. Wistfulness turned into *saudade*.

As I stood there listening I couldn't help remembering that the quality the Brazilians call *saudade* goes back to the homesickness the slaves felt for Africa. A Brazilian friend of mine told me this a few years back and it struck me that Badi must have known it as well, so apt was the evocation of "going home" to the occasion. What got to me was what almost always does with bossa nova, the mix of compliance, complication and complaint it brings off. The piece, that is, was one in which longing, heavily

　　　　　　　　　　　　　　　Making Callaloo

tinged with regret, became complicit with a no-regrets furtherance of itself or beyond itself, a self-possessed rhythmic advance which, when it
was on, ran the line between "of" and "beyond."

But I've gotten caught up with something I really didn't mean to go
on about so long. Suffice it to say that we were there, Badi's trio reminded
us, to see Monk home, that their reading of the piece more than rose to
the occasion, so gently thrusted was its mating of tendency with touch,
that they more than made it live up to its title. Which is also to say that
they put us in just the right mood, just the right frame of mind. They put
us in touch with a well of affection to which we repeatedly had recourse
throughout our set (though "put us in touch" wasn't so much what it
was as that they variously apprised us we already were).

Penguin chose to show up at the gig, as I've already said, but we were
well into our set by the time he did. We had just finished "Reflections,"
our rendition of which, though I hate to brag, was a killer. With Aunt
Nancy on violin and Djamilaa doubling on harmonium and bandoneon,
we gave it an Indo-Argentine reading which, by way of tempo changes
here and there, insisted on links between tango and Baul. Lambert and I
both played tenor, both of us heavily indebted to Sonny Rollins's Blue
Note recording of the piece, most notably the sense of alarm he gets from
the leap to high D in the fifth bar. We gave it that same quantum sense of
duress but added a touch of our own, pulling back as if to declare the
alarm false. If you can imagine the acoustical equivalent of a fade-away
jumpshot you've got a good idea of the approach we took. Aunt Nancy
complicated the figure once or twice with a sirenlike shooting-pain
bowswipe recalling Piazzolla's violinist Fernando Paz. Anyway, it all
added up to murder—so much so that Onaje joked with us later that
he'd considered calling the coroner's office. Things got even more lethal
with our next and, as it turned out, final number, "In Walked Bud." I
went over to alto, Djamilaa switched to piano and Aunt Nancy went
from violin to bass. Djamilaa played the first eight bars unaccompanied,
the rest of us joining in on the first repeat. It was at the beginning of
the second repeat that we heard an oboe join in from near the club's
entrance, perfectly in tune and right on the beat. We looked out over

the heads of the audience, all of whom had turned around to see who the oboist was, and there was Penguin playing away while slowly making his way toward the stage. We went into yet another repeat and still another and, before it was over, several more—an impromptu vamp-till-ready as we waited for Penguin to reach the stage.

Once Penguin was onstage one couldn't help noticing how disheveled he was. He hadn't shaved, his hair hadn't been combed and his clothes looked as if he'd slept in them. What's more, he appeared to have slept outdoors. Twigs, bits of dry grass and even leaves clung to his clothes and to his hair. (We later learned he'd spent the time he'd been away camping out near the Hollywood Reservoir.) One also couldn't help noticing how different he sounded, the expansive, magisterial sound he got from the horn, a voluminous thrust and dimensionality which was all the more pronounced now that he blew into a mike. This was a bigger, rounder, more hollowed-out, holier sound than he'd ever gotten, a sound he sought to surround us with. It was as if he sought to house us in a celestial cave. It was what I can't help calling a *world* sound, a ringing sound which went well beyond the pinched, piercing sound the oboe normally has. This Penguin later attributed to the time he spent practicing during his retreat, his time in what he insisted on calling the "wouldshed." (This apparent concession to the "high would" pun which has more and more come to be common coinage among us, given the manifest advance we'd all heard with our own ears, had a not so subtle smirk woven into it.)

Shortly after Penguin made it onstage we brought our vamp to an end. We went on to the next eight bars and then returned to the first eight, after which Djamilaa tore into a solo which honored Monk in so wincingly dexterous a manner it made one's fingers ache just to be in the same room. What hit was its tolling, tangential resonances, the off-to-one-side ringing she coaxed from the keys, the oblique "bell" she had a way of resorting to now and again, a "bell" which confounded alloy with allure (as though "belle" was much more what it was). Aunt Nancy followed with a bass solo which took alloy farther toward its limit by accentuating "alien" wood. Her right hand, that is, repeatedly left the strings to give the body of the bass a percussive tap or a number of taps, the play between plucked and percussed her way of having some fun with Penguin's heart-throb Drennette. For her part, however, Drennette showed no sign of noticing, going on in as blasé, matter-of-fact, businesslike a way as ever. Penguin, though, did seem to take note, albeit ever so briefly, recovering quickly, adopting a duck's back's attitude to water.

During Djamilaa's solo Lambert had whispered to each of us that Aunt Nancy would solo next, that I'd follow her and that Penguin would, as he put it, "bat clean-up." Penguin then came over to me and whispered that rather than soloing one after the other he and I should do so at the same time, trade choruses and so forth, make it a dialogue, a duet. This I agreed to. When Aunt Nancy finished her solo the two of us took up what turned out to be an extended, increasingly conten-tious conversation. Penguin, I quickly found out, took exception to "E Po Pen," felt it trivialized his retreat. It made too much of his aborted rap to Drennette, too much of the torch it alleged he carried for Djean-nine. This he insisted by way of a bold, falsetto run which embraced "high would" in order to complain of my "low blow." He ended the run by quoting the stuttering, low-register croak Wayne Shorter gets into towards the end of his solo on "Fee-Fi-Fo-Fum," one of the pieces on the *Speak No Evil* album, the point of neither title missing its mark. With that we were off on what ended up being duet, duel and dozens rolled into one. Though a bit surprised at first, Aunt Nancy, Drennette and Djamilaa egged us on, as tight and on-top-of-it a rhythm section as one could want, and Lambert threw in an exhortative two or three notes every now and then. It was somewhat like Freddie Hubbard and Lee Morgan's exchanges on *The Night of the Cookers*, Hawkins and Rol-lins's on *Sonny Meets Hawk*, Mingus and Dolphy's on "What Love" or "So Long Eric." What it came down to was an old-time cuttin' session.

I won't attempt to give you a detailed account. Let me let it go at saying that I held my ground as best I could, arguing that "E Po Pen" struck me as being dictated to me by him (to which he replied I was blaming the victim), that, in any case, a little humor never hurt anyone (to which he replied we'd see who'd laugh last), that, even so, it was his Djeannine dream and only his which had the broken-tooth ending (to which he replied so what), and so forth. It was some of the hottest, heaviest going I've ever taken part in. We worked what seemed like a million variations on "In Walked Bud" and by the end had come up with a new tune that you'll find on the tape I've enclosed. Penguin and I recorded it yesterday, just the two of us, unaccompanied. We set out to recapture what we did at Onaje's and, allowing for the inevitable variances, we succeeded. We call the piece "In Walked Pen."

The thing worth pointing out about both the tape and our duel/duet at Onaje's is that Penguin ultimately prevailed by turning my "low blow" against me. Somehow during his retreat he managed to add a full octave to the bottom end of the oboe's range. Towards the end of our duel/duet he lured me into what amounted to a limbo match, a test of who could go lower. (It was this match, in fact, which brought both our duel/duet and the piece to a conclusion. It also, that night at Onaje's, ended our set, "In Walked Bud" having gone on longer than we'd planned as a result of Penguin showing up.) The alto being pitched over half an octave lower than the oboe, I figured I had it made. He surprised me and everyone else, though, by working his way down past the horn's low B-flat to an even lower B-flat, almost half an octave lower than mine. As he did so I could've sworn I heard the rafters rattle and felt the floor shake. I made the futile gesture of putting my knee in the bell of my horn to play A, though I knew that didn't even come close to making up the difference. Penguin had beat me at what he insisted was my own game, deftly augmenting "high would" with "low would," a stunning move to which my A was a lame comeback, next to none at all. Had it been knives rather than horns we battled with I'd have bled to death.

As ever,

N.

———————————— 27.II.82

Dear Angel of Dust,

Thanks for writing back so soon. What a surprise to receive your "liner notes" to "In Walked Pen." I appreciate your once again encouraging us to put out a record, even more your willingness to write the notes for it. The idea of a "test run" is a good one and I'm glad you thought of it, glad you acted on it as well. I've read your "run" a couple of times and I'm very excited. I particularly like the use you make of narration. Yes, every tune does tell a story. The coy, contingent yarn you spin teases out—instructively so—"In Walked Pen" 's oblique, centrifugal drift. I also like the length you give it. Do you remember those Limelight albums in the 1960s, the ones that opened up sort of like a book and had several pages of liner notes? That's the kind of thing I'd want done with what you've written.

There's one thing, though, I have problems with: the way you belabor the relationship of Penguin's boastful, magisterial sound to rap music. It's not that your play on his would-be rap to Drennette is lost on me, nor that rap isn't the latest in a long tradition of black (male mostly) self-praise and contestual display, a tradition of which our duel/duet is obviously a part. No, it's more a matter of scale and perspective. I wouldn't want anyone to get the idea we were pandering to fashion, putting undue emphasis on something simply because it's in. I'd feel more at ease with your notes if you gave more attention to the wider matrix rap's a part of, were you to drop a few of the rap references for some mention of, say, Memphis Slim's "Sweet Root Man," Bo Diddley's "Who Do You Love," Dexter Gordon's "Soy Califa" (or, for that matter, Pete "El Conde" Rodriguez's "Soy La Ley"), John Lee Hooker's "I'm Bad Like Jesse James," Lord Invader's "Me One Alone" or any number of others too numerous to list. There's nothing new about swagger.

What *is* new is that since I last wrote there's begun to be talk about changing the name of the band. It was Drennette who brought it up. She complained at rehearsal the other day that "Mystic Horn Society" privileges the horns, emphasizes them at the other instruments' expense. She went on to say that since our sound wouldn't be what it is were *any* of the instruments missing she saw no reason to single out the horns as in some way worthy of special notice. It was a point none of us could disagree with. Aunt Nancy was quick to chime in that not only was Drennette right but that the problem went farther, that the name smacks of male privilege, given that the horns are played primarily by the men in the group. "To say nothing," she capped it off by saying, "of the phallic associations horns have."

This last remark had a funny effect on me. I had no problem with Drennette's complaint, nor with Aunt Nancy's addendum apropos male privilege. Something inside me, however, instinctively objected to the "phallic associations" bit, the easy, one-sided equation it rested on, the reductiveness of it. The phrase triggered—antithetically triggered—the recollection of a dream I hadn't thought about in years. Almost before I knew it I found myself speaking up to say that while I agreed with almost everything that had been said I thought the phallic bit was going too far. I then proceeded to recount, as a counter example, the dream which had just come back to me again, a dream I'd had when I was about eight, the circumstances surrounding which I recounted as well. I explained that as a kid I was a big fan of rock and roll—Little Richard, Chuck Berry, Bill Haley and the like—and that I was also under the influence of the church, that my mother, at my grandmother's insistence, had started me going to Sunday school when I was five. I explained that I thought about Judgement Day a lot and that having heard that to listen to rock and roll was a sin had me worried. I found it hard to believe it was and different people gave different opinions, but, I explained further, I worried about it anyway. I then recounted how one night I decided to settle the question, how when I said my prayers that night I asked God to send me a sign: to make me dream of pirates if it was true that listening to rock and roll was a sin, to make me dream of cowboys if it wasn't. I went on to how it ended up I dreamt about neither pirates nor cowboys that night but dreamt instead I was in a dark room in which I heard a sinuous, arresting piece of music played on what sounded like a cross between a trumpet and a bassoon; how it went on that way for a while, me standing in the dark, unable to see anything, caught up in the music; how finally a spotlight came on and illumined a figure quite some distance away from me and how with that it became clear that this figure was where the music was coming from; how I knew now I was in a large auditorium and began walking towards the spotlighted figure; how as I got closer I could tell the figure was a woman and, closer yet, that she had no clothes on and that the music was as much a scent as it was a sound, a synaesthetic mix (part music, part musk), a penetrating mist of sound which was earthy, ethereal, refined and funky, all at the same time; how as I got even closer I could tell the music emanated from a horn between the spotlighted woman's thighs, a cornucopic horn without the grapes and so forth, though I couldn't make out whether it was a part of her body or simply held in place by pressure put on it by her legs; how when I reached the stage and finally stood in front of her I couldn't resist sticking my nose up over the lip of the horn to "smell" the music better; how when I did my eyes crossed and rolled around before closing and my head shot back in slow motion as I went into a swoon.

Once I finished there was a silence lasting a moment or two before Aunt Nancy, nonplussed, rolled her eyes in mock motherly amazement and exclaimed, "Such a precocious child! Yes, the Lord does work in mysterious ways." Everyone laughed and I blushed a bit. She went on to add, however, that, all joking aside, even though my dream might simply be the exception which proves the rule she was willing to back off on the phallic business, that that wasn't the main point anyway and that if no one could come up with a reason not to we should start thinking about a new name for the band. No one could. Neither could anyone come up with a new name that all of us liked. We're still thinking about it.

Thanks again for the notes.

Yours,

N.

_____ 11.III.82

Dear Angel of Dust,

I found myself going back to your "liner notes" again and again over the past few days. The ipseic surmise they engage the music with kept calling me back—that along with a wish to have my own way with what you'd written, a wish I couldn't quite shake even though I told myself I should. It's not so much that I had quarrels with your take on the piece as that the more I read your notes the more it seemed I stood on revisionary ground, so exponential the seismic suzerainty ipseity served. Sesame squared I'm tempted to call it, Earth of sesame to the second power, ground grown rich with susurrant seed, an open aliquance insisting on emendation. (One of Cecil Taylor's titles, "Chorus of Seed," comes to mind.) Seismic seed not only fed me but, as if I were a muscle, flexed me. I found myself changing words here and there, making notes in the margins, putting my own stylistic spin on this, that and the other. That spin bore an antithetical bent, the ongoing gist or gestation of an *opera contra naturam*. Your notes were clearly lecture/libretto material. The results you'll find enclosed.

As you can see, the changes are not that radical. I followed your lead at all points. Your notes ended up, it seems to me, not so much rewritten as differently pitched. Seismic seed's pneumatic sprout, however much it recast or reconceived your tack, for the most part reconfirmed it.

Anyway, let me know what you think.

Yours,

N.

In Walked Pen or, The Creaking of the Word: After-the-Fact Lecture/Libretto (A.D. Version)

Penguin's return coincided with the news of Monk's death. Newly descended from an ancient line of authority figures, he came back having crowned himself King Pen. Some, he knew, would think of King Oliver,

King Pleasure, King Curtis, Nat King Cole. Duke, Prez, Count, Prince Lasha and others would also come to mind. It went, in fact, much farther back than any of them, farther back than he himself had initially suspected. It went farther back than the 'Lection Day fifes and drums he'd heard the moment the crown touched his head, farther back than the Pinkster eelpot he'd heard not more than a split-second after that.

King Pen had come into antiphonal play with "monastic flight," Penguin's loose, euphemistic term for Monk's death. A funereal wedding of church and state, nominal kingship heralded the end of charismatic retreat. The quality Lambert once referred to as Monk's "renunciative harmonics" had long struck a mendicant chord deep within. Even so, Penguin seized upon the occasion of "monastic flight" (a further phase of the mock-awkward mantle, the gnostic shrug Monk so regally wore) to inaugurate a new recourse to power, a return to the world.

"I went off," Penguin announced on his return, "to prepare a place. The alternate authority of would-be kings no longer sufficed. Gassire's lute-song notwithstanding, I went after an order of metathetic spin which would, pardon the expression, cash in on a eurythmic aplomb typically consecrated to forfeiture, debility, loss." He stopped, feeling he sounded too rhetorical. N. had already heard it all anyway.

Penguin had gone off to Wouldly Ridge but he'd kept N. abreast of his thoughts off and on, getting in touch by telepathic dispatch when some such incident of note as his coronation came up. N. too had heard the fifes and drums and the Pinkster eelpot the moment the crown touched Penguin's head. They'd both also heard a voice—a faint, far-away voice which asked, "Who are our true rulers?" Possessed of a strong 19th-century accent, the voice, barely pausing a beat, went on to answer, "The Negro poets, to be sure. Do they not set the fashion, and give laws to the public taste? Let one of them, in the swamps of Carolina, compose a new song, and it no sooner reaches the ear of a white amateur, than it is written down, amended (that is, almost spoilt), printed, and then put upon a course of rapid dissemination, to cease only with the utmost bounds of Anglo-Saxondom, perhaps with the world. Meanwhile, the poor author digs away with his hoe, utterly ignorant of his greatness." That they'd both heard it had to do with the odd bond

Penguin's retreat had brought to the surface, the otherwise Atlantislike relational "glue" which took the place of place. It was as if the "place" he'd gone off to prepare was not so much a place as a certain rapport, a "place" neither wholly here nor wholly there. It was a "place" which was more than one place at once, a utopic ubiquity which, though always there, was never all there.

Nonetheless, Penguin's hideaway had indeed been a place. Tucked away in a wooded area near the Hollywood Reservoir, Wouldly Ridge overlooked the L.A. Basin. It was there Penguin had pitched his tent after taking a run around the reservoir. Indian vision quest and early American camp meeting rolled into one, his retreat had begun with an unbased ring shout, the atavistic shuffle he took his jog around the reservoir to be.

Before going off Penguin had suffered a romantic setback. This was widely known to be the reason he went off. Going into hiding near the reservoir was an attempt to get back in touch with something he feared had begun to get away. His womanly thought-soul he called it, adopting the Dogon idea of a female intelligent kikínu held in reserve in the family pool—an idea N. had turned him on to some time ago. Perhaps it was this which had made for the brotherly rapport which telepathically kept the two of them in touch.

" 'Cash in,' " Penguin resumed after a pause, "isn't quite the right way to put it." He paused again. His mouth was dry. He was no longer sure he had N.'s attention. Afraid he'd see that he didn't, he looked away, out the living room window, deliberately avoiding eye contact.

As the two of them sat there in N.'s living room the odd, psychosomatic thirst from which he'd suffered while on Wouldly Ridge again, for a moment, parched his mouth and throat. It had been a thirst he couldn't shake no matter how much he drank, a thirst made all the more intransigent, it seemed, by the nearness of the reservoir. It had been as if water was there in too much abundance, as if the thought of so much held in reserve refuted satiety. If, as he'd once read, thirst proves water's existence, wasn't the converse also true? The whole time on Wouldly Ridge he'd felt like a dying man on a desert, his thirst seeming at times, deliriously, like a thirst for diminution, a wish that the reservoir were smaller, the watery, womanly thought-soul he sought to replenish notwithstanding. "A spoonful," he'd found himself muttering, "just a spoonful." "Spoonful" had become a kind of mantra he often resorted to over the course of his retreat. "Spoonful, spoonful," he'd intone from time to time, seeking to soothe (and to some degree succeeding) his parched mouth and throat's insatiate "fling" with proximate water.

N. looked at Penguin, who continued gazing out the window. He wondered what had made him fall silent. No longer telepathically in touch, he had no way of knowing that Penguin's thoughts were on Wouldly Ridge, that he sat absorbed in recollecting the spill he'd suffered three days into his retreat. Even so, he himself felt a slight centrifugal rush as a somewhat stronger centrifugal rush took hold of Penguin, an ultimately phantom centrifugal sense of being swirled or swung or, "ec" to "centric" water, flung. This was the sense Penguin had had during his run around the reservoir on day three of his retreat—not so much a mere sense, though, as an outright force causing his legs to cross and him to go tumbling to the ground.

"At first I felt it had to be that I was being punished," Penguin muttered, more to himself than to N. but breaking the silence none-theless. He continued to not make eye contact, gazing out the window. "My centrifugal fling with womanly water had led to a fall. An ever so faint atavistic voice pointed out that my legs had crossed and for a moment I'd been dancing. My head hit the ground and I saw the Big Dipper, the 'drinking gourd' the same voice had said I should follow. It seemed to rebuke the diminution I sought, cosmically magnify the man-tric spoonful I'd invoked. Oddly enough, it was then, I think, that my accession to the throne began, adumbrated by the 'starry crown,' to use the voice's expression, I saw swirling right above my head. There was something baptismal about the astral splash my spill brought me abreast of. Yes, my head hit the ground and I saw stars. This was the wet celestial seed of which King Pen appears to've been born."

N. wasn't sure he got Penguin's drift but he went on listening with-out interrupting. Penguin had sent no telepathic dispatch on this matter. This was the first he'd heard of the spill. It gave him a lot to think about and he was having a hard time keeping up. Did Penguin mean to suggest, he wondered, that he himself (that is, Penguin) had assumed the role of womanly water? Did he mean to say that he'd been dipped into, that the "starry crown," the magnified spoonful, capped an interior, "southern" sky? The long journey from humble gourd to coronal spoonful he could follow, though he'd have wanted it to be a northward one. Was it, after all, merely sublimation, he wondered, couvade?

Drennette, N. remembered, had suffered a spill she credited with revelatory impact, an epiphanous bicycle accident she said had turned her sense of things around. Did Penguin seek to spark some sort of parallel with her by claiming to have similarly suffered a revelatory spill? Did he mean to show that he too could invoke a blow to the head, that the initiatic tie between spill and spirit was an experiential truth to which he too was now privy? If so, in what spirit did he seek to do so? Was it rapport or was it one-up-manship he sought? Did he mean to install himself as King to Drennette's Queen or was he claiming a throne all to himself? Why had he so far made no mention of her? These were the questions N. sat asking himself while Penguin made such pronouncements as "I gave birth to myself on Wouldly Ridge," "King Pen is for real and it's him I really am," "Monk died so King Pen could be born."

After a while N. could sit quietly no longer. "What about Drennette?" he interrupted to ask.

Penguin stopped talking but went on gazing out the window. He himself realized he'd suffered multiple blows. The blow to his head when he fell while jogging had been followed the next day by the news of Monk's death. The problematic turn his interest in Drennette had taken, he had to admit, was the blow to which those two were like aftershocks. The looped allusion to womanly water to which his run around the reservoir amounted he continued to conceive as a ring shout—unbased because of Drennette's anti-antiphonal silence. Her non-response had sent him off in search of inner resources, the atavistic, "southern" chorus whose antiphonal support placed him on the throne. He caught the point of N.'s question at once and wanted to answer that the throne was solely the King's, that it rested on antiphonal authority which wasn't hers, that Drennette could in no way be said to be his Queen. On the other hand, he quickly admitted to himself, Drennette's non-response had mothered his need to give birth to King Pen, his need to break womanly water to become his own unmatched body of water—to *thirst*, outward water notwithstanding. "Yes," he said, turning at last to look at N., "for a time the throne I sought was the oceanic sway of Drennette's hips. I'm way beyond that now. King Pen sits on his own." It was a surprising way to put it, surprising even to himself, and he paused to reflect a moment before going on. "The fifes and drums and the Pinkster eelpot I heard made it clear I'd made it north, that no matter how compensatory it appeared it was no mirage. No, this was no 'southern' sky lit by an illusory Dipper, no wishful pursuit of illusory depth, no illusory spoonful's putative plunge. No, this was true north."

N. felt he'd been caught out. He himself had heard the fifes and drums and the Pinkster eelpot, a fact which didn't leave much room for the kinds of questions he'd been entertaining. The slight centrifugal rush he'd felt should also have taught him something. What was at stake was the nature of true rule, the circumambular cast of an antiphonal north natively known to be true, quixotic needle notwithstanding. Penguin had apparently picked up on this, apparently read his thoughts or in some other way known that "What about Drennette?" was a loaded question. His powers were not to be dismissed or taken lightly. King Pen had to be reckoned with.

All of this N. already knew. Penguin did nothing more than make him admit it. Native knowledge went a long way to "explain" circumambular north but in the end had not really gone anywhere. What had gone was explanation itself, the tangential demand put on perimetric spill by centric water.

For a short while they sat silently looking at one another. Penguin then turned his head and went back to gazing out the window, whereupon N. once more felt a slight centrifugal rush. The inexplicable sense of having been flung caused a shiver to run up his back, a sharp, anti-explanatory twinge which made him sit up straight. "Explanation," he found himself saying, "is the pail of water we used to dance with atop our heads in slavery times. Would you agree that post-explanatory spillage's 'Hush now, don't' takes the cake nowadays?"

Penguin turned and looked at N. again, a look on his face which seemed to ask what was going on. N.'s tangential comment had touched on the limits of explanatory truth, the perimetric defects of circumambular persuasion, circular trope and treadmill rolled into one. Even so, N. again found himself tempted. An explanatory model proposed itself in which the would-be bond between phallic plunge and philosophic spoonful surfaced again. Before he could stop himself he gave in to it, taking advantage of Penguin's non-response to insist, "You've still got a chance with Drennette if you'll only come down from Would-Be Ridge."

No sooner had N. said this than they both felt a further centrifugal rush, an oblique furtherance of an emergent prospect or principle whose outline remained obscure. The lateral drift accelerated by N.'s pointed play on "Wouldly" was not without a vertical aspect, a sense of tilt, disorientation or erosion which made it feel as though as they slid they lost elevation as well. "Would-Be Ridge" 's intimation of unreliable support, much to N.'s own chagrin, fostered a sense that the floor sank as they slid across it. He himself couldn't shake the feeling that he slid upon a precipitous ledge, inexplicably dependent upon a hypothetic surface which might not have been there. Thus it was that epithetic "Would-Be" boomeranged against him. He found he'd cast a more inclusive net than he'd intended. Not only had he reversed his earlier position regarding Drennette (encouraging Penguin to pursue her whereas before he'd urged him to cool it), he'd also cast aspersions on Wouldly Ridge. Neither of these had he intended to do. It was this, the irrelevance of intention, which undermined his living room floor, made it more and more hypothetic. Hypothetic floor, moreover, might as well have been epithetic Ridge—a reversal which was by no means lost on him.

Penguin, on the other hand, endured the further centrifugal rush and the sense of tilt with the firm conviction that they were evidence of King Pen's power. Tangential drift and the loss of elevation paradoxically bolstered the throne on which he sat. Tilt and slide recalled the oceanic sway he'd spoken of in regard to Drennette's hips, an ironic accession to the "throne" he'd earlier insisted he'd gone beyond. With this he rubbed N.'s innuendo in his face, tilt and slide taking less time than the blinking of an eye, at the end of which he sat grinning with satisfaction. "I didn't come here to be insulted," he told N. He'd made it clear that King Pen didn't play.

N. understood he'd been put in his place. The pail of water crowning the slave's head, he reflected, might as well have been a dunce's cap. Penguin had answered with an antiphonal spoonful, an ever so slight bit of spillage he'd endowed with the movement of a wave about to break. Crest, crown and womanly rump rolled into one, the tilting, sliding sense of a "spilling" floor had brought N. up short. That this had occurred at all would've been wonder enough. That it was done with a mere spoonful of water—spilled water—humbled him all the more.

Having made it clear that King Pen didn't play, Penguin now went on to insist that "What about Monk?" was much more to the point. "Monastic flight," he said, "brought home to me the fact that in retreating to Wouldly Ridge I was looking for a meeting of would-be king with worldly king, the fact that wouldly reign sought to reconcile the two. Monkish, renunciative accent unquenchably thirsted after wouldly rule. That this was the case was all the more obvious now that Monk was gone. When I heard the news I couldn't help thinking of 'New Monastery,' Andrew's piece. The title of the album it's on, *Point of Departure*, ratified my sense of tangential vocation. Call it the rendezvous of *tendency* with *point*, or, better yet, say that the prospect of punctual access *lifted*, possessed of a centrifugal 'high.' "

Penguin fell silent, his head slightly tilted like a bird's. The implications of lifted access caused him to pause and reflect a while. Tendency and point's conjunctive capture, their joint possession by centrifugal "high," felt as if point no longer yielded to explanatory pressure.

N. studied the look on Penguin's face while giving some thought to what he'd said. It was an odd, not entirely convincing take, he thought, having more to do with Monk's name than with the music or the man. Still, the Andrew Hill piece to which Penguin had referred happened to be one of his favorites. The mix of watery verticality and angular surge it pulled off had taken hold of him what seemed like ages ago. The mere mention of it now filled his head with the synaesthetic images of staggered ignition which had filled it the first time he heard the piece—subaquatic fountains and jets, underwater fireworks giving Penguin's pursuit of womanly thought-soul all the more oomph. Even so, N. continued to apply a grain of salt to Penguin's take on Monk's death, a take he increasingly felt to be offbase—deliberately so, thera-peutically so perhaps, but bordering on disrespect all the same. He had a hard time not meeting disrespect with disrespect, a hard time refrain-ing from asking, "What about Djeannine? What about lilac time?"

Repressing the question hurt the tip of his tongue. It was a question alluding to a song which had recently come to his attention, a song Gene Austin recorded in the 1920s, "Jeannine, I Dream of Lilac Time." That the song had been featured in a movie, *Lilac Time*, a movie starring Colleen Moore and Gary Cooper, made the question all the more sar-castic. Behind its dig lay the lines "Jeannine, my queen of lilac time, / When I return, I'll make you mine." Penguin's return, the question implied, was mere fantasy resolution; King Pen's throne a mere would-be seat beside his dream-queen Djeannine.

It was an allusion, however, whose bite would've been lost on Pen-guin. N. himself had only recently learned of the song, having happened upon Austin's recording on an album he found in a used record store. He had no reason to believe Penguin had ever heard of it. The question was thus one whose dig he'd have to explain—all the more reason, he admitted, not to ask it. Even so, it took an immense effort to hold it back, so immense he literally bit his tongue, applied a steady, clamplike pressure with his teeth. As he did so he couldn't help wondering was reverse bite, boomeranging bite, yet another demonstration of King Pen's power.

N.'s nose now began to twitch. The smell of lilacs wafted in from some abrupt, immediately suspect source he thought of turning his head to try to catch offguard—a thought it took no more than a moment to reject. Years ago he'd read liner notes on an Eric Dolphy album, notes which spoke of Dolphy's "impatience," his wish to "sneak" past limits. "He implies beyond the horn," the notes had asserted. "He tries to sneak through its limitations at some swift, flat angle." The passage had stayed with him, stuck in his mind, more or less verbatim. It was exactly that "swift, flat angle" from which he now felt himself addressed, an obtuse, tangential angle thru which the lilac scent made its way. The resistance of any such angle to attribution argued against turning his head. He knew too well it would've done no good.

The clamplike pressure of his teeth on his tongue and the angular advent of lilac scent made for a synaesthetic wad of apprehension to which the eelpot's return was now added. The sound of it came in loud and clear, entering at exactly the same "swift, flat angle" the smell of lilacs took. Smell, touch and hearing were rolled into one by the lilac vibe, an unsettling mix which made it evident that Penguin had not only read his thoughts but succeeded in turning them against him again. The eelpot completed the combination which took him out, an epiphanous "click" not unlike sesame access except that it was clamp-lilac-eelpot access instead.

Yes, he now knew for sure, reverse bite, boomeranging bite, was another demonstration of King Pen's power. A split-second before he passed out he glimpsed a spoon spinning slowly like the blade of a fan just above Penguin's head, a suspended "crown" which, hovering halolike, confirmed the now uncontested majesty of King Pen.

from The River People

BY JOHN MCCLUSKEY, JR.

The River People *is a novel-in-progress which treats the trials and triumphs of a small band who have achieved fellowship and seek a land for the sustaining of that fellowship. Julian, their reluctant leader, comes across a crude map during his travels in the American West. That map and the group's commitment to find a home lead them to West Africa and Brazil. They wind up near Cincinnati where Julian is rehearsing his story for the press.*

"SO THAT WAS THE END OF THE BEGINNING WHEN YOU WERE CALLED TO THE CITY, TO SUFFER A SEASON IN ITS WILDERNESS? WHAT OF THE TEMPTATIONS AND HOW DID YOU FIND YOUR WAY? AND, STILL WHAT OF FAITH?"

The scribe would sit, pen poised.

A city can cruelly test faith, break it down. Strangers watch while you gather pieces from the gutter.

That year the snows came early to northern Ohio. In November, just after Soviet Premier Khrushchev had vowed to have a Russian on the planet Mars by 1984, thirteen inches of snow covered Cleveland in two days. Julian arrived in that snowstorm, the Soviet leader's words bracketed in red in a torn column folded deeply in a jacket pocket. Three days later while leaving a White Castle diner and with the job listings from the morning *Plain Dealer* in hand, Julian suddenly stopped in the middle of the sidewalk. A gust of wind made him squint as he looked up.

"You! Teacher!" His mouth fell open. A finger was pointed directly under his nose. The finger, the frayed cuff and now the dirty sleeve belonged to a short wiry man with watery red eyes. The bottom edges of his mustache were crusted. His light grey jacket was too short, grimy around the pockets. In the fist of his other hand the man held a cigarette which he brought slowly to a corner of his mouth. At the same time he lowered the accusing finger. A panhandler, Julian concluded. He relaxed.

"How about a light, chief?"

"OK, but what's the jive about 'teacher'?" he asked as he fished through his pockets.

"You're a teacher, though you don't know it yet. You were born on the Aquarius-Pisces cusp. You tried your hand at basketball once, but gave it up because of your lousy jumpshot. You settled for baseball, at shortstop to be specific, and you could have been better than Pee Wee Reese and Jackie Robinson put together." The man was seized by a fit of coughing, spat brown against the snow. "Your favorite color is deep blue and your taste in women favors those who are fine, the color of a puddle of maple syrup on a white saucer, and extra big in the right places. You look for sweetness in melancholy. And you're running away from a marriage."

Julian rocked on his heels, wheeled around for some partner with his bio sheet flashing this to the panhandler. But there were only laborers rushing through the cold, while pulling up their collars as they passed, blowing into their fists and cursing low. He offered the matches as if surrendering ransom.

"How can you tell so much? How do you know what you know? You from Union City?"

The man tapped his head, then his chest twice. "Just something I've always had since I was a jitter-bug, just yea-high. A gift, they calls it. They claim I was born with a cawl over my eyes and black cat bones in both of my little fists. A seventh son got nothing on me. I've done everything but make money from my gift."

Julian was past simple curiosity. The jobs could wait for a minute or so. "Here let's get out of the cold. I'll buy you a cup of coffee." He folded the newspaper and led the man back into the White Castle.

Over a packet of french fries drowned in ketchup and a steaming cup of coffee, the man narrowed one eye and pulled at one end of his mustache. "The thing you have to understand, youngblood, is that you have to trust your instincts at the same time you study. There is no contradiction in that."

from The River People   225

Julian had been starved for conversation those first days away from home. He accepted it anywhere he found it—busses, street corners, laundromats, checkout lines in cramped grocery stores. He needed other voices to drown out his doubt about walking into the wilderness. He had yearned for the bright and clear path. Imagined himself in those first days away as walking into his college classes, certain and clean explanations waiting. Or in a spaceman's suit of fabric to be invented with a name he would imagine he must mispronounce, strapping on his helmet. Such things were definite, solid. How far could he trust the advice of this stranger who talked so familiarly to him and who belched loudly after his second sip from his coffee?

"Excuse that one," the man said, tapping his stomach and pushing on before Julian could comment. "I can tell that you are studying. What—I cannot say. I done studied a little myself over the years. A little mathematics here, some Islam there. Architecture, poetry. I ain't bragging, but I done brushed up against most things. Down at the library there's this fine little librarian who calls me 'The Hook' because of the way I go through there latching onto books. I'd like to latch on to that fine foxy young thing if you really want to know the truth about it."

His low laughter erupted into another coughing spell. Julian waited still, searching for the con lurking among the man's words, the trapdoor beneath his prophecy and easy familiarity. Had he simply strung together some lucky guesses? With a cat's patience the man licked ketchup from his fingers. Julian decided on the surprise attack, the same approach he had used with the palm reader.

"What are you after?" he asked.

"Hmm?" The man was caught with a finger in his mouth.

"This reading of everything, this prophesying—what does it add up to?"

The man relaxed, blew into his coffee, kept his eyes to its surface. "I don't raise that question no more. The search is an end in itself. Let's just call it nervous energy. I hope that the things I learn, my little bit of knowledge, can benefit others especially he who has come with knowledge far greater than mine." He paused and looked up. "Course, most folks think I'm nutty, but I think we know better, eh? I think we on the same wavelength, you and me. It came to me clear as everything out there on the sidewalk. We know that there are protests and disciples and the great army of gropers and the even greater army of the indifferent. Most things in the world is tied together by only a few messengers of love. Well, I been a disciple waiting by the side of the road for the real messenger."

"And you will know him when he comes?"

"He has come. And I follow."

Through the window Julian could see a knot of people, about fifteen or so waiting for a bus. A steady stream of people moved past the window now—out of these dozens why was he picked? Was there something about the way he stood on the sidewalk? About his coat or cap? Why so elaborate a scheme for a cup of coffee and french fries? "The Savior," anyone who sits patiently and listens to rambling? He tried again.

"Stop jiving, man. It's too early in the morning."

The man raised his right hand. "I swear before the Creator." The last time he had heard an oath delivered so solemnly was Reynaldo's pledge about the safety of his condoms. "How can you doubt? Wasn't I right about your sign, the jumpshot? The honey in your blues? You can't deny any of that . . ."

"Lucky guesses don't add up to any kind of gospel."

"Call it what you will, chief, but there's a whole army of souls out here waiting on your word." He leaned closer. "And I'll tell you something else. You want to fly and soar and do. You will, inside. But there's more of a riverboat captain than an astronaut in your soul. Yep, more than you know."

"All this is flattering, but, see, this morning I have a job to find. I've got to eat."

"You will be fed."

"I barely have a decent roof over my head."

"You will be sheltered." The man dug into his jacket pocket and pulled out a soiled pouch. He loosened the drawstring, glanced around, then emptied the contents on their table. Two gold watches, a diamond ring, and sapphire pendant sparkled.

Julian quickly stood. "I think you have the wrong guy. Last week I was a foreman in a factory, had a nice house. I don't know you or what you're talking about."

"Wait! These ain't stolen. They's mine. I had them for years. They part of the family treasure. You studyin' wrong if you think I'm a common thief."

He walked away. When he turned to see the man gathering his things and trying to follow, Julian pushed through the door and started to jog.

"No, wait!"

As if responding to someone who had just whispered his name, he awoke in a dingy room he had rented in a three-story rooming house. The room smelled of fried onions and damp newspapers. The roaches were bold, sauntered to their hiding places when the light was pulled on. The lumpy mattress offered cruel fists to his back and sides. Just as insistent had been the dream: he eased through the dimly-lit maze of hallways, hands reaching from the walls pulled at him, his arms, his legs. The hands were warm and when he moved on the fingers would not clutch at his clothing. Near the ends of each hall he heard muffled voices but when he came close there was only silence. He would find another hallway, again the hands, again the smear of voices until after many such wanderings he entered a hallway, hands starting up again, and he heard his name and he started a slow jog to the source. In mid-stride he awoke. His mouth tasted of wood ashes and a burst of imagined fleas worked up his stomach from his groin.

The second floor was graced with a communal/common bathroom, so the morning's hottest water belonged to the earliest risers. He had just jumped from his bed when he heard the bathroom door slam and the lock click into place. Ten minutes wait, at least. As he dressed and gathered his towel, he charted his moves through the morning. The corner drugstore for the newspaper, coffee and donuts at the counter as he read the job listings. Today he must find work.

At home his family would be stirring, school awaiting the two children, work for Iris. The children would then sit down to oatmeal at 7:15 and Iris would finish getting ready. What would the neighbors be saying by now? ("He run off with some younger woman?" "Was he fired?" "Just no 'count, no good nigger.") Iris could handle it, deflect it, but for how long? He figured that she would never be caught alone without one of the children and would bend to attend to the child when the questions grew too pointed.

When he heard the toilet flush and the door open, he grabbed his soap and toothbrush and sprinted into the hallway. Then he slowed. The White Castle disciple was squatting next to his door and carefully lighting the butt of a cigarette.

"How long have you been out here?" Julian asked, still inching toward the bathroom.

The man straightened and yawned. "Not long." Breath of stale coffee, eyes of pain.

Julian walked from him and locked the bathroom door behind him. This man, this strange man tailing him, might he be not a free-lance disciple, but some definite evil stalking him? Was his guilt trying to nag him into the confession of sin? He showered, gargled, spat. Then tried to comb at his hair. He smiled into the mirror. Maybe the man is just a harmless drifter, a little loose upstairs is all. Bad grapes can do that to you over the long haul. Outside Julian did not bother to even talk with the man. He walked quickly, hoping to tire the grizzled shadow that whispered drily. But the same wind that tore at his face, the same flying grit from the wake of trucks and buses must have caught the shadow's face and eyes.

"Damned dirty city," Julian could hear him say from behind. "The first pure-D important step is to get land far from this grimy city. Land that you can work with your hands, that leaves the character of your handprint. We all need to sniff the smell of dirt from our palms."

Julian grunted and hopped a bus heading downtown. The man got on and took a seat behind him, close, hot breath across the back of his neck.

Julian turned slightly. "What's your name? We really haven't gotten to names yet."

"Some call me Groundhog because I can call down the spring, never see no shadow. Now others have called me Old Crazy Nigger. Then I done gone by 'The Hook'—I told you about that one, yeah. Been called Old—Bad—Foot-Man-Blocking-The-Sidewalk, Case Number 44612, Sweet Meat, Daddy, Soldier. Before all them I was Royal Mickens. But I like Groundhog the best 'cause it tells you about my potential." He ran the back of a hand across his mouth.

"I ask for a name and you give me your history," Julian said.

"A name is a history." Short brown teeth for a smile.

The bus moved through quiet, neat neighborhoods of old, two-story frame houses. Clerks and saleswomen got on. Riot of perfumes. Julian smiled at one woman who sat across from him, her thick legs crossed, a foot in red leather, rocking.

Then: "How did you find me, Groundhog?"

"Contacts. I got eyes and ears all over the colored neighborhoods. Plus I knew you wasn't downtown at the Plaza. I knew you'd slip into town humble-like. So I had you figured two ways. When you ran off yesterday, I knew it'd be just a matter of time."

Julian smiled a grudging smile. "You don't believe in straight answers. . . ."

"Ask me a straight question."

Julian dug into his pocket, turning. "You want to hit me for a dollar? OK, here's a dollar and save us both some time and breath."

Groundhog gently pushed away the hand that held the dollar bill just under his nose. "You know that ain't it. You know that way deep down, if you know anything. Would I follow you around and wear out good shoe leather when I can get me a dollar in forty-seven different ways? I ain't a beggar."

"Well, what then?" At Julian's shout a few glanced around sharply. Across the aisle the woman sat up, a finger tapping her chin. The man called Groundhog stiffened, then leaned back in his seat. "How come you keep following me? You don't know me. I don't know you. How come?"

The man was silent for awhile, scratching his neck. Up front the driver's look of concern could be seen in the mirror above his head. A stickup on number 6? Then Groundhog spoke in a tiny voice, threaded off by phlegm. Julian wanted to clear his own throat for him.

"But I've already told you how come. Don't deny me."

They rode the rest of the way in silence. Julian got off at a busy intersection near the center of the shopping district, weaving through the gauntlet of panhandlers, past battalions of hurrying secretaries, turning on occasions without slowing to admire anonymous legs.

He wound up in the offices of an employment agency he had applied to. A bleached blonde woman who seemed too young for conducting interviews told him there was a job open.

"Selling shoes just three blocks from here. You're lucky." She had studied her bright red nails through most of the interview and now as he paused she tapped a nail with a pencil.

"Yes, I'll take it."

She handed him the card with the store's address typed on one side. "Good luck," she said as methodically as she might say "take a seat."

Outside the glare of the sun hit him with the suddenness of a slap. He was also met by Groundhog, his sole supporter in this city. Without a word he started for the shoe store. He saw himself forcing the latest style pumps on the feet of thick-ankled matrons, saw himself sliding wingtips on the feet of frowning businessmen. Well, it's a way to make a living. Never spit on honest work, he always told himself.

Without looking back he knew that his shadow darkened the face of Groundhog, could smell the familiar breath against his neck. He began to weave through the crowd like a loping halfback. Then he jogged, stopped quickly and raced into a bar.

He headed through the dim room and found the men's room. Locked it. Waited. "Dude must have needed to go pretty bad," he heard. Waited. Could hear commotion clearly from the street. "Ain't you got no manners ol' half-blind fool?" Minutes later the doorknob turned twice, once slowly, then quickly. Then he heard footsteps moving away. Waited still and heard the roll of a coin into the jukebox slot, heard the whir of the selector, the pause, the touchdown of the needle. There was a moment's crackle before the first bars of a blues, Albert King's "Crosscut saw." He could smell now the fresh bar of deodorizer in the pit of the urinal. He had not paid much attention to the kind of bar he had rushed into. It was just the first open building available to give the slip to the strange man trailing him.

He hoped that Groundhog was back on the sun-splashed street, scratching his chin and looking for another savior. The doorknob rattled again and this time a deep voice boomed.

"Don't make your home in there, slick."

"Hold tight, OK?" he shouted.

"I'm holding the best I can, but I can't hold off all morning."

He came out and nodded to a stocky reddish-brown man in a mail carrier's uniform. Several other mailmen sat at the bar laughing loudly as the music played. As he moved past them, he half-expected a hand to emerge from the wall, a tap on his shoulder, and a voice, "How about a little guidance and direction, captain?" He was chuckling to himself by the time he stepped outside into the cold.

He paused in the doorway and scanned the street. He saw no disciple in run-down, knob-toed shoes nearby so he started off again to the shoe store. He couldn't be late. He was certain that he would prove a dazzling salesman and move up in no time. Then he would find another, bigger job and in a few months he would send for the family. He and Iris would work their schedules in such a way that both would finish with their degrees, then Iris would go on to medical school and he would begin his flying career modestly as, say, an air force reserve pilot. If only they could be patient, they could regain their path and the ascent before they reached thirty-five. Looking over his shoulder now, walking quickly, almost loping, he had made three blocks with such thoughts. At an intersection a fire truck, its siren screaming, roared past. By the next intersection he was wondering about other ways to prepare himself, about local space research sites he could visit and query about such things. Then there was a sudden squeal of tires, followed by two long screams. A car, fishtailing, slowed just in front of him and he met squarely the frightened look of a teen-aged driver. His dark hair whipping, the boy looked over his shoulder. Then the car jerked forward, his head snapped back, and the car made the next corner on two screaming, smoking wheels.

Julian turned back to join a crowd gathering along the curb. Like others standing at the rear he stood on tiptoes for a look at what must be the seriously hurt, judging by the terror in the boy's eyes. He elbowed his way to the front, then stopped. In the street and on his side, one arm spread as if pulled and twisted back, the other forward like a signal to ward off a blow to the chest, lay the man who called himself Groundhog. Blood oozed from the slightly opened mouth and from under his hand. His trousers fluttered across the back of his legs.

"Is he dead?" a woman asked near Julian. "Is there a doctor? Somebody, won't somebody help that poor man?"

Head reeling, Julian did not know how long he stood there nor when he stepped forward to kneel and reach toward Groundhog's hand. He noticed that one of Groundhog's shoes had been knocked off by the impact.

"Get back, get back now!" A policeman was a blue storm upon him, his bulk cutting off the sun. "You two know this man?"

Staring at the shoe, newspaper squares lining the sole and the heels run down to nothing, Julian had not noticed another man checking for a pulse. Julian shrugged and stood. "Not really. I saw him around, that's all. I mean . . ."

The cop was gruff with swagger, tried to tame the crowd but could not disguise the nervousness in his voice. A few women in bright wool coats trotted off, one with a handkerchief to her mouth as she wept. A siren could be heard approaching from far away. There would be a story of death, swift and brutal, to spread during that morning's first coffee break. Who would know of this man's strange quest, the gleam of his last intention? Was there a family or a friend who endured his moods? Would anyone in this world miss him, claim him? In a few weeks would that pretty librarian he talked about look up from the file cabinet one afternoon, consider the snow falling slowly past her window and discover that the limping man had not been in recently to flatter her?

Julian looked down at his own trembling hands, then clenched them into fists. In the dead man's other hand was a slip of paper. He reached again for the hand, decided against it. He turned and moved away. A few were describing the car to the officer, one even getting part of the license plate number. "Some punk kid, officer," he heard someone say. "I saw him speed up to make the light."

Julian wandered the streets for an hour. What was in that hand? He would think of it years later during reveries in other parts of the world. Could it have been a map of his own destiny? And if it were, would it have made any difference to have it then before he had started on even the second step of his journey? He could not know. He only knew that he was taking a feeble step to direct his life, to feel it whole again, and up popped a stranger to nudge him toward some mystery. You could be minding your own business, whistling as you walked down the street, glancing in shop windows like any solid citizen, and someone would come along and fit you with a custom-made plan. He had to be careful, alert.

Thick clouds swallowed the sun. Before night the edges of rivers would melt and the sky would cry. He stopped to blow his nose, then hurried to find his job.

Ma'Dear

(for Estelle Ragsdale)

BY TERRY MCMILLAN

Last year the cost of living crunched me and I got tired of begging from Peter to pay Paul, so I took in three roomers. Two of em is live-in nurses and only come around here on weekends. Even then they don't talk to me much, except when they hand me their money orders. One is from Trinidad and the other is from Jamaica. Every winter they quit their jobs, fill up two and three barrels with I don't know what, ship em home, and follow behind on an airplane. They come back in the spring and start all over. Then there's the little college girl, Juanita, who claims she's going for architecture. Seem like to me that was always men's work, but I don't say nothing. She grown.

I'm seventy-two. Been a widow for the past thirty-two years. Weren't like I asked for all this solitude, just that couldn't nobody else take Jessie's place is all. He knew it. And I knew it. He fell and hit his head real bad on the tracks going to fetch us some fresh picked corn and okra for me to make us some succotash, and never come to. I couldn't picture myself with no other man, even though I looked after a few years of being alone in this big old house, walking from room to room with nobody to talk to, cook or clean for, and not much company either.

I missed him for the longest time, and thought I could find a man just like him, sincerely like him, but I couldn't. Went out for a spell with Esther Davis' ex-husband, Whimpy, but he was crazy. Drank too much bootleg and then started memorizing on World War I and how hard he fought and didn't get no respect and not a ounce of recognition for his heroic deeds. The only war Whimpy been in is with me for not keeping him around. He bragged something fearless about how he could'a been the heavyweight champion of the world. Didn't weigh but 160 pounds and shorter than me.

Chester Rutledge almost worked ceptin he was boring, never had nothing on his mind worth talking about; claimed he didn't think about nothing besides me. Said his mind was always clear and visible. He just moved around like a zombie and worked hard at the cement foundry. Insisted on giving me his paychecks, which I kindly took for a while, but when I didn't want to be bothered no more, I stopped taking his money. He got on my nerves too bad so I had to tell him I'd rather have a man with no money and a busy mind, least I'd know he's active somewheres. His feelings was hurt bad and he cussed me out, but we still friends to this very day. He in the home you know, and I visits him regular. Takes him magazines and cuts out his horoscope and the comic strips from the newspaper and lets him read em in correct order.

Big Bill Ronsonville tried to convince me that I shoulda married him instead of Jessie but he couldn't make me a believer of it. All he wanted to do was put his big rusty hands all on me without asking and smile at me with that big gold tooth sparkling and glittering in my face and tell me how lavish I was, lavish being a new word he just learnt. He kept wanting to take me for night rides way out in the country, out there by Smith Creek where ain't nothing but deep black ditches, giant mosquitoes, loud crickets, lightening bugs and loose pigs, and turn off his motor. His breath stank like whiskey though he claimed and swore on the Bible he didn't drank no liquor. Aside from that his hands were way too heavy and hard, hurt me, sometimes left red marks on me like I been sucked on. I told him finally that I was too light for him, that I needed a smaller, more gentle man and he said he knew exactly what I meant.

If you want to know the truth, after him I didn't think much about men the way I used too. Lost track of the ones who upped and died or the ones who couldn't do nothing if they was alive nohow. So, since nobody else seemed to be able to wear Jessie's shoes, I just stuck to myself all these years.

• • •

My life ain't so bad now cause I'm used to being alone, and takes good care of myself. Occasionally I still has a good time. I goes to the park and sits for hours in good weather; watch folks move and listen in on confidential conversations. I add up numbers on license plates to keep my mind alert unless they pass too fast. This gives me a clear idea of how many folks is visiting from out of town. I can about guess the color of every state now too. Once or twice a month I go to the matinee on Wednesdays, providing ain't no long line of senior citizens cause they can be so slow; miss half the picture show waiting for them to count their change and get their popcorn.

Sometimes, when I'm sitting in the park, I feed the pigeons old cornbread crumbs, and I wonders what it'll be like not looking at the snow falling from the sky, not seeing the leaves form on the trees, not hearing no car engines, no sirens, no babies crying, not brushing my hair at night, drinking my Lipton tea and not being able to go to bed early.

But right now, to tell you the truth, it don't bother me all *that* much. What is bothering me is my case worker. She supposed to pay me a visit tomorrow because my nosey neighbor, Clarabelle, saw two big trucks outside, one come right after the other, and she wondered what I was getting so new and so big that I needed trucks. My mama used to tell me that sometimes you can't see for looking. Clarabelle's had it out to do me in ever since last spring when I had the siding put on the house. I used the last of Jessie's insurance money cause the roof had been leaking so bad and the wood rotted and the paint chipped so much that it looked like a wicked old witch lived here. The house looked brand new, and she couldn't stand to see an old woman's house looking better than hers. She know I been had roomers, and now all of a sudden my case worker claim she just want to visit to see how I'm doing, when really what she want to know is what I'm up to. Clarabelle work in her office.

The truth is my boiler broke and they was here to put in a new one. We liked to froze to death in here for two days. Yeah, I had a little chump change in the bank, but when they told me it was gonna cost

$2,000 to get some heat, I cried. I had $862 in the bank. $300 of it I had just spent on this couch I got on sale; it was in the other truck. After twenty years the springs finally broke and I figured it was time to buy a new one cause I ain't one for living in poverty, even at my age. $200 was for my church's cross-country bus trip this summer.

Jessie's sister, Willamae, took out a loan for me to get the boiler, and I don't know how long it's gonna take me to pay her back. She only charge me fifteen or twenty dollars a month, depending. I probably be dead by the time it get down to zero.

My bank wouldn't give me the loan for the boiler, but then they keep sending me letters almost every week trying to get me to refinance my house. They must thank I'm senile or something. On they best stationery, they write me. They say I'm up in age and wouldn't I like to take that trip I've been putting off because of no extra money. What trip? They tell me if I refinance my house for more than what I owe, which is about $3,000, that I could have enough money left over to go anywhere. Why would I want to refinance my house at fourteen and a half percent when I'm paying four and a half now? I ain't that stupid. They say dream about clear blue water, palm trees and orange suns. Last night I dreamt I was doing a backstroke between big blue waves and tipped my straw hat down over my forehead and fell asleep under an umbrella. They made me think about it. And they asked me what would I do if I was to die today? They're what got me to thinking about all this dying mess in the first place. It never would've layed in my mind so heavy if they hadn't kept reminding me of it. Who would pay off your house? Wouldn't I feel bad leaving this kind of a burden on my family? What family they talking about? I don't even know where my people is no more.

I ain't gonna lie. It ain't easy being old. But I ain't complaining neither, cause I learned how to stretch my social security check. My roomers pay the house note and I pay the taxes. Oil is sky high. Medicaid pays my doctor bills. I got a letter what told me to apply for foodstamps. That case worker come here and checked to see if I had a real kitchen. When she saw I had a stove and sink and refrigerator, she didn't like the idea that my house was almost paid for, and just knew I was lying about having roomers. "Are you certain that you reside here alone?" she asked me. "I'm certain," I said. She searched every inch of my cabinets to make sure I didn't have two of the same kinds of food, which would've been a dead giveaway. I hid it all in the basement inside the washing machine and dryer. Luckily, both of the nurses was in the islands at the time, and Juanita was visiting some boy what live in D.C.

After she come here and caused me so much eruptions, I had to make trip after trip down to that office. They had me filling out all kinds of forms and still held up my stamps. I got tired of answering the same questions over and over and finally told em to keep their old food stamps. I ain't got to beg nobody to eat. I know how to keep myself comfortable and clean and well fed. I manage to buy my staples and toiletries and once in a while, a few extras, like potato chips, ice cream and maybe a porkchop.

My mama taught me when I was young, that no matter how poor you are, always eat nourishing food and your body will last. Learn to conserve, she said. So I keeps all my empty margarine containers and stores white rice, peas and carrots (my favorites) or my turnips from the garden in there. I can manage a garden when my arthritis ain't acting up. And water is the key. I drinks plenty of it like the doctor told me and I cheats, eats Oreo cookies and saltines. They fills me right up too. And when I feels like it, rolls homemade bisquits, eats them with Alga syrup if I can find it at the store, and that sticks with me most of the day.

Long time ago, used to be I'd worry like crazy about gaining weight and my face breaking out from too many sweets, and about cellulite forming all over my hips and thighs. Of course, I was trying to catch Jessie then, though I didn't know it at the time. I was really just being cute, flirting, trying to see if I could get attention. Just so happens I lucked up and got all of his. Caught him like he was a spider and I was the web.

Lord, I'd be trying to look all sassy and prim. Have my hair all did, it be curled tight in rows that I wouldn't comb out for hours till they cooled off after Connie Curtis did it for a dollar and a Budweiser. Would take that dollar out my special savings which I kept hid under the record player in the front room. My hair used to be fine too: long and thick and black, past my shoulders, and mens used to say, "Girl, you sure got a head of hair on them shoulders there, don't it make your neck sweat?" But I didn't never bother answering, just blushed and smiled and kept on walking, trying hard not to switch cause mama told me my behind was too big for my age and to watch out or I'd be luring grown mens toward me. Humph! I loved it though, made me feel pretty, special, like I had attraction.

Ain't quite the same no more though. I looks in the mirror at myself and I sees wrinkles, lots of them, and my skin look like it all be trying to run down towards my toes but then it changed its mind and just stayed there, sagging and lagging, laying limp against my thick bones. Shoot, mens used to say how sexy I was with these high cheeks, tell me I looked swollen, like I was pregnant, but it was just me, being all healthy and everything. My teeth was even bright white and straight in a row then. They ain't so bad now, cause ain't none of em mine. But I only been to the dentist twice in my whole life and that was cause on Easter Sunday I was in so much pain he didn't have time to take no x-ray and yanked it right out cause my mama told him to do anything he had to to shut me up. Second time was the last time, and that was cause the whole top row and the fat ones way in the back on the bottom ached me so bad the dentist yanked em all out so I wouldn't have to be bothered no more.

Don't get me wrong, I don't miss being young. I did everything I wanted to do and then some. I loved hard. But you take Jessie's niece, Thelma. She pitiful. Only twenty-six, don't think she made it past the tenth grade, got three children by different men, no husband and on welfare. Let her tell it, ain't nothing out here but dogs. I know some of these men out here ain't worth a pot to piss in, but all of em ain't dogs. There's gotta be some young Jessies floating somewhere in this world. My mama always told me you gotta have something to give if you want to get something in return. Thelma got long fingernails.

Me, myself, I didn't have no kids. Not cause I didn't want none or couldn't have none, just that Jessie wasn't full and couldn't give me the juices I needed to make no babies. I accepted it cause I really wanted him all to myself, even if he couldn't give me no new bloodlines. He was satisfying enough for me, quite satisfying if you don't mind me repeating myself.

I don't understand Thelma, like a lot of these young peoples. I be watching em on the streets and on t.v. I be hearing things they be doing to themselves when I'm under the dryer at the beauty shop. (I go to the beauty shop once a month cause it make me feel like thangs ain't over yet. She give me a henna so the silver have a gold tint to it.) I can't afford it, but there ain't too many luxuries I can. I let her put makeup on me too if it's a Saturday and I feel like doing some window shopping. I still know how to flirt and sometimes I get stares too. It feel good to be looked at and admired at my age. I try hard to keep myself up. Every weekday morning at 5:30 I do exercises with the t.v. set, when it don't hurt to stretch.

But like I was saying, Thelma and these young people don't look healthy, and they spirits is always so low. I watch em on the streets, on the train, when I'm going to the doctor. I looks in their eyes and they be red or brown where they supposed to be milky white and got bags deeper and heavier than mine, and I been through some thangs. I hear they be using these drugs of variety and I can't understand why they need to use all these things to get from day to day. From what I do hear, it's supposed to give em much pleasure and make their minds disappear or make em not feel the thangs they supposed to be feeling anyway.

Heck, when I was young, we drank sarsaparilla and couldn't even buy no wine or any kind of liquor in no store. These youngsters ain't but eighteen and twenty, and buys anything with a bite to it. I've seen em sit in front of the store and drank a whole bottle in one sitting. Girls too.

We didn't have no dreams of carrying on like that, and specially on no corner. We was young ladies and young men with respect for ourselfs. And we didn't smoke none of them funny cigarettes all twisted up with no filters that smell like burning dirt. I ask myself, I say Ma'Dear, what's wrong with these kids? They can read and write and do arithmetic, finish high school, go to college and get letters behind their names, but everyday I hear the neighbors complain that one of they youngsters done dropped out.

Lord, what I wouldn'ta done to finish high school and been able to write a full sentence or even went to college. I reckon I'da been a room decorator. I know they calls it be that fancy name now, interior designer, but it boil down to the same thang. I guess it's cause I loves so to make my surroundings pleasant, even right pretty, so I feels like a invited guest in my own house. And I always did have a flair for color. Folks used to say, "Hazel, for somebody as poor as a church mouse, you got better taste in thangs than them Rockefellers!" Used to sew up a storm too. Covered my mama's raggedy duffold and chairs. Made her a bedspread with matching pillowcases. Didn't mix more than two different patterns either. Make you dizzy.

Wouldn't that be just fine, being an interior designer? Learning the proper names of thangs and recognizing labels in catalogs, giving peoples my business cards and wearing a two piece with white gloves. "Yes, I decorated the Hartley's and Cunningham's home. It was such a pleasant experience. And they're such lovely people, simply lovely," I'da said. Could'a told those rich folks just what they needed in their bedrooms, front rooms and specially in the kitchen. So many of em still don't know what to do in there.

But like I was saying before I got all off the track, some of these young people don't appreciate what they got. And they don't know thangs like we used to. We knew about eating fresh vegetables from the garden, growing and picking em ourselves. What going to church was, being honest and faithful. Trusting each other. Leaving our front door open. We knew what it was like to starve and get cheated yearly when our crops didn't add up the way we figured. We suffered together, not separately. These youngsters don't know about suffering for any stretch of time. I hear em on the train complaining cause they can't afford no Club-Med, no new record playing albums, cowboy boots or those Brooke-Shields-Calvin-Klein blue jeans I see on t.v. They be complaining about nonsense. Do they ever read books since they been taught is what I want to know? Do they be learning things and trying to figure out what to do with it?

And these young girls with all this thick makeup caked on their faces, wearing these high heels they can't hardly walk in. Trying to be cute. I used to wear high heels mind you, with silk stockings, but at least I could walk in em. Jessie had a car then. Would pick me up, and I'd walk real careful down the front steps like I just won the Miss America pageant, one step at a time and slide into his shiny black Ford. All the neighbors peeked through the curtains cause I was sure enough riding in a real automobile with my legitimate boyfriend.

If Jessie was here now I'd have somebody to talk to. Somebody to touch my skin. He'd probably take his fingers and run em through my hair like he used to; kiss me on my nose and tickle me where it made me laugh. I just loved it when he kissed me. My mind be so light and I felt tickled and precious. Have to sit down sometime just to get hold of myself.

If he was here, I probably woulda beat him in three games of checkers by now and he'd be trying to get even. But since today is Thursday, I'd be standing in that window over there waiting for him to get home from work, and when I got tired or the sun be in my eyes, I'd hear the taps on his wing tips coming up the front porch. Sometime, even now, I watch for him, but I know he ain't coming back. Not that he wouldn't if he could, mind you, cause he always told me I made him feel lightning lighting up his heart.

Don't get me wrong, I got friends, though a heap of em is dead or got tubes coming out of their noses or going all through their bodies every which-a-way. Some in the old folks home. I thank the Lord I ain't stuck in one of them places. I ain't never gonna get that old. They might as well just bury me standing up if I do. I don't want to be no nuisance to nobody and I can't stand being around a lot of sick people for too long.

I visits Gunther and Chester when I can, and Vivian who I grew up with, but no soon as I walk through them long hallways, I get depressed. They lay there all limp and helpless, staring at the ceiling like they're really looking at something, or sitting stiff in their rocking chairs, pitiful, watching t.v. and don't be knowing what they watching half the time. They laugh when ain't nothing funny. They wait for it to get dark so they know it's time to go to sleep. They relatives don't hardly come visit em, just folks like me. Whimpy don't understand a word I say and it makes me grateful I ain't lost no more than I have.

Sometime, we sits on the sun porch rocking like fools; don't say one word to each other for hours. But last time Gunther told me about his grandson what got accepted to Stanford University and another one at a University in Michigan. I asked him where was Stanford and he said he didn't know. "What difference do it make?" he asked. "It's one of those uppity schools for rich smart white people," he said. "The important thang is that my black grandson won a scholarship there which mean he don't have to pay a dime to go." I told him I know what a scholarship is. I ain't stupid. Gunther said he was gonna be there for at least four years or so, and by that time he would be a professional. "Professional what?" I asked. "Who cares, Ma'Dear, he gonna be a professional at whatever it is he learnt." Vivian started mumbling when she heard us talking, cause she still like to be the center of attention. When she was nineteen she was Miss Springfield Gardens. Now, she can't stand the thought that she old and wrinkled. She started yacking about all the places she'd been to, even described the landscape like she was looking at a photograph. She ain't been but twenty-two miles north of here in her entire life and that's right there in that home.

Like I said, and this is the last time I'm gonna mention it, I don't mind being old, it's just that sometime I don't need all this solitude. You can't do everything by yourself and expect to have as much fun if somebody was there doing it with you. That's why when I'm feeling jittery or melancholy for long stretches, I read the Bible and it soothes me. I water my morning glories and amaryllis. I babysit for Thelma every now and then, cause she don't trust me with the kids for too long. She mainly call on holidays and my birthday. And she the only one who don't forget my birthday: August 19th. She tell me I'm a Leo, that I got fire in my blood. She may be right, cause once in a while I gets a churning desire to be smothered in Jessie's arms again.

Anyway, it's getting late, but I ain't tired. I feel pretty good. That old case worker thank she gonna get the truth out of me. She don't scare me. It ain't none of her business that I got money coming in here besides my social security check. How they spect a human being to live off $369 a month in this day and age is what I wanna know. Everytime I walk out my front door it cost me at least two dollars. I bet she making thousands and got credit cards galore. Probably got a summer house on the Island and goes to Florida every January. If she found out how much I was getting from my roomers, the government would make me pay back a dollar for every two I made. I best to get my tail on upstairs and clear everything off their bureaus. I can hide all the nurses's stuff in the attic; they won't be back till next month. Juanita been living out of trunks since she got here, so if the woman ask what's in em, I'll tell her, old sheets and pillowcases and memories.

On second thought, I thank I'm gonna take me a bubble bath first, and dust my chest with talcum powder, then I'll make myself a hot cup of Lipton's and paint my fingernails clear cause my hands feel pretty steady. I can get up at five and do all that other mess; case worker is always late anyway. After she leave, if it ain't snowing too bad, I'll go to the museum and look at the new paintings in the left wing. By the time she get here, I gotta make out like I'm a lonely old widow stuck in a big old house just sitting here waiting to die.

from Cambridge

Without rank and order any society, no matter how sophisticated, is doomed to admit the worst kind of anarchy. In this West Indian sphere there is amongst the white people too little attention paid to differences of class. A white skin would appear passport enough to a life of privilege, without due regard to the grade of individuals within the range of that standing. The only exception I have so far observed was the modesty displayed by the book-keeper who first conveyed me here. However, sensible to propriety, he has subsequently maintained his distance. The other men, perhaps because I am a woman, have shown little courtesy in affording the attentions proper to my rank. They converse with me as freely and as openly as they wish. This is barely tolerable amongst the whites, but when I find the blacks hereabouts behaving in the same manner I cannot abide it, and see no reason why I should accommodate myself to the lack of decorum which characterizes this local practice.

Today I arrived at the luncheon table and yet again found Mr. Brown's strange and haughty black woman, Christiania, seated opposite me. I ordered her to retire from the table, for I am not accustomed to eating my meal in the company of slaves. Further, I informed this coal-black *ape-woman* that I desired her to put on a serving gown and take up a role among my attendants, male and female, who properly circled the table to wait upon their mistress. On a property belonging to Christian owners, this was her rightful place. Unfortunately, she seemed to display a total lack of concern at my words, and showed no sign of quitting her chair, so I asked her again if she would kindly remove her person in order that I might commence my luncheon. The wench cast on me a look of intense passion that indeed appeared unhinged, her eyes blazing with a malice the source of which I imagined to reside deep in her bosom, springing from some other hurt than that which I had inflicted upon her. Her manner becoming frivolous, she then tossed her

246   Making Callaloo

head in seeming annoyance. "Massa say I can eat at table. Why missy not like me?" This, as you might imagine, only served to compound the insult of her presence. That she was asking after me an explanation of my behavior caused my blood to overheat, and I began to tremble with indignation.

Again, this time in a more uncompromising voice, I ordered her to rise and leave my table. When it became clear that she was set on her stubborn course, I turned to the chief butler, a slight-looking fellow greying around the temples who, it must be admitted, appeared at least as outraged as I by this woman's display of intransigence. I ordered this black retainer to escort the negress from my table. He immediately set down his burnished silver platter and approached her, whereupon she began to scream in the most reckless and foul-spoken manner, spitting out words whose meaning I dared not imagine. It proved sufficient to cause the butler to back away. The unfortunate lackey turned to me, pleading for clemency, "Missy, she too dangerous, altogether too dangerous." For a third time, now beside myself with fury, I shouted my commands at the black woman, but her lungs were better fitted for the occasion than mine, as she loosed her invective upon me, howling and hurling abuse like some sooty witch from *Macbeth*. At this juncture, I am sorry to admit, my cue was to flee into the sanctuary of my bedchamber where I concealed both my tear-stained face and my impotent rage.

I had determined to isolate myself in my soft and feminine chamber, uncharacteristic of the Great House, until the merciful day of my departure, which I knew I would welcome much as a prisoner might greet the end of his hated sentence. It was then that I heard a knock upon the door, and the quiet voice of my companion Stella. I drew back the bolt and admitted her to my chamber, whereupon I noted that she seemed equally afflicted by the events that I had recently been compelled to endure. Further, she appeared distressed that she had not been in attendance to offer me support both moral and practical. Quickly I shut in the door and bade her rest in a large basket-chair, while I reclined upon the Holland sheet. "Missy," she began, "Christiania is obeah woman, but massa do like she and that is enough." Well, this was information too rich for me to comprehend at once, so I asked her to explain.

According to Stella's testimony, the negro belief in *obeah* involves the possession of a variety of strange objects which are used for incantations: cats' ears, the feet of various animals, human hair, fish bones, etc., all of which make their vital contribution to the practice of the magical art. One skilled in the practice of obeah is able to both deliver persons to, and retrieve them from the clutches of their enemies. Such practitioners hold great sway over their fellow blacks, and they sell medicines and charms in profusion, thus acquiring a status unsurpassed within the community. It would appear that this traffic in charms and remedies is the business of Christiania, which manifestly explained the reluctance of my other slaves to cross the woman, but assuredly did not explain Mr. Brown's desire to have her share his table.

Putting aside all modesty, I felt it only proper that I investigate further. I asked if the black Christiania was indeed a slave and the property of my family. "Yes, missy. She in your service." *But what is her role on the estate?* "Missy, she just in the house. She don't have no use as such." I began to grow impatient. I asked if she was something to Mr. Brown, but Stella professed ignorance of what I was suggesting. I informed Stella that I had been sufficiently alert to realize that it is sometimes the custom for white men to retain what they term *housekeepers*. These swarthy dependents elevate their status by prostrating themselves. Stella was vociferous, in defense of whom I am not sure. She spoke against these liaisons with such force that I recalled the proverbial saw that "the lady doth protest too much." I did not think that I imagined a conspiracy of black womanhood against white, but I knew that I would find this difficult to prove. Therefore I thought it best to reveal to Stella my awareness of such *amours*, in the hope that she would realize that by speaking frankly, she was unlikely to cause me grief.

Apparently such illicit relationships came about because comparatively few wives journey out to the tropics, and those that do are often distinguished by the meagerness of their conversation with their husbands. As a result concubinage appears to have become universal. I revealed to Stella that I was also aware that the highest position on which a sable damsel could set her sights was to become the mistress of a white man. They seek such unions with planters, overseers, book-keepers, doctors, merchants and lawyers, and when their beauties fail, they seek similar positions for their daughters, knowing that success will assure them of a life of ease and prestige among their own people. This much I have gleaned from my brief perusal of the tawdry newspapers, from conversation, and from a knowledge of human conduct observed not only in these parts but in England also. Naturally, the children of such unions receive the status of the slave mother, unless manumitted by their fathers. They seldom achieve recognition as full heirs, and rarely rise above the skills of the artisan. These hybrid people, who hold themselves above the black, but below the white, abound throughout these island possessions as physical evidence of moral corruption.

All of this I conveyed to Stella in the hope that she might be persuaded to share her knowledge with me, but I succeeded only in arousing her ire. It appeared that she took offense at the manner in which I portrayed the ambitions of black womanhood, but she manifested her rage not by overt onslaught, but by covert smoldering. I asked her if it were not true that young black wenches are inclined to lay themselves out for white lovers, and hence bring forth a spurious and degenerate breed, neither fit for the field nor for any work that the true-bred negro would relish. She would not answer. I asked her if it was not entirely understandable that such women would become licentious and insolent past all bearing because of their privileged position? Again, she would say nothing in response. I informed her that I have even heard intelligence that if a mulatto child threatens to interrupt a black woman's pleasure, or become a troublesome heir, there are certain herbs and medicines, including the juice of the cassava plant, which seldom fail to free the mother from this inconvenience. At this point Stella seemed ready to quit my chamber. Her insolence fired me, and I resolved to cast my accusatory stone where it properly belonged. I demanded that Stella immediately conduct me to Mr. Brown. At this Stella protested that it was the height of the afternoon, and that I should not be exposed to the vertical rays from on high, but I insisted. The arrogance of the inky wench, who had dared publicly to preside at my table, still burned within me. I wished to quiz Mr. Brown as to her status.

Indeed the sun was high. I had but stepped ten paces from the Great House before I knew that I ought not to be so exposed. Stella was correct. We were attended by Hazard and Androcles, two inferior lackeys who carried our parasols and sauntered along with an air which belongs to creatures unfettered by those responsibilities which are the familiar burden of rational humanity. Stella carried herself with comical self-assurance, quite as if she were a white. I can remember little of the walk to the fields, where according to *fair* Stella our Mr. Brown was supervising his drivers, but I do recall that on more than one occasion I felt sure that I should expire before we reached our destination. Inwardly I cursed myself for even attempting such a journey, but after what seemed an eternity Stella finally pointed out Mr. Brown. As we approached, a flight of birds rose in the air and cast a shadow like that of a cloud, causing the sun to darken for a few seconds. I found new resolution, and stormed ingloriously across the field, leaving instructions that Stella was not to follow.

The slaves ceased their Sisyphean labors and inclined their heads towards the wild Englishwoman charging across the denuded cane-piece. Noticing this, Mr. Brown understood that something was amiss. He too turned and watched, waiting, hands upon hips and whip in hand, for my approach. "Mr. Brown," I demanded, "what is the meaning of this black woman sharing my dining table?" Mr. Brown stared at me as though I had finally taken leave of my senses in this inhospitable climate. "I will not tolerate such a vile and offensive perversion of good taste," I cried. "I demand your assurance that she will never again be allowed to disgrace my table." Mr. Brown raised a hand to block the sun from his face. He seemed rather confused by my performance, and he nodded as though uncertain of why he was doing so. For sometime we stood, toe to toe, two solitary white people under the powerful sun, casting off our garments of white decorum before the black hordes, each vying for supremacy over the other.

I played my final card. "Mr. Brown, if you do not display more consideration for my position, immediately upon my return I shall have you replaced." Mr. Brown, with no discernible movement of his body, and certainly without taking his eyes from my face, called to his trustee, Fox. He ordered this black man to bear me back to the Great House. Fox, a somewhat docile but evidently sturdy negro, positioned himself before me. I repeated my threat, but Mr. Brown simply uttered the word "Fox," at which point the nigger laid his black hands upon my body, at which I screamed and felt my stomach turn in revulsion, at which its contents emptied upon the ground. Despite the heat of the day, I felt a cold shudder through my body, and I tried desperately to keep back a sob of distress. Thereafter, I have to confess that my memory remains blank until I regained consciousness in the coolness of my chamber with my Stella in attendance on me.

I judged from the sounds of nature without, and the darkness within, that the later hours of the evening were upon us. I was pleased to see the loyal Stella hover over me with concern writ large and bold across her sooty face. How far she has come in matching the loyalty of the dearly departed Isabella! Although sadly lacking the natural advantages of my former companion, and incapable of mastering even the most elementary intellectual science of the alphabet, my sable companion has virtue still. Her smiling ebon face and broadly grinning lips, which display to good advantage her two rows of ivory, offer a greeting that has helped make tolerable my sojourn on this small island in the Americas. I have been thinking seriously of taking her back with me to England, but my fear is that she may be mocked as an exotic, as are the other blacks who congregate about the parish of St. Giles and in divers parts of our kingdom. However, when the time is ripe I will suggest to her that she might wish to meet with her master in his own country, the prospect of which, I am sure, will delight her. I cannot believe that any West Indian negro would spurn the opportunity of serving their master a quart of ale and a tossed tea-cake on a wintry English night.

On my regaining fuller awareness, my first enquiry of Stella brought forth the much feared response. Indeed there was much to regret. It would appear that Fox carried me bodily back to the Great

House, and Stella has sat with me since. Stella informed me that Mr. McDonald was summoned to attend, and that having done so he has stayed on in the hope that he might be present once I had recovered my senses. I instructed Stella to send him away, which she proceeded to do. She returned within the minute, a light smile etched upon her sable countenance. It seems that she is no longer fond of our physician, having detected a certain warmth in his passions towards me which she is happy to see dowsed by my new coolness. Stella served me yet another glass of the medicinal *sangaree* and began to inform me of Mr. Brown's concern for my condition. I said nothing, thus giving her the chance to release from within whatever was troubling her mind. She paused, and then seized the opportunity. Stella suggested that Mr. Brown is in a difficult situation, having neither wife, nor children, and he has been upon this plantation for many years, first as bookkeeper, lately as assistant, and now as overseer and manager. I let her continue. Stella added that nobody knows the plantation as Mr. Brown does and that although he is hard, and perhaps a little coarse and unconventional, he is generally known to be a fair man, the implication behind the black woman's peroration being that my conduct had been somehow improper to interfere in his smooth running of the estate. I sighed. What this sooty illiterate could never hope to understand is that by coming to visit I was far exceeding the duties that most proprietors set for themselves. And without a visit, I could never have discovered that my father's deputed authority was being abused and his property, including dear Stella, exploited. I held my tongue and let her continue. Her final words on the subject were poignant, if somewhat offensive, although I took it that they were not meant to be interpreted as being disrespectful. "Here is no place for missy. Missy have a better life in her own country." I smiled at Stella, even as I felt my eyelids grow heavy with sleep's ever-increasing burden. So missy have a better life in her own country? Perhaps Stella thinks that missy ought to hurry back to Mr. Thomas Lockwood? Perhaps Stella thinks missy is jealous of Christiania and her obeah? Who knows what she thinks. I asked Stella to sit with me, worried as

I was that my dreams might become over-populated with dark incu-bae. She turned down the light, folded her hands into a comfortable bundle, and dropped them into her dark lap. I knew she would not desert me, not this evening.

Ascent by Balloon from the Yard of Walnut Street Jail

BY JOHN EDGAR WIDEMAN

I am the first of my African race in space. For this achievement I received accolades and commendations galore. Numerous offers for the story of my life. I'm told several unauthorized broadsides, purporting to be the true facts of my case from my very own lips, are being peddled about town already. A petition circulates entreating me to run for public office.

Clearly my tale is irresistible, the arc of my life emblematic of our fledgling nation's destiny, its promise for the poor and oppressed from all corners of the globe. Born of a despised race, wallowing in sin as a youth, then a prisoner in a cage, yet I rose, I rose. To unimaginable heights. Despite my humble origins, my unworthiness, my sordid past, I rose. A Lazarus in this Brave New World.

Even in a day of crude technology and maddeningly slow pace, I was an overnight sensation. A mob of forty thousand, including the President himself, hero of Trenton and Valley Forge, the father of our country as some have construed him in the press, attended the event that launched me into the public eye.

The event—no doubt you've heard of it, unless you are, as I once was, one of those unfortunates who must wear a black hood and speak not, nor be spoken to—the event that transformed me from convict to celebrity received the following notice in the Pennsylvania Gazette:

"On January 19, 1793, Jean-Pierre Blanchard, French aeronaut, ascended in his hydrogen balloon from the yard of Walnut Street Jail in Philadelphia to make the first aerial voyage in the United States. In the air forty-six minutes, the balloon landed near Woodbury, New Jersey, and returned the same evening to the city in time for Citizen Blanchard to pay his respects to President Washington, who had witnessed the ascension in the morning."

Though I am not mentioned by name in the above, and its bland, affectless prose misses altogether the excitement of the moment, the notice does manage to convey something of the magnitude of the event. Imagine men flying like birds. The populace aghast, agawk, necks craned upward, every muscle tensed as if anticipating the tightening of the hangman's knot, its sudden yank, the irresistible gravity of the flesh as a trap door drops open beneath their feet. Men free as eagles. Aloft and soaring over the countryside. And crow though I was, my shabby black wings lifting me high as the Frenchman.

I was on board the balloon because little was understood about the effect of great height upon the human heart. Would that vital organ pump faster as the air grew thinner? Would the heart become engorged approaching the throne of its maker, or would it pale and shrink, the lusty blood fleeing, as once our naked parents, in shame from the Lord's awful gaze? Dr. Benjamin Rush, a man of science as well as a philanthropic soul, well known for championing the cause of a separate Negro church, had requested that a pulse glass be carried on the balloon, and thus, again, became a benefactor of the race, since who better than one of us, with our excitable blood and tropically lush hearts, to serve as guinea pig.

The honor fell on me. I was the Frenchman's crew. Aboard to keep the gondola neat and sanitary, a passenger so my body could register danger as we rose into those uncharted regions nearer my God to thee.

Jean-Pierre Blanchard was not my first Frenchman. Messrs. De Beauchamp and De Tocqueville had visited my cell in the Walnut Street Jail on a humanitarian, fact-finding mission among the New World barbarians to determine whether this Quaker invention, "the penitentiary," reformed criminals and deterred crime. The Frenchmen were quite taken with me. Surprised to discover I was literate. Enchanted when I read to them from the dim squalor of my cage the parable of the Good Shepherd, the words doubly touching, they assured me, coming from one who was born of a degraded and outcast race, one who, they assumed, had experienced only indifference and harshness.

No. Beg pardon. I'm confusing one time with another. Events lose their shape, slide one into another when the time one is supposed to own becomes another's property. An excusable mistake, perhaps inevitable when one resides in a place whose function is to steal time, rob time of its possibilities, deaden time to one dull unending present, a present that is absolutely not a gift, but something taken away. Time drawn, quartered and eviscerated, a sharp pain hovering over the ghost of an amputated limb. Too much time, no time, time tormenting as memories of food and blankets when you lie awake all night, hungry, shivering in an icy cell. No clocks. Only unvarying, iron bars of routine, solitary confinement mark your passage, your extinction outside time.

I would meet De Tocqueville and De Beauchamp years after the flight with Jean-Pierre Blanchard. By then I'd been transferred from Walnut Street Jail to the new prison at Cherry Hill. There, too, I would have the distinction of being the first of my race. Prisoner Number One. Charles Williams: *farmer; light black; black eyes; curly black hair; 5' 7 1/2"; foot, 11"; flat nose, scar on bridge of nose, broad mouth, scar from dirk on thigh; can read.*

First prisoner of any race admitted to Cherry Hill. Warden Samuel Wood greeted me with no acknowledgment nor ceremony for this particular historic achievement. Later that day, when I complained of dampness in my cell, he reminded me that the prison being new, on its shakedown cruise so to speak, one could expect certain unanticipated inconveniences. The good Warden Wood allowed me a berth in the infirmary until my cell dried out (it never did), but unfortunately the infirmary was also dank and chilly, due to lack of sunlight and ventilation, the cold miasma from marshy soil sweating up through the prison's foundation stones. So I began my residence with a hacking cough, the subterranean air at Cherry Hill as thick and pestilential as the air had been wholesome and bracing in the balloon.

I'm complaining too much. All lives are a combination of good times and bad, aren't they. We all suffer a death sentence. Today I wish to celebrate the good, that special time rising above the earth. So up, up, and away then.

A cloudless morning. In minutes we drift to a height that turns

Making Callaloo

Philadelphia into a map spread upon a table. The proud steeple of Christ Church a pen protruding from an ink well. After the lazy, curved snake of river, the grid of streets laid straight as plumb lines. I pick out the State House, Independence Hall, the Court House, Carpenters Hall, the market on High Street. And there, the yard of the Walnut Street Jail, there at 1, 2, 3, . . . count them . . . 4, 5, Sixth Street, the Jail and its adjacent yard from which we'd risen.

People are ants. Carriages inch along like slugs. Huge silence beats about my ears. A wind, clear and safe as those rare dreams that enfold me, slip me under their skirts and whisk me far from my cell.

But I must not lose myself in the splendor of the day until I execute the task that's earned me a ride. Once done, I can, we can, return to contemplating a world never seen by human eyes till just this unraveling, modern instant.

I place the glass on my flesh, count the pulse beats 1, 2, 3, . . . as I practiced counting rungs on the ladder of streets rising, no, *sliced* one after another, beginning at Water Street along the Delaware's edge.

Near the end of that momentous year, 1793, a plague of yellow fever will break out in the warren of hovels, shanties and caves along the river and nearly destroy Philadelphia. My Negro brethren, who inhabit that Quarter in large numbers, will perform admirably with enormous courage, skill and compassion during the emergency. Nursing the afflicted, burying the dead. One measure of the city's desperation in that calamitous year, a petition that circulates (unsuccessfully) suggesting we, the inmates of the jail, be allowed to serve and, thereby risking our lives, purchase freedom. This is the year that famous prisoner, the French King, is executed and my brethren will build their separate church, the African Episcopal Church of St. Thomas at Fifth and Walnut, a location empty at the moment, though cleared and ready. See it, a mere thumb print opposite the Jail from this elevation.

The Quakers, with their concern for the state of my soul, their insistence I have boundless opportunity to contemplate my sins, to repent and do penance, arrange matters in the Jail so I have ample time to consider things consequential and not. I've often pondered late at night when I cannot sleep, the symmetry between two events of that busy year, 1793: the separation of black from white in God's House, the plague that took so many citizens' lives. One act, *man's*, an assertion there is not enough room in the house of worship; the second act, *God's*, making more room.

During the terrible months when the city teetered on the brink of extinction, when President Washington together with all Federal and City officials decamped to more salubrious locations, various treatments, all futile, were prescribed for the deadly fever. Among the treatments, phlebotomy, the opening of a vein to draw blood from a victim, was quite popular until its opponents proved it killed more often than it cured.

My brethren, trained and guided by the ubiquitous Dr. Rush, applied his controversial cure: an explosive purge of mercury and calomel, followed by frequent, copious bleedings. Negro nurses became experts, dispensing pharmaceutical powders and slitting veins with equal dexterity. Out with the bad air. In with the good. I couldn't resist a smile when I pictured my brethren moving through white peoples' houses during broad daylight as freely as I once glided through the same dwellings after dark. Emptying purses, wallets, pockets, desk drawers, I, too, relieved my patients of excess.

In the prison also, we must drive out bad blood. Though all of us are infected by the fever of lawlessness, some prisoners are incurably afflicted. One such wretch, Matthew Maccumsey, Number 102. His crime: speech. Too much talk and at the wrong times and often in an obstreperous, disruptive, disrespectful manner, threatening the peace and economy of the entire system of absolute silence.

Ice water ducking, bagging with black hood, flogging, the normal and natural deterrents all applied and found wanting in lasting effect, the iron gag was prescribed. Number 102 remanded for examination and treatment to Dr. Bache, the nephew, I've heard, of the famous Dr. Franklin, the kite-flyer.

A committee, convened a decade later to investigate continuing complaints of questionable practices at the prison, described the gag in these words: a rough iron instrument resembling the bit of a blind bridle, having an iron palet in the center about an inch square and chains at each end to pass around the neck and fasten behind. This instrument was placed in the prisoner's mouth, the iron palet over the tongue, the bit forced back as far as possible, the chains brought round the jaws to the back of the neck; the end of one chain was passed through the ring in the end of the other chain drawn tight to the "fourth link" and fastened with a lock.

Rousted out of sleep before first light, groggy, frightened, I knew by the hour, the hulking stillness of the figures gathered into the narrow corridor outside my cell, I was being summoned for a punishment party. Seeing the faces of other prisoners of color in the glaring torchlight, I rejoiced inwardly. This night at least I was to be a punisher, not the punished. The guards always enlisted blacks to punish whites and whites to punish blacks, by this unsubtle stratagem, perpetuating enmity and division.

We forced No. 102's hands into leather gloves provided with rings, crossed his arms behind his back and after attaching the rings to the ends of the gag chain drew his arms upwards so their suspended weight pulled the gag chains taut, causing the chains to exert pressure on jaws and jugular, trapping blood in the averted head, producing excruciating pain, the degree of which I could gauge only by observing the prisoner's eyes, since the gag at last had effectively silenced him.

Niggified, ain't he, a guard exclaimed, half in jest, half in disgust as 102's lifeless, once pale face, blackened by congealed blood, was freed of the gag.

Again, I'm muddling time. The pacifying of 102 came later at Cherry Hill. My job on the balloon was to record the reaction of my own African pulse to heavenly ascent. Higher and higher it rose. The striped French balloon. The stiff, boat-shaped basket beneath it, garlanded with fresh flowers, red, white and blue bunting. Inside the gondola the flags of two great republican nations. We intended to plant them wherever we landed, claim for our countrymen joint interest in the rich, undiscovered lands far flung across the globe.

Watching the toy town shrink smaller and smaller beneath me, all its buildings and inhabitants now fittable on the end of a pin, for some unfathomable reason as I rose irresistibly to a heretofore undreamed-of height for any person of my race, as I realized the momentousness of the occasion, all the planning, sacrifice and dumb luck that had conspired to place me here, so high, at just that fantastic, unprecedented, joyous moment, as I began to perceive how far I'd risen and how much further, the sky literally the limit, still to rise, a single tear welled out from God-knows-where.

From my swaying perch high above everyone I watch our shadow eclipse a corner of the yard, then scuttle spider-like up the far wall of the Walnut Street Jail.

Observed from the height of the balloon I'd be just another ant. Not even my black hood pierced with crude eyeholes would distinguish me as I emerged from the night of my cell, blinking back the sudden onslaught of crisp January sunlight.

My eyes adjusted to the glare and there it was, finally, the balloon hovering motionless, waiting for someone it seemed, a giant, untethered fist thrust triumphantly at the sky.

From the moment it appears, I am sure no mere coincidence has caused the balloon to rise exactly during the minute and a half outdoors I'm allotted daily to cross the prison yard, grab tools, supplies and return to my cell. If Citizen Blanchard's historic flight had commenced a few seconds sooner or later that morning, I would have missed it. Imagine. I could have lived a different life. Instead of being outdoors glancing up at the heavens, I could have been in my cell pounding on the intractable leather they apportion me for cobbling my ten pairs of shoes a week. In that solitary darkness tap-tap tapping, I wouldn't have seen the striped, floating sphere come to fetch me and carry me home.

How carefully I set the pulse glass above a vein. Register the measured ebb and flow, each flicker the heart's smile and amen.

POETRY

Blue Suede Shoes

A Fiction

BY AI

1

Heliotrope sprouts from your shoes, brother,
their purplish color going Chianti
at the beginning of evening,
while you sit on the concrete step.
You curse, stand up, and come toward me.
In the lamplight, I see your eyes,
the zigzags of bright red in them.
"Bill's shot up," you say.
"Remember how he walked
on the balls of his feet like a dancer,
him, a boxer and so graceful
in his blue suede shoes?
Jesus, he coulda stayed home, Joe,
he coulda had the world by the guts,
but he gets gunned,
he gets strips of paper
tumbling out of his pockets like confetti."

Is Bea here? I say
and start for the house.
"No," you say. "This splits us, Joe.
You got money, education, friends.
You understand. I'm talking about family
and you ain't it.

The dock is my brother."
Lou, I say and step closer,
once I was fifteen, celestial.
Mom and Pop called me sweetheart
and I played the piano in the parlor
on Sunday afternoons.
There was ice cream.
Your girl wore a braid down the center of her back.
The sun had a face and it was mine.
You loved me, you sonofabitch, everybody did.
In 1923, you could count the golden boys on your fingers
and I was one of them. Me, Joe McCarthy.
I gave up music for Justice,
divorce, and small-time litigation.
And you moved here to Cleveland—
baseball, hard work, beer halls,
days fishing Lake Erie,
more money than a man like you
could ever earn on a farm
and still not enough.
Pop died in bed in his own house
because of my money.
Share, he always said, *you share*
what you have with your family
or you're nothing. You got nobody, boys.
Will you cut me off now
like you did
when I could have helped my nephew,
when you hated the way he hung on to me,
the way he listened when I talked
like I was a wise man? Wasn't I?
I could already see a faint red haze
on the horizon;
a diamond-headed hammer
slamming down on the White House;

a sickle cutting through the legs
of every man, woman, and child in America.
You know what people tell me today,
they say, *You whistle the tune, Joe,*
and we'll dance.
But my own brother sits it out.

2

A man gets bitter, Lou,
he gets so bitter
he could vomit himself up.
It happened to Bill.
He wasn't young anymore.
He knew he'd had it
that night last July
lying on a canvas of his own blood.
After a few months, he ran numbers
and he was good at it, but he was scared.
His last pickup
he stood outside the colored church
and heard voices
and he started to shake.
He thought he'd come all apart,
that he couldn't muscle it anymore,
and he skimmed cream for the first time—
$10s, $20s.

You say you would have died in his place,
but I don't believe it.
You couldn't give up your whore on Thursdays
and Bea the other nights of the week,
the little extra that comes in off the dock.
You know what I mean.
The boys start ticking—
they put their hands in the right place

and the mouse runs down the clock.
It makes you hot,
but I just itch
and when I itch, I want to smash something.
I want to condemn and condemn,
to see people squirm,
but other times,
I just go off in a dream—
I hear the Mills Brothers
singing in the background,
Up a lazy river,
then the fog clears
and I'm standing at Stalin's grave
and he's lying in an open box.
I get down on top of him
and stomp him,
till I puncture him
and this stink rises up.
I nearly black out,
but I keep stomping,
till I can smell fried trout, coffee.
And Truman's standing up above me
with his hand out
and I wake up always with the same thought:
the Reds are my enemies.
Every time I'm sitting at that big table in D.C.
and so-and-so's taking the Fifth,
or crying, or naming names,
I'm stomping his soul.
I can look inside you, Lou,
just like I do those sonsofbitches.
You got a hammer up your ass,
a sickle in between your percale sheets?
Threaten me, you red-hearted bastard. Come on.
I'll bring you to heel.

3

Yesterday Bill comes by the hotel
and he sits on the bed, but he can't relax.
Uncle, he says, and points at his feet,
all I ever wanted was this pair of blue suede shoes,
and he takes out a pawn ticket,
turns it over in his hand, then he gets up,
and at the door holds it out to me
and says, *Yes keep it.*

Today I go down to the pawnshop
and this is what I get back—a .38.
Bill didn't even protect himself.
You have to understand what happened to him,
in a country like this,
the chances he had.

Remember Dorothy and the Yellow Brick Road?
There's no pot of gold at the end,
but we keep walking that road,
red-white-and-blue ears of corn
steaming in our minds: America,
the only thing between us
and the Red Tide.
But some of us are straw—
we burn up like Bill in the dawn's early light.
He didn't deserve to live.
This morning, when I heard he was dead,
I didn't feel anything.
I stood looking out the window at the lake
and I thought for a moment
the whole Seventh Fleet was sailing away beneath me,
flags waving, men on deck,
shining like bars of gold,
and there, on the bow of the last ship,

Dorothy stood waving up at me.
As she passed slowly under my window,
I spit on her.
She just stared at me,
as if she didn't understand.
But she did.
She gave up the Emerald City
for a memory.
I'd never do that, never.
I'm an American.
I shall not want.
There's nothing that doesn't belong to me.

The Venus Hottentot
(1825)

I. CUVIER

Science, science, science!
Everything is beautiful

blown-up beneath my glass.
Colors dazzle insect wings.

A drop of water swirls
like marble. Ordinary

crumbs become stalactites
set in perfect angles

of geometry I'd thought
impossible. Few will

ever see what I see
through this microscope.

Cranial measurements
crowd my notebook pages,

and I am moving closer,
close to how these numbers

signify aspects of
national character.

Her genitalia
will float inside a labelled

pickling jar in the *Musée
de l'Homme* on a shelf

above Broca's brain:
"The Venus Hottentot."

Elegant facts await me.
Small things in this world are mine.

II.
There is unexpected sun today
in London, and the clouds that
most days sift into this cage
where I am working have dispersed.
I am a black cutout against
a captive blue sky, pivoting
nude so the paying audience
can view my naked buttocks.

I am called "Venus Hottentot."
I left Capetown with a promise
of revenue: half the profits
and my passage home: A boon!
Master's brother proposed the trip;
the magistrate granted me leave.
I would return to my family
a duchess, with watered silk

dresses and money to grow food,
rouge and powders in glass pots,
silver scissors, a lorgnette,
voile and tulle instead of flax,

cerulean blue instead
of indigo. My brother would
devour sugar-studded non-
pareils, pale taffy, damask plums.

That was years ago. London's
circuses are florid and filthy,
swarming with cabbage-smelling
citizens who stare and query,
"Is it muscle? bone? or fat?"
My neighbor to the left is
The Sapient Pig, "The Only
Scholar of His Race." He plays
at cards, tells time and fortunes
by scraping his hooves. Behind
me is Prince Kar-mi, who arches
like a rubber tree and stares back
at the crowd from under the crook
of his knee. A professional
animal trainer shouts my cues.
There are singing mice here.

"The Ball of Duchess DuBarry":
In the engraving I lurch
toward the bellesdames, mad-eyed, and
they swoon. Men in capes and pince-nez
shield them. Tassels dance at my hips.
In this newspaper lithograph
my buttocks are shown swollen
and luminous as a planet.

Monsieur Cuvier investigates
between my legs, poking, prodding,
sure of his hypothesis.
I half-expect him to pull silk

scarves from inside me, paper poppies,
then a rabbit! He complains
at my scent and does not think
I comprehend, but I speak

English. I speak Dutch. I speak
a little French as well, and
languages Monsieur Cuvier
will never know have names.
Now I am bitter and now
I am sick. I eat brown bread,
drink rancid broth. I miss good sun,
miss Mother's *sadza*. My stomach

is frequently queasy from mutton
chops, pale potatotes, blood sausage.
I was certain that this would be
better than farm life. I am
the family entrepreneur!
But there are hours in every day
to conjur my imaginary
daughters, in banana shirts

and ostrich-feather fans.
Since my own genitals are public
I have made other parts private.
In my silence I possess
mouth, larynx, brain, in a single
gesture. I rub my hair
with lanolin, and pose in profile
like a painted Nubian

archer, imagining gold leaf
woven through my hair, and diamonds.
Observe the wordless Odalisque.

I have not forgotten my Xhosa
clicks. My flexible tongue
and healthy mouth bewilder
this man with his rotting teeth.
If he were to let me rise up

from this table, I'd spirit
his knives and cut out his black heart,
seal it with science fluid inside
a Bell jar, place it on a low
shelf in a white man's museum
so the whole world could see
it was shriveled and hard,
geometric, deformed, unnatural.

An Audience of One

BY GERALD BARRAX

It's all very friendly
the way the night is shrieking
a joyful noise unto itself.

My area light is a baton
against the green that's too brilliant
and the absolute-black interstices of the wall of trees,
all in their perfect places: willows on the left,
oak to the right, maple, pine, and dogwood
orchestrated between, all leaning hungrily toward it,
swallowing the light
that goes into the woods and never
out again.
In there the hunger rages,
so close to my domicile,
things in combat to devour
one another, not at all
the way lovers do.

As an audience of one
it must be me to cough
and applaud the crickets, tree
frogs, and God knows what else
out there.
And I'm discovered.
Monitored,
I'm a terminal whose readouts are taken
and my internal processes fed back into the dark

where it is computed that you are gone from me,
in another part of the world.

Nothing stops completely,
not even the sanest music;
but in sympathy that great heartbeat slows down
and there is a diminuendo in the dark
while the trees and I lean toward
that cool artificial light
as though it were you or the sun.

All My Live Ones

BY GERALD BARRAX

Penny accepted the Alabama neighbor's green meat,
Died in our swept-dirt back yard
Near the black wash pot, her brown spot penny-
Side up. My mother's dog, but like
All pets, with no sense of justice:
After forty years she still haunts
Me, innocent of her death, with
These images. My mother en-
Trusted to me the folly of love,
The daily care of caring for them,
And the rest were all mine to lose,
Mockery in their dying
And more than fear in running away.
Rex, ears clipped, tail bobbed, escaped
Into Pennsylvania nowhere
In a cloud of flea powder for no reason
That a twelve-year-old could know.
Micky Midnight, the stray gift to me,
Sick in bed from school, black
As only cats can be, stuck it out
Only long enough for the perfect name
And took it with him.
Fulton (after Sheen the bishop
For his round skull cap), my one canary,
Died so soon after he'd learned to sing,
Finally, that I wondered if song
Were worth the cost. And last: Sinbad.
One morning before Pharmaceutical Latin
In nineteen fifty-two I watched him die

My nearest death between my absent brother's
Bed and mine, stretched out, rasping, so closely
Watched I knew and remember which half-second
Distemper tore the last breath out.
But the people: how different.
Since nineteen thirty-three
I've been the key to immortality:
All it takes is loving me:
Both parents, who had me
When they were young; the brother
Who left me there that morning
Alone when that dog died;
A wife who let me go
With her life, our three sons;
Another wife bringing
Her hostages to fortune,
Two daughters; all the lovers.
What will I do?
They are all here. At my age what will I do
With only a bird and a dog long ago?
I cried for days. For days and days.

Dissidence, I

BY ROBERT BERROUËT-ORIOL

bookmarker
      the bald island hoisting its breasts
      active memory
      its percussions on the high railing
my retina leaning.
here a frizzy breaking away   sides along   a slow
measure   the recitative of hopscotch

aerial

daybreak
          decibel

cracked matrix   I salute you
barbed poets
in you   the palaverous ink
nearest the bars
wears away in new words
in the alphabet of the day
water   labor
         ventriloquistic dread

       I
migrant leaping
to survive

my broken flute once more on the alert
at the familiarity of the streets
rusty saliva
I cheat three-times-is-a-charm
the sail of hopscotch courts

ABC primer
a city-rumbling vacillates

the conquered trough
beautiful
to be preserved
                    I salute you from Mont-Royal
Florville-palette
Manuel-Mute E   surveyor of Carib languages
Bélance-the-source
lighting
Trouillot-the-sap
Charles christophing caravel-dreams
speak
Chassagne-lamppost
Philoctète of the limping islands
thundering Etienne   fresco on the Dézafi[1] sea

elsewhere
here
geometry of the bow

I salute you
poets of the sunrise towing the night
the austral jib
the boreal index
                    he the numinous son of America
at the noon of voices   Carib dissidence

I am   of the wind   the pregnant mistress
one-armed gestures
a programmed word
o   geographer   tide   fording   you seam up
link   and   liana
our mortiferous couplings

undoes the dream
                    says the retina

place without a place
obese
an adulterous city
sweats
Tropics in distress

sweats
cadaverous   your hymn   limping
stinks
        Port-aux-Putes[2]
impure
your memory   powdered with the shipwreck of shades
drowses
trauma   my wrinkles   childhood at half-mast

Port-aux-Putes
Port-aux-Putes
                    bloodless
I love your gall   its deafness
vain suture of premeditated dreams
lone hiccough of a chorale
remains
        here
                my marigraphic dissidence

in a reverent score   my polar viol
grafts its salt

MONTREAL, SUMMER 1989

—Translated by Carrol F. Coates

NOTES

1. *Dézafi* is the title of Franketienne's first novel, in Creole (Port-au-Prince, 1975) [translator's note].
2. Port-aux-Putes: Port of Whores, a play on the name of Haiti's capital [translator's note].

from Clips

BY EDWARD KAMAU BRATHWAITE

II
Plantation
Dat harf-assed inherited plantation
left as his benefice by some disgruntled guilty massacouraman

was up to wreck and ruin
weeds were killing the cane waves and there was no one to pull
them out

bury them then or burn them

but the fires destroyed auras and auroras of unpaid-for-sweat
contours of flesh that had been shaped by love

in the middle of the trash bone sticks when you stepped on crackle
the shimmering landscape ignored you

take the boy from school

and so years after dust silverworm cratered but hardly dog-eared
i found your latin primer quarter touch unsteadied

  you clearly would not understand
  those regular irregulars like *do.dare.dedi.datum*

  the archaic algebra the undernourished shakespeare
  merchant of venice and surprising *cymbelene*

you spent months with soot on your fingers (the black
would not rub off) not knowing what to do with the asp

that was itching your eyes. your pants were slack
and baggy often too long frayed at the heels

sluggish with yard-dirt and hurt or
sometimes too short: showing the skin where the sun

didn't torch through the holes of your old fashioned shocks.
the buggy that you loved and played at driver in was

sold: the horse, thin chestnut stallion with the bruised and bony
haunches
slipped and broke a fretlock and was shot . dead .
cold . by your insensitive half-brother

he who talked with his mouth full a dumplin
who ate with his hat on at table except sundees

you remembered feathers a broken pillar in the wind and the sad
drone of flies

if you had liked the bottle you could have started drinking from
upwards to now. and why

not: there were rumshops everywhere: ambivalent as chapels: their
captains

would have trusted you: there were two elder brothers at the
mount gay factory

had you liked women you could have had them picked and
pregnant in

no fuckin time at all. they black-eyed ex-slave smooth-thighed
giggles

passed by you slowly strong-necked sweating softly heading cane or ground provisions: balancing their water-buckets with

their doom

cast eyes. stopped when you spoke, their voices like a cloud across
the canefields

yet when they laughed you heard the hair-springs of their ecstasy
their scythe shaped backs and buttocks of the goddess

and they were keen on brown-skin fathers. for them plantation
wreck
and ruin still meant pride and prejudice and certain in-

grained customs and a relationship and attitude and distance use
of eye
they call respect. and of course there was the house and horse

and buggy

and the treasure-chest of money underneath your father's door
while they lived with their mothers in those one-room huts of
wood and thatch

and shingle rut

man: had you liked women: *wow:* but you were careful. *sir-cumspectacles*
your tie-head great-aunt called it: one or two little
tings, you know, from time to time, korblimeman

but not like the brothers

for you no squealing bastards hugged-up by show-off patient
leather mothers
their wet-nose nipples jerking juice at clinics

no pay-day pilgrims at your debtors door no loud-mout would-be
breddas

bawling out how they gine lick you dung an leave you tangle-up

upside-down in de eddoes

Sally Hemings to Thomas Jefferson

BY CYRUS CASSELLS

*for Barbara Chase-Riboud and for my family, reputed to be the direct
descendents of Hemings and Jefferson*

Je m'appelle Sally:
How simply my first French lesson
Returns to me,
The stern and exacting gaze of my tutor,
Monsieur Perrault,
And your rich, commanding voice
—The voice of one
Both demigod and father:
Tell me Sally, what did you learn?
Master, I learned to say
My name.
Now, years later, I repeat the French,
As if to yield
All that I am,
And open the locket to find,
Cached in the tiny, gold-lined womb,
A lock of your red hair:
It happens, your face
Looms again in my lifetime.
If I could go to the doorway,
And stand, waiting for you
As you take the hall, your leonine figure
Assembling in the longest mirror
As in my eyes.
But you are dead, Thomas Jefferson,
And I can only sit,

Motionless, my heart pounding
At your phantom,
For today I learned
The census-taker made me white
To absolve you of the crime
Of having loved a slavewoman.
So I burned our correspondence
—The diaries and *billet-doux* an ash
Clinging to my skirts,
A smoke in my hair. Each word
A swatch of myself, a forbidden history:
The Hôtel de Langeac, the Palace of Marly,
The Capitol, Monticello—
Now I am robbed of everything,
Even of my color.

I was fifteen when you took me,
Your daughter's nursemaid;
You brushed my cheek
With your red-plumed chest,
Whispering *Martha, Martha*
—Piercing me with the name
Of your dead wife, my white half-sister
Whom I resembled.
I was so frightened by you then,
So overawed and unbelieving
Of your love.
I would stand before my mirror,
Cupping my breasts
In my two hands, amazed: no fledgling
But a woman—
Je t'aime, Sally, Je t'aime,
I heard you say,
And in Paris I mislaid
My slavery.

Sally Hemings to Thomas Jefferson

So home to Monticello, I met
My mother's loving, though accusatory face,
And knew I should have chosen freedom.

*

The battlecries,
Your glittering words of revolution
Have been recorded,
But in a secret wing of Monticello,
Against your will, I marked
The dreams and follies of our seven children,
The shocked faces of our foreign guests.
But O what I could not capture
Was your silence
As all the country crowned me
Black Lillith, Sooty Chatelaine.
In your pain and ravaged pride,
You clung to me.
Love me, stay with me, you whispered.
They say a man cannot free what he loves:
Is it your truth, your story,
I hear in these words?
Love me and remain a slave?

*

In the recurrent dream,
I stand on the steps of Monticello,
And see what blinds me:
Our children like hunted deer,
In a dead run—our children
You could never acknowledge.
I recall pausing on the Pont de Neuilly,
And absently dropping
A key into the Seine,

As I watched the word *enceinte*
Darken your gaze:

Return with me to Virginia,
You pleaded, a great man,
Lonely in your aegis,
But I refused, knowing I was unfettered
As long as I remained in France.
You would love me;
We would return to Paris,
And my child would be given
Freedom at adulthood
—A perilous, vouchsafed freedom, surely,
To pass from slavery
Into a forged whiteness
That begs amnesia.
I looked into your eyes, two sapphires
Set in a human face,
And met a suffering so vast, what else
But to take your hand
And whisper, *Yes*...
My love and master, I need to believe
I would choose this way again,
Though as property
I had no choice
'Cept to give myself
But I, Mademoiselle Sally,
Gave you my heart,
And returned to slavery.
Nothing could free me from you.

The Times

BY LUCILLE CLIFTON

it is hard to remain human on a day
when birds perch weeping
in the trees and the squirrel eyes
do not look away but the dog ones do
in pity.
another child has killed a child
and i catch myself relieved that they are
white and i might understand except
that i am tired of understanding.
if these
alphabets could speak their own tongue
it would be all symbol surely;
the cat would hunch across the long table
and that would mean time is catching up,
and the spindle fish would run to ground
and that would mean the end is coming
and the grains of dust would gather themselves
along the streets and spell out

these too are your children   this too is your child

Lazarus

BY LUCILLE CLIFTON

first day

i rise from stiffening
into a pin of light
and a voice calling
"Lazarus, this way"
and i walk or rather
swim in a river of sound
toward what seems to be
forever   i am almost
almost there when i hear
behind me
"Lazarus, come forth" and
i find myself swiveling
in the light for this
is the miracle Mary Martha,
at my head and at my feet
singing my name
is the same voice

second day

i am not the same man
borne into the crypt.

as ones return from otherwhere
altered by what they have seen,

so have i been forever.

lazarus.
lazarus is dead.

what entered the light was one man
what walked out is another.

   third day

on the third day i remember
what i was moving from
what i was moving toward

light again and
i could feel the seeds
turning in the grass   mary
martha i could feel the world

now i sit here on a crevice
in this rock   stared at
answering questions

sisters stand away
from the door to my grave
the only peace i know

The Promise

BY TOI DERRICOTTE

I will never again
expect too much of you. I have
found out the secret of marriage:
I must keep seeing your beauty
like a stranger's, like the face
of a young girl passing on a train
whose moment of knowing illumines
it—a golden letter in a book.
I will look at you in such
exaggerated moments, lengthening
one second and shrinking eternity
until they fit together like man and wife.
My pain is expectation:
I watch you for hours sleeping, expecting
you to roll over like a dead man
and look me in the eye;
my days are seconds of waiting
like the seconds between the makings
of boiling earth and sweating rivers.
What am I waiting for if not
your face—like a fish floating
up to the surface, a known
but forgotten expression that
suddenly appears—or like myself,
in a strip of mirror, when, having
passed, I come back to that image
hoping to find the woman
missing. Why do you think I sleep
in the other room, planets away,

in a darkness where I could die solitary,
an old nun wrapped in clean white sheets?
Because of lies I sucked
in my mother's milk, because
of pictures in my first grader reader—
families in solid towns as if
the world were rooted and grew down
holding to the rocks, eternally;
because of rings in jewelers' windows
engraved with sentiments—*I love you
forever*—as if we could survive
any beauty for longer than just after . . .
So I hobble down a hall
of disappointments past where
your darkness and my darkness have
had intercourse with each other.
Why have I wasted my life
in anger, thinking I could have more
than what is glimpsed in recognitions?
I will let go, as we must
let go of an angel called
back to heaven; I will not hold
her glittering robe, but let it
drift above me until I see
the last shred of evidence.

Holy Cross Hospital

BY TOI DERRICOTTE

In my ninth month, I entered a maternity ward
set up for the care of unwed girls and women.

couldn't stand to see these new young faces, these
children swollen as myself. my roommate, snotty,
bragging about how she didn't give a damn about the
kid and was going back to her boyfriend and be a
cheerleader in high school. *could we ever "go back"?*
would our bodies be the same? could we hide among the
childless? she always reminded me of a lady at the bridge
club in her mother's shoes, playing her mother's hand.

i tried to get along, be silent, stay in my own corner.
i only had a month to go—too short to get to know them.
but being drawn to the room down the hall, the t.v. room
where, at night, we sat in our cuddly cotton robes and
fleece-lined slippers—like college freshmen, joking
about the nuns and laughing about due dates: jailbirds
waiting to be sprung . . .

one girl, taller and older, twenty-six or twenty-seven, kept
to herself, talked with a funny accent. the pain on her face
seemed worse than ours . . .

and a lovely, gentle girl with flat small bones. the
great round hump seemed to carry *her* around! she never
said an unkind word to anyone, went to church every morning
with her rosary and prayed each night alone in her room.

she was seventeen, diabetic, fearful that she or the baby
or both would die in childbirth. she wanted the baby, yet
knew that to keep it would be wrong. but what if the child
did live? what if she gave it up and could never have another?

i couldn't believe the fear, the knowledge she had of
death walking with her. i never felt stronger, eating
right, doing my exercises. i was holding on to the core,
the center of strength; death seemed remote, i could not
imagine it walking in our midst, death in the midst of
all that blooming. she seemed sincere, but maybe she
was lying . . .

she went down two weeks late. induced. she had decided
to keep the baby. the night i went down, she had just
gone into labor so the girls had two of us to cheer about.
the next morning when i awoke, i went to see her. she
smiled from her hospital bed with tubes in her arms. it
had been a boy. her baby was dead in the womb for two
weeks. i remembered she had complained *no kicking*. we
had reassured her everything was fine.

meanwhile i worked in the laundry, folded the hospital
fresh sheets flat three hours a day. but never alone.
stepping off the elevator, going up, feeling something,
a spark catch. i would put my hand there and smile with
such a luminous smile, the whole world must be happy.

or out with those crazy girls, those teenagers, laughing,
on a christmas shopping spree, free (the only day they
let us out in two months) feet wet and cold from snow.

i felt pretty, body wide and still in black leotards
washed out at night. my shapely legs and
young body like iron.

i ate well, wanted lamaze (painless childbirth)—i
didn't need a husband or a trained doctor—i'd do it
myself, book propped open on the floor, puffing and
counting while all the sixteen-year-old unwed children
smiled like i was crazy.

one day i got a letter from my cousin, said:

> *don't give your baby up—*
> *you'll never be complete again*
> *you'll always worry where and how it is*

she knew! the people in my family knew! nobody died
of grief and shame!

I *would* keep the child. i was sturdy. would be a better
mother than my mother. i would still be a doctor,
study, finish school at night. when the time came, i
would not hurt like all those women who screamed and
took drugs. I would squat down and deliver just like the
peasants in the field, shift my baby to my back, and
continue . . .

when my water broke, when i saw that stain of pink blood
on the toilet paper and felt the first thing i could not
feel, had no control of, dripping down my leg, i heard
them singing mitch miller xmas songs and came from the
bathroom in my own pink song—down the long hall, down
the long moment when no one knew but me. it was time.

all the girls were cheering when i went downstairs, i was
the one who told them to be tough, to stop believing
in their mother's pain, that poison. our minds were
like telescopes looking through fear. it wouldn't hurt

like we'd been told. birth was beautiful if we believed
that it was beautiful and good!

—*maternity*—*i had never seen inside those doors.*
all night i pictured the girls up there, at first hanging
out of the windows, trying to get a glimpse of me . . .
when the pain was worst, i thought of their sleeping faces,
like the shining faces of children in the nursery, i held
onto that image of innocence like one light in the darkness.

Heartbeats

BY MELVIN DIXON

Work out. Ten laps.
Chin ups. Look good.

Steam room. Dress warm.
Call home. Fresh air.

Eat right. Rest well.
Sweetheart. Safe sex.

Sore throat. Long flu.
Hard nodes. Beware.

Test blood. Count cells.
Reds thin. Whites low.

Dress warm. Eat well.
Short breath. Fatigue.

Night sweats. Dry cough.
Loose stools. Weight loss.

Get mad. Fight back.
Call home. Rest well.

Don't cry. Take charge.
No sex. Eat right.

Call home. Talk slow.
Chin up. No air.

Arms wide. Nodes hard.
Cough dry. Hold on.

Mouth wide. Drink this.
Breathe in. Breathe out.

No air. Breathe in.
Breathe in. No air.

Black out. White rooms.
Head out. Feet cold.

No work. Eat right.
CAT scan. Chin up.

Breathe in. Breathe out.
No air. No air.

Thin blood. Sore lungs.
Mouth dry. Mind gone.

Six months? Three weeks?
Can't eat. No air.

Today? Tonight?
It waits. For me.

Sweet heart. Don't stop.
Breathe in. Breathe out.

Climbing Montmartre

BY MELVIN DIXON

Take these thousand steps, these up-running shoes,
the orange / red / brownstone rooftops
studded like Arab faces in the sun. Take
my one African eye.

Take these white steps, these ladders up-growing
from the green, the marble-head dome with eyes
the flicking cameras of tourists, the franc rusted
fountains, the postcards, the translated prayers.

Take the beaded stained glass and the false
night naked inside, the nuns singing, the
statues looking cool, the candies leaning from light.

Langston in the twenties and old Locke too,
Cullen from the Hotel St. Pierre,
Wright from rue Monsieur le Prince, even too,
Martin came to climb Montmartre.

Take the fast breathing, the up-going,
the wide plane of rooftops frozen in a Paris mist.
the dignity of trodden stone descending to
subway sleepers, take my primitive feet
danced out and still.

Take the iron colored dust from *Gare du Nord*,
the pigeon feeders, the hundred smelling vendors,
the fast hands, the begging. Take jazz in

twisted TV antennas and wire clotheslines, or
my lips quivering, hands watching, holding.

Take this hill into the mind as you look
all over Europe; your clogged ears can't hear
the screaming, your pointed noses snuff out
blood and urine smells, your green eyes
don't see this body drop on angry gargoyles.

Straw Hat

BY RITA DOVE

In the city, under the saw-toothed leaves of an oak
overlooking the tracks, he sits out
the last minutes before dawn, lucky
to sleep third shift. Years before
he was anything, he lay on
so many kinds of grass, under stars,
the moon's bald eye opposing.

He used to sleep like a glass of water
held up in the hand of a very young girl.
Then he learned he wasn't perfect, that
no one was perfect. So he made his way
North under the bland roof of a tent
too small for even his lean body.

The mattress ticking he shares
is brown and smells
from the sweat of two other men.
One of them chews snuff:
he's never met either.
To him, work is a narrow grief
and the music afterwards
like a woman
reaching into his chest
to spread it around. That's when

he closes his eyes. He never knows
when she'll be coming but when
she leaves, he always
tips his hat.

Motherhood

BY RITA DOVE

She dreams the baby's so small she keeps
misplacing it—it rolls from the hutch
and the mouse carries it home, it disappears
with his shirt in the wash.
Then she drops it and it explodes
like a watermelon, eyes spitting.

Finally they get to the countryside;
Thomas has it in a sling.
He's strewing rice along the road
while the trees chitter with tiny birds.
In the meadow to their right three men
are playing rough with a white wolf. She calls

warning but the wolf breaks free
and she runs, the rattle
rolls into the gully, then she's
there and tossing the baby behind her,
listening for its cry as she straddles
the wolf and circles the throat, counting
until her thumbs push through to the earth.
White fur seeps red. She is hardly breathing.
The small wild eyes
go opaque with confusion and shame, like a child's.

Headdress

BY RITA DOVE

The hat on the table
in the dining room
is no pet trained
to sit still. Three
pearl-tipped spears and Beulah
maneuvering her shadow
to the floor. The hat
is cold. The hat
wants more.

(The customer will be
generous when satisfied
beyond belief. Spangled
tulle, then, in green
and gold and sherry.)

Beulah
would have settled
for less. She doesn't
pray when she's
terrified, sometimes, in-
side her skin like
today, humming
through a mouthful of pins.

Finished it's a mountain
on a dish, a capitol
poised on a littered shore.
The brim believes

in itself, its
double rose and feathers
ashiver. Extravagance
redeems. O
intimate parasol
that teaches to walk
with grace along beauty's seam.

Heroes

BY RITA DOVE

A flower in a weedy field:
make it a poppy. You pick it.
Because it begins to wilt

you run to the nearest house
to ask for a jar of water.
The woman on the porch starts

screaming: you've plucked the last poppy
in her miserable garden, the one
that gave her the strength every morning

to rise! It's too late for apologies
though you go through the motions, offering
trinkets and a juicy spot in the written history

she wouldn't live to read, anyway.
So you strike her, she hits
her head on a white boulder

and there's nothing to be done
but break the stone into gravel
to prop up the flower in the stolen jar

you have to take along
because you're a fugitive now
and you can't leave clues.

Already the story's starting to unravel,
the villagers stirring as your heart
pounds into your throat. Why

did you pick that idiot flower?
Because it was the last one
and you knew

it was going to die.

Middle Ear Recitation
(a transcription of Cecil Taylor's "Erzulie Maketh Scent")

BY BRENT HAYES EDWARDS

1. INTROIT

entering a cave, you   Ascends
   to where a garden
      considered heat,
terrible sharp grins, ecstatic chattering:
three steps down in.

    "it's like" three
steps down.
without moving   the shudder of an eyelid
   in too much light,
or shutter:

   rustled, rummed ascent

"it's like water"   (her comment upon
     hearing it)

   Water, when light moves
in it, has no corners
     "like" a mobile fulcrum, coy:

a cave entering you

2. DANCE

the sensing of what is most remote. begins
in the smallest seed. the smallest fossil.
silence before a mirror where the dream
strikes a chain of miles.

                              the ear precedes
the dance. to hear its way from falling
a droplet jostles in a frame of bone. here
its way blown from shifting, blown smooth,
blown into a lucent way of moving. blown
covert, then, unintentioned ply proves motive,
blown with shifting motive. the ear proceeds
to dance its water

                    still. before the dance
she lowers herself, slender ossuary,
down into it. her entrance propped with splinters
of perfume. what rises, something ceded
to the air. something cut with light
and pried up, rummed out. to prepare
the ground. blown seeds dance the air
like severed ears

3. SALLE D'ATTENTE

A cave, entering   it's like
     scent unfurled   too much of her sent too close
for comfort. water in your blood-

        shot eyes

     feet tendrilled to find their way
from falling. in the air the stench of sulfur, now.
tendrilled hair

                        flung out
                        down your back

each dread tendril
        swinging down
for a root
        each massed arm of hair
        straining down

   to bob and weave the cicatrix
        of an immemorial divorce

   their eccentric orbits
        glancing down
          an approach
     to imaginary points

   singeing a romance
    of the unseen

       breath
     a loony pirouetted descent——

4. MODE DE MONTER

—Your right hand is crumbling into dust and blowing away;
your left foot implants itself in something that feels like mud
but doesn't smell like it; your left shoulder is covered with plaster
which is drying in the sun and hardening; someone has come by
with a short sword and gracefully cut your eyeballs out of your skull,
you grope for them on the asphalt; you are sitting on a toilet,
constipated again, you hear her call from the other room; there is an egg
swelling in your armpit, something inside is straining to break out.

This must be dancing.

        You balance in the thirst of it,
troll for balance, await the inundation of the ride *manqué*,
the ocean's rhythm and the ear's corrective

blasts foretold
and buffets, and the promise of thighs speaking astride
you, and that edge of feeling before the drum is audible:
down in the middle, voice's antecedent is a tuning:

The bulrush is edible.
Castor oil is edible.
Baneberry and hemlock are inedible.
Sloe gin poured over vanilla ice cream is edible.
White mangrove will blind you.
Wild potatoes are edible.
The ashengray morel mushroom is edible.
(Under its umbrella, its pockmarked face
is like a moon.)
Nightshade and bitter cassava are inedible.
Black eyed peas and collard greens are edible.
Jimson weed is inedible.
Horse hair is inedible.

5. RECITATIVE
our hands are pick and shovel enough
our teeth are knife enough—
languid thing
tolling in an invisible bell
carve your message into my skin

our hands are pick enough
our hands are shovel enough—
languid tolling thing

lash your terrible sweetness
lacerate your terrible answer
into the back of my throat

our teeth are knife enough—
take my tongue
ride me with your song

6. CODA (AS FROM A DISTANCE)

The dream leaves an instrument
behind like a dropping in its wake:
a big black piano,
the finish scratched and disfigured,
the soundboard cracked, strings frizzled
away from hammers into the air.
Its guts brim with dust like a swamped boat.
In the frenzy of the dream someone's given hell
to the action—the ivory's chipped in jagged
shards, some hand has beaten a few keys off.
A crazy black cactus
in this desert.

What stirs behind its dusty husk?

Something comes down to look:
an enormous spider, pale
with big sad eyes, jostling the air
down an invisible thread.

She gingerly fingers the black wood,
imbibes an agitation with a shiver.
Patient, as though she's paused to read a pooled
reverberation in the broken black frame.
The dust eddies, the dungeon of the strings
shakes around her.
Her eight legs bow at sharp angles.
She balances, oddly translucent against
the black's faint dust-choked glimmer Wavers
    then holds firm

to a fragile web of light.
In her tender clutch, the black finish
tinkles like a pocket full of change.

Fatal April

Thomas Leon Ellis, Sr. (1945—1991)

BY THOMAS SAYERS ELLIS

The phone rang. It was Doris,
Your sister, calling to say
April had taken you, where,
In your bedroom, when, days ago,
How, murder, no, a stroke.

You left a car (but I
Don't drive) and enough cash
In your pockets to buy
A one-way train ticket
From Boston to Washington.

Let's get one thing straight.
I didn't take the money, but
I did take your Driver's License
And the Chuck Brown album,
Needle to groove,

Round and round,
Where they found you.
Both were metaphors.
The license I promised, but knew
I'd never get—now I have yours

And the album because
Of what you may have been
Trying to say about writing,

About home. James keeps
Asking me to visit your grave,

When will I learn to drive
And why I changed my name.
He's your son, stubborn with
An inherited temper. I keep telling him
No, never, there's more than

One way to bury a man.

A Kiss in the Dark

BY THOMAS SAYERS ELLIS

In our community everything was kept quiet,
behind closed doors. When dogs got stuck
it was because one was hurt and the other
was a friend helping it home—just like a friend.
Once Reverend Gibson ran from the church
with a bucket of hot water and when it separated them,
they sang. That's why it was such an event,
a mistake equivalent to sin, when my parents
left their bedroom light on, door open.

Mistakes are what gave light to that tiny apartment
darkness tried to conquer. And imagination,
how there had to be more to it than the quick
& crude *He put it in and he took it out.*

A naked bulb on the dresser next to where
they made me made them celebrities, giants, myth.
I watched their black shadows on the wall,
half expecting fade out and something romantic
as the final scene of *Love Crazy*, my father
a suave William Powell, my mother's slender body
a backwards C in the tight focus of his arms—
close-shot, oneiric dissolve, jump-cut to years
before their separation and the arrival of hot water.

A Ride to the Wedding

BY PHEBUS ETIENNE

I said goodbye to another piece of childhood,
watching the bride, pretty in organza bows and orchids.
She was billowed in joy, not like the morning
when she finally opened the door after I had knocked
for an hour, fearing she had overdosed. The woman
who had offered me a ride to the church turned up
the air conditioning in her apartment. I groped
for small talk as she rubbed her brown shoulders,
and leaned forward on the couch
to finish her cigarette, a tall can of beer.
She grabbed her wrap, walked into her kitchen,
stirred sugar into her ice water.

On my way to her bathroom,
she directed, "Don't sit on my toilet!" I obeyed.
We trailed the speeding limousine
ribboned in turquoise and she complained
about having cramps. When she asked me how I got
to her house, I said I took a cab. Six blocks
in heels was a long walk in the heat. She'd never
take a cab in this town, she ranted. She *hated* Haitians,
especially the taxi drivers. Using what
was left of her middle and index fingers,
nubs without fingernails,

she found a rhythm and blues station
on the radio. I pulled the tulle on my hat
closer to my eyes and hoped it wasn't
a Haitian who maimed her. Maybe I should have said

that our chained relatives could once
have been heading for the same auction block.
Maybe her peoples' ship docked in the Caribbean
where the captain sold my ancestor as he waited
for the end of an autumn storm.
But she did not want to hear me link us.
I didn't say that sometimes we drink
poor man's soda, sweeten our ice water, too.
I hid myself, as if defending what I am.

Goldsboro Narratives

GOLDSBORO NARRATIVE #4
MY FATHER'S VIET NAM TOUR NEAR OVER

The young dead soldier was younger
than they thought. The 14-year-old passed
himself as seventeen, forged
a father's signature. In the army no more
than months, he was killed early
the week before a cease-fire.
The boy was someone-I somewhat-knew's
older brother and someone-my-mother-
had-taught's son, and, lying
in the standard Army casket, an American
flag draped over the unopened half,
the boy didn't look like anyone
anybody would know—a big kid his dark skin
peached pale, lips pouted. I was sure
I hadn't recognized him.

When kids older than us
closed down one campus after another,
I thought they'd close all colleges down,
and there would be no place for me
when it was my time. It didn't seem fair.

Capt. Howell's wife answered
the door one day, and two men
in military dress asked to come in.
She had no choice, I suppose,
but once they came into her living room,

she no longer had a husband, and
the three boys and the girl no longer
had their father. *So this is how
it happens*, I thought: two men come
to your house in the middle of the day,
ringing a bell or rapping on the door.
And, afterwards, there's nothing left
to look forward to.

GOLDSBORO NARRATIVE #7

Time was a boy, specially a black boy,
need to be whipped by his kin, teach him
not to act up, get hisself killt.
Folks did this cause they loved them boys.
The man laughs. And boys would do what all
they could to get out of them whippings,
play like they was getting tore up,
some play like they was going to die.
My grandmama the first one that whipped me,
and she made me go get my own switches.
If I come back to her with a switch too small,
she make me go right back and get a big one.
And she whipped me for that, too. He laughs.
I loved that woman, though. Sho did.

GOLDSBORO NARRATIVE #28

When folks caught on to what was happening
between Rev. Johnson and Sister Edna,
the grown-ups went back to speaking
in front of children as if we couldn't spell.
It was easy to figure out, though:
Rev. Johnson's wife didn't get happy; and,
after service, she wouldn't shake hands
with Sister Edna or any of her kin.
And Sister Edna's husband, Mr. Sam,

who never came to church, began waiting
in the parking lot to drive his wife home.
Now the age Rev. Johnson was then, I doubt
he was concerned with being forgiven.
But when I was 12 and kept on falling
from available grace, I began dismissing him
and mostly all of what he said he meant.
I went witnessing instead to Mr. Sam,
his truck idling outside the paned windows,
him dressed in overalls and a new straw hat.

Modulations on a Theme: For Josephus Long

BY MICHAEL S. HARPER

Not far from Harvard Square
between New Years and Xmas
we file in to the sanctity
of your name: Josephus Long,
long on the details
of nuance and residue.

I met you in the winter
of 1964, in the snow
of Wiltwyck School for Boys,
in Esopus, New York;
you'd commute to New Paltz
at odd hours,
counseling your charges,
boys from 8–14,
who craved the structure
and elegance of your laugh,
but could not hear the perfidy.

At basketball you were silk,
sometimes brought down by brute
power, the elbows of equality
you would not stomach
as you swept for the goal;

your bright, black face
was like the best Brazilian
coffee, without cream,
and so creamy women

came to your doorstep
with all they had to give,
an estuary aflutter,
an estuary forsaken
on the remnants of the Hudson River.

And so we came to Bard
and Vassar for the scent,
and the scent came;
though the girls came for crafts
to teach to children,
their wombs spoke differently
and so we had to talk of solace,
and how to resist the symbolism
of flesh, ours and their own:
we swam on those rivers,
were instructed by the suckholes
and rapids of a shallow river,
ran our tongues over placenames
still forbidden, and anchored
in the speech of Coltrane,
who talked exclusively in song.

Driving on the Taconic
in the blue-dark of spray,
and fearing oncoming traffic,
we headed for the "Half-Note,"
after work, to catch the last sessions.

You were awed by Elvin,
McCoy was young, aesthetic,
almost your age, and Jimmy,
Jimmy was learning to play
in the steam of subway cars—
and Coltrane came.

No need for sleep!
We checked, in team meetings,
the virtue of *enrichment*,
saintly period of custodial
control, when we could get the kids
to write letters;
and there were the tailors,
exclusive domain of local women,
who sat like cranes in the buzzard's
roost of the administration building,
but they were white,
unafraid of black/Hispanic
mafia kids,
more afraid of the Mennonites
who ran errands everywhere,
and what they said
counted in more than needles and thread.

They lived for character,
and from where they sat,
they saw everything:
you would bring your charges
into the courtyard
in a straight line,
in clean clothes,
ready for the routine
of the 600 School Review—
600 schools were remedial schools—
and so when the herring ran
we would have runaways;
we had runaways on good days
and on bad;
we would report to the shrinks

and the social workers
what little we knew of design,
for in the files, the psychiatric
files we were not supposed to read,
we found the answers,
cost commentary on the underclass,
the vacuums and votive candles
of the future
for they were sacrificial lambs.

Still, we fought for them,
and when we drove to Grand Central
into the general population,
all their canteen money
as carfare home,
we wept for them,
but we wept secretly:
we had put them to bed,
soothed their nightmares,
retrieved them from the runaway
streams, fed them with pointless
forks, bathed their predatory
sores, patched them up with needle,
thread, and the buttons
of timeless assault,
our institutional homeland.

We did not speak of *bantustans*,
for this was before the jargon
of oppression,
we spoke of a chance;
the girls from Bard and Vassar,
they brought their softness,
and the shrinks met monthly,
with reports on the reserves.

We live by analogy:
I told you to keep your hands off
of what you couldn't support
for a lifetime;
these are the seeds of love.
We drank *Antiquary* scotch
from an Irish stream
in Catskill, New York
where my father was born—
I pointed out the Day Line
where my grandfather worked,
how he lost his eye
to a pop bottle
that blew up in his face;
how he *made* the sweet strings
and palate of the mandolin,
and wouldn't let his wife
work, for anything,
took pride in being 'the only one'
in town, took pride in *battle royales*
for spending money to feed his family.

And so we battled on the riverways
in Rome, New York, where you were born,
and where my uncle traipsed on
Griffiss Air Force Base—
lost his life driving friends to Utica.

So when I heard the mortifying
word, carcinoma,
I came to attention
as a coach runs ascant
to a star running back,
or shortstop, or to the tennis
net where you laid out your habit

in celestial whites,
for you were ruthless at the net,
and in the forecourt,
and your serve was coming around
into the corporate empires
of the inner sanctum:
now there was time for :fun.

You had the faith of your mother, Eva;
you had the intuition of Alex, your father,
who sits in his Town Car
waiting for dialysis,
which is the sight of your face
in the speedlane of the Thruway
coming home; home is your sister,
Rosalyn; it is the beauty of children
at play where all pulled their punches;
all played by the ubiquitous rules.

Deception in your brilliant facades,
and in the mechanics of cooptation,
you met your match in New Mexico,
spirit center of the Navajo,
the high winds of andeluvial change,
and her fealty was the law
and how to count
even your foibles
and property-gain.

The salon opens into the magical sound
of a sunroof in the stars
as a shield is made from Orion,
from Big Bear, from Asia Minor.

Mysteries

BY CLAIRE HARRIS

and   at this moment   the accidental world
why   in the foreground   a framed
wire fence   cat's weathered step-ladder
in the dandelions   cat himself
rampant   considering intently this butterfly
its fluttering yellow statement at the grid
what does cat   butterfly
in mutual revelation

and I with them

beyond us poplars   dawn shadows wind-teased
in the middle ground
my feet released in wet grass   the fresh motion
of snails   earth-scent mingling
with the rising day that should be enough
on the valley floor trucks and cars fan out
sun-gleam whispering on hood/roof
an annunciation of other   of possible
unfathomable brightness

these and I we absorb each other

a jogger labours past   an old man bends to frail
steps   a woman grey bleared
from the night shift   rungs
on which I bruise my feet towards
some curious perfection   no doubt as casual
as these hills

rounded   scorched green   mauve shadows
dark gashes of fir in cluster
the delicate tracery of pylon reaching above
a clutch of unfinished houses

to contain what/how   and these to bear
all unknowing on this one span

mine and not mine

the sky is russet   there is birdsong
far down the hillside a dog's bark opens
onto thunderless oceans   *all this* in infinite
stretches of time   still rising
even as we stand still splitting
towards what   why

Framed

BY CLAIRE HARRIS

She is in your painting   the one you bought when the taxi
snarled in market lines   you jumped out and grabbed
a picture of stilted wooden houses against the vivid island
even then there was recognition

She is the woman in a broken pair of men's shoes   her
flesh slipped down like old socks around her ankles   a tray
of laundry on her head   I am there too   but I would not
be like her   at supper she set the one plate and the whole
cup at my place   for herself a mug a bowl my leavings
they said I resembled her   I spent hours before the mirror
training my mouth to different lines

At night while I read   she folded the blanket on her
narrow board   coalfire smooth on her face   she boiled
scrubbed   ironed   musk of soap and others soil like
mist around her head   often she dreamed   I would have
a maid   like her   she laughed   I studied harder harder
she grieved   I was grown a woman   I was grown
without affinity

For the calling   her eroded hands   cupped like a chalice
she offered me the blasted world as if to say   this is our
sacrament   drink   I would not   this is all there is   I
could not   I left school   I left   she faded
the island faded   styles changed   you hid the dusty
painting in the attic   But I am still there   the one in
middle ground   my face bruising lines of soft white
sheets   my hand raised as if to push against the frame

Touch

BY TERRANCE HAYES

—for Y.K. & brothers playing football in the parks, in the streets, in the dark

We made our own laws.
I want to be a Hawk,
A Dolphin, a Lion, we'd say

In stores where team logos hung
Like animal skins.

Even by moonlight,
We'd chase each other
Around the big field

Beneath branches sagging
As if their leaves were full of blood.

We didn't notice when policemen
Came lighting tree-bark
& our skin with flashlights.

They saw our game
For what it was:

Fingers clutching torso,
Shoulder, wrist—a brawl.
Some of the boys escaped,

Their brown legs cut by thorns
As they ran through the brush.

It's true, we could have been mistaken
For animals in the dark,
But of all possible crimes,

Blackness was the first.
So they tackled me,

And read me my rights without saying:
You Down or Dead Ball.
We had a language

They did not use, a name
For collision. We called it Touch.

The Love of Travellers

(Doris, Sandra and Sheryl)

BY ANGELA JACKSON

At the rest stop on the way to Mississippi
we found the butterfly mired in the oil slick;
its wings thick
and blunted. One of us, tender in the finger tips,
smoothed with a tissue the oil
that came off only a little;
the oil-smeared wings like lips colored with lipstick
blotted before a kiss.
So delicate the cleansing of the wings
I thought the color soft as watercolors would wash off
under the method of her mercy for something so slight
and graceful, injured, beyond the love of travellers.

It was torn then, even after her kindest work,
the almost-moth exquisite charity could not mend
what weighted the wing, melded with it,
then ruptured it in release.
The body of the thing lifted out of its place
between the washed wings.
Imagine the agony of a self separated by gentlest repair.
"Should we kill it?" One of us said. And I said yes.
But none of us had the nerve.
We walked away, the last of the oil welding the butterfly
to the wood of the picnic table.
The wings stuck out and quivered when wind went by.
Whoever found it must have marveled at this.
And loved it for what it was and

had been.
I think, meticulous mercy is the work of travellers,
and leaving things as they are
punishment or reward.

I have died for the smallest things.
Nothing washes off.

Some Kind Of Crazy

BY MAJOR L. JACKSON

It doesn't matter if you can't see
Steve's 1985 Corvette: Turquoise-colored,
Plush purple seats, gold-trimmed
Rims that make little stars in your eyes

As if the sun is kneeling at
The edge of sanity. Like a Baptist
Preacher stroking the dark underside
Of God's wet tongue, he can make you

Believe. It's there; his scuffed wing-
Tips—ragged, frayed, shuffling
Concrete—could be ten-inch Firestone
Wheels, his vocal chords fake

An eight cylinder engine that wags
Like a dog's tail as he shifts gears. Imagine
Steve, moonstruck, cool, turning right
Onto Ridge Avenue, arms forming

Arcs, his hands a set of stiff C's
Overthrowing each other's rule,
His lithe body and head snap back
Pushing a stick shift into fourth

Whizzing past Uncle Sam's Pawn
Shop, past Chung Phat's Stop & Go.
Only he knows his destination,
His limits. Can you see him? Imagine

Steve, moonstruck, cool, parallel
Parking between a Pacer and a Pinto—
Obviously the most hip—backing up,
Head over right shoulder, one hand

Spinning as if polishing a dream;
And there's Tina, wanting to know
What makes a man tick, wanting
A one-way trip to the stars.

We, the faithful, never call
Him crazy, crackbrained, just a little
Touched. It's all he ever wants:
A car, a girl, a community of believers.

Venus's-flytraps

BY YUSEF KOMUNYAKAA

I am five,
   Wading out into the deep
     Sunny grass,
Unmindful of snakes
   & yellowjackets, out
     To the yellow flowers
Quivering in sluggish heat.
   Don't mess with me
     'Cause I have my Lone Ranger
Six-shooter. I can hurt
   You with questions
     Like silver bullets.
The tall flowers in my dreams are
   Big as the First State Bank,
     & they eat all the people
Except the ones I love.
   They have women's names,
     With mouths like where
Babies come from. I am five.
   I'll dance for you
     If you close your eyes. No
Peeping through your fingers.
   I don't supposed to be
     This close to the tracks.
One afternoon I saw
   What a train did to a cow.
     Sometimes I stand so close
I can see the eyes
   Of men hiding in boxcars.

Sometimes they wave
& holler for me to get back. I laugh
   When trains make the dogs
      Howl. Their ears hurt.
I also know bees
   Can't live without flowers.
      I wonder why Daddy
Calls Mama honey.
   All the bees in the world
      Live in little white houses
Except the ones in these flowers.
   All sticky & sweet inside.
      I wonder what death tastes like.
Sometimes I toss the butterflies
   Back into the air.
      I wish I knew why
The music in my head
   Makes me scared.
      But I know things
I don't supposed to know.
   I could start walking
      & never stop.
These yellow flowers
   Go on forever.
      Almost to Detroit.
Almost to the sea.
   My mama says I'm a mistake.
      That I made her a bad girl.
My playhouse is underneath
   Our house, & I hear people
      Telling each other secrets.

Red Pagoda

BY YUSEF KOMUNYAKAA

Raised against the green
morning, the lodestone
landmark pulls us to it:
our eyes on the hill,
we have to get there
somehow. Three snipers
lasso us in a silver
crossfire, singing out
our names like hornets.
The red pawn
is our last move—
green & yellow squares
backdropped with mangrove
swamps, against all
feeling left naked,
something to hold to. Hand
over hand, following frayed
invisible rope to nowhere,
we duck walk through
the tall blooming grass
& nose across the line
of no return. Remnants
of two thatch huts stand,
half trembling to the heavy
sound of running feet,
luteous against the day.
We make it to the hill,
fall down & slide rounds
into the mortar tube;

smithereens of light
& leaf debris cover
the snipers. Unscathed,
with arms hooked through each other's,
like men on some wild
midnight-bound carousel,
in our joy, we kick
& smash the pagoda
till it's dried blood
covering the ground.

Birds on a Powerline

BY YUSEF KOMUNYAKAA

Mama Mary's counting them
Again. Eleven black. A single
Red one like a drop of blood

Against the sky. She's convinced
They've been there two weeks.
I bring her another cup of coffee

& a Fig Newton. I sit here reading
Frances Harper at the enamel table
Where I ate teacakes as a boy,

My head clear of voices brought back.
The green smell of the low land returns,
Stealing the taste of nitrate.

The deep-winter eyes of the birds
Shine in summer light like agate,
As if they could love the heart

Out of any wild thing. I stop,
With my finger on a word, listening.
They're on the powerline, a luminous

Message trailing a phantom
Goodyear blimp. I hear her say
Jesus, I promised you. Now

He's home safe, I'm ready.
My travelling shoes on. My teeth
In. I got on clean underwear.

Slam, Dunk, & Hook

BY YUSEF KOMUNYAKAA

Fast breaks. Lay ups. With Mercury's
Insignia on our sneakers,
We outmaneuvered the footwork
Of bad angels. Nothing but a hot
Swish of strings like silk
Ten feet out. In the roundhouse
Labyrinth our bodies
Created, we could almost
Last forever, poised in midair
Like storybook sea monsters.
A high note hung there
A long second. Off
The rim. We'd corkscrew
Up & dunk balls that exploded
The skullcap of hope & good
Intention. Bug-eyed, lanky,
All hands & feet . . . sprung rhythm.
We were metaphysical when girls
Cheered on the sidelines.
Tangled up in a falling,
Muscles were a bright motor
Double-flashing to the metal hoop
Nailed to our oak.
When Sonny Boy's mama died
He played nonstop all day, so hard
Our backboard splintered.
Glistening with sweat, we jibed
& rolled the ball off our
Fingertips. Trouble

Was there slapping a blackjack
Against an open palm.
Dribble, drive to the inside, feint,
& glide like a sparrowhawk.
Lay ups. Fast breaks.
We had moves we didn't know
We had. Our bodies spun
On swivels of bone & faith,
Through a lyric slipknot
Of joy, & we knew we were
Beautiful & dangerous.

Fishing the White Water

BY AUDRE LORDE

Men claim the easiest spots
stand knee-deep in calm dark water
where the trout is proven.

I never intended to press beyond
the sharp lines set as boundary
named as the razor names
parting the skin
and seeing the shapes of our weakness
etched into afternoon
that sudden vegetarian hunger for meat
tears on the typewriter
tyrannies of the correct
we offer mercy   forgiveness
to ourselves and our lovers
to the failures we underline daily
insisting upon next Thursday
yet forgetting to mention each other's name
the mother of desires
wrote them under our skin.

I call the stone   sister   who remembers
my grandmother's hand
brushed   on her way to market
to the ships
you can choose   not to live
near the graves where your grandmother sings
in wind through the corn.

There have been easier times
for loving   different richness
if it were only the stars
we had wanted
to conquer
I could turn from your dear face
into the prism light makes
along my line
we cast into rapids
alone   back to back
laboring the current.

In some distant summer
working our way farther from bone
we will lie in the river
silent as caribou
and the children will bring us food.

You carry the yellow tackle box
a fishnet over your shoulder
knapsacked
I balance the broken-down rods
our rhythms pass through the trees
staking a claim   in difficult places
we head for the source.

1984

Jessehelms

BY AUDRE LORDE

I am a Black woman
writing my way to the future
off a garbage scow knit from moral fibre
stuck together with jessehelms'
come   where Art is a dirty word
scrawled on the wall
of Bilbo's memorial outhouse
and obscenity is catching
even I'd like to hear you scream
ream out your pussy
with my dildo called Nicaragua
ram Grenada up your fig hole
till Panama runs out of you
like Savimbi a-flame.

But you prefer to do it
on the senate floor
with a sackful of paper pricks
keeping time to the tune
of a 195 million dollar
military band
safe-sex dripping from your tongue
into avid senatorial ear-holes
later you'll get yours
behind the senate toilets
where they're waiting for you jessehelms
the white boys with their pendulous rules
bumping against the rear door of Europe
spread-eagled across the globe

their crystal balls poised over Africa
ass-up for old glory
your turn now jessehelms
come on   it's time
to lick the handwriting
off the walls.

Difficulty with Perspective

BY CLARENCE MAJOR

I am in the coach, waiting
for the other passengers.

They're coming now.
I watch.

My mother
as a black-and-white
photograph.
The girls
in long dresses
from the brothel,
Mme. Ginoux,
two old ladies
from Etten.
Cabbage pickers.
Lovers of dahlias
and cypress-sway.
My doctor
with his leather
bag. A stock-holder
with interest
in the Oskar Reinhart.

I wait self-consciously:
with blue gloves,
a basket of lemons, very
chic, a cypress branch
on my lap.

Here comes a young girl
against a red background,
chinless high-stepper
with brooding face
borrowed from somebody
else. My mother
as a child? My child?

The doctor helps
my mother up. Then
the girls from the whore-
house. Enchanted.

The horses
are restless: shifting
and kicking. I wait.

Others still come
out the station:
its doors folding out
and falling back,
with these walkers
coming through
like the careful
arrangement
of music.

Approaching
is the rock-star,
a girl with ruffled hair
from Burlington. My mother
says Minneapolis. She saw
it on TV. Vince called
her a mudlark! Monticelli?
Florentine angel

with dirty hair,
savior rebel spirit!

Now: all the dancers
from last night's dance
with lights still
suspended above them
and the darkness too.

Here, sailors and lover-
silhouettes returning
from the drawbridge
with the sun big
as Texas behind them.

I'm patient.
Potentially, I am
a good passenger, too.
I slide over.

I keep sliding over.

Unwanted Memory

BY CLARENCE MAJOR

My memory of myself has become
a drawbridge to ancient catcalls
left echoing in my brains.
I was the worthless victim
of a jihad: dead. I pause.
I pause before plunging in:
once inside, there is no elbowroom.
Memory speaks: inside
me there's a catatonic ape
trying to get a grip on his mate.
His failure is respectable
without being a violation
of nature. Perverse, grim,
pure? It is not like working
for the film industry: he does
not simply plug along for fear
of not getting another gig.
Part of the script has to do
with a churning mixture of bad
memory and using one's finger
when the dike is about to
show its tendency. I forgot
what I was going to say.
Oh, yes: see
this window? I'm going to take it,
unscrew the entire frame,
and ram my head through the glass.
I will march with it around my neck
like this along the river down

to the drawbridge and stop
at the dike. Here, I will
have no trouble remembering
what to do.

Country After Country

BY KAREN MITCHELL

My mama threw her falafel at him
because he wouldn't put any red cabbage
on her naked pita—
he put everything
on the others. Everything
for those who stood with cameras, passports—
visitors assured like sweat in June.

When she threw her curve,
I could see the onion grow roots,
my mama swearing, asking, remembering
her cattail brew
to make the lamb roast faster
than a reluctant kiss,
to transform the bread into Saltine crackers,
to summon the firepeople
for a tango of smoke
as he tried to explain
that some foreigner
had tried to remake his recipe.

After she didn't leave for twenty-two minutes,
I knew she could tie them up.
Those that knew:
the boy who fumbled for the word
water, coming out of unconsciousness;
the woman who mumbled that "everything had been nice,"
wonderful, like the tour of churches
built with in-house tombs.

She would tie them up with barbed wire,
potent enough to convince the goddess
to take them in absence
of basil and thyme.
But when she sat down on the sidewalk,
pressing her belly like untimed
labor, she cried.
She said it was like the time when she
had to buy those shoes.
The saleswoman, explaining that those were the only
pair left, exhibited
them like they were the tips
of the last unicorns.

She had to buy them for the recital,
the choir of white
dresses singing like angels
manufacturing sheen—*And now this*:

The American coke.

She didn't drink, but
threw it at him, watching
the ice hit
like hail on pane.

Forgiveness

BY KAREN MITCHELL

He heard that she had drowned,
candles lit, sonata on pause,
soap floating from one end to another, a
vagabond in water.
He knew there wouldn't be anyone
to hear her heeltaps announce
that she had reached the mirror,
then turned to see her hair unravel
like a rope
being thrown
from a window.
He didn't linger; she didn't relax,
but kept shoving the dirt
away from the sucking,
the groans
of some child
bewitched in an underwater cave. . . .
When he took his bath, he read
his wife's letters, telling her
she could do better.
A five-year contract. The university
that kept writing to her
like a boy proposing.
She wouldn't write back,
and so he had to warn her,
tell her that she had to be
the girl with just one wish
because he knew
how men were

with a woman who declared
her birth as Paris.
So when he heard that she had died,
he told those French-speaking morticians
to be ready to call the police
after they had drained her body
and saw that her blood
had been nothing but poison.

Richard Brought His Flute

BY NANCY MOREJÓN

I
soundlessly
his veins bursting with cognac and Romeu's danzón
Papa Egües firmly and with an air of astonishment appropriates
                                            his chair
"there isn't a single musician of my generation left
            in Placetas
            a damnable dirge
            over all the band"
we're all here but the one we're waiting for doesn't come
and outside it rains steadily

each night
legends of *Juan Gualberto* in the old country
reappear
like the wind through the trees

meanwhile we kept playing records

"the swing's in the drums"

it thunders and rains
        and rains enough to drown us all in our
            fourteen and fifteen year-old memories

there's death and then where will we be?

we look out the window facing the narrow street
that leads to the church of San Nicolás

(we never liked priests)
it's dinner time and we nibble bread
and drink beer

II
the piano is in the living room

the good thing about having the piano in the living room
is that we can see everything else clearly
the living room isn't large just the place where the piano sits

"how do you feel about listening to a little music?"

everyone agrees to that

good afternoons or good evenings
suspend thought
we're all here what else?
    just together
even if nettled Papa Egües
    and his spectacles
want to tie us down and teach us
every note on the flute
    as well as solfège

of course we lack the necessary breeding
to understand the music
and without knowing why
it's clear that our attention is wandering at this hour
at this moment of sound and secular discipline

the piano is in the living room

(it is Monday and someone has lit a candle
    the large seven day candle for Elegba

there's nothing to say
just sit by the door drinking a bottle of rum)

all of us virtuous and well-mannered
the little girls with their folded hands
the little boys practicing solfège
growling away on the sticky drunken violin
the paltriness of our every act was summed up
in knowing perhaps that we could easily recognize a Picasso
and that perhaps hispanics and blacks lived better in New York

through a first cousin we had bought
Count Basie Duke Ellington and the Nat Cole trio
and by December it was possible to get
Mozart's concerto for flute
among all the marvels of the living room the piano rests

a serpent rises as night falls

it is time

the invention of legends

III
the day that two old ladies dissected two birds
         in some room in a museum
we came home empty anxious to hear some jazz
our happiness lay wholly in the pleasure of listening
         lost in the spell of a black art

for me it was the first time
the first time
the first time I knew a clarinet so fierce
         so smoky
         hot

thanks to Papa Egües that was the beginning of an age
for us childhood restored
        begun so alone

that clarinet alone like a bridge

(and Gladys   her coppery gaze   a little heavier)

we needed to hear the faintest whisper
the *chack* of the dust-caked needle

Mozart and Europe laughed in the distance
but we were also dancing desperately
listening to a *timbal* a bass a trumpet a gourd a flute
all playing together
or listening to drumbeats rising from the same fire

it was my first time my first big moment
and the silence resolved into listening
        into listening

IV
we're all here

the music plays

congratulations Gladys

Gladys

but Gladys won't dance

no

never that

V

soon we were all talking at once

"my shoes are the prettiest, dear"

our eyes sorted out the table and the painting of the white swan

we felt the evening's weight

at times we felt an urge to blow everything
        willy nilly
in the end *papa* would understand

we got Papa Egües's help
just by letting him tell us about our family
and his youth

we wound up later in the kitchen
trying to control the house from there
returning afterwards to our books
with such desire to devour dictionaries
looking at each other face to face
only to realize much later that some of us would plunge
        into life
        others into a living death
into madness and others
would collapse at the end of a garand or a mauser

VI

when we looked at our skin we switched our glance
        toward the television
at least that pleasure cost nothing
when we looked at our teeth we began to laugh like madmen
hurting each other for no reason

when Papa Egües wrenched the ring from his finger
or complained of insufferable arthritis
        we sang a hymn to his elegance
stifling our laughter trying not to hear his reprimands

when we arrived in a frenzy for Zaira's French class
                        —a little late—
the black washerwoman scolded us loudly

(*a Girl's education must first take place in her head*)

when we talked about Jorge's eyes
someone who was daydreaming with us
would say "he's Dr. Milián's son"

when we looked at our neighbors
        black like us incidentally
well
        "no reason to worry that's the way things are"
finally
        everything becomes that living room the piano
everything weighs upon us
like someone who shuns a distant dead relative

VII
the sun fell on the park packed with children
a lot of bicycles
I used to accompany Gladys on a walk
        every afternoon
such noise
she would ask about my parents
whether they disappeared at night
if something caught in their throats when they mentioned me

the afternoon was suffocating
as usual Gladys and I
took in a movie
went shopping for a closet full of clothes
        just to show them off

"you have to be in style"

we returned home

VIII
the orishas never echoed our voices
        we knew they surrounded the house
and like güijes frightened all evil away

there was someone around or living there
        all powerful
a simple stick or reed was his attribute
he blew through it with all the strength of a black man in love

the orishas vibrated quietly around his fingers
the fingers of his right hand diminished the rhythm
        slowly
the one we were waiting for brings his flute

we all craved his presence around the mahogany table
the gold light of the hearth shattered on his shoulders
mysteriously
it's miraculous Richard is with us
        with his solitary flute

                    —*Translated from the Spanish by Lois Wright*

One for All Newborns

BY THYLIAS MOSS

They kick and flail like crabs on their backs.
Parents outside the nursery window do not believe
they might raise assassins or thieves, at the very worst
a poet or obscure jazz musician whose politics
spill loudly from his horn.
Everything about it was wonderful, the method
of conception, the gestation, the womb opening
in perfect analogy to the mind's expansion.
Then the dark succession of constricting years,
mother competing with daughter for beauty and losing,
varicose veins and hot water bottles, joy boiled away,
the arrival of knowledge that eyes are birds with clipped wings,
the sun at a 30° angle and unable to go higher, parents
who cannot push anymore, who stay by the window
looking for signs of spring
and the less familiar gait of grown progeny.
I am now at the age where I must begin to pay
for the way I treated my mother. My daughter is just like me.
The long trip home is further delayed, my presence
keeps the plane on the ground. If I get off it will fly.
The propellor is a cross spinning like a buzz saw
about to cut through me. I am haunted and my mother is not dead.
The miracle was not birth but that I lived despite my crimes.
I treated God badly also; he is another parent
watching his kids through a window, eager to be proud
of his creation, looking for signs of spring.

Holding

BY THYLIAS MOSS

Evening comes
and it is the only promise
the day has kept.

Nobody knows about the wig
and she doesn't look at herself
taking it off. Then she feels
for her own stubby braids, unbraids
them, liking the coarseness
like a working man's hand. It's been so long
simulation will do just fine, thank you.
But not liking it enough.
The wig is smooth.

She braids them again, obeying
a tradition in Ghana, in Guinea
in a D.C. home business so skilled in
managing three worlds of hair, blending
them into one unit of braid without
juggling or favoring, the skill is questioned
by those who cannot braid, who spend
a hundred hours learning to shampoo
and untangle for their licenses: and thousands
of women are queens for days and—days
when they leave, for the braids last and last.

She tucks the stubby braids under a tight-
fitting crown, a stocking cap. Then

she talks to God, getting down on her knees
as if the room is full of smoke.

Her face shines with night cream, pinkish,
mother-of-pearlish; this nacreous effect
is almost precious; it comes off in the morning.
God talks to her. She hears every word
he says even those without words. The God
she pictures is white headed, his eyes are oceans,
his muscles are trees; his knuckles, mountain
ranges; there are escarpments where the cuticles
drop down to nails, valleys between his toes
and that is how he holds the whole world.

She sleeps well. She holds her dreams well
although she is sleep, her grip does not weaken.

She wakes ready, really all gaga with faith
and all God does is hold, hold,
put her on hold.

Fable

BY HARRYETTE MULLEN

When the crow fell in love
with a scarecrow
the possibilities seemed endless.
Such strangers,
they could teach each other.
Crow was not afraid
and scarecrow,
though dressed like a working man,
had nothing better
to occupy the time.

Actually there was little
they could do—
with scarecrow staked out
in the corn,
fastened to a silly grin,
wearing clothes that once belonged
to a real person.
Only tatters now,
an imperfect skin trying to contain
innards of straw,
the hay spilling out.

That bird sits on one shoulder,
cocking her head to the side,
Crow, bright-eyed,
glossy-feathered.
Know the way rainbows thrive
in the black shine of oil?

Raucous bird
thinks she can sing.
Scarecrow seems pleased,
unable to cover its ears
or change its expression.
Easy critic dances in the breeze
while the blackbird whispers
notes toward a song.

Unspoken

BY HARRYETTE MULLEN

I'm holding on to you, but you're gone already,
halfway up the mountain, maybe,
in a dream I cannot climb.
I lie awake outside the door
that leads to my own dreams of houses
with bookshelves in every room.

I'm holding your body the color of walnuts—
brown shell you've left behind,
a code I cannot crack—
and wishing you talked in your sleep,
so I could listen in.

Always, when I want to know what you're feeling,
you put your hands on me:
"Here, let me show you,"
and you let your hands do the talking.
Oh yes, I like it and it feels good,
but of course that isn't what I meant.

"We don't need words for this," you tell me.
I wonder if that's what you like best
about our bodies side by side,
together and strange,
like words of two languages
trying to form a sentence.
There I go again,
talking of words and languages

while you've gone to sleep,
leaving me to find a message in your snoring.

Holding you,
I concentrate on the arcane language of your breathing.
Holding your hands in the dark,
I finger the lines of each curling palm,
as if they were a braille I could learn to read.

Finally, I put my ear to your chest,
thinking I can eavesdrop on your heart,
hoping to hear a meaningful pattern of beats—
a telegram you stop to send
on your way down the far side of that mountain.

Setting Loose the Icons

BY BRENDA MARIE OSBEY

this is the year i have given up old icons
or else had them rudely snatched from my hands
making the two-day trek eastward by train
all my belongings in sealed parcels
or the loaded baggage
the cabbies refused to lift
coming finally to a stopping place
where the pain continues
and i am left with oddly turned streets
only vaguely like home
volumes of biography
weighting the front-end of my brain.

the first one:
i search among the junk and jewelry shops
for the right stone
smooth and cool
like your hands those thursday evenings
because we never were together weekends
because i wanted you well enough to accept it all
without becoming the hero
of an affair i built from scratch
inventing as i went along.
how well you played it
like a blues your best friend listens to again
because it masks his growing fear
of being abandoned on some dance floor
around three a.m.
going home to the empty house

no one waiting up
sheet music strewn across the piano bench
in his house that smells only
of a man who lives alone.

small rituals you go through uptown after midnight
rooms shrouded in palms
the pine tree i left you
your shadow strewn across a glass of scotch
too strong for your aging constitution.
onyx set in silver
a lover i took some years ago
because i was young and firm
because i could
because i was beautiful and you would not refuse me.
so much has happened
between then and the hospital stretcher
where they force-fed me oxygen
two lovers looking on
the numbness in my hands and feet
my eyes running tears of shock perhaps self-pity
the young animal in me wounded
the groan like a broken record
no one bothers to correct.
small retribution for the intensity of my life—
the smell of you as near to me as death.
tell the truth
what did you see that night?

what did you see?
something says you will not tell.
it will perhaps cease to matter
while the japanese girl behind the counter
smiles as i finger each stone
bringing it to my face

my lips
rubbing it along
the red-brown skin along the back of my hand
i make the uneven exchange:
paper money
for the smooth stone that binds you to me
binding fast the wanga
no one has set free in years and years.

the second one:
the telephone receiver lies dead in my right hand
the childhood smell of cold new plastic
distance
distance
there is nothing i can exchange for you
my heart strung round with glass beads
counted like a rosary
in the empty half of your house there on burgundy
death walking like a grown woman
searching through the miscellany
of your dead and dying parents' belongings.

give me back my life
give me back my life damn it.

i fold up the edges of the photograph
and place it face down in its little grave
the glass beads around my heart
like the prayers of a young widow

the hardest thing
is the turning away
the hardest thing
to live long enough
to bury your own dead.

the other one:
father father father
it becomes a kind of song
beneath bright lights
across a hardwood floor.
when the choir in me dries up
like dust from an indian clay vessel
tossed casually to the floor
when i stop dancing
my legs confined to the corridors
of the insane ward of the private hospital
uptown where no one knows me
where a lover's mother lies speechless
preparing to die
when i am no longer the precious fledgling
but a grown woman whose life hurts and breaks
a grown woman scraping the blues for some answer
that is nothing but a cry
that comes as close to saying help me
as a proud woman can manage
there is only that stillness in your voice
the eyes that look away
like the proverbial louisiana creole
bastard children
scattered from one small town or city to the next
substitution becomes such an easy thing.

and so i go packing up my life again
leaving no visible traces
nothing to be discarded
taking up residence
as far from anything like home as possible
for a woman like me
using rootworking and the past
proper antidotes to life.

it takes a while to accept
such rude transformations.

the ritual:
this is the year the idols are all placed
beneath the altar
cracked and broken
some missing even eyes and limbs

no one must see me
fondle them close to my private parts
no one must see me
float them in the indian clay vessel
saved for just this purpose
no one must see me put them down inside my shoes
crushing them softly
walking the charles river
among the innocent
and the unsuspecting
blood in my shoes
blood in my shoes
along the backs of a water
that carries me only
farther away
from the icons i have constructed
from willing human flesh.

this is called dying.
i am told the young do it
with true grace.

Calunga Lungara

BY EDIMILSON DE ALMEIDA PEREIRA

I am going to put into words
what is not possible.
They are water-words
that dissolve.

I am speaking of Calunga.

It can be large or
small depending
on who crossed it.

Its name changes
according to the tongue.
In some it kills
in others it is ocean.

On it is traveling
someone who has no body.
We are sailors
in a land of pilgrimage.

Calunga goes around at night
studying dreams.
It accompanies captive
marks in the dust.

It brings present fears
family fears.

The oldest does not show
that even he would die.

I put into words
what should not have been spoken.

What one says is not Calunga.

—Translated from the Portuguese by Steven F. White

Moving Target

BY CARL PHILLIPS

If to be patient were less
an exercise

and more a name to be worn, say,
in the middle—

that he might wear it—

Of the linen sash to
his robe, of linen,

that his hands have
fashioned a knot such that
the knot suggests now a dragonfly in

flight from what is harmless and

not, entirely—
that he might, if at all, know this

only as when without understanding it
we know we have and have come to

expect we shall have always

upon others
an effect we do not
intend—

His face:

a face, turning. And
then a turned one.

The Clearing

BY CARL PHILLIPS

Had the light
changed, possibly—or,

differently, was that how I'd
seen it

   always, and not
looking? Was I meant for

a vessel? Did I only
believe so and,

so, for a time, was it true but

only in that space which belief makes
for its own wanting?

What am I going to
do with you
   —Who just

said that?

Whose the body—where—that voice
belongs to?

   Might I turn,
toward it, whinny

into it?

      My life
      a water,

      or a cure for
      that which no water
      can cure?

      His chest
      a forest, or a lush
      failure—

Even now, shall I choose? Do I
get to?

Dearest-once-to-me

      Dearest-still-to-me

Have I chosen
already,

      or is choice a thing
hovering yet, an

intention therefore, from
which, though
late, could I hurry back?

What am I going to do with you—   or

how?
Whom for?

If stay my hand—where

rest it?

Elegy for a White Cock (after Mei Yao-ch'en, ca. 1002–1060)

BY ED ROBERSON

With suburban real estate rising

anywhere it's snug up
    the butt of the rural,

the roosters who used to

make all those promises
    are fewer and fewer.

       Lifters of the dark, nightblooming labia,
       Comers of the light,   et cetera.

Any birds you can call are less.
    Call them   messengers or angels,

ring or flight announcers in the laddered wrestling

up through dumbness . . .
    Our deepest carriers   in specie planes

go down, blow up   like birds nor angels never

       could admit, get hijacked . . .
       And the unit

of the morning, measure of temples,

how could it
        matter to a plumb-line fired by we   unfeathered

that in its infancy cracks an orbit whip

off Jupiter's
        huge head?   matter

            to this shining semblance we
            spot in a glide for setting

down,   eastern's early coach at dawn,
        our morning star?

that silent cock of the spectrum,

up   at our changed limit . . .
        Our fires once our horizons. Now out past stars,

what started at the simple reds of roosters.

                        **

But
        There is no one   from this apartment   who you'd expect
            to hear morning   chanticleerly   with any sense
                since wake-up radio and traffic
                            reports
                    abruptly shortened as by the neck
                by live transmission of one crash
            into the Hudson off 44th   some mechanism loosely acting
                        your fox.

But that is gone, too, that red, too. Some tale of water closing
            about it, white as ice   because,   in a moment
                the last attention failed. Everything

got across
        that water in its brief window as footing
     but the loss at the end, the end of the red
   tail   touched down with cold white.   Like black blood is
in the western light   where it touched the sea.

**

old farmer, poor as dirt, maybe older even than dirt is,
surely older than these kind of stories,

had a rooster got to be his pet, his friend . . . one night
he hear it holler, something had done snatch it . . .

he run outside to chase whatever . . . he end up saying, "who
could use cinnamon and ginger on him now?" that exactly

that exactly where we at.

**

Our wolf at our door   or earlier
        our cave entrance   or closer in such distances
of time to us   just outside our fires,

a wolf of minute just night's side of ebb,
        those barely eyes twice the morning star as cold
and more unmoved than heavens were ever wished,
        fixes a hunger into blue hairs
            and disappears in this direction
                as a day.

The cock crow which rules   that night hungers have eaten
        all that earth has turned
up,   the meaning of wolves   dissolving already
        into light, the quick of foxes'

fire just so much flesh, so much material
of suns,

recalls the sides into position.
That exactly where we at.

Where,   as that call goes down, every revenge, each justice
unreturned by then to the balance
we thought we made as a fire,   it dawns
each scheme again that these are periods not any
understandable score
of resolution we can study;

where,   around a fire we thought would keep the fox
the wolf the chaos off
like the timekeeper crowing on our side,
we sit with loss, the unreturned or absence for timekeeper
and only the summary embering to study before,
far on the burning horizon,   foreign pictoglyphs

begin arriving written in the broken dazzling.

**

You could wake up with the set still on,
still in the process of drawing
the pictureless, blue brightness from the dark
through the antenna   it seems

until, too much,   a clot of day hangs there.
Vacuumed tightly to the teats of the antenna,
a blue static backs up from the little window
into day,   pressure after frameless pressure,

emptiness after emptiness.
Halting,   in that counter-telescopic

squeal of static,   our star
entropies into place

among the waves,   the blue echoic waves
that thin and feral lips of the event horizons
pull upon and break along
a spectral line like shore at sea at dawn

clear as the line of the antenna is
the perch for birds
to finish the extension of their wing
come down to this

                                    **

Birds are taken in through the t.v. antenna
to the screen. Only the squawks of pain

and the shout of eyes in the darkness against
some fox of broadcast.

Some favorite and antique hope is silenced.
                        . . . You lose your damn rooster,
we lose our commons' farm to suburban imageries,
then lose our images to speculation in returns on anomie.

The land, the vane, its bird who names the sun up, lost
in a traffic of the windshield's focus, lost, the morning, star,
                        the very morning itself.

What spices could you use on this death
when it   in every pot   is tuned empty

an iron bell in your stomach spooned against?

See how the thinned blood day uprises
hungry over the hills in reply.

Book Review

BY LUCINDA H. ROY

I.

Amid the whir of estrogen,
my finger marking the last page
of this book I've written by mistake,
I repeat the question like a mantra:
*How can suffering be translated
into flight?* until the skin divides
and fluffs into the sweep
of feathers, and arms lengthen
out of yearning,
and what I was before I entered heaven
becomes a speck in the eye—
calcium deposits in the sky
of the intellect.

But pain cannot be thrown off like a cloak;
it is scraped from backs with razorblades.
Listen. In the geographic warps
which scar the globe like seams
on a lunatic quilt,
my people are not screaming.
In extremity, lyricism mutes itself
and a violent hush—the split
second after the guillotine
splits the head from the shoulders,
the moment before the mushy crash
to the ground, in between
the clicks of needles;
the quiet after the compelled ejaculations

of the hinged niggers when the bodies
swing once in a smile line
from left to right and birds
are shocked out of music;
that millimeter of time between
the locked door and the gas explosion
crawling into Semitic lungs like whirling spiders;
that peace prior to departure
when the brown and hungry child lies between
the breasts in sweet imitation of serenity
before the camera's click for the West
and the mother's howl blasts from her mouth—
at that moment poetry is prayer
and language a flagrant disregard
of what we seem to have to be.
No one recreates the omnisecond—
the extended empathy for the void.
Women come closest to it when their screaming
ricochets off holes as deep as rape.
They come closest when children tunnel
from between them covered in the blood-and-mucous
heritage of kings and slaves.
The seam down the meridian is flanked with despair
like runway lights. Inside the fold
is the key to aerodynamics.
If I have the guts to follow it.
If I have the nerve to ponder the edge.

II.
Lucy took a needle
And sewed her lady's clothes.
Her head in plaits of suffering,
Like corn, in rows, in rows.

She sewed until her thumb was gone
Her eyes were crossed and blind;
She didn't sing a sorrow song
Her words were far behind

Between the coast of Africa
And the Carolina shore
Her alphabet is floating like the corpse
Her body wore

When the sea began its rhythm
In her back and in her head
When she knew her eyes were open
To the clamor of the dead.

Lucy took a needle
And sewed her lady's clothes.
Her head in plaits of suffering
Like corn—in rows, in rows.

III.
1st voice:
Love is not a meritocracy, and those who claim
it for the meritorious are wrong.
Love is simple in its devastation.
The wings it gives us are strapped on
with leather bands that cut into the flesh
if the breeze doesn't blow just right
and the great wings are thrown back against the air
like insidious umbrellas and the filaments
of pain are incandescent and love tears
tears from the dryeyed and the Stoic
and makes women mad.

2nd voice:
Love need not be infestation.
In that rare instance when desire and fulfilment
fuse, wet is warm and sex a dialogue between
good friends, then love is a path through
elements and what is sentimental merely
what is true.

IV.
When everything's projection,
integrity is lost,
and now I'm afraid
that all she's seen is manufactured
and all she's written down a fabrication.
Between the sheets of where she is
lies a continent. If it had a name
it would be Africa Omega where the early bones
of early tribes were laid bare—
the femurs white "I's" in the red earth.
These are not ideas but actualities—
this white noise from the dark.
Her features are a descant
to the sun—the flat nose
and the full lips an interplay between
the who and where.
Between
her lips the moist tongue
works to climax,
and in her hands the woman takes
a shape against the day,
blending with the sun's set
like photosynthesis.
In her are the girls
of Europe with history bells
around their necks, ambling

from the pastoral with a rustic need.
And the urban girls pursuing the highheeled
drama of the bank. And the ravaged girls
of humanistic fiction of whom tragedies
are made. And her white mother
and her black father, and her skin's
antithesis.

Brimful as Whitman,
private as Emily's ghost,
I want to wrench flight from the sky
and pin it to my full breasts like medallions.

I have flown up to Hades and back again.
The going up is sweet.
The lifting off
the best that I have known
of joy.

A Poem for My Father

BY SONIA SANCHEZ

how sad it must be
to love so many women
to need so many black
perfumed bodies weeping
underneath you.
      when i remember all those nights
i filled my mind with
long wars between short
sighted trojans & greeks
while you slapped some
wide hips about in
your pvt dungeon,
when i remember your
deformity   i want to
do something about your
makeshift manhood.
i guess
        that is why
on meeting your sixth
wife, i cross myself
with her confessionals.

Sequences

BY SONIA SANCHEZ

1.
today I am
tired of sabbaths.
I seek a river of sticks
scratching the spine.
O I have laughed the clown's air
now my breath dries in paint.

2.
what is this profusion?
the sun does not burn
a cure, but hoards
while I stretch upward.
I hear, turning
in my shrug
a blaze of horns.
O I had forgotten parades
belabored with dreams.

3.
in my father's time
I fished in ponds
without fishes.
arching my throat,
I gargled amid nerves
and sang of redeemers.
       (o where have you been sweet
          redeemer, sharp redeemer,
       (o where have you been baroque

shimmer?
i have been in coventry
where ghosts danced in my veins
i have heard you in all refrains.)

4.
ah the lull of
a yellow voice
that does not whine
with roots.
I have touched breasts
and buildings answered.
I have breathed
moth-shaped men
without seeds.
(O indiscriminate sleeves)

(once upon an afternoon
i became still-life
i carried a balloon
and a long black knife.)

5.
love comes with pink eyes
with movements that run
green then blue again.
my thighs burn in crystal.

Childhood

BY SHARAN STRANGE

Summer brought fireflies in swarms.
They lit our evenings like dreams
we thought we couldn't have.
We caught them in jars, punched
holes, carried them around for days.

Luminous abdomens that when charged
with air turned bright. Imagine!
mere insects carrying such cargo,
magical caravans flickering beneath
low July skies. We chased them, amazed.

The idea! Those tiny bodies
pulsing phosphorescence.
They made reckless traffic,
signaling, neon flashes forever
into the deepening dusk.

They gave us new faith
in the nasty tonics of childhood,
pungent, murky liquids promising
shining eyes, strong teeth, glowing skin,
and we silently vowed to swallow ever after.

What was the secret of light?
We wanted their brilliance:
small fires hovering,
each tiny explosion
the birth of a new world.

Offering

BY SHARAN STRANGE

In the dream I am burning the rice.
I am cooking for God. I will clean
the house to please Him. So I wash the dishes
and it begins to burn. It is for luck.
Like rice pelting newlyweds,
raining down it is another veil,
or an offering that suggests
her first duty: to feed him.

Burning, it turns brown, the color
of my father, who I never pleased.
Too late, I stand at his bed,
calling. He is swathed in twisted
sheets, a heavy mummy that will not
eat or cry. Will he sleep when
a tall stranger comes to murder me?
Will I die this fourth time, or the next?

When I run, it is as if underwater,
slow, sluggish as the swollen grains
rising out of the briny broth to fill
the pot, evicting the steam in low
shrieks like God's breath sucked back in.
Before I slip the black husk of sleep,
I complete the task. The rice chars,
crumbles to dust, to mix with
the salty water, to begin again.

Letter Home—New Orleans, November 1910

BY NATASHA TRETHEWEY

Four weeks have passed since I left, and still
I must write to you of no work. I've worn down
the soles and walked through the tightness
of my new shoes calling upon the merchants,
their offices bustling. All the while I kept thinking
my plain English and good writing would secure
for me some modest position. Though I dress each day
in my best, hands covered with the lace gloves
you crocheted—no one needs a *girl*. How flat
the word sounds, and heavy. My purse thins.
I spend foolishly to make an appearance of quiet
industry, to mask the desperation that tightens
my throat. I sit watching—

though I pretend not to notice—the dark maids
ambling by with their white charges. Do I deceive
anyone? Were they to see my hands, brown
as your dear face, they'd know I'm not quite
what I pretend to be. I walk these streets
a white woman, or so I think, until I catch the eyes
of some stranger upon me, and I must lower mine,
a *negress* again. There are enough things here
to remind me who I am. Mules lumbering through
the crowded streets send me into reverie, their footfall
the sound of a pointer and chalk hitting the blackboard
at school, only louder. Then there are women, clicking
their tongues in conversation, carrying their loads
on their heads. Their husky voices, the wash pots
and irons of the laundresses call to me. Here,

I thought not to do the work I once did, back bending
and domestic; my schooling a gift—even those half days
at picking time, listening to Miss J—. How
I'd come to know words, the recitations I practiced
to sound like her, lilting, my sentences curling up
or trailing off at the ends. I read my books until
I nearly broke their spines, and in the cotton field
I repeated whole sections I'd learned by heart,
spelling each word in my head to make a picture
I could see, as well as a weight I could feel
in my mouth. So now, even as I write this
and think of you at home, *Goodbye*

is the waving map of your palm, is
a stone on my tongue.

Vignette—from a photograph by E. J. Bellocq, circa 1912

BY NATASHA TRETHEWEY

They pose the portrait outside
the brothel—Bellocq's black scrim,
a chair for her to sit on. She wears
white, a rhinestone choker, fur,
her dark crown of hair—an elegant image,
one she might send to her mother.
Perhaps the others crowd in behind
Bellocq, awaiting their turns, tremors
of laughter in their white throats.
Maybe Bellocq chats, just a little,
to put her at ease while he waits
for the right moment, a look on her face
to keep in a gilded frame, the ornate box
he'll put her in. Suppose he tells her
about a circus coming to town—monkeys
and organ music, the high trapeze—but then

she's no longer listening; she's forgotten
he's there. Instead she must be thinking
of her childhood wonder at seeing
the contortionist in a sideshow—how
he could make himself small, fit
into cramped spaces, his lungs
barely expanding with each tiny breath.
She thinks of her own shallow breath—
her back straining the stays of a bustier,
the weight of a body pressing her down.

Picture her face now as she realizes
that it must have been harder every year,
that the contortionist, *too,* must have ached
each night in his tent. This is how
Bellocq takes her, her brow furrowed
as she looks out to the left, past all of them.
Imagine her a moment later, stepping out
of the frame, wide-eyed, into her life.

On Stripping Bark from Myself

(for Jane, who said trees die from it)

because women are expected to keep silent about
their close escapes I will not keep silent
and if I am destroyed (naked tree!) someone will
   please
mark the spot
where I fall and know I could not live
silent in my own lies
hearing their "how *nice* she is!"
whose adoration of the retouched image
I so despise.

No. I am finished with living
for what my mother believes
for what my brother and father defend
for what my lover elevates
for what my sister, blushing, denies or rushes
to embrace.

I find my own
small person
a standing self
against the world
an equality of wills
I finally understand.

Besides:

On Stripping Bark from Myself   403

My struggle was always against
an inner darkness: I carry within myself
the only known keys
to my death—to unlock life, or close it shut
forever. A woman who loves wood grains, the color
    yellow
and the sun, I am happy to fight
all outside murderers
as I see I must.

Yellow Wolf Spirit

BY RON WELBURN

It is the wolf running
across lightbeams that underscores
the powers of vision.
All else may fail out here on the road.
All else may become perilously a search
for meaning, in the way a theorist
can count only the yellow lines,
unable to learn the dark.

That wolf is meaning enough.
Its yellow spirit lopes across view;
the yellow lights sing to its iron coat.
What is learned from this witness
no book can attempt in words,
for the vision consecrates spirit
as the wolf runs through the heart.

Often we play out its maneuvers
admiring how wolfhair cloaks our intentions,
misreading instructions kindling the yellow eyes,
the music of its speaking.

Often, we become foul shouters and whistlers
or pursue careless quests of chaos to the woman
with the wolf's carpathian eyes
who would read us the cards.

From it we learned how to hunt and
invented the cunning of seduction,

the body language of stealth and
the lowered heads of pretentious desire.

Then it runs the dark through
our burnt out forests of identity, cajoling
our secrets and weakened essence
with its song, lyrics to the fear of
resonating sentience.

Wolf running, wolf songs.
We follow yellow wolf to edges of light
where the night world swallows its coat
and where its chest heaving resplendid
and strong drives the force of a lance
bolting with life.

Naming the Asturian Bird

BY JAY WRIGHT

"Me casó mi madre
con un pícaro pastor ..."

I would be carried away
by my name, adrift
in a sound that only wind
could secure and draft.
I know that I have sprung, head
first, bereft of signs,
glabrous, mute and spiky hard.

I stand apart from the law
of graves and thrifty
sacrifices, the dew
of devotion—my deftness.
Once I thought death alone held
secrets so feigned
I need not stand to be healed.

Nomen, cognomen, the straw
of a faith so scruffy,
so fallen, so swiftly wed
to a loss uplifted.
Why should I, unfrocked, now hide,
and then be impugned
by the death they apprehend?

Why should I see the flaw
in my mother's craft,

the torn seam in her blue shawl,
the rage gone spendthrift?
There must be a bead hidden,
a link that designs
the soul's unbidden heraldry.

I must find faith in the swell
of vowel, the deft
plowing of consonant, awe
dampened angels, love's crafters.
Faith seeds me in custom, holds
me to the slogans
of my house, and binds my hands.

I know my mother has strewn
her skill in my croft
and set me all softly down,
my soul's own grafter.
Seated now, I am haunted
by the magnitude
of the earth I have harrowed.

I turn, ready to bestow
my nomadic gifts
upon a pícaro, wi-
ly, and derelict.
I must accept these hurried
tokens and the reign
of another's holiday.

My name will be a weaver's
cloth, adorned with grief
and pressed beside my dowry,
to serve as my shrift.
I now turn to the haunted

Making Callaloo

page and signature
of a free song I have heard,

and awake to a wedding
song, the blessed script
of testament and sorrow,
light in the soul's cleft,
and recall all the hunted
—the significant
other, wearing a bird's hood.

The Economy of Power

BY JAY WRIGHT

"La bellísima luna
se ha alzado . . ."

The song is forever false,
though the words are true,
and a lover with a faith
obscured by trust

feels the power in a flash
of limestone. The tramp
festivity of night flees,
and the soul construes

its own deception, falls,
on its way, to treat
a flowered heart and to flaunt
the gemlike turtle

shell of a nomadic faith.
I await the terse
exchange my heart, fearless
after its triumph,

matches with that instant flare
that sustains, travels
the weave love's figure fledges,
the soul's swift trouvaille.

When every shadow that falls
is desire's own trope,
arché that moves and might fleece
the raven and tropic

promise of night, lift the fault
of a betrothal
to power out of the flesh,
death sets its trifling

indifference in our flawed
forest of rapture,
there to engage the twin's lais
and to reconstruct

an allusive hymn to flint.
So we must destroy
your rose shawl and all those fables
of the blue treasure

your name hides, the mayflower
by which you suture
your presence to the faltering
flare of a lost tree.

I am now bereft of face,
and the tremulous
consent you give my failings
can only betray

a legacy that will fail
to hold and transcend
the thrifty soul that follows
and cries its tribute.

The Escape Artist

BY KEVIN YOUNG

beyond the people
swallowing fire   past the other acts
we had seen before   we found the escape
artist   bound to a chair   hands tied
behind his back   we climbed onstage
to test the chains   around his ankles
and tongue   watched on
as they tucked him   in a burlap sack
and lowered it   into a tank of water
he could get out of   in his sleep

imagine the air   the thin
man   his skin   a drum   drawn
across bones   picture disappearing
acts   the vanishing middles
of folks from each town
the man who unsaws them
back together again   dream
each escape   is this easy   that all
you need   is a world full of walls
beardless ladies   and peeling white
fences   that trap the yard   that neighbors
sink their share of ships over   sketch
each side gate   the dirt roads leading
out of town   the dust that holds
no magic   here your feet are locked
to the land   to its unpicked
fields   full of empty
bags of cotton   that no one

ever seems   to work
his way out of

after the hands
on the clock   met seven
times   in prayer   they drew
the artist up   unfolded his cold
body from the sack   and planted
it quietly   on the way out
of town   at home we still hear
his ghost nights   guess he got free
from under the red earth   but what
no one ever asked   is why
would anyone want to

Cassius Clay by Basquiat

1982, acrylic & oil paintstick on canvas

BY KEVIN YOUNG

I'm pretty!
I shook up

the world! Clay shouts
to the announcer

after trouncing
Sonny Liston—

the next day he
will turn Ali.

Butterfly,
bee—none stung

or swole carpet-red
as the paint B covered

this canvas, drawing
blood—not even Cassius

called out his name.
Refusing to recognize

Allah—like Terrell
or fool Floyd Patterson—

will get you a new haircut,
whether you want one

or not. How
he hounds

Liston, waving
his prize belt—

a noose for Sonny's ex-
con neck. Petty crook.

Ali just bout serves
time himself

—title stripped
like paint

—Army taking away
his right to fight

when he won't fight
them Viet Cong

who've done him
nothing wrong.

Houston, we gots
a problem—will not

bow or stand
when his no-longer-

name the Draft
Board calls. Lords

over Liston
—*Get up, you bum!*

—who will fall to a phantom
punch 1st rd, forget

to get up. (Died,
Liston did, five

years later, in Vegas,
the needle in

his arm, the neon.)
Ali, now he could hit you

into next year—
but apart from the flogging,

his flaunting, were the taunts
challengers heard ringing

Uncle Tom! Come on
Come on White America!

even above the ten count
& crowd—his undented smile—

that smarts still.

Afterword

BY CARL PHILLIPS

Be it at the level of style, vision, content, or some combination of these, what makes for a lasting (that is, memorable) poem is the fact of its difference—not so much its ability to stand out from the rest, but its inability *not* to. And yet, for all of its contributions to broadening and redefining what poetry can be, a large part of the history of American poetry (paralleling, of course, the country's social history) has been and continues to be one of resisting differences from the presumed norm, or of finally accepting a particular difference, yes, but then championing that difference over and to the exclusion of all others (what is called, in this country, variously patronage, literary criticism, and editorial vision).

In the case of African-American poetry especially, this problem with difference has seemed to come as much from outside as from within the African-American literary community. The same questions that particularly distinguish the American sensibility have also, from at least the time of the Harlem Renaissance, haunted the African-American artist: Who is the African-American, and what are we to do with him or her? What is meant by a term like African-American, and what to make of it when coupled with such big and slippery terms as Vision, Psyche, and Art? If this kind of interrogation has led to white America's attempts to set parameters for African-American identity, it is no less true that factionalism has arisen with the African-American community itself as—under headings like "movement," "collective," and "school"—African-Americans have taken stands on what African-American poetry is and on what the responsibilities of its makers must be, each faction predictably excluding whatever can't be made to fit neatly within that faction's definition.

The mistake has never been in asking questions about identity but in assuming a limit to the number of possible answers. Diversity, necessarily, *has* no limits; this is what makes it dangerous, on one hand: its inability to be controlled entirely, its constant reminder that power shifts easily and can therefore afford no complacency. Diversity's lack of limits is also, on the other hand, what makes it exciting—even as, to any danger, there is somewhere thrill—as well as the only guarantee, finally, against stagnation in art itself. Diversity helps make possible the resonance that distinguishes tradition from artifact and literature from curio or mere document.

The vision of Charles Rowell, in its manifestation as *Callaloo*, has been for twenty-five years the single most powerful and reliable upholder of the need for difference and a constant, unflinching reminder of the *fact* of difference. In an age where literary journals increasingly resemble stables that the same horses never leave, *Callaloo* makes clear that contemporary African-American poetry has as much range as does—and should—poetry of any kind; and that, if there is a single responsibility for a literary journal, it's surely to showcase, as best it can, all that it can. Rather than a record of what has been done, *Callaloo* continues to be a gauge of what is being done and—just as inspiring—of what *can* be done. Which is to say that *Callaloo* has never been one of those journals that publishes a writer only after said writer's talent has been confirmed in the form of numerous other publication credits and prizes; instead, a crucial and distinguishing element of the *Callaloo* tradition has been the discernment of its founder and editor, Charles Rowell, whose ability to identify undiscovered gift is matched by his eagerness both to take a risk on and put faith in that gift. It's a generosity of vision that serves as antidote, as well, to the threat of literary factionalism, since the criterion for *Callaloo* has from the start been excellence—not only all facets of it, but its many dimensions, even as identity is multidimensional.

It is with the latter in mind that *Callaloo* continues to remind us that the term "African-American" is itself, more and more, inadequate. Ever evolving, the journal has gone from being a resource and showcase for African-American poetry to serving to trace and highlight the important and varied influences of the African diaspora more generally. Hence the widening of focus to include the poetry of the Afro-Caribbean, of Brazil and Cuba, to name but a few. The devotion, as well, of entire issues of the journal to subjects ranging from gay, lesbian, bisexual, and transgender literature and culture to the examination of the historical and contemporary resonances of that stubborn bugbear, the Confederate flag, points to yet another concern of *Callaloo*: namely, that we remember that race, if it is an inevitable lens through which we experience and therefore know not only ourselves but all of the world that includes us, is but one of many other lenses; and without taking each of these lenses into account, all knowing is flawed, because incomplete.

To read the poetry collected in *Making Callaloo* is to understand how seriously the journal has taken its responsibility to make as complete a representation as possible of the African diaspora's literary tradition. From Mullen and Etienne to Hamer and Moss, from Morejón to Young, this volume makes it impossible to ignore the richness of that tradition, its vitality, its refusal to be pinned—permanently, anywhere—down.

I am grateful to have been among those in whose work Charles Rowell had faith from the start. That belief meant everything, as it does to any beginning writer. But just as critical, if a writer is to continue to develop further, is the constant exposure to difference, to what is new, given the very nature of art: It grows in direct proportion to the number of challenges put before it. And nothing so challenges intellect as that which, being genuinely new and therefore original, resists the initial grasp of intellect, and consequently forces intellect to extend its reach. It is what I call athletic thinking; and for the poet whose work is worth reading, such thinking, far from burdensome, is in fact welcomed precisely because its limits are as unknowable as are those of identity and of identity's reflection—art itself.

Contributors

Ai is the author of numerous books of poetry, including *Cruelty* (1973), *Killing Floor* (1979), *Sin* (1986), *Fate* (1991), and *Greed* (1993). Her most recent work, *Vice: New and Selected Poems* (1999) won the National Book Award.

Elizabeth Alexander is currently a fellow at the Whitney Humanities Center, Yale University. She is the author of two collections of poems, *The Venus Hottentot* and *Body of Life.*

José Alcántara Almánzar, fiction writer, scholar, and literary critic, is the author of five collections of short stories dating from the early 1980s, many of which are gathered in a recent anthology, *El sabor de lo prohibido* (1993). He lives and works in Santo Domingo, Dominican Republic.

Gerald Barrax was Professor of English, Poet-in-Residence, and Editor of *Obsidian* at North Carolina State University at Raleigh. He is the author of five volumes of poems, *Another Kind of Rain, An Audience of One, The Deaths of Animals and Lesser Gods, Leaning Against the Sun,* and *From a Person Sitting in Darkness: Selected and New Poems.* He is retired and lives in West Chester, Pennsylvania.

Robert Berrouët-Oriol was born in Port-au-Prince, Haiti, where in 1991 he returned from Canada to work with the media. He is a poet and linguist, and the author of *Lettres urbaines* [Urban Letters], a collection of poems.

Edward Kamau Brathwaite is Professor of Comparative Literature at New York University. Born and raised in Barbados and educated in England, he is the author of a wide array of poetic collections, including *Arrivants* (1973), *Black + Blues* (1979), *Roots* (1993), and *Ancestors* (2001), collecting in one volume a trilogy—*Mother Poem, Sun Poem* and *X/Self*—first published by Oxford University Press between 1977 and 1987. Brathwaite is the recipient of numerous honors, including the Neustadt International Prize for Literature, the Casa de las Américas Premio, the Guggenheim Fellowship, and the Fulbright Fellowship. His scholarly works include *The Folk Culture of the Slaves in Jamaica* (1970), *The Development of Creole Society in Jamaica, 1770–1820* (1971) and *History of the Voice* (1984).

Octavia E. Butler, who lives in California, is author of a number of books of science fiction, including *Mind of My Mind, Kindred, Clay's Ark,* and *Patternmaster,* as well as the Parable series (*Parable of the Sower* [1993] and *Parable of the Talents* [1998]). She is a recipient of the Mac-Arthur Foundation Fellowship.

Cyrus Cassells has, in the course of his career, been a film critic, an actor, a teacher, and a translator. He has received numerous fellowships and awards, including the Pushcart Prize, a Rockefeller Foundation fellowship, and a Lambda Literary Award. *Beautiful Signor, Soul Make a Path Through Shouting,* and *The Mud Actor* are some of his publications.

Lucille Clifton, Poet Laureate of the State of Maryland (1975–85), was recently awarded the National Book Award for her *Blessing the Boats* (2000). For her numerous books of poetry she has received many fellowships and awards, including the Shelley Memorial Prize, a Charity Randall Citation, an Emmy Award from the American Academy of Television Arts and Sciences, a selection as a Literary Lion by the New York Public Library, a Lannan Achievement Award in Poetry, and the 1999 Lila Wallace-Readers' Digest Writers' Award. She serves on the board of Chancellors of the Academy of American Poets and was recently elected as a Fellow of the American Academy of Arts. Her poetry collection, *The Terrible Stories* (1996), was a finalist for the National Book Award, the Lenore Marshall Prize and the Los Angeles Times Book Award.

Maryse Condé was born in Guadeloupe. She is the author of several novels, including *Hérémakhonon, Ségou: les Murailles de terre, Moi, Tituba, sorcière noire de Salem, La vie scèlérate,* and *Traversée de la mangrove.* She is also author of *La parole des femmes: essai sur de romancières de Antilles de langue française, La civilisation du bossale,* and other studies of literature and culture. A new book, *Tales from the Heart,* is scheduled to appear in late 2001.

Edwidge Danticat is author of two novels, *Breath, Eyes, Memory* (1994) and *The Farming of Bones* (1999), as well as *Krik! Krak!* (1995), a short story collection which was a finalist for the National Book Award. When she was twelve, she emigrated from Haiti to the U.S. to join her parents in Brooklyn. A graduate of Barnard College, she received the M.F.A. degree in creative writing from Brown University in 1993.

Samuel R. Delany, a four-time winner of the Nebula Award from the Science Fiction Writers of America, is a professor of English at Temple University. His numerous books of prose fiction and nonfiction prose include *Dhalgren, Silent Interviews: On Languages, Sex, Science Fiction, & Some Comics, Atlantis: Three Tales,* and *The Mad Man.*

Toi Derricotte is author of four books of poetry and a memoir, *The Black Notebooks. The Black Notebooks* won the Annisfield-Wolf Award in nonfiction and the nonfiction award from the Black Caucus of the American Library Association in 1997. Her latest book of poems, *Tender,* won the Paterson Poetry Prize in 1998. She is co-founder (with Cornelius Eady) of Cave Canem, the first workshop for African-American poets.

Melvin Dixon (1950–1992) was a professor of English at Queens College in New York. His numerous publications include *Love's Instruments* (poems) and *Vanishing Rooms* (novel). He died of complications of AIDS-HIV in 1992.

Rita Dove, Commonwealth Professor of English at the University of Virginia, is former Poet Laureate of the United States. *Thomas and Beulah* won her the Pulitzer Prize in 1987. Her seventh collection of poems, *On the Bus with Rosa Parks,* was published by W. W. Norton in 1999. The most recent of her many honors are the 1996 Heinz Award in the Arts and Humanities, the 1996 National Medal in the Humanities, the 1997 Barnes and Noble Writers for Writers Award, the 1997 Sara Lee Frontrunner Award, and the 1998 Levinson Prize for Poetry magazine.

Ms. Dove's song cycle *Seven for Luck,* set to music by John Williams and featured with the Boston Pops on PBS, was premiered by the Boston Symphony Orchestra at Tanglewood in July 1998, and her play *The Darker Face of the Earth* has been performed at the Fountain Theatre in Los Angeles, the Oregon Shakespeare Festival, the Crossroads Theatre of New Jersey, and at the Kennedy Center in Washington.

Brent Hayes Edwards is an assistant professor in the English Department at Rutgers University in New Brunswick. He is currently completing a book called *The Practice of Diaspora,* which will be published by Harvard University Press. He is an associate editor of *Callaloo.*

Thomas Sayers Ellis teaches African-American literature and creative writing at Case Western Reserve University in Cleveland, Ohio. He received the MFA in creative writing at Brown University and is a co-founder of the Dark Room Writers Collective. Ellis is the author of the chapbook *The Genuine Negro Hero* (2001). He is a co-editor of *On the Verge: Emerging Poets and Artists* and one of the three poets collected in *Take Three.*

Ralph Ellison (1914–1994) is author of the novel *Invisible Man* (winner of the 1952 National Book Award), two books of non-fiction prose, *Shadow and Act* (1964) and *Going to the Territory* (1986), and numerous essays, reviews, speeches, and pieces of short fiction. He received many other awards, including the National Medal of Arts (1985), the Chevalier de l'Ordre des Artes et Lettres (1970), and the Medal of Freedom (1969). He was a member of the Carnegie Commission on Public Television, a charter member of the National Council on the Arts and Humanities, a trustee of the Colonial Williamsburg Foundation (1971–84), and a trustee of the John F. Kennedy Center for the Performing Arts (1967–77). He was Visiting Professor of Writing at Rutgers University (1962–64) and, from 1970 to 1980, he was Albert Schweitzer Professor of the Humanities at New York University. A part of his last novel, unfinished at his death, was published posthumously in 1999 as *Juneteenth* by his literary executor, John Callahan.

Phebus Etienne, who studied at Rider University and New York University, was born in Port-au-Prince, Haiti, and reared in East Orange, New Jersey. She has also published poems in *Poet Lore, Mudfish, Caribbean Writer,* and the *Beacon Best of 2000.*

Percival Everett is a professor and the chair of the Department of English at the University of Southern California, Los Angeles. His numerous books of fiction include *Frenzy, God's Country,* and *Glyph.*

Leon Forrest (1937–1997) was a professor of English and African American studies at Northwestern University, where he taught from 1973 until his death. He is the author of four novels, *There Is a Tree More Ancient Than Eden, The Bloodworth Orphans, Two Wings to Veil My Face,* and *Divine Days.* His last novel, *Meteor in the Madhouse,* was published posthumously in 2001.

Thomas Glave is the author of *Whose Song? and Other Stories* (City Lights Books, 2000). The recipient of a 2000–01 New York Foundation for the Arts Fellowship in fiction, Glave was named a "Writer on the Verge" by *The Village Voice* in June 2000. He is an assistant professor of English and Africana Studies at the State University of New York, Binghamton.

Forrest Hamer is a lecturer at the University of California, Berkeley, and a practicing psychologist in Oakland. *Call & Response* (1995) was his first collection of poems, followed in 2000 by *Middle Ear.*

Michael S. Harper, the first Poet Laureate of Rhode Island (1988–1993), is University Professor and Professor of English at Brown University and author of several volumes of poems. His *Honorable Amendments* (1995) won the George Kent Award selected by Gwendolyn Brooks, and his collected poems *Songlines in Michaeltree* was published in the spring of 2000. He is also co-editor (with Anthony Walton) of the *Vintage Anthology of African American Poetry, 1750–2000* and *Every Shut Eye Ain't Asleep.* He has also edited *The Collected Poems of Sterling A. Brown* and *Chant of Saints* (with Robert B. Stepto).

Claire Harris, a native of Trinidad, is a resident of Calgary, Canada, where she has taught high school English and drama. She began her writing and publishing career in 1975, during a leave of absence in Nigeria. A winner of The Writer's Guild of Alberta Award, she has also received the Alberta Culture Poetry Prize for her book of poetry, *Traveling to Find a Remedy* and the Commonwealth Award for the Americas region for her book *Fables from the Women's Quarters.* Her other books include *Translation into Fiction, The Conception of Winter, Drawing Down a Daughter,* and *Dipped in Shadow.*

Wilson Harris, a native of Guyana, lives in England. He is the author of numerous books of fiction and essays, including *The Palace of the Peacock, Da Silva Da Silva's Cultivated Wilderness, The Eye of the Scarecrow, Carnival, Genesis of the Clowns, The Age of the Rainmakers, The Whole Armor, The Infinite Rehearsal, Resurrection at Sorrow Hill,* and *The Radical Imagination.* His newest novel, *The Dark Jester,* was published in 2001.

Terrance Hayes is author of *Muscular Music* (1999) and the recipient of a Red Brick Review Award, a Whiting Writers Award, and a Kate Tufts Discovery Award for his poetry. He is an assistant professor of English at Xavier University in New Orleans, Louisiana.

Angela Jackson is a poet, fiction writer, and playwright, as well as Chair of the Organization of Black American Culture (OBAC) Writers Workshop. Awarded the American Book Award for her *Solo in the Boxcar Third Floor E* (poems), Jackson is also the author of *Dark Legs and Silk Kisses* (poetry), *And All These Roads Be Luminous: Poems Selected and New* (nominated for the National Book Award), and *Shango Diaspora* and *Comfort Stew* (plays).

Major L. Jackson is a graduate of the creative writing program at the University of Oregon. His poems have appeared in *American Poetry Review, Boulevard, Obsidian II,* and *Painted Bride Quarterly.* He is the recipient of scholarships and fellowships from Bread Loaf Writers' Conference, MacDowell Artist Colony, and Pew Fellowships in the Arts.

Currently, he serves as Assistant Professor of English at Xavier University of Louisiana.

Charles Johnson is author of three novels, *Faith and the Good Thing*, *Oxherding Tale*, and *Middle Passage* (winner of the 1990 National Book Award); a collection of short stories, *The Sorcerer's Apprentice*; a work of aesthetics, *Being and Race: Black Writing Since 1970*; and two collections of comic art, *Black Humor* and *Half-Past Nation Time*. He co-edited with John McCluskey, Jr., *Black Men Speaking*. Johnson was also instrumental in the PBS series and companion volume, *Africans in America* (1999). He teaches creative writing at the University of Washington (Seattle), where he is the Pollock Professor for Excellence in English.

Gayl Jones is the author of *Corregidora*, *Eva's Man*, *Mosquito*, and *The Healing*, which was nominated for a National Book Award. She lives in Lexington, Kentucky.

Randall Kenan, winner of a 1994 Whiting Writer's Award, is author of *A Visitation of Spirits* (a novel), *Let the Dead Bury the Dead* (short stories), *James Baldwin: Author* (a biography for young adults), and *Walking On Water: Black American Lives at the Turn of the Twenty-first Century* (social criticism). He has taught creative writing at the University of Mississippi, Sarah Lawrence College, and Columbia University. He is currently teaching at the University of Memphis.

Yusef Komunyakaa is the author of twelve books of poems, including *Talking Dirty to the Gods* (2000); *Thieves of Paradise* (1998), which was a finalist for the National Book Critics Circle Award; *Neon Vernacular: New & Selected Poems 1977–1989* (1994), for which he received the Pulitzer Prize and the Kingsley Tufts Poetry Award; *Dien Cai Dau* (1988), which won The Dark Room Poetry Prize; *I Apologize for the Eyes in My Head* (1986), winner of the San Francisco Poetry Center Award; and *Pleasure Dome: New & Collected Poems, 1975–1999*. A decorated Vietnam veteran, Komunyakaa recently received the 2001 Ruth

Lilly Prize. He serves as a Chancellor of The Academy of American Poets and is currently a professor in the Council of Humanities and Creative Writing Program at Princeton University.

Helen Elaine Lee, who teaches at the Massachusetts Institute of Technology, is author of two novels: *The Serpent's Gift,* winner of the American Library Association Black Caucus First Novelist Award in 1995, and *Water Marked,* published in 1999. A magna cum laude with Highest Honors graduate of Harvard College, she received a J.D. from Harvard Law School.

Audre Lorde (1934–1992), who died of cancer in the Virgin Islands, is author of more than eight volumes of poems and four collections of essays, including *Zami, Chosen Poems: Old and New, A Burst of Light, Sister Outsider,* and *Our Dead Behind Us.* She taught at Tougaloo College (Mississippi), John Jay College of Criminal Justice, and Hunter College.

Nathaniel Mackey is the author of *Discrepant Engagement: Dissonance, Cross-Culturality, and Experimental Writing, Whatsaid Serif, School of Udhra, Bedouin Hornbook, Djbot Baghostus's Run,* and, most recently, *Atet A.D.,* which is volume three of *From a Broken Bottle Traces of Perfume Still Emanate,* and *Four for Glenn,* a chapbook of poems. He teaches at the University of California, Santa Cruz.

Clarence Major is the author of several award-winning novels, including *Such Was The Season, Painted Turtle: Woman With Guitar, Dirty Bird Blues* and *Reflex and Bone Structure, My Amputations,* as well as stories collected in *Fun & Games* (1990), a new edition of poetry, *Configurations: New and Selected Poems 1958–1998* (a finalist for the National Book Award in 1999), and nonfiction, *Afterthoughts: Essays and Criticism* (1998) and *Necessary Distance* (2001). He has also edited a number of anthologies, including *Calling The Wind: Twentieth Century African-American Short Stories* (1993) and *The Garden Thrives: Twentieth Century African-American Poetry* (1996). He has received numerous awards, among them a National Council on the Arts Award (1970), a Fulbright

(1981–1983) and two Pushcart prizes (1976/1990). He teaches at the University of California, Davis.

John McCluskey, Jr., is author of two novels, *Look What They Done to My Song* and *Mr. America's Last Season Blues.* He has also edited a number of books, including *Blacks in Ohio History, The City of Refuge: The Collected Stories of Rudolph Fisher,* and (with novelist Charles Johnson) *Black Men Speaking.*

Terry McMillan is an associate professor at the University of Arizona and the editor of *Breaking Ice,* an anthology of black writers. She is the author of *Mama* (1987), *Disappearing Acts* (1989), *Waiting to Exhale* (1992), *How Stella Got Her Groove Back* (1996), and *A Day Late and a Dollar Short* (2001).

Karen Mitchell was born in Columbus, Mississippi. She is the author of *The Eating Hill* and has published in several magazines.

Nancy Morejón, Cuban scholar and poet, is Director of Caribbean Studies at Cuba's premier cultural studies institute, Casa de las Americas. She is the author of *Mutismos* (1962), *Amor, ciudad atribuída* (1964), *Richard trajo se flauta* (1967), *Parajes de una época* (1979), *Poemas* (1980), *Elogio de la danza* (1982), *Octubre imprescindible* (1983), and *Cuarderno de Granada* (1984), in addition to critical works focusing particularly on Cuban poet Nicolás Guillén (1974) and translations of poems by Paul Eluard, Jacques Roumain and Aimé Césaire.

Thylias Moss, an associate professor of English at the University of Michigan (Ann Arbor), is author of numerous volumes of poems: *Last Chance for the Tarzan Holler, Hosiery Seams on Bowlegged Woman, Pyramid of Bones, At Redbones, Rainbow Remnants in Rock Bottom Ghetto Sky* and *Small Congregations.* Her memoir, *Tale of a Sky-Blue Dress,* appeared in 1999. She has received numerous awards and fellowships for her poetry—most recently the Whiting Writer's Award, the Witter Bynner Prize, and the MacArthur Foundation Fellowship.

Harryette Mullen is Professor of English and Afro-American Studies at the University of California, Los Angeles, where she teaches African-

American literature and creative writing. She is the author of four poetry books, including *Trimmings* (1991), *S*PeRM**K*T* (1992), and *Muse & Drudge* (1995). Her critical book on slave narratives *Freeing the Soul* is forthcoming from Cambridge University Press.

Brenda Marie Osbey teaches in the honors program at Southern University in Baton Rouge, Louisiana. A native of New Orleans, she is the author of four volumes of poems, the most recent of which, *All Saints: New and Collected Poetry,* received the American Book Award in 1998.

Edimilson de Almeida Pereira lives in Juiz de Fora in the state of Minas Gerais, Brazil. He has published poetry and studies of Brazilian culture which include *Corpo vivido, A roda do mundo* (with Ricardo Aleixo), *Negras raízes mineiras: Os arturos,* and *Mundo encaixado: Significação da cultura popular.* He teaches Brazilian literature at the Federal University in Juiz de Fora.

Carl Phillips is the author of *From the Devotions,* a finalist for the National Book Award, *In the Blood,* winner of the Samuel French Morse Poetry Prize, *Cortége,* finalist for a National Book Critics Circle Award, *Pastoral,* and his most recent collection, *Tether* (2001). He teaches at Washington University (St. Louis), where he has also served as the director of the Creative Writing Program.

Caryl Phillips grew up on St Kitts, in the Eastern Caribbean, and in Leeds, England, where he spent his teenage years. Since 1998 he has been Henry R. Luce Professor of Migration and Social Order at Barnard College, Columbia University, in New York. Phillips is the author of two book-length travel essays, *The European Tribe* (1987) and *The Atlantic Sound* (2000), and is the editor of the Faber Caribbean Series and *Extravagant Strangers: A Literature of Belonging,* an anthology of British writers born outside Britain. Widely celebrated as a novelist, his fiction includes *The Final Passage* (1985), *A State of Independence* (1986), *Higher Ground* (1989), *Cambridge* (1991), *Crossing the River* (1993), and *The Nature of Blood* (1997).

Ed Roberson is assistant director of special programs at Cook College, Rutgers University, and is the author of *Voices Cast Out to Talk Us In* (1994 Iowa Poetry Prize winner). His works include *When Thy King Is a Boy, Etai-Eken, Lucid Interval as Integral Music, Just In/Word of Navigational Challenges,* and, most recently, *Atmospheric Conditions.*

Lucinda H. Roy, the daughter of Jamaican writer and artist Namba Roy, is Alumni Distinguished Professor in English at Virginia Tech in Blacksburg, Virginia. Her works include *The Humming Birds* (winner of the 1995 Eighth Mountain Poetry Prize), *Lady Moses: A Novel* (1999), and, most recently, *The Hotel Alleluia: A Novel* (2000).

Sonia Sanchez is the Laura Carnell Professor of English at Temple University, where she serves as Director of Women's Studies. She has published 13 books of poetry, the most recent being *Does Your House Have Lions?, Like the Singing Coming Off the Drums,* and *Shake Loose My Skin.* She has won several awards for her poetry, including the Lucretia Mott Award, a Pew Fellowship, and the Governor's Award for Excellence in the Humanities (Pennsylvania). *Does Your House Have Lions?* was nominated for the National Book Critics Circle Award in 1998.

Sharan Strange teaches at the Parkmont School in Washington, D.C., and has recently been writer-in-residence at Fisk University, Spelman College and the California Institute of the Arts. Her poetry has been widely published in journals and anthologies, and her first collection of poetry *Ash* (Beacon Press) was published in 2001.

Natasha Trethewey, an assistant professor of English at Emory University, was born in Gulfport, Mississippi. Her first book of poems, *Domestic Work,* which won the 1999 Cave Canem Poetry Prize, was published in 2000 by Graywolf Press. For her poetry, she has also won a number of other prizes and has been awarded several fellowships, including the Grolier Poetry Prize, the Jessica Nobel-Maxwell Memorial Award, a National Endowment for the Arts Fellowship, and a Bunting

Fellowship to the Radcliffe Institute for Advanced Study at Harvard University. She has published poems in a number of periodicals, including *The Southern Review, Gettysburg Review, Agni, New England Review,* and *American Poetry Review.*

Alice Walker has received numerous awards and honors for her work. Among her books of poetry are *Her Blue Body Everything We Know: Earthling Poems, 1965–1990 Complete* (1991), *Horses Make the Landscape More Beautiful* (1984), *Goodnight, Willie Lee, I'll See You in the Morning* (1979), *Revolutionary Petunias and Other Poems* (1973), and *Once: Poems* (1968). Her prose includes *The Way Forward is with a Broken Heart* (2000), *By the Light of My Father's Smile* (1998), *Possessing the Secret of Joy* (1992), *The Temple of My Familiar* (1989), *The Color Purple* (1982, winner of the Pulitzer Prize and American Book Award) and *In Search of Our Mother's Gardens: Womanist Prose* (1983).

Ron Welburn teaches American literatures at the University of Massachusetts in Amherst. His published works include *Roanoke and Wampum: Topics in Native American Heritage and Literatures* (2001), *Council Decisions* (1990), and *Heartland: Selected Poems* (1981).

John Edgar Wideman, a MacArthur Foundation Fellow, is author of numerous award-winning books of prose fiction and nonfiction prose, including *Fever, Philadelphia Fire* (1990 PEN/Faulkner Award), *Reuben, Damballah, Hiding Place, Sent for You Yesterday* (1984 PEN/Faulkner Award), *Brothers and Keepers, The Cattle Killing, Fatheralong,* and *Two Cities.* He teaches at the University of Massachusetts (Amherst).

Jay Wright is the author of *Transfigurations: Collected Poems* (2000), *Boleros* (1991), *Selected Poems of Jay Wright* (1987), *Explications/Interpretations* (1984), *Elaine's Book* (1986), *The Double Invention of Komo* (1980), *Dimensions of History* (1976), *Soothsayers and Omens* (1976), and *The Homecoming Singer* (1971). He is the recipient of an American Academy and Institute of Arts and Letters Literary Award, a Guggenheim Fellowship, a MacArthur Fellowship, an Ingram Merrill Foundation Award, and a National Endowment for the Arts grant.

Kevin Young is Ruth Lilly Professor of Poetry at Indiana University, Bloomington. He is the author of *To Repel Ghosts* (2001) and *Most Way Home* (1995), selected by Lucille Clifton as part of the National Poetry Series and winner of the John C. Zacharis First Book Prize from *Ploughshares*.